As It Ends

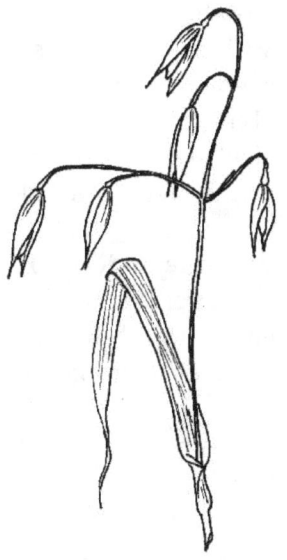

Denise Terriah

Happy Duck Publishing
103 East 3rd Street
Belle, MO 65013

Genre: Fiction, General
ISBN: 978-0-9861182-7-2
First Edition.

To my husband

Acknowledgements

First and foremost I want to thank my family for their patience and support while I tried to get this book out there. This process has involved me hiding behind a closed door more than I'd like to admit. It's taken a lot of encouragement and forgotten responsibilities to make this book a reality. My husband Robert, and my daughters Katelyn and Amber, forgave me anyway. For that I am in their debt… and no, lunch isn't ready.

I would also like to thank my friends and editor, Edward and Eva Gehlert for having had their eyeballs all over this story's nooks and crannies to help bring order to the chaos. They were on the front lines of spelling errors, misused words, and missing punctuation so nobody else has to be. Hey Ed, you don't have to remind me that I should be working on this project anymore. I appreciated the encouragement. Go us!

A special thanks to Brandy for always listening to my ramblings about characters and plot. She was one of the first brave souls to read the earliest chapters of the earliest version of this book. Don't worry; those pages are locked away where they can't hurt anyone anymore. Your insights and opinions have improved this story and its characters in a myriad of ways.

Wes, you may not know this, but you were the first person that helped me believe those many, many years ago that I might one day write something worth reading. Thanks for treating me like a fellow writer even when I didn't feel like one.

I'd like to thank my first fans: my mom and my niece Allison. I appreciate your enthusiasm.

And, lastly, I'd like to thank any long suffering friend, family member, enemy, or stranger, whom I've forgotten to mention, that has ever had to hear me babble at length about the novel I was hoping to finish one day.

CHAPTER 1

"What makes you feel that you are uniquely qualified for this position?"

The woman sitting across the table from Tara watched her with boredom.

Tara opened her mouth, but nothing came out. She felt neither unique nor qualified. The only reason she was in this room was because it was the only call back for a job she'd had in weeks. Tara had practiced her answer in the mirror this morning, but now she just sat looking at the woman.

"Miss?" the interviewer cleared her throat impatiently.

"Sorry," Tara smiled weakly under the weight of the older woman's hawkish glare. She continued with a deep breath, "I'm a highly motivated person who works well individually or as part of a team. I have good people skills and I learn new things quickly so I can adapt to nearly any situation."

The woman behind the desk rubbed her eyes; pushing her glasses out of the way. It was obvious that she wasn't impressed. "Now, Missus Hillcrest, can I get you to tell me in plain language what that means for this company? Do you have prior experience in a bakery or in management?"

"I don't," Tara admitted, shifting uncomfortably. Her toes were still cold from standing outside. She tugged nervously at the hem of her gray wool skirt under the table. Needing to say something, she decided on the truth.

"I need this job." Tara leaned forward earnestly. "I'll take minimum wage. I can get along with anyone, and learn to do anything."

The woman looked at her stone-faced and Tara instantly regretted being so blunt. The interviewer's thin lips drew back into a frown before she spoke again.

"Thank you, we'll be in touch," the woman recited distractedly already looking at the next name on her list as she leaned across the table to shake Tara's hand.

Tara met her halfway. "Thank you for your consideration," she nodded, shaking the woman's hand before heading out the door.

In the lobby a jagged line of nervous-looking applicants fidgeted and watched her walk through. She understood how they felt. Tara had stood in line for her name to be called for a little over an hour.

This morning she'd been excited and hopeful because the advertisement she'd answered in the paper said they were looking to fill five positions. Now, getting one of those five seemed about as likely as winning the lottery.

Tara pushed the heavy door open and pulled her coat tightly around her body to block the biting wind that whipped right through her interview suit. She might as well have been naked. Overhead the sky was dark and threatened snow. It looked the way she felt.

Tara walked from Main Street to Fourth Street where she found herself standing in front of a little blue house with white shutters on a corner lot. She hated to drop in without calling, but it was much too cold to stay outside and she couldn't think of anywhere else she could go to use a phone that was near enough to walk to in high heels.

The doorbell was answered by Kate, a woman short enough to be mistaken for the average eleven-year-old. She was petite in every sense of the word, and as usual, looked lovely. Kate's dark hair was perfectly smooth and shiny, and her equally dark eyes sparkled. She wore jeans, a t-shirt and a loose sweater. On a different woman it could have looked unkempt, but somehow Kate always managed to look put together.

Tara envied that. She didn't feel put together with her hair done, in her somber interview suit, pantyhose, and high heels.

"What brings you here?" Kate asked, allowing a smile to spread across her face as she stepped back and gestured Tara through the door.

"My cold aching feet," Tara smiled wiggling her toes to encourage blood flow. "I had an interview at that place at the end of Main Street," she said tugging her arms free from her coat in the front entry.

"The doughnut place?"

"That's the one. I hope you don't mind me dropping in. I was hoping to use your phone to call my husband so he can pick me up."

"Not a problem," Kate smiled, digging her cell phone out of her purse. She exchanged it for Tara's coat; hanging it in the closet next to the door.

Tara scrolled quickly through the phone book to Jasper's number and hit the call button, but there was no answer.

"This is Tara. I'm at the Miller's house. Call this number or just come get me when you get this message." Tara hung up and handed the phone back to Kate. "Thanks."

Tara liked Kate's place. The living room was a mix of overstuffed furniture and clusters of family pictures. In the corner was a Christmas tree decorated with blinking lights and little plastic ornaments. It was tied to the ceiling with wire.

"Make yourself comfortable," Kate beamed as she led her back to the house's small kitchen. It was furnished with fifties era appliances and could have been really charming if it was intentional. Instead the turquoise clashed with the seventies countertops and linoleum.

Kate set a plate of macaroni back on the tray of the high chair that her two-year-old daughter Kylie was strapped in, a blonde, curly, giggling mess.

As she wiped the cheese off the wall next to the high chair with a cloth Kate smiled. "How'd the interview go?"

Tara cringed, "It was a disaster."

"I'm sure it wasn't that bad,"

"You weren't there," Tara sighed tugging the wisps of hair at her temples while she watched Kate rinse the cloth in the sink.

"Fair enough," Kate admitted, "How about that gorgeous husband of yours? Has he had any luck with his job search?"

"Not even a little," Tara sighed again. "I wish I had better news. He put up fliers all around town and has had a few calls for odd jobs. There's just not that much out there right now."

Kate nodded sympathetically. "They've been talking about laying off some of the city employees too."

"Not Alex?" Tara asked hopefully.

"Not that I've heard, but the wife is always the last to know these things, am I right?" Kate lifted Kylie out of the high chair and proceeded to wipe her face and hands clean.

A loud pounding at the door made both women jump. Kate hurried to the door and flung it open, stepping back out of the way with Kylie on her hip.

Kate's husband Alex shuffled slowly backwards into the room. In his arms he held one end of a large cardboard box.

Alex was a bear of a man with sandy blonde hair and strikingly beautiful eyes with long lashes that looked totally out of place on his rugged face. He was easily twice the height of his wife. He was the kind of man to look up to, both literally and figuratively.

"Tip it a little more to the left," a voice called from the other end of the box. With the adjustment Pete came through the door supporting the box's back end.

Pete was a man of much more average height, making the box lopsided. He smiled when he saw Tara and Kate. Pete had a friendly smile, the kind that was infectious, making Tara smile back without thinking about it. Under his smile a small smudge of gray in his trimmed beard made him look older than the late twenties that Tara guessed him at. The rest of his hair was a plain shade of brown. Otherwise he was reasonably handsome and trim in a way that made him hard to describe by virtue of being unremarkable.

"Where are we going with this, boss?" Pete asked Kate.

"Kylie's room," she gestured down the hall. "Somebody's getting her big-girl bed today," she cooed to the toddler before kissing the little girl's cheek.

"Do you need any help?" Tara asked Alex as he shuffled away.

"No, are you kidding?" Alex snorted. "We want to be manly

and build things without reading directions."

"Let's just leave them to that," Kate grinned.

Tara and Kate listened with amusement to some cursing and cooperation after which the guys came out to announce the bed was assembled.

"Piece of cake," Alex bragged, polishing his fingernails on his chest before blowing on them and giving his wife a wink.

Pete held up his palm where there were several pieces of hardware and a screw. "We even had extras." He smiled while Alex whistled and looked at the ceiling.

"How inventive of you dear. Leave it to you to put it together with less parts than it called for," Kate mocked.

"They were extras," Alex insisted before turning to Pete. "Thanks for that, buddy."

Kate kissed Alex on the cheek. "I'm sure you did a fine job."

Alex looked at the clock on the wall, "Speaking of jobs. I hate to be rude, but I need to get ready for work," he announced. "They have us working swing shifts." Alex kissed his wife again and she followed him around the corner into their bedroom with Kylie on her hip, leaving Pete and Tara standing in the kitchen.

Pete studied the tabletop while Tara listened to the clock ticking. Of the group, Tara knew the least about Pete. He tended to stay busy and keep to himself, so she seldom ran into him at all. The only thing she really knew about him was that he was Alex's best friend. Tara waited patiently, but Pete made no attempt at small talk.

"So," Tara said finally. "What have you been up to?"

Pete looked up. "Just being a beast of burden today," Pete shrugged his broad shoulders in a slow lazy gesture. His answer didn't tell her anything and didn't invite further discussion.

"Such a fine beast he makes," Kate smiled as she breezed back into the room, having laid Kylie down for a nap. Tara was relieved that Kate was back. At least she had talked to Kate more than a handful of times.

"He's nearly housebroken," Kate winked.

"I try," Pete said shuffling and looking down at his feet in mock humility. He paused then leaned back to look at the clock on the wall. "I hate to do this to you guys, but I've got to run too."

"You late for a hot date?" Kate teased.

"How'd you know?" he said sliding on his tweed flatcap with a flourish. He didn't linger and was out the door without another word.

"Did I run him off?" Tara asked

"No, he's always like that," Kate assured her.

Alex walked back into the room in his police uniform with the shirt unbuttoned over his undershirt. Kate watched him sit down to lace up his boots before she spoke.

"Pete left for his hot date."

"What and he didn't even kiss me goodbye?" Alex winked at Tara.

Leaning back against the counter, Kate paused looking thoughtful. "What do you think he's really doing?"

"You don't know that he doesn't have a hot date," Alex offered. "Stranger things could happen. The faucets could suddenly start pouring gold, or the neighbor's Chihuahua could spontaneously combust."

"I'd take either happily," Kate smiled.

"You are wonderfully wicked," Alex remarked, pulling her towards him with a growl and kissing her. Tara smiled, hoping they would remember she was in the kitchen before things got out of hand.

Thankfully Alex looked at her after pawing his wife only briefly. "You need a ride home?" he asked.

"It's so far out of your way," Tara shook her head.

"Nonsense. I don't mind. I'll give Jasper a call and let him know I'll bring you home."

"Thanks." Tara pulled her coat out of the closet and shrugged it on. She really did appreciate it. It wasn't that she didn't want to spend time with Kate. It was just that she didn't know either of them well enough to impose on their time for an entire day.

Her husband Jasper was a personable guy who made friends fast. A skill she found enviable. Fast everything really. Jasper and Tara had only been married four months and had only dated for two before he surprised her with a trip to the courthouse to buy a marriage license at the end of a date. Tara surprised herself by saying yes. He was so witty and intriguing, not to mention the fact that he was tall and tan with brown eyes and dark strait hair pulled back into a low ponytail which he'd since cut off as part of his job search. Jasper was a bit too slender, but well-muscled with several elaborate tattoos. He had smoldering good looks and a scar on his left cheek that made him look dangerous.

He was frankly everything she wished she could be: Confident, likeable, impulsive, and beautiful. Jasper's interest had taken her off guard, she was basically his opposite. Pale skin, with a dusting of freckles, green eyes, and a face her father had made sure she understood wasn't attractive. He'd told her many times that she was going to have to have one hell of a personality with her looks. She'd always taken her father at his word, but Jasper disagreed. He'd told her he loved her full pouty lips, striking large eyes, and hourglass figure. Tara had always taken this to be the nice way of telling her she had a big bottom. The only thing she and Jasper did agree on, and her main point of pride, was the hair that cascaded down her back almost to her hips in waves of the color of honey.

Jasper had lost his job as a maintenance technician for a heating and cooling repair company just after they got married. Soon after that, they'd left St. Louis to return to Tara's hometown located about two hours away. When he couldn't find work right away, Jasper had put up fliers.

Jasper's fliers for work as an odd-jobs man were how they'd met Alex and Kate. The Millers landlord had called Jasper to fix a damaged duct under the house.

When Jasper knocked on the door, Kate had been in the shower so she didn't hear him. Figuring she wasn't home he'd gone to work under the house. When Alex had come home from work for lunch he found Kate in the bedroom wearing a robe and started tearing the room apart looking for her gentleman caller because of the truck in the driveway. She had no idea Jasper was even there. They eventually found him in the crawlspace under the house and Alex had ordered him out because he thought he was trying to steal the copper water pipes. Jasper thought he was getting arrested. After a phone call to the landlord they got it all sorted out and Alex invited him out to buy him a beer in apology.

Tara had met them when Pete and Alex dropped off her very drunk husband. Alex and Kate were the first friends they'd made since they'd move to town only a few months ago.

"Here you are!" Alex's voice was cheerful as he pulled to a stop in her driveway.

"Hey," he called as she climbed out of the car. "If you ever need a ride, just give me a call. It's no trouble really."

"Will do, thanks." Tara waved.

As Alex backed down the driveway, Tara dug her keys out of her purse. Jasper didn't like their home. It was a cottage on the edge of her mother's fifteen acres. He complained that it was a ten minute drive to town, and that her mother was a nasty woman who only had her there to keep Tara under her thumb.

Tara had to keep reminding him that it didn't matter because they were staying there rent-free until they could get back on their feet. This arrangement had been her mother's wedding present to them, which was much more generous than she had expected. The cottage itself was originally put up for her younger brother, and would be his again when he returned from college.

Tara found it charming. It had a stucco exterior and a cheerfully blue door. The interior was the picture of simplicity. It consisted of a single large room with two doors leading to a bedroom and bathroom along the back wall. The decorating scheme had left a lot to be desired, but after she'd taken down the pin-ups and cleaned the place it seemed livable enough.

Admittedly, none of the appliances or furniture matched and nearly everything inside was damaged, torn or threadbare. It looked about the way one would expect a teenage boy's party pad to look, but it didn't matter to Tara. The entire main room and bathroom were covered in linoleum for easy clean-up. The fridge, stove, cabinets, sink, washer, and dryer lined up against one wall. The tiny red kitchen table with four mismatched chairs were next, then at the other end of the room was a brown oval braided rug and a threadbare blue gingham sofa that had a slash repaired with duct tape on one of the cushions. In one corner was a small computer desk where Tara kept her laptop. In the other corner was an entertainment center with their unreasonably small television. Tara always tried to think of it as cozy.

Today it wasn't cozy. When Tara opened the door water cascaded out, soaking her already cold feet.

"Shit!" Tara jumped back. She turned immediately and tried to flag Alex down, but he was backing out of the driveway talking on the radio and didn't notice her before he drove on.

Now would be the perfect time to have my cell phone back, Tara thought with irritation. She and Jasper had turned off their phone plan over a month ago in favor of a single pay-as-you-go cell phone that Jasper always carried with him. It was the only thing they could afford.

"Shit!" Tara squealed as she waded through the frigid water in the main room to change out of her nice clothes.

In the bedroom, the mystery-stained carpet squelched underfoot.

"Shit!" she spat as she fell on the carpet while trying to peel her hosiery off. Tara flung her now sopping wet suit onto the bed, and then she wiggled into a pair of jeans and pulled on a t-shirt and sweater. Before she got off the island that the bed now made, she wiped her feet dry on the coverlet and stuffed them into some wool socks and her waterproof work boots.

It didn't take her long to trace the leak to the supply line for the toilet. As Tara suspected it was about an inch below the shutoff valve so that valve was of no use to her. That's where the waterline had been kinked, a pair of fuzzy purple handcuffs were still attached to the line when she had moved in.

"Shit," Tara breathed, wiping her hands on the front of her thighs. All their tools were with Jasper.

Tara wandered around inside the house, then outside trying to trace the plumbing, but she couldn't find where to shut off the water. Tara opened the door in the bathroom that contained the furnace, water heater, and pressure tank. Inside was a lever near the pressure tank, but she couldn't get it to budge.

She couldn't just let the water keep running, so she headed into the bedroom and opened the top drawer of Jasper's dresser. Inside was their last condom. Tara held it for a minute. If this didn't work Jasper was going to be pretty upset with her. She shrugged, she had to do something. Determinedly, Tara wrapped it tightly around the water line in multiple loops before knotting it. Over that she wrapped duct tape from the junk drawer. This slowed the water from a spray to a gentle dribble.

"Oh shit, look at this mess," Tara sighed.

Hours later, Tara was still down on her knees trying to get the water out of the carpet with the wet-dry vacuum. She had already mopped everything else. The rug from the living room hung dripping on the porch and a towel was soaking up the water that still drooled out of the water line.

"Jesus Christ, Tara. What happened?" Jasper demanded from the bedroom doorway. She hadn't even heard him come in over the sound of the vacuum.

Her sense of relief made her sway slightly when she saw him. "Water line busted, I have it sort of under control."

"Show me." Jasper pinched the bridge of his nose, like the sight of the ruined carpet was giving him a headache.

Tara led him into the bathroom and showed him the tightly wrapped water line.

"Use your brain, Tara!" Jasper scolded.

"What?" she asked, startled by his response.

Jasper opened the door to the utility room and opened the fuse box where he flipped a switch. Then he came out and turned on the faucet in the sink until it ran dry.

"What did you do?" Tara asked surprised.

"I cut the power to the well pump; like you should have. How hard was that?"

"I didn't think about that," Tara stammered. "I'm sorry."

"Why didn't you think about that?" he demanded. "You're the one who grew up in the country."

"I grew up in town. We were on city water." Tara whispered while her cheeks burned. She felt stupid. "Mom didn't buy this place until she got the insurance money when Dad died. That was after I moved out."

"Hey, it's okay," Jasper soothed when he looked at her face. "At least you tried."

"I did," Tara nodded, but his acknowledgement didn't make her feel less stupid.

"What do you have that wrapped with? It did a pretty good job of slowing the water down."

"Duct tape and a condom," Tara admitted looking at the floor.

"Oh, Tara. The last condom. Really?" Jasper rebuked her, making Tara's cheeks burn even hotter.

"I'm sorry. I couldn't think of anything else to do. I didn't even think of the well. I'm really sorry."

Jasper ran his fingers through his short hair several times while she tugged on the wisps of hair by her temples. Finally he smiled.

"It's okay, honey," he soothed, letting his voice become mellow again. "It's just not how I pictured using that."

Tara continued to look at the floor. She'd thought she did a good job at the time. Then she worked so hard to get everything cleaned up. Now she was ashamed of herself for not thinking of the well. It was like being a kid again. She did everything wrong.

"How'd the job interview go?" Jasper asked as he began cutting the tape off the water line with his knife.

"Well, I bombed my interview. But if they liked that maybe I have a chance against the other hundred people who were there."

"It's okay, we know how you can be," Jasper told her, standing up and kissing her forehead.

"Yeah," she whispered. Tara waited while he went to the truck. He came back with a square of rubber and an adjustable hose clamp.

"Did you have any luck?" she asked while he tightened the clamp with a screwdriver.

Jasper shrugged, "Nothing's available at the temp agency. They promised me I'm still on the list, just like last week, but," he brightened, "I did make some money working on a roof leak for an old fella' who called this morning. It was an easy fix too; just had to sort out some flashing."

"If it was easy, why did it take you so long to get home?" Tara asked. It had been dark for hours. He couldn't have been working on a roof.

Jasper turned the water back on and watched the patch to see if it would leak. "That'll have to do until we can replace the line."

He turned towards her. "It turns out the guy whose roof I worked on was career Navy. I know this because he must have told me thirty times. Anyway, he tried to get me to take some old pin-ups instead of cash," Jasper finished, smiling.

"Did he really or are you just being silly?" Tara prompted.

"Scout's honor, it really happened."

"I didn't know you were a scout."

"I wasn't," he admitted, "but it sounded better than non-scout's honor."

"Really?" Tara rolled her eyes at him.

"He really did have several trunks full of pin-ups that he insisted on showing me while he told me some rather off-color tall tales." Jasper chuckled.

"What you're saying is that you left me here crawling around on my hands and knees mopping up this mess while you sat around looking at nudie pictures?" Tara asked raising an eyebrow.

"I had a beer, too. That's important," he corrected. "I left you here alone while I ogled nudie pictures and drank beer."

"Thanks, honey," Tara grumbled.

"Anytime dear," he smiled kissing her cheek.

CHAPTER 2

When Tara opened her eyes, her breath floated out of her like tiny clouds and her cheeks stung with the intensity of the cold. The small bedroom was bathed in the gray morning light, giving the room the feel of a monochrome photograph. Along one wall were their dressers, standing side by side. On top of her dresser was a wooden box a little smaller than a footlocker with some foreign writing printed on the side of it that had faded to illegible long before it belonged to her. The only other piece of furniture in the room was the bed they slept on that someone had made rather crudely from two by fours. There was a small closet, but the only clothing that hung in it were their interview suits. She'd already sold her nice clothes and shoes, including her wedding dress.

Tara groaned. She was so cold her joints hurt and her muscles were stiff. The only sounds were the ticking of the battery-operated clock on the wall and Jasper's slow rhythmic breathing. She couldn't remember the last time the house had been so quiet. It was eerie, even in the growing daylight.

"Jasper," she hissed giving him a nudge. "There's something wrong with the furnace."

In response he mumbled something she suspected wasn't very kind. Tara slid out of bed and stuffed her feet into her slippers then wrapped up in a robe that was shockingly cold.

The air in the house was painful to breathe and by the time she reached the bathroom Tara was shivering so hard her teeth were chattering. She wasn't going to make the same mistake twice.

Tara opened the utility room and carefully reset all the breakers. Nope, the furnace failed to come to life. The light switch also didn't respond to her. This was why the house had seemed so quiet. She didn't hear the compressor on the fridge, the water heater, the pressure tank, and most upsettingly the furnace blower.

"Now what?" she moaned. Hopefully this newest setback didn't have anything to do with yesterday's flood.

Tara wandered back into the bathroom. The water in the toilet bowl had a layer of ice on the surface. She closed the lid. Hopefully they could figure out what to do with it before it cracked the porcelain. When Tara twisted the handle on the sink she wasn't surprised that nothing happened. No power, no well. She moved stiffly to the kitchen and pulled a pitcher of water out of the fridge, at least that wasn't frozen. Back in the bathroom she poured water into a cup and began brushing her teeth.

Tara needed to call the power company soon. If it was a power outage they could tell her when it was estimated to be back on.

When Jasper walked in, Tara looked up from the drain that she didn't even realize she'd been staring at. He was already wearing his hat, coat, and boots. His cheeks and nose were still rosy with the cold.

"Can't use the toilet, it's pretty much frozen," Tara murmured after she spit her rinse water down the drain and put up her toothbrush. "We don't have any power." Tara fidgeted before she began to brush her long hair.

"I noticed." Jasper grabbed his toothbrush.

Tara stood in silence waiting for him to continue; instead he stared into his eyes in the mirror, never glancing in her direction. Tara took this as her cue to leave.

Back in the bedroom she dug out as much cool-weather gear as she could find: Long underwear, followed by heavy jeans, several shirts, a thick sweater, and some heavy wool socks.

Over them she laced her boots before adding a scarf, stocking cap, and gloves. After all of this, she still didn't feel warm. Her gray wool coat hung on its hook by the front door, so she added it to everything else. She felt uncomfortable being dressed this way in the house, but it was definitely necessary.

In the kitchen, Tara opened the refrigerator and took stock of what they had: Leftover macaroni, a stick of butter, and some condiments. At least she didn't have to worry about any of their food going bad. In this weather she could leave it out on the counter. The pantry hadn't magically created more food than was there the night before either. Still only a can of beets that Tara didn't buy

Cold macaroni was going to have to be breakfast.

When Jasper had finished his share he stared absently at his plate, tapping it with his fork.

"What's up?" Tara asked when she finished chewing.

Jasper set the fork down. "I think one of us should stop in at the food bank tomorrow. They open at eight in the morning and it's first come, first served according to the flier in the temp agency."

"Didn't you just get paid?" Tara asked quietly. "Can't we use that to buy food?"

Jasper leaned back, pulling his stocking cap tighter over his ears while he watched the plumes of his breath. "I didn't get much. Gas just went up again, so I'll need to put all of what I made in the truck."

Tara fidgeted with the ends of her hair. "It said first come first served. That means they don't have enough for everyone..." Tara paused while Jasper looked at her. "That food needs to go to families and the elderly. People who really need help."

"We are people who need help. Why should we go hungry just because someone had more brats than they can afford."

Tara gasped, "You don't mean that?"

Jasper's face went as cold as the room. "People who can't afford children shouldn't have them."

"How is someone with a five-year-old supposed to know before they had that child that we were going to find ourselves in a recession today? How was a mom who got laid off or a dad who got fired supposed to know what was going to happen in the future?" Tara looked at the chipped red tabletop because she didn't want to look at him.

"Why are you trying to make me angry?" Jasper asked

calmly.

"I'm not."

"Then what are you doing?"

"I just don't want to take food away from people who really need it. I don't want to walk out of there past hungry children who might not get a meal because of me," she pleaded.

Jasper rubbed his hands together and blew into them for warmth. "Why do we deserve help less than other people?"

"Because we don't have kids," she insisted before taking a couple of shaky breaths.

"Well it's nice to see that you and the government agree about that," Jasper taunted.

"About what?" Tara asked, genuinely confused.

"When I went in to apply for food and energy assistance the lady at the desk told me there was a huge waiting list and if we didn't have kids we shouldn't even bother applying."

"You applied for aid without even talking to me?" Tara asked shocked.

"I didn't think you'd want me to do it," Jasper grumbled. "You have crazy ideas about what's best for us. Someone has to be rational."

Tara blinked quickly. "I'm rational."

"No, you're not! You can barely act like an adult. You do stupid things, make stupid decisions…" Jasper huffed. "I'm the one holding this house together at the moment."

Tara stared at him. This was not her definition of holding things together. They were living in a borrowed house, eating a cold breakfast, wearing their coats, and unsure what they were going to eat tomorrow. She didn't say any of what she thought, instead she asked, "Why did you do it?"

"Because we got a notice in the mail about our power getting disconnected if we didn't get the bill paid," he sighed

Tara stood up and paced to the door of the bedroom and back. She needed to be calm. She needed to control herself. "We sold the rest of my jewelry; my grandmother's pearls to have enough to cover that bill." Tara held up her ring finger where the gold band of her wedding ring sat. "This is all I have left."

Jasper's mouth set in a hard line. "What are you implying?"

"I'm implying that the money should have been there. I'm implying that I'd like an explanation."

"Oh, I'm sorry I didn't keep any receipts. I didn't realize I was going to be audited." Jasper mocked, trying to push his chair back. Instead, he shoved the table several feet away from himself.

Tara flinched. "I don't know what you're getting angry about. I don't think it's unfair of me to ask where that money went."

Jasper stared at her without saying anything for several heartbeats. "You're so controlling! Why don't you trust me?"

"This isn't about trust!" Tara shot back.

"Damnit, Tara." Jasper interrupted getting up so abruptly that the chair he'd been sitting in bounced when it landed on the floor.

Tara staggered backwards.

"Oh, now you're scared of me? You're so dramatic. I've never laid a hand on you and you know it. I hate when you act like this." Jasper kicked the chair, making it bounce against the wall.

Tara stood motionless, pressed against the opposite wall; eyes wide. She barely dared to breathe and said nothing.

"I don't have to take this shit!" he raged. "I'm not the monster you make me out to be." He stormed out the door, slamming it so hard that the clock fell off the wall and broke.

Tara's body didn't relax until the truck was bouncing out of the end of the driveway. Once it was out of sight she moved forward and picked up the chair. Thankfully it wasn't broken. That's why she tried so hard not to make him mad. He had such a temper. This wasn't the first time he'd broken things, but he'd warned her that he was passionate about everything.

Calmly, she got the broom out of the corner and started to sweep up the clock. It had been the only clock that was actually in the house. Now that no numbers showed on the stove, and Jasper always had the cell phone, it was going to be difficult judging the time.

Tara gathered up the breakfast dishes, thankful that they

hadn't fallen to the floor when Jasper shoved the table. They couldn't afford to replace them and they were more necessary than the clock. When she set them in the sink and turned the faucet she remembered that the well wouldn't run without power. How were they going to wash dishes? They didn't have any water.

"Use your brain, Tara!" she mumbled to herself. Tara took a pot into the utility room and drained some of the water from the water heater then set it on the stovetop.

The house had a gas range, so Tara decided to give it a try. When she turned the knob there was no spark, so she just listened to the hiss of escaping gas before she turned it off.

"Now what?" she asked the empty room while she let out a loud sigh. Then she remembered there was a book of matches in the box where she kept her treasures.

The wooden box that should have been under her bed was sitting on the top of her dresser until the carpet dried. When she opened it, she sorted through photos of her childhood; the few good memories that she cherished. Under this was her sewing box and an old stack of journals that went back to when she was a small child. Near the bottom she found the book of matches from the first bar that Jasper had taken her to.

The bar had been a dark little hole in the wall with watered down drinks and music kept loud enough to make conversation impossible. Tara smiled when she thought of how shy she'd been to go on the dance floor with Jasper. She'd kept the matchbook as a souvenir, but if there was anything that Tara had learned in the last few months it was that nothing was sacred.

Tara used one of the matches to light the burner of the stovetop. Unfortunately, the oven was controlled by an electrical gate instead of a pilot light; so that would be useless until they got the power turned back on. Tara sighed, *Why does everything have to be so hard?*

Tara washed the breakfast dishes in one pot and rinsed them in another. When she was finished she was still agitated. She needed to do something to relieve her stress other than pacing the house. What if Jasper was right? What if she couldn't take care of herself? What if he was the only one holding the place together. She could barely do the dishes. They couldn't bake, or vacuum, or do laundry, or mop the floors, or take a shower. They couldn't even flush the toilet.

Tara didn't know what else to do, so she starting using some of her energy to restlessly sweep the floor. She stabbed at the dirt in the corner while she thought about the towels draped over the railing, frozen on the porch, and about the fact that she had no idea what they were going to eat for lunch. She didn't even know where Jasper was, or if he intended to come back. What if he left her here in this little nightmare all by herself? *Why shouldn't he*, she wondered, *I can't even get a job.* She really was useless. Tara stepped out on the porch and flung the broom as far into the yard as she could manage. Then she began to cry as she crept, defeated, to go pick it up.

Twilight came early this time of year, so Tara set about looking for some light. Jasper still hadn't returned and part of Tara felt guilty for making him so mad that he left in the first place. She wasn't any better than her mother. Tara's father had stormed out many times when she was growing up. Normally he'd stumble back in angry and drunk. She had to physically shake her head to get her father's face out of her mind.

On the wall above the sofa was an old oil lamp hanging in a wall bracket that had been there since before they moved into the place. She lifted it out of the bracket, but it seemed too light to contain anything. With some effort she unscrewed the burner hoping there was still some lamp oil. A sharp smell like paint thinner escaped, but the reservoir was empty. As she began her search for candles the shadows in the room deepened, but all she found were five birthday candles in assorted colors. The first one gave her only enough light to search hopelessly for more, but it burned out too quickly. She'd have to save the other four for emergencies.

When it was nearly too dark to see, Tara sat down with some

blankets on the couch and huddled under them listening to herself breathe and the utter stillness of the house.

She must have dosed off because she woke to the door opening.

"Tara?" Jasper whispered into the cold darkness.

Her bones ached and the air was so sharp it stung when she breathed in. "I'm here on the couch."

"Gimmie' a minute," he called as the door shut.

When it opened again he was carrying a flashlight that was so bright it hurt her eyes. He set it down on the coffee table that wobbled in front of the couch. The beam bounced off the ceiling, lighting the room in a dim glow.

Tara fidgeted under the blanket.

"I'm sorry I yelled at you. I've been under so much stress lately."

Tara nodded.

"When I went into the agency, I did that for you." Jasper ran his hand across his face as if he could wipe the words away from him, then he visibly slumped. "I'm sorry, I just feel like such a failure."

Startled, Tara looked at him before her features relaxed and she smiled. "We're doing the best we can," she soothed. "Don't think for a second that I don't know how hard you try. I'm out there getting rejected time and time again, too."

"Yeah, but you don't have any useful job experience. You've only been a clerk and some stuff like that."

Tara didn't say anything. Instead she gave him a space of silence while he stared at his threadbare sneakers.

"I never wanted us to live like this," he spoke without raising his eyes to hers.

Tara pushed an arm free of her blankets and placed her hand on his elbow, leaving it there until he looked into her eyes. "I can't imagine anyone wanting to live like this."

CHAPTER 3

As the truck pulled to a stop in front of the factory, Tara frowned. It looked abandoned except for the cars in the parking lot, the hum of machines, and some billows of smoke that curled into the cold gray sky. It matched the rest of the run-down park where more than half of the industrial buildings had boarded up windows and in their parking lots tufts of shriveled brown grass lay dead in the cracks of the pavement. Those were abandoned.

"Call me when you're done," Jasper commanded as she slid from the truck. She nodded then watched him drive off towards town.

Tara knew from experience which buildings stood empty and which housed industry. As she walked into the first one she smelled the familiar factory smell of iron filings, machine oil, and coffee.

"Morning, Tara," a plump blonde woman behind the desk called out.

"Morning, Brenda." Tara leaned against the counter and sighed.

"We have just as much nuthin' available today as we had last week," Brenda intoned sweetly.

"I figured," Tara sighed, fiddling with a pen that was tied to the counter. "You know I still want to fill out an application."

"This ain't a drawing honey. Having your name in more times won't increase your chances. We don't have any positions available."

"I know," Tara groaned. "I just have to do something."

Brenda's brow wrinkled between her eyes, "I know honey." The older woman opened her desk drawer and set an application in front of Tara. "You do what you gotta' do."

"Thanks."

"You have the truck today?" Brenda asked, making small talk while Tara wrote her name and address again. Tara liked Brenda. She only knew her from this office, but she already knew the woman had two grown sons that she was very proud of, three grandkids (one of whom ate bugs at every opportunity), and a tiny puppy who refused to housebreak.

"Nope, just out walking," Tara answered distractedly while she paused over the phone number of her previous employer. She had them all memorized, she wrote them twenty times per week or more.

"In this weather? It's not more than fifteen degrees out there."

"You don't have to tell me," Tara shook her head. "I've been out there."

"Can't you do this on a warmer day?" Brenda asked her as Tara neatly printed her references.

"I wish." Tara handed her the finished application.

"You're welcome to stay and have some coffee."

"That's nice of you," Tara smiled, "but, this is my first stop and I have a long way to go."

"Take care of yourself honey," Brenda called as Tara headed for the door.

"You too," Tara called back over her shoulder as she stepped out into the bone chilling cold.

Tara worked her way through three more factory offices making small talk and filling out applications that she suspected were going straight into the trash when she was finished.

A book bindery was her last stop in the industrial park. The receptionist wasn't at her usual spot behind a gray countertop smeared with colorful fingerprints from the ink covered employees.

"Linda?" Tara called. Nobody answered, so she peaked her head through the door that led to the factory floor. To her left was a break room, where Linda could sometimes be found having a cigarette. Tara was always surprised when she saw the woman smoke, she seemed too young.

Instead of Linda she found a crowd gathered at the edge of

the factory floor. People were agitated and there was a disjointed clamor of angry voices that she caught in snippets.

"What am I supposed to do… Son's medical bills… nearly Christmas… only three years to retirement… rent and all my bills… you fat sons of bitches… just bought a house… no jobs anywhere."

In front of the crowd stood a fat balding man wearing a button-up dress shirt with the sleeves rolled up and some expensive-looking slacks. His hands were raised making a gesture for everyone to settle down.

"When corporate makes up their mind I have no say!" he shouted over the din.

Tara spotted Linda near the back of the crowd. She was scowling.

"What's happening?" Tara asked.

"We just got shit-canned," Linda snapped. "Not so much as a day's notice."

"That's awful," Tara moaned. It was awful, but Tara felt a pang of guilt because the first thing she thought about was that she and Jasper now had what looked like another two hundred people to compete with in the local job market.

That was when a can of soda hit the wall and exploded in sticky fizz just above the head of the man who stood in front of the crowd.

"Damn it!" he shouted, "You bunch of goddamn animals."

A hush rippled through the crowd that made the hair on the back of Tara's neck stand up.

"Get the hell out!" the fat man shouted, wiping the top of his balding head with a handkerchief from his pocket.

The crowd stood defiantly while angry murmuring began. Another can of soda was thrown. This one broke the man's office window.

"I'm calling the cops you pieces of shit!" the man shouted, backing into his office as members of the crowd swarmed forward.

"Time to go, Linda!" Tara shouted as a small machine that Tara couldn't identify was pushed over on its side. Linda looked at Tara's face as if she hadn't seen her before, rushed forward, and picked up a metal bar that she smashed repeatedly against the side of another machine.

Tara stood staring at Linda open-mouthed in shock. What was wrong with her? What were these people thinking? Tara needed to get out of here before she got hurt. As she made that decision a machine showered sparks nearby and someone started screaming. Tara turned and fled with some of the employees who had obviously come to the same conclusion. In the doorway into the front office she slid, landing hard on her knees and wrists on the floor. The heel of her shoe was lying on the floor where she'd taken the corner too quickly. When Tara reached for it she was kicked hard in the side by a man trying to get out past her. She didn't really need the heel. She just needed to get out of there. As she scampered to her feet a crashing sound was followed by a loud cheer.

When she was clear of the parking lot, Tara slowed her pace. Limping unevenly on her broken shoe she heard the sirens, and then watched three police cars fly into the parking lot. Tara wondered if Alex was there. If so she hoped he would be safe, but she didn't want to go back and give a statement. What if she was mistakenly scooped up as one of the agitators? No way could she afford that mess. So she kept walking. It was a mile back to town from here; surely she could find a phone somewhere that she could use.

Thankfully, less than five minutes passed before a familiar blue vintage Chevy pulled over just in front of her. She'd admired the truck before with its late fifties curved hood and rounded fenders. The passenger door swung open before she ever got close to it so she approached the truck from that side.

"Are you okay?" Pete asked as she stepped into the space between the door and the truck.

"I'm fine, why?" she answered him, trying to smile so that he would believe her.

"Your knees are dirty, one is bleeding, and your stockings are torn up. Your shoe is broken and your coat is ripped at the shoulder," Pete pointed out matter-of-factly.

"Is it?" Tara felt her shoulder and found a rip in the shoulder seam on the left side. Pete was also right about her knees. One was bleeding a little from a scuff and her stockings had holes at both knees; with runs up and down in stripes of various lengths.

"Were you mugged?" Pete asked as if it was the most normal thing in the world.

"No," she shook her head vigorously, "I just fell down."

Pete stared at her without speaking, like he was trying to figure out what to say next. At least she hoped he was. He had a bad habit of silence.

"Can I give you a ride somewhere?"

Tara thought about it, but realized she didn't want to admit where she'd just been. She'd fled the scene of a crime. Since she was unsure of where the law would come down on that, she felt it was better not to ride with Alex's best friend.

"Can I just borrow your phone to call my husband? He can come get me."

Pete patted the seat next to him in the truck. "At least warm up for a minute while you do. It's freezing out today and you're not dressed for the weather."

Tara nodded while she climbed into the truck and took the cell phone he offered her. It was already dialing her husband's number. She wondered briefly if he was being nice or he didn't want her to rummage through his phone contacts.

When the answering system picked up she left a message. "I'm done and was hoping you could come get me. Come on Jasper pick up. I'll be making my way to Main Street. Jasper?"

Pete took the phone from her abruptly. "Don't worry about it. This is Pete, I'll drive Tara home." Pete was frowning when he hung up the phone. "Have you had lunch yet?"

"No, but I can have something when I get home," she lied enjoying the heat from the vent. She rubbed her legs to warm them through her ruined pantyhose. She was starting to get sensation back in her toes and it was unpleasant.

"I was on my way to lunch anyway. We can stop and get a bite."

Tara panicked. She didn't want to admit that she didn't have a penny to her name. "Gosh no, I really need to be heading back."

"I'll pay," Pete offered.

Tara shook her head vigorously. "I don't want to impose more than I already am." She offered him an embarrassed smile.

"I don't want to drive out to your house first. I'm hungry. So we'll stop for a bite."

"You're not going to take no for an answer are you?" she asked crossing her arms.

"I'm not going to force feed you. I can't make you eat. I'm going to stop at the diner and I'm going to have lunch. If you don't order, I'll order for you. Then if you don't eat it's purely a matter of choice. Personally I think it would be a shame to waste good food," he smiled as he pulled the truck to a stop in the diner's parking lot, turning off the engine like a punctuation mark.

Inside, the diner was warm and smelled mostly of gravy. The walls were a glossy white with generic artwork consisting of barnyards, cowboys, and one inexplicable cartoon frog. Tables and booths were both an unnatural shade of burnt orange. The seats had some splits in the vinyl patched with brown tape. On each table were sets of novelty salt and pepper shakers. The table they were seated at had a pair of sad-eyed hound dogs.

The waitress was at the table before Tara had even finished pulling her coat off. A perky young blonde set down two menus. Her hair was up in a neat ponytail and her nametag said, "Elizabeth."

"What can I get you and your...?" The girl trailed off and waited for Pete to fill in the word while she pulled her order book and a pen out of her red apron.

"Friend."

"Right," the waitress continued looking at Tara with narrowed eyes. "What would you and your friend like to drink?"

"Coffee," Pete answered

"And you?" Elizabeth turned to Tara.

"Just water, please."

"Sweetie, would you like your coffee the way you like your women?" Elizabeth winked at Pete.

Pete shook his head, "I like coffee more than that. Just bring it to me, I'll fix it myself."

The young woman's smile faded and she seemed to deflate.

Tara opted for a burger and fries since it was one of the cheapest things on the menu.

Then the silence began. Pete was texting someone on his phone while she watched him. When he looked up at her he shrugged and said, "Work stuff."

Tara blushed. He didn't owe her an explanation so she nodded and turned away. Tara studied all the nearby salt and pepper shakers, and then she decided to look out the window since Pete seemed perfectly content for them not to talk at all.

Once their food came Tara realized she was being watched. "Do I have something on my face?" she asked Pete.

"No, why?" he responded, barely looking at her. He had put his phone down and was now concentrating on eating.

"Our waitress keeps staring at me," she whispered to him as she made eye contact with their server; who quickly looked away to continue folding silverware into napkins.

Pete shrugged.

"She looks like she's annoyed with me for something. It's making me feel a bit uncomfortable," Tara frowned.

"Then I suggest not paying attention, you'll feel better in no time."

Even after thinking about what Pete said for a few minutes Tara couldn't decide if he was being sarcastic, or blunt.

When they were both finished with their lunch Pete leaned in and asked quietly, "I know it's none of my business, but how are you guys holding up with no power. Are you warm enough?"

Tara looked back at him shocked. "What?" Her cheeks burned with embarrassment.

"Do you guys have some way of keeping warm?" Pete asked

again as he pulled out his wallet and began counting a tip onto the table, "It's really too cold not to have something."

"Who told you we don't have any power?" Tara asked instead of answering.

Pete seemed surprised for a moment, and then cleared his throat. "A reliable source," he assured her.

Tara looked down and scratched her neck before reflexively pulling on the ends of her hair to find some calm. "I'd like to say that we have a plan and everything is under control, but then I'd be lying. I've been everywhere in town, nobody's hiring," she paused just long enough to drop the strand of hair she'd been playing with before the rest came out in a rush. "We can't get food or energy assistance. Jasper's unemployment ran out months ago and I wasn't even eligible. We've sold everything we owned of value except my wedding ring," she confided in him, holding up her left hand. "I only have that because Jasper insisted we keep it. He sold his months ago."

Tara dropped her hand onto the table with a loud smack that made a lot of heads swivel in their direction. Tara blushed and waited to speak until the others had turned back to their own conversations. "I don't know what to do anymore."

Pete watched her longer than she was comfortable with. Was he judging her? Why had she blurted all of that out to him in the first place? It's not like any of this was his problem.

"Okay," he nodded.

Tara bit her lip thinking about his dismissive reply. But he continued, "You're not alone. A lot of people are having the same problems as you right now."

Tara looked around the restaurant. It was true that nobody in here looked well off, but at least they could still afford to eat at a restaurant. She couldn't afford to eat at all. She dropped her cheeks into her hands to hide her embarrassment.

Pete frowned, "When things get hard it's important to be adaptable. If finding a job isn't working for you is there something else you can do? If you don't have money for the grocery store can you find somewhere else to get food?"

Tara blinked at him. What was he talking about? "Do you

want me to dig through trash cans like a raccoon?"

Pete smiled, "Not exactly. I was just wondering if you'd looked into any methods of self-sufficiency or barter?"

"What do you mean?"

"Self-sufficiency is a movement that has gained some popularity since the recession started," Pete responded, standing up from the booth. "I'm sorry," he said glancing at his phone. "I hate to do this, but I'm going to need to be getting back to work so we need to get going."

Tara nodded and grabbed her coat as she slid out of the booth.

"Have a nice day, Pete!" Elizabeth waved as he headed out the door.

Pete gave the woman a brief wave without looking back over his shoulder at her on his way out.

Tara was watching Elizabeth so she was shocked when the woman mouthed something at her slowly and carefully. "Dumb slut."

Tara turned her back and walked out of the restaurant, but said nothing to Pete as she climbed in the truck. Maybe Tara had misunderstood what Elizabeth had tried to say. After all she couldn't think of a single thing she'd ever done to this waitress. She wasn't rude while she was at the restaurant and she couldn't recall having met her before.

"Could you do me a favor and drop me off at the library instead of taking me all the way home?" Tara asked.

"Sure, but I can take you all the way home. I have time."

"No, really. I want to go to the library," Tara spoke firmly.

Pete looked at her suspiciously before he turned on his blinker to head back towards Main Street.

"I have a little research I want to get done."

"Suit yourself." He pulled to a stop in front of the library so that Tara could climb out.

"Thanks for lunch," Tara told him shyly.

"Not a problem, anytime. I'll let your husband know where you are."

Tara didn't get to thank him again before he drove away.

CHAPTER 4

The library door was heavy and made a whoosh and an electronic beep as Tara walked in. The librarian was a surprisingly young man who looked up at her. His smile faltered only for a moment.

"Nasty day out there. Anything I can help you find?"

"Boy is it," Tara admitted, enjoying how friendly his round face seemed as he began to stand up from behind an ancient-looking wooden desk. She wiped her broken and unbroken shoe on the commercial welcome mat and advanced toward him. "I'm looking for some information on self-sufficiency."

"Self-sufficiency," he confirmed. "We'll see what we can find." The librarian swiveled to face the old computer sitting on his desk. The menu looked ancient as he jumped through a series of screens typing in information. "If we have anything it should be this way." He motioned her to follow him, pushing out his chair and leading the way towards the back of the library to a set of shelves on the right.

"Thanks you for your help," she whispered to him as she began scanning the titles. The librarian stood watching her for a few moments before she turned to him and smiled politely.

He seemed briefly embarrassed then stammered, "Well, if you need anything else just ask." He smiled quickly and walked off toward the front of the library.

Tara took her time perusing the shelves. It was a general farming and livestock section. Some of the books were quite old, others were new glossy paperbacks. She flipped through each book in turn, but she couldn't find anything specifically about the self-sufficiency movement.

"Can I use the computers online?" Tara asked the librarian after she'd made her way to the front of the library.

Startled, the man nearly dropped his phone that he'd been staring at. "Sure, just sign the log, and use the headphones provided."

Tara sat down and after a quick search found herself drowning in a sea of information. She settled on watching some videos so that her mind could wander. "Self-sufficiency" appeared to span a whole spectrum of things from tiny homes, with toilets made out of buckets, to gardening, canning, and baking. The videos that Tara enjoyed watching the most were the ones about chickens and baby animals. Goats, sheep, cows, pigs, and even horses seemed to feature prominently. It was about farming, but more than that it appeared to be a lifestyle.

Tara sat like this until Jasper walked in the door of the library looking for her.

"Ready to go?" he asked.

"Yeah, just let me sign out." Tara jotted her log out time on the clip board and waved goodbye to the librarian who acknowledged her with only the briefest nod.

Tara couldn't stop thinking about the things she'd watched and read the whole way home, but that didn't stop her from noticing Jasper. He kept looking at her sideways and taking a deep breath like he was going to say something before looking back to the road again. It made her tense.

"Something the matter?" Tara finally asked as they were pulling into the driveway of their perfectly dark house. It was going to be a miserable night anyway; she might as well get this over with.

"What were you doing at the library?" Jasper asked her quietly.

She watched his face in the truck's dome light when she opened the door. This wasn't what he wanted to talk about, but maybe she could distract him.

"I was looking up self-sufficiency."

Just after the door on Jasper's side of the truck banged shut the flashlight clicked on. "Why?"

"It was something Pete and I were talking about at lunch. He thought it might help us get back on our feet."

"Isn't that what self-sufficient means?" Jasper asked as Tara pushed the door open.

"What?"

"Able to take care of ourselves." Jasper seemed irritated.

"Basically," Tara nodded. "But it's like a lifestyle. Did you know that you can raise chickens in a backyard?"

Jasper set the flashlight pointing towards the ceiling on the table where it lit the room with a dim glow. "No," he frowned, looking in the pantry. "I've never thought about where chickens can live. I barely think about eating them."

"Well, what do you think about raising some?" Tara asked.

"Some what?"

"Chickens," Tara reiterated.

Jasper stared at her. "You're not expecting me to buy this crap are you?"

"What?"

"I'm supposed to believe that you and Pete spent all morning talking about chickens and that's how you tore the knees out of your stockings?"

It was Tara's turn to stare. She couldn't figure out how raising chickens had anything to do with Pete or what any of it had to do with her stockings.

"Are you sleeping with him?" Jasper asked in a voice like the ice crystals covering the windows.

"What?"

"Don't play dumb with me. Are you sleeping with Pete?"

"I've barely spoken to Pete. We weren't together all morning like you seem to think, and he has nothing to do with my torn stockings." Tara shot back, shocked by Jasper's accusation.

"Really? You don't think I've noticed how quiet he is around you, how uncomfortable he seems around me." Jasper slammed his fist down on the counter. "So, don't lie to me!"

"This morning I was filling out job applications like I said I was. When I got to the printing company some sort of riot started. I broke my heel when I fell down trying to stay out of the middle of it."

"You're trying to tell me you were there for the riot. They arrested something like fifty people. They had to call in both county and state. They rounded up another one hundred and fifty for questioning. I call bullshit. If you were there you would have been in the group."

Tara was shocked. "You knew what happened in the industrial park and when you saw the way I look you didn't ask if I was okay?" Tara kicked her shoe off. "You accused me of sleeping with Pete?" Tara kicked the second shoe off with such force that it bounced off the wall.

"Pete didn't mention any riot when he talked to me, and Alex didn't see you there."

"That's because, like I told you, I ran away. Was I supposed to stick around? I was scared of getting hurt, and of getting arrested for being in the wrong place at the wrong time."

Jasper frowned. "So why didn't Pete tell me about it. My wife being in a riot seems noteworthy."

Jasper still didn't seem like he believed her. "I didn't tell him."

"Why?"

"He's friends with Alex and it's none of his business."

Japer still looked suspicious, but he unclenched his fists.

"Why didn't you answer the phone when I called you?" Tara asked carefully.

Jasper plopped down on the couch still wearing his coat. "I was doing a repair." He smiled before he reached into his coat and pulled out an envelope. "I got paid in cash. We should get some dinner."

"Shouldn't we save the gas? We have beets." Tara volunteered, happy that Jasper seemed ready to drop the accusations.

"I don't like beets," Jasper groaned.

"We can still eat them."

Tara wandered into the bedroom and came back out with her sewing kit. She needed to fix her coat before she could apply for more jobs. The shoes were unfortunate; she was going to have to get rid of them. Now the nicest thing she had was her black boots. If she polished them they might still be acceptable. When she sat down with the kit Jasper stared at her.

"Beets aren't dinner."

Tara pulled her gloves off and threaded the needle. "You said gas went up again."

Before she could continue, headlights flashed across the room briefly sweeping across Tara's face and casting a monstrous shadow on the wall. Jasper jumped up and looked out the window then glared over his shoulder at Tara before heading for the door.

"Now what?" Tara muttered to the empty room as she followed.

The blue Chevy sat in the driveway and Pete climbed out of the driver's seat. As Tara stepped out onto the porch snowflakes were just beginning to drift lazily out of the sky.

"What's up Pete?" Jasper called cheerfully as if he hadn't just accused Tara of an affair with the man.

Pete waved as they approached the truck. He was still in his work uniform, a navy blue shirt tucked into pants of the same color. His heavy work boots were caked with mud, as were the knees of his pants. On his chest were two embroidered patches, one said his name, the other belonged to the company he worked for.

"Just thought I would drop off a couple of things I'm not using at the moment. Hoped you might find them useful," he called as he pulled a kerosene heater off the back of the truck.

"Oh my God! I could kiss you!" Jasper laughed.

"Please show some self-control man. At least wait until your wife isn't watching," he teased with a smile in Tara's direction. This earned the briefest scowl from Jasper whose pleasant countenance recovered quickly.

Four five-gallon containers of kerosene followed the heater off the back of the truck. He pulled them out two at a time and carried them to the porch while Jasper grabbed the heater and Tara picked up one of the containers, which were uncomfortably heavy and awkward.

Something struck Tara. "You had twenty gallons of kerosene you just happened to not be using sitting around?" Tara asked setting the plastic container of kerosene on the porch.

"I..." Pete began, but stopped. "I mean..." Pete paused like he needed to give her a very precise response.

"Do you still need the heater?" Tara asked. "Seems like a lot of kerosene for something you're not using.

"Stop it Tara," Jasper scolded. "You can be so stupid sometimes. Use your head. He just bought this stuff and doesn't want to embarrass us."

Tara's cheeks burned. She hated it when Jasper scolded her in front of other people. Pete gave her a sympathetic look before turning away, which somehow made it feel worse.

"I think you owe him an apology," Jasper insisted.

Tara hadn't meant to insult Pete, and she wasn't sure she had, but he did seem uncomfortable about answering the question. "I'm sorry Pete. I really do appreciate you doing this for us. I didn't mean to seem ungrateful."

"It's fine," Pete assured her though his face looked pained. He turned back to Jasper. "I know you guys would never have asked me to do this."

"Thanks man." Jasper clapped Pete on the back.

"I'm sorry if I embarrassed you." Pete looked at Tara. "You guys aren't the only ones down on your luck right now. Besides," Pete smiled, "when I was last down on my luck a good-guy cop that we all know did an awful lot to help me out. I haven't been able to pay him back, so I thought I might pay some forward."

Tara gave him a half-smile while she studied the red embroidery of his nametag. She couldn't look him in the eye. She was humiliated about her situation, and Jasper's behavior. "I'm really glad you did, we've been freezing. Is there anything we can do for you? Any way we can pay you back?"

Jasper glanced at Tara and it felt like an accusation. Did he think she was going to screw Pete for some kerosene now? Had she been upgraded from slut to whore?

"No worries," Pete assured her as he closed the tailgate of his truck. I know you'd do the same if the roles were reversed and that's all that really matters. You don't owe me a thing."

"Wanna' come inside?" We're gonna light this baby and celebrate with a fabulous dinner of beets," Jasper offered.

"I'd like to," Pete glanced at Tara then back to Jasper, "but, I have someplace I have to be. Otherwise I'd stay longer."

It was an excuse. Tara suspected they couldn't have paid Pete to step inside their house with them. She didn't blame him. She didn't really want to be here either.

Jasper held out a hand to Pete. When he took it Jasper pulled him in for a crushing hug. "You don't know what this means to us. I can't thank you enough!" He released Pete and clapped him on the back hard.

Pete's brow furrowed while he stared at Jasper, then he headed to the driver's side door of the truck and waved goodbye to them.

Jasper's macho display was clearly meant to intimidate Pete, but he seemed more confused than intimidated when he left.

Jasper bent down to unscrew the cap of the heater's fuel reservoir. "What an unexpected surprise."

Tara wrinkled her nose at the sharp smell of kerosene, but said nothing.

Jasper replaced the cap and rocked the heater, which sloshed back and forth. "He already filled it, how nice of him to make it so easy on you."

"What are you implying?"

Jasper pressed the button to light the heater in silence as a ring of light began to form on the wick. About the time Tara assumed he was going to drop it, he continued, "I just think it's weird that he brought this out here after spending some time with you."

"I didn't beg him for charity if that's what you are implying." Tara knew it wasn't what he was implying. "He already knew we didn't have power. Does everyone in town know? Are we being gossiped about?"

Jasper looked momentarily sheepish, "I wasn't looking for

charity when I told him about that this morning. I was hoping he'd mention something to his boss about hiring me. They have an open position where he works right now."

Tara stared at him for a moment, "You're the one who told him?"

"Yes."

"It never occurred to you that he was bringing this over for you. You were the one asking for help."

Jasper stared at Tara quietly. "Yes, that's possible."

Heat shimmered from the top of the heater in the quiet space between the two of them. Jasper picked it up and carried it inside.

Tara huffed as he disappeared through the doorway. He wasn't going to apologize. Snow tickled her cheeks as she stepped forward to the edge of the porch and looked at the moon just above the horizon, she didn't want to fight.

Everything was a fight now. Ever since they lost their jobs Tara felt like she was stuck in the lake that she had nearly drown in as a child. Every day she flailed, all day, and if she dared to rest she would go under and never see the surface again.

"Hey, get in here and close the door," Jasper called through the open doorway.

Tara joined him next to the heater while she listened to the little creaks and snaps made by warming metal. A dim light illuminated Jasper's knees and a ring of dashes undulated on the ceiling.

"So, chickens?"

Tara looked up. It appeared to be a question.

"Yeah."

"Why?"

"They make eggs, live on kitchen scraps, and you can eat them when they don't lay anymore." Tara shrugged. "They seem to be what everyone starts out with."

"Fine. Where do we put them?"

"Fine as in we're going to get chickens?" Tara asked surprised.

"Sure. Where do we get a coop?"

"I've been thinking about that." Tara smiled. "Do you know of any construction sites in the area? We could see if they want to get rid of any scrap lumber."

"That's not a bad idea," he shrugged, "except that I don't recall seeing anything new being built around here."

Tara considered this for a few moments while she rubbed her hands to warm them next to the heater. "If nothing is going up, maybe things are coming down. We could offer to take down and haul away old buildings."

"I suppose I have no argument. I'll write up some fliers saying we'll take down sheds and outbuildings for free. I'm not doing houses, too dangerous."

"So we're getting chickens?"

"Yeah, but they're going to be your responsibility," Jasper sighed as he curled up on the couch.

"That's fair," she admitted, easing down next to him on the sofa and closing her eyes.

"Tara?"

"Yeah?"

"I don't want you spending time with Pete anymore."

"Okay," Tara nodded. Jasper didn't trust her and that hurt.

CHAPTER 5

Tara jumped when the phone rang. She had become so used to the silence over the past week that any noise was intrusive. Jasper crossed the room quickly but Tara had already glided her finger across the green arrows to accept the call.

"Hello, this is Tara Hillcrest," she said in her most professional tone.

"Hi. Are you the folks with the ad at the supermarket offering to remove outbuildings for free?" a small frail voice asked.

"Yes, ma'am we are," she answered.

"Dear, in all my life I've found that nothing is really free. I don't mean to sound cynical, but why?"

Surprised by the woman's candor Tara admitted, "My husband and I have decided to raise some chickens. Money's tight so we need usable lumber to build a coop."

"Excellent," the little voice quavered, "My great-grandson is always telling me that everyone is crooked. When I told him about the ad he said you were going to come by and rob me blind."

Tara couldn't stop herself from chuckling. "No, ma'am. I wasn't planning on it."

"When can you start?" the tiny voice asked.

"Whenever you want, we can head over right now if you'd like."

"Okay I'll see you soon, but I'm not in town," she warned, giving Tara the address.

"You're less than five minutes away from us. We'll be there shortly."

Tara hung up the phone and smiled at Jasper who had been hovering since she picked the phone up. "We have a shed to take down."

"Don't do that again," Jasper snatched the phone from Tara.

"Do what?"

"Answer my phone. What if that was a job for me? What if they'd hung up because they thought they had the wrong number?"

Tara stared at him confused. "I use that number for my job applications too."

Jasper's nostrils flared and his mouth pinched. "Just don't do it again."

"Fine," Tara held her hands up in submission.

When the tools were loaded the couple got in Jasper's truck and headed to the address that they were given. Several miles down a gravel road they reached a mailbox with chipped and faded roses painted on it right above of the words, "The Penderton's."

The driveway was two dirt tracks with dead grass in the middle that crossed a concrete slab over a little creek. It was probably impossible to cross in a heavy rain, which Missouri got all too often in the spring. Overhead the bare tree branches nearly touched, it would be a beautiful tunnel of shade in the summertime. The house itself was small and in need of a coat of paint, but all around were planters which only held dirt this time of year. When Jasper parked the truck the two of them climbed out and headed up the front steps to the porch.

Even a light knock rattled the screen door in its frame. Just inside when the door opened stood a tiny little old lady, but she looked younger than Tara had pictured when she spoke of her cynical great-grandson. The woman was wearing a puffy red coat with a small rhinestone brooch on the collar. Her white hair was short and smooth while her face was set with the lines of a lifetime of smiling.

"Hello, dears."

Tara's husband stepped forward. "I'm Jasper, it's nice to meet you, ma'am," he smiled, taking her fingertips in his hand.

"My, but you do seem like a healthy young fella'," she said, looking him over as if she was thinking of buying a horse. "Young men nowadays are so soft. All that sitting on the couch playing those video games. Men used to do things when I was a girl. You, sir, look like you do something. Nice strong hands too."

Jasper looked to Tara obviously at a loss for words, but Tara couldn't help him. She had to look away and was biting her lip struggling not to laugh. Finally Tara took a deep breath to compose herself and stepped forward.

"I'm Tara Hillcrest. It's very nice to meet you." She tried not to imagine this little old lady climbing up and examining Japer's teeth.

"Rose Penderton," the elderly woman replied with a smile. "Follow me, I'll show you where the shed is."

Rose shuffled with careful, deliberate steps off the porch and down a path around the back of the house. They walked past an old clothesline and an empty doghouse to a clapboard shed with a sagging roof whose door Rose opened and gestured them inside.

Inside was barely space to stand amongst the cardboard boxes, old metal bits, scraps of wood, and jars of nails. Jasper looked at Rose with eyebrows raised.

"Okay, I know it needs to be cleaned out first, but you can't expect a ninety-year-old woman to be hauling boxes," she admitted with a small smile on her face.

"I fear we should have been the ones questioning your motives instead of the other way around," Jasper replied lightly.

Rose gave a small shrug. "When my nephew sent a real estate agent over; that soft young man told me that I would need to take down this old shed to increase the value of the property. That little vulture wants to make sure that I've done all the improvements to the place before I croak so that he can put it directly on the market and make as much money as possible from it."

Jasper and Tara stood in shocked silence.

"It's okay dears. I understand I'm not as young as I used to be. My great-grandson is no better than my nephew, but they are all that's left of my family. What they don't seem to understand is that my brain still works just fine. I'm happy to clean up the house. But if anyone is going to sell it, it's me. Then," the little old lady winked in a way that was so animated she might as well have been a cartoon, "I think I'll do some gamblin' and drinkin' until I find myself so broke that I have to go stay with one of them." Rose burst out in a loud belting laugh that made both Jasper and Tara smile.

"In that case," Tara beamed at her, "We'll be happy to help you out."

"So where do you want all these things?" Jasper asked.

"Honestly," Rose said looking around, "I'll pay the fees if you'll take it all to the dump. What do I need all this stuff for in my time of life?"

"Is there anything of sentimental value that you want us to save for you?" Tara asked.

"Nope, get rid of it all. If I haven't missed it by now; I won't. I don't need the clutter."

"Then please feel free to head inside where it's warm," Jasper gestured toward the house. "My wife and I will work on this for you."

"If you need anything dear, just come on up to the house," Rose smiled at them before she headed slowly back the way they'd come.

After a few minutes of silence Tara looked at Jasper. "That sucks," she whispered solemnly.

"It does," he agreed.

Tara looked down and smiled. "I like her attitude though. She seems like quite a piece of work."

"She's a piece of work all right," Jasper agreed.

Tara got the impression that Jasper didn't approve of Rose's attitude but Tara didn't care. Tara already adored the little old lady.

She sighed and looked around. "Where do we even start?"

The shed was full of dust and piles of knick-knacks. In the

corner were some holiday decorations that looked like they hadn't moved since before Tara was born. Spider webs grew like dust blankets and the boxes had the curly quality of years of neglect.

"How about we separate things into piles? One for things that can be scrapped or sold, one for the things that obviously need to go to the dump, and one for things we might want to keep."

"We're going to sell her things?" Tara asked surprised.

"Why not? She doesn't want any of it. She said to take it all to the dump. We might as well get paid for all this extra work."

Tara nodded. It made sense, but it still felt wrong. "What do you have in mind to keep?" Tara asked.

"Those jars of screws and nails would be awfully useful to build our chicken coop," he said pointing to the collection sitting on what was probably a workbench.

Tara nodded.

The first thing they did was carry out as much of the truly ruined furniture as they could fit into the back of Jasper's truck. This way they would have some room to start sorting things into piles. Next, they carried out the bundles of mildewy mouse-eaten magazines and newspapers that it appeared someone had been meticulously saving for quite some time.

While loading the last of the magazines, Tara caught sight of Rose standing by the back door waving for her. Tara stuffed her bundle between two broken chairs and headed that direction.

"You folks must be plum frozen through by now," Rose said. "Why don't you two come in and have a warm drink."

"We couldn't impose, we're filthy," Tara gestured vaguely at herself.

"Nonsense, nothing's wrong with some good honest dirt. Now get that tall drink of water you came here with and let yourself on in. It's too cold for my old bones out here. I'll be waiting on you folks in the kitchen. Just come right on in."

"Alright we'll be in shortly," Tara agreed, heading back toward the shed for Jasper.

The back door led directly into a brightly scrubbed kitchen. It looked exactly like a grandmother's kitchen was expected to look. All the cabinets and appliances were gleaming white. On the windows were pink gingham curtains with a rose border. On the gray countertop was a set of metal canisters, each emblazoned with a title, "Sugar," "Flour," "Coffee," "Tea," and "Lard." On the top of the refrigerator, right where you would expect it to be, was a green cookie jar which also boldly announced its contents. In the middle of the room was a small table with four chairs around it. Two of the chairs were already pulled out in welcome. Rose stood behind the third. Rose herself was wearing a gaily printed floral dress and a very warm smile.

"What can I get you two to drink? Coffee, tea, bourbon, or any combination thereof?"

"Just tea for me, thanks," Tara hazarded a look at Jasper, who seemed as amused as she was.

"Same for me," Jasper nodded.

Rose looked at them for a moment. "Suit yourselves dears," she said putting the kettle on and pouring herself a glass of bourbon.

Tara couldn't help noticing that something smelled wonderful.

"We're having meatloaf for dinner. There's pie in the oven for dessert." Rose explained.

"We don't expect you to feed us." Tara shook her head quickly, caught off guard.

"Dinner's already all but done. It's no trouble at this point," Rose replied. "Besides, I didn't mention how much extra work you would be doing. The least I can do is feed you. My husband Chester, rest him, fancied himself quite the handyman. Couldn't bring himself to throw a damn thing away. By the time he died he had that whole damn shed crammed full."

"I'm sorry for your loss," Jasper said solemnly.

Rose stared at him a moment before she grinned. "You kidding me? Best years of my life have been since he was gone!" Rose crowed. Then she began to laugh when she saw the look of disgust that had crept onto Jasper's face. "I don't care what you may think of me for saying that, young man. You never met Chester."

"Thank you for dinner." Tara moved forward to one of the empty chairs and Jasper followed.

Rose smiled back and forth at the two of them before she took a deep breath. "I'm sorry you folks are a hard luck story. There are so many of them now that I can't help thinking back to when I was a girl," she paused seeing into the past instead of the kitchen. "The great depression didn't end when they said it did, you know. I didn't know that things were getting better until the first time I saw a rabbit runnin' through the field with nobody chasing it," she joked as they began to dish out dinner. "We were lucky. We had a little farm and a big garden. My mom canned everything we didn't use fresh, and she could make a meal out of just about anything." Rose paused to look at Tara. "Do you can?"

"No," Tara admitted, "but I want to learn."

Rose smiled. "Good. I'm glad to hear you say that. Young ladies don't seem to know a thing about keeping a house anymore. Ever since they glorified going off to work everyone treats women's work like it doesn't matter anymore. It's all fine and good if you can go earn the money for a can of peas, but you'd save a bunch if you grew and canned em' instead. Besides, you could count on it. When us ladies canned we'd have a winter's worth of food in the house. Now people are lucky if they have a week's worth. How do you make it a few weeks without a job without a little food in the pantry? A real winter storm would starve half this town." Rose sighed, and then brightened. "Did you happen to come across my canning supplies in the shed?"

Tara looked at Jasper who shrugged, and then she shook her head no.

"You're welcome to them when you do. I had a whole mess of jars, some big pots, and a good pressure canner too. It doesn't take a gasket, but it will probably need an overpressure plug. You'll also need new canning lids, mine probably ain't no good anymore."

Tara nodded, she didn't want to interrupt.

Rose continued, "I used to can a lot when I was a young wife and mother. I got back into it when I was a young grandmother, but when you're my age a garden really is more trouble than it's worth and canning itself is a lot of long, hot hours. My old body just isn't up to it anymore."

Tara waited a moment to make sure Rose was finished. "I would be happy to have your canning supplies, thank you. Now I just need to learn how."

"Young man," Rose said turning to Jasper, "how about you hop up and open the cabinet over there," she pointed. When he complied she continued, "Top shelf, red book on the right... that's the one!" Rose let him know when he had his hand on the right book spine. "Bring that on over and give it to your adorable wife."

Jasper handed the book to Tara as ordered. It was a thick volume on food preservation. When she opened the front cover the table of contents showed sections for canning, freezing, smoking, drying, fermenting, and root cellaring.

"You keep that. It's got most anything you'd want to know in it. If you have any questions you can just give me a call."

"Thank you so much," Tara gushed.

"Just a bunch of old junk to me now. Good if someone's getting some use out of it."

"Thank you just the same," Tara breathed, grateful.

Jasper and Tara thanked Rose for dinner and promised to come back soon and keep working on cleaning out the shed. Rose apologized again for not telling them the whole truth and offered dinner as part of the deal when they came back next time too.

Once they were home the two of them unloaded the furniture, stripping any fixtures and salvageable parts, before making a pile and lighting it on fire.

In the circle of firelight in the fading twilight they enjoyed the warmth while the upholstery burned with acrid black smoke.

"Are we heading back tomorrow?" Tara asked, sliding her arm around Jasper's waist and laying her head against his shoulder.

"Nope, I have a clogged drain to work on tomorrow morning and I thought we could head down to the bulk store and get some shopping done"

"The next day?"

Jasper smiled devilishly. "Nope, I didn't tell you I got a call while you were re-arranging the truck bed. It was from some guy at that Properties Inc. Auctions place; the one outside of town that set up in the blue barn."

"I know the one you're talking about," she nodded.

"The manager told me he saw my ad at the supermarket. He offered me a house cleanout job. They said it's huge, some old guy who died a hoarder. They need a couple of extra guys to get it done."

"Really?" Tara squealed.

"He said it would be maybe a week's work. I told him I would be glad to. I get nine dollars per hour under the table," Jasper smiled.

"That's great news!" Tara hugged him. "Any chance it could lead to steady work?"

"I don't know," he admitted, "He did imply that the company might have an opening for a good worker."

Tara kissed Jasper, suddenly feeling buoyant. Having steady money coming into the house would be such a relief. Tara imagined hot showers, a toaster, coffee maker, microwave, doing dishes with running water that didn't need to be hauled from town, and a flushing toilet. She kept letting her mind wander through that euphoria as the fire burned down to ashes. They raked it out before throwing dirt over it all.

CHAPTER 6

On the morning of Jasper's cleanout job they both got up much earlier than they needed to. They had a lot riding on Jasper making a good impression.

Tara bustled around the kitchen packing a lunch of beans and rice for Jasper that she had pre-cooked the night before. It felt good to have food back in the house even though it was only the basics. They'd bought big bags of rice, beans, and some of the other staples, but it seemed like their money bought less at the store every time they went. The price of everything was going up again. A few pennies here, a dollar there, but it was starting to really add up.

Tara rearranged the containers in Jasper's lunch box twice. This felt like the only thing she could do to help out. She really wanted him to get a regular job from this trip.

When Jasper walked into the living room she met him on the couch with a steaming bowl of oatmeal at their usual place by the heater. They ate in silence. Tara was too nervous to talk. She was full of hope, but if she'd learned anything in the last months it was that hope was useless and just caused hurt feelings.

Jasper wore a hopeful smile when he kissed her on his way out the door twenty minutes earlier than necessary.

When the truck pulled out of the driveway Tara milled aimlessly around the kitchen. She needed this to work out, but it was all out of her hands now.

Finally Tara sat down on the couch and pulled out a basket she had abandoned there several nights before. Inside was a tangle of cheap red acrylic yarn and the toe of a sock she'd started knitting. It was knitted from the toe up by a formula her aunt had taught her to keep her busy one summer. The toe was formed in gray. After that she had added red for the foot. Tara was a little fuzzy on the way the heel was made, but if she couldn't remember it this would have to be a tube sock. Either way it would be warm.

Tara had only knit a couple of stitches when she heard the sound of tires crunching on the driveway so she hurried to the window. Jasper's truck was easing to a stop, and Jasper was talking to a young woman with short dark hair in the cab next to him.

He turned off the engine and hurried to the passenger door where he pulled a backpack off the floorboard and swung it onto his shoulder by one strap. The young woman slid out of the truck and Tara stared in shock as Jasper swept an arm under the petite woman and began carrying her towards the house.

Tara pushed the front door open just in time to meet Jasper and stepped back out of the way so he could carry the woman in.

Jasper set the woman down gently on the couch, and then bent down to untie her sneakers. Tara could only watch the scene unfold from the door in silence as she pushed the door until it latched shut.

Easing the first shoe off caused the woman to gasp. The heel and toe of her socks were bloody.

Inspecting the woman's face, Tara realized that she may not even have been old enough to use the term woman. The girl on the couch couldn't have been more than nineteen years old.

The girl's features were striking, with a perfect little nose and full wide lips. Her figure was lost in layers of dirty torn clothing, but her cheeks were sunken and she must have been almost painfully thin.

"Are you okay?" Tara asked. She didn't know what else to do.

"Just couldn't walk no further," the young lady replied with a heavy southern drawl that Tara wasn't expecting.

Jasper had begun the slow process of peeling the young lady's socks off while she gasped.

"Honey, the first aid kit," Jasper prompted.

"Right," Tara acknowledged unable to take her eyes off the

bloody socks.

"Tara?"

"Right away." Tara hurried out of the room. The first aid kit was in the cabinet under the sink in the bathroom.

When Tara slipped back into the main room she went straight to the stove where she started some water in a kettle. As Tara approached them, the girl looked down at her hands in her lap.

"Where are my manners, my name's Tara," Tara introduced herself as she handed the first aid kit to Jasper.

"I'm Melody," the girl winced as Jasper set her foot down on his lap.

"What a lovely name," Tara murmured as she inspected the girl's feet over Jasper shoulder.

Melody's feet were a series of sores, some blisters, and a couple of deep gouges. Tara didn't know how she was walking at all.

Tara hurried back to the kitchen and poured the warm water into a pan and grabbed a clean cloth. When she got back to Jasper he began cleaning the wounds as carefully as possible.

"If you don't mind my asking, how did you do that to your feet?" Tara asked, feeling useless while she watched Jasper.

"Well," Melody replied finally looking into Tara's face. "I've been walking for weeks because I have to make it to my great auntie's place. When my husband died he didn't have no insurance so I ended up spending everything I had on his funeral," she drawled quietly. "From there everything went wrong. I lost the house, the car… everything. He and I had moved there from Georgia so I didn't know no one in the area." Melody grunted when Jasper placed her feet in the water to loosen the dirt.

"Where did you move to from Georgia?" Jasper asked leaning back from what he was doing.

"Texas," she sighed.

"Where are you headed?" he asked.

"I heard that there are a lot of jobs available in Chicago and since it's where my auntie lives, I figured I'd go there for a fresh start. I couldn't afford no bus ticket or nothing so I figured I'd hitchhike…" Melody trailed off as her brow creased and she bit her lip.

Jasper shot Tara a worried look as he dabbed gently at the girl's wounds.

"You look like you've done a lot more walking than hitchhiking." Tara spoke quietly in what she hoped was a soothing tone of voice.

Melody closed her eyes and shook her head several times as she wrapped her arms around herself in a bear hug and looked at a point on the wall somewhere behind them both.

"I was attacked by a nice-looking man who offered me a ride on the first night." Melody's voice broke and she started to sob as she finished the sentence.

Jasper leaned forward and wrapped his arms around the girl and held her for a span of minutes until she stopped crying and was taking fast shuddering breaths.

"I've been avoiding the roads ever since," Melody said between gasps. "I was just so hungry, and cold, and I couldn't walk no more. I stopped at the first road I saw and waited."

"You're safe now," Jasper murmured into the girl's hair as he rocked her gently like a child. Tara watched him as a series of emotions flickered across his face. He bounced from anger, to pain, to determination in a matter of seconds. "Don't you worry," he wavered, clearing his throat before he started again, "Don't you worry, you're safe here."

Melody watched him as she pulled back from their long embrace. "Thanks for saving me."

The poor creature. The girl's story pulled at Tara's heart while she brought Jasper a towel to dry Melody's feet.

Tara started another kettle of water while Jasper started covering the girl's feet in antibiotic ointment.

"You should get her set up in the bathroom so she can get cleaned up," Tara advised Jasper while giving a nod towards the kettle on the stove. "I'll go get her something clean to wear."

"Could you make it some pajamas?" Melody asked as meek as a mouse. "I could really use a nap."

"Pajamas it is," Tara agreed as she went back into her room. She dug a soft pair of flannel pants that were gray with red polka dots out of the dresser before finding the shirt. The long-sleeve t-shirt that matched it had a sleeping cartoon coffee cup on the chest.

By the time Tara reached the bathroom Jasper had already set Melody on the closed lid of the toilet and was situating a pan of warm wash water on the sink. Tara set the folded pajamas along with a fresh towel on the floor next to Melody. Then she placed a wash cloth and a bar of soap on the sink next to the wash pan.

"You can leave your clothes in here. I'll get them washed for you when I next head into town," Tara offered, backing out of the bathroom door. "Just give a shout when you're dressed and ready to be helped to bed."

"It's freezing in here. Why can't I just take a shower?" Melody asked, staring at the dishpan of water on the sink.

"Sorry," Jasper answered as he stepped back out of the small bathroom after Tara. "We don't have any running water right now."

"What kind of house doesn't have running water?" Melody asked suspiciously. "Are y'all one of those weird religions, or like a cult, or something?"

Tara pressed her lips together. "No, we're just broke." She exhaled loudly. She didn't like to admit it.

"I don't know if I want to take no bath in a pan." Melody eyed it as if it was going to tip off the edge of the sink all over her.

"Then don't," Tara shrugged. "We can help you to bed."

"Isn't there no other options? Can't you fill the bathtub or something?"

"We can only carry about ten gallons of water from town at a time," Tara frowned. "It's not enough to fill the tub."

"Never mind, this works," Melody shrugged, looking unhappy.

"I'm sorry," Jasper apologized again.

"It's not a problem," she smiled at him. "I didn't mean to seem ungrateful. I just really wanted a shower. I haven't had no shower in weeks."

Jasper shut the door and gestured Tara out onto the porch. Once they were outside he stood with his back to Tara staring at the sky.

"That poor woman," he murmured without looking at Tara. "This world makes me sick sometimes."

Tara laid a hand on his shoulder. The girl was hardly more than a child and was already lost, alone, raped, and a widow besides.

Jasper turned to look at her suddenly. "It's okay I brought her here right?"

"Why wouldn't it be?" Tara asked.

"I don't know," Jasper slouched rubbing his face with his hands. "We're barely getting by as it is, and now we have another mouth to feed."

Tara leaned on the railing next to him. "She needs our help."

"I love you," Jasper kissed Tara on the forehead and pulled her in tight for a hug. Tara hugged him back as tightly as she could until he pulled away to look at her.

"What time is it?" he demanded, suddenly panicked.

Tara stared at him blankly. "I don't know."

Jasper pulled his phone out of his pocket and looked at it. "Shit. This is just great. I'm late. I'm already late!" he shouted as he sprinted off the porch towards the truck. Tara watched him drive away and sagged against the porch railing.

When Melody called for help from the bathroom Tara did her best to move her as carefully as possible. When she had Melody tucked in bed Tara dropped onto the couch to pass the day quietly knitting, that had been the plan anyway. Unfortunately she got frustrated pulling out the heel of her sock over and over again. Instead she began reading about canning. The procedure seemed simple enough. When she finally put the book down, more time had passed reading then she'd intended.

Tara busied herself making some potato soup for dinner. She

didn't have the cheese or milk that the recipe called for, but they had bought a few bags of potatoes and onions since they would keep. By the time Tara had finished it was more like the bland ghost of potato soup, but it would have to do.

Tara checked the heater's fuel level and carried it outside to refill it before it went out. When she came back in she was surprised to see Melody standing stiffly in the doorway of the bedroom. Tara had nearly forgotten about the girl. She'd been so quiet all day.

"Hey hon, could ya' help me to the bathroom?" Melody asked smoothing her sleep tousled hair back from her face.

"Not a problem." Tara hurried forward to help the child to the bathroom then she stepped back out of the way.

"Yuck! This toilet is disgusting!" The girl squealed from behind the door.

"Sorry, we can only flush it once per day with the dish water."

"That's nasty," Melody shouted.

"Sorry," Tara called back.

Just as Tara turned back to the stove Jasper came in stomping a light dusting of snow off his boots onto the front mat. It must have just started snowing.

"Oh that smells wonderful," he exclaimed, breathing deeply. "Sorry I'm a bit late. I stopped over at Alex and Kate's to get a shower. The house I was working at is filthy."

"I'm afraid dinner isn't quite as good as I'd like it to be." Tara kissed him on the cheek as she helped unwrap his scarf.

"Anything would taste good right now," he smiled. "If you made that with cardboard and glue I'd still eat it. I'm that hungry."

"Good, because that's a pretty good description of how it tastes." Tara smiled.

As he stepped back the bathroom door opened and Melody waved at Jasper. He moved quickly forward to pick her up and carried her to the couch. While he did that Tara ladled soup into three bowls and carried the first one in to Melody while Jasper scooted the coffee table closer to the couch for her. The two of them pulled chairs up to the coffee table, and then dragged the heater closer. The temperature had dropped and it was starting to get chilly around the outer edges of the room.

Melody brought the first spoonful of soup to her lips and grimaced. "What is this?" she asked swallowing hard.

"Potato soup." Tara smiled as sweetly as she could.

"Don't taste like potato soup," Melody complained.

"I'm sorry if you don't like it. I had to substitute half of the ingredients," Tara shrugged determined not to take offense.

"It don't taste good this way," Melody complained while eyeballing the soup as if she expected dirty socks to float to the surface.

"I'm sorry it doesn't meet with your approval." Tara's voice came through gritted teeth.

Jasper, who had been watching the two of them, interrupted before anything else could be said. "You have to admit, Tara, this isn't the best soup you've ever made."

Tara nodded in agreement. It was true, but Tara still didn't appreciate Melody being so blunt about it. She'd done the best she could with what she had.

They finished the rest of their dinner in silence with Jasper looking back and forth between the women. Afterwards they got Melody settled onto the couch for the night. She admitted that even after having slept all day she thought she could sleep another whole day if she got the chance.

In the bedroom, as Jasper and Tara shivered into their pajamas, Jasper pulled an envelope out of his pocket and handed it to Tara.

"What's this?" she asked

"They paid me in cash today. That's your chicks and whatever feed and things they might need," he smiled at her.

Tara threw her arms around her husband's shoulders and hugged him tightly. "You really mean it?" she asked.

"Of course," he assured her. "If those chicks will make you feel better about our situation than you deserve them."

"Thanks." She slid the wooden box out from under the bed. She slipped the envelope of cash carefully inside and slid it back in place.

"I'm happy to do it," he hugged her again before they both crawled under the covers.

Tara shivered. The mound of blankets was much smaller with Melody here since half of them were now on the couch. Tara pushed herself tightly against Jasper's body heat. It didn't' matter, Melody's stay with them would only be temporary after all.

CHAPTER 7

Jasper dropped onto the kitchen chair and began taking off his boots with such ferocity that Tara wondered if they had broken or otherwise assaulted him in some way.

"What's the matter honey?" Tara asked as she continued to dry the breakfast dishes she'd just finished washing.

"You didn't notice that I'm home early," Jasper spat.

"I noticed, but I wasn't making any assumptions as to why you're home," Tara chose her words carefully. She knew she'd just stepped into a minefield and any misstep on her part would make him blow up.

"Oh you make no assumptions. Is that how we're going to do this?" he demanded throwing his boot with such force that it bounced off the door.

Boom! Tara sighed. "What happened, honey?"

"I was just told that I'm no longer needed at the auction company, that's what. The other guy that started the same day as me was given a permanent job."

"That doesn't seem fair at all," Tara soothed, putting a stack of plates in the cabinet.

"But do you know why I didn't get a job?" Jasper asked his voice suddenly dripping sickly sweet from his mouth.

"No, why?" Tara asked. She could tell this was going somewhere awful.

"Because I was late to work the first day. They told me they needed dependable guys."

"Oh," Tara sagged against the counter behind her.

"You make our lives so hard sometimes," Jasper turned away from Tara.

Tara stepped forward, surprised. "I what?"

"Stop playing innocent! If you knew how to take care of

anything I wouldn't have had to stay home and hold your hand while we got Melody situated!" Jasper paced away from Tara. "Then I wouldn't have been late on that first day and maybe I would still have a damn job."

Tara stood shocked. "But you picked Melody up."

"Oh! So now you're going to blame this on Melody. Like this is her fault?" Jasper slid his chair quickly under the table as he paced back towards Tara.

Tara flinched, she hadn't meant to, it always seemed to make him mad. Thankfully he didn't seem to notice her reaction. "I wasn't blaming Melody," she offered.

"You know that's a lie. I don't want to talk to you when you're pulling this bullshit!" Jasper stuffed his feet into his sneakers and grabbed his coat before he stormed back out the door.

Tara watched him stomp to his truck amazed. How was it that anything she said was always the wrong thing? She leaned against the sink as tears began to well up in her eyes. She was silently scolding herself for running Jasper off again when a hand touched her shoulder and Tara shrieked.

"I didn't mean to scare you," Melody drawled stepping back. "Y'all know I could hear you guys."

Tara rubbed her eyes before she began to tug absently at the ends of her hair. "Yes?" Whatever Melody had to say, Tara wasn't ready to hear it. Melody had been settling in for the last few days and Tara felt like all she'd been doing in that time was running around caring for the girl's needs. The girl, for her part, had gotten increasingly rude to Tara as if she was some sort of servant to be ordered around. Except when Jasper was around; when Jasper was around the girl had been minding her manners and remembering her "pleases" and "thank-yous."

"Sorry that Jasper lost his job, but it's not my fault ya' know," Melody told her calmly as the girl hobbled stiffly over to the couch.

"I didn't say it was," Tara replied just as calmly, but she couldn't look at the girl.

"That's not what I heard," Melody countered smoothly.

"Fine," Tara answered dismissively. She didn't have the will to fight.

Silence filled the room. The kind of silence that amplifies the slightest click until it's louder than thunder. The women stared at each other until Melody exhaled loudly.

"I'd like some clothes today. I don't like these nasty pajamas." Melody tugged at the leg of her pajama pants.

"Sorry they're not to your liking. Did you bring anything with you that I can get for you?" Tara asked gesturing vaguely towards the girl's bag.

"I wore everything I owned in layers since midway through Arkansas."

"I see," Tara answered slowly, thinking about the stained pile of rags she hadn't taken anywhere to wash yet. "I'll find something in my clothes that might fit you."

"I really doubt that, but I've never minded loose clothing. It's comfortable." Melody looked Tara up and down.

It was like a physical blow, but Tara managed to keep control over her features. Melody smiled at her. Tara took a deep breath and then another. Melody wasn't actually wrong; she was what Tara would describe as willowy. Tara said nothing, but went into her room and came back out with a pair of jeans, socks, a white t-shirt, and a comfortable wool sweater.

Melody sniffed. "Let me pick what I think will fit," she said taking the clothes from Tara and heading back into the bedroom to shuffle through the dresser herself.

Tara considered stopping her. She honestly hated the idea of someone going through her things, but she figured that for the sake of some sort of peace she could let this happen. Tara leaned against the doorway with folded arms watching the girl.

After rummaging through Tara's drawers for a few minutes Melody looked over at her, "Where's the rest of your clothes. All ya' have is a few boring t-shirts, jeans, and what are these… dresses. Don't ya' own anything that didn't come from the boring old lady store?"

"The rest of my clothes were sold to keep the lights on," Tara replied as blandly as she could manage while a quiet spark of rage wavered inside her chest.

"How'd that work out for ya'?" Melody smiled.

"Fine until last month actually," Tara answered with a poker face.

When Tara didn't take the bait Melody quit prodding her. "Do ya' have a belt I could use?"

Tara took one out of the closet where it hung on a hook by the wall and handed it to the girl.

Melody dropped the belt on a newer t-shirt and slightly darker pair of jeans than Tara had originally given her. She tossed the sweater to the side.

"I don't wear wool," she said.

"Suit yourself, it's warm." Tara refolded the sweater and put it back in her drawer.

"I'll take this," Melody grabbed one of Jasper's hooded sweatshirts from where it was draped over the end of the bed.

"That's Jasper's," Tara informed her coldly.

"I know." Melody buried her nose in the collar and took a deep breath. "It smells like him."

Tara's nostril's flared, but she said nothing. What was she supposed to say to the little girl who was obviously trying to make her mad?

"I'll take these too." Melody picked up Tara's only pair of sneakers.

"You can wear shoes?" Tara asked suddenly excited by the prospect. If Melody's feet were doing well enough for her to walk again then maybe they could have her on her way soon.

"No, but I don't want to have to beg ya' for stuff later. How do I know y'all won't sell these too? All ya' have are those ugly boots," she pointed to Tara's feet.

Tara frowned. Her boots were warm and waterproof.

"I'll need these too." Melody picked up Tara's slippers and hobbled out of the room.

It's fine, Tara told herself. *At least it means the girl is thinking about leaving.*

Back in the living room Melody had arranged herself on the couch wearing Tara's clothes. They were much too big for her.

Tara frowned.

"I'm bored," Melody announced. She sounded like a spoiled child.

"Maybe you want to help me patch your clothes?" Tara asked as she got up to fetch her sewing basket.

"Those clothes are ruined. Ya' should just throw 'em away." Melody made a face.

"We might be able to fix them."

"They're all stained, ripped and gross." Melody shrugged. "I can wear your clothes until we can buy me some new ones."

Tara frowned. How much did this child expect from them? Wasn't it enough that they were feeding and taking care of her? Now she expected them to buy her new clothes too? Tara sighed and came back to the center of the living room.

"Do you want to read a book?" Tara asked

"I don't like to read," Melody shook her head. "Can't we watch television or something?"

"We don't have power." Tara rubbed her temple then tugged the tips of her hair.

"Everyone has generators and stuff. Can't you run the generator for a bit?"

"I don't have one," Tara sighed again. "Do you want to learn to knit?"

"That's too fiddly, and I'm not an old lady." Melody shrugged tugging at a loose thread on the blanket she had pulled onto her lap.

Tara watched the destruction with irritation. "Why don't you tell me something about yourself? What did you used to do for fun?" Tara asked dropping onto the arm of the couch.

"Normally I watched television, or went shopping, or went to lunch with my girlfriends, or got my nails done. I really like going out and doing things. I also loved being active in my local church."

Tara's eyebrows shot up. She had a really hard time imagining Melody engrossed in any good works since she'd been acting like a spoiled child for days.

"Sounds like a fun life." Tara smiled though it was insincere.

"It was before Martin died," Melody pouted, biting her lip.

"Martin was your husband?" Tara asked.

"Yeah, he was amazing. He loved me so much, and Mom didn't like him which made me happy."

Tara couldn't help smiling when she thought about her own rebellion against her father.

"Why didn't your mom like him?" Tara asked. Maybe they finally had some common ground.

"Oh, Martin was older than me, a lot older, and kinda' married when we started dating,"

Tara's head snapped up and she looked at the girl who winked back.

"It's fine, don't worry. His wife was a real gold-digger. She didn't even like him, and he definitely didn't love her the way he loved me," Melody reminisced.

"Is that so?" Tara asked, trying to keep her voice even while she picked up her sock and busied herself counting stitches. This girl was a real piece of work.

"You should have seen the beautiful gifts he used to buy for me. He didn't buy his wife pretty things like that. He was such a sweetheart," Melody said wistfully.

"Sounds like quite a catch," Tara mumbled unwilling to look at the girl.

"We dated for nearly a year before I told him we were pregnant."

Tara's head snapped up to look at the girl again.

Melody smiled fondly while she rubbed her belly. "Do you know what he did when he found out?" she asked.

"What?" Tara was surprised by this new development. Where was the girl's child?

"He filed for divorce the very next day. Boy was his nasty old wife surprised. Their kids were all grown up anyway so it's not like she had anything to complain about. Can you imagine, she tried to get alimony?" Melody looked genuinely annoyed. "With me pregnant and all. The nerve of some people," she said shaking her head.

Tara waited quietly for Melody to explain the elephant in the room, but she didn't, so Tara asked, "Did you lose the baby?" Tara was sympathetic. Even this girl didn't deserve to lose a baby.

Melody stared at her surprised. "No. I was never pregnant."

"What?"

"Are you kidding?" Melody snorted. "I just wanted to give him a little push to leave his wife. You know how men are." Melody looked at Tara sideways. "They always feel some kind of obligation to stay with the wrong woman just because they married her." Melody looked Tara up and down.

"So you lied to him?" Tara frowned at the girl.

"I saved him from continuing to live a miserable life with a miserable woman," Melody shrugged. "I told him I lost the baby and you should have seen all the beautiful things he bought me to cheer me up. He was wonderful."

Tara wanted to tell the child how disgusting she was, but what good would it do now? The man was dead. The girl was still a widow.

Melody leaned out and grabbed her bag that was sitting on the floor next to the couch. "You wanna' see a picture of us together?" Without waiting for an answer the girl held out a wrinkled photograph. In it were two people grinning widely, but a more mismatched pair would have been hard to find. Martin was a paunchy balding man with salt and pepper hair. Next to him was melody with a veil on, showing off a very big diamond on her finger.

"Cute," Tara lied.

"I know," Melody replied oblivious to Tara's feelings. It's the only picture I have of the ring. I had to sell it before I left Texas.

Tara didn't know what to say. She knew what she wanted to say, she wanted to tell the girl she was a horrible person. She wanted to call her a gold-digging home-wrecker, but that wouldn't make a dent in the girl's point of view. Instead Tara excused herself to make some lunch before she said something she shouldn't.

Jasper walked in the door calm and freshly showered.

"Did you stop in to see Alex?" Tara asked barely looking up from the knitting in her hands. She was hoping that he was in a better mood than he had been that morning.

Instead of answering he glared at her. "Always a thousand questions when I get home. Can't I ever come here and not get grilled like you don't trust me."

Tara stopped knitting and stared at her hands. "I'm sorry."

"It's okay, dear," Jasper leaned forward and kissed Tara's forehead. "I just want to be able to be happy to come home."

Tara nodded. "Dinner is on the stove. It's rice and beans."

"Mixed or separate?" Jasper grimaced.

"Mixed."

"Oh well, I'll eat it anyway," he smiled, "But first I have some things for you ladies."

"For us?" Melody asked.

Tara could hear the excitement in the girl's voice.

Jasper placed a large black metal box on the table in front of Tara. It had a handle on the top and in the front was a glass viewing window and a thermometer. Inside was a wire rack shelf.

"I got you a camp oven. You set this on the burner and it works like an oven. I know the oven doesn't work without electricity, but I thought this way we might be able to have something home baked." Jasper turned to Melody. "Do you know how to bake?"

"Not really," she shrugged.

"That's a shame," Jasper leaned towards Melody and spoke in a stage whisper. "What Tara bakes is normally only fit for the trash."

Tara hated it when he talked about her like that in front of other people, but with Melody it was especially galling. The girl smiled at Tara in an unpleasant way.

Jasper laughed as if what he'd said was clever.

Tara flashed as radiant a smile as she could muster. She couldn't let them see her pain. Showing weakness was blood in the water and sometimes it felt like everyone was a shark but her.

"I don't know how to bake but I'm probably still better than her," Melody winked at Jasper while they both laughed.

Jasper picked up the oven and offered it to Melody. "Looks like I should have gotten this for you."

"What's my actual present?" Melody asked.

"Oh, I nearly forgot," Jasper said putting down the oven and picking up the bag. He handed it to Melody.

"For me?" the girl lilted.

Inside the bag were a few pairs of lacy white underwear.

"Oh they're so pretty!" Melody cooed.

Tara gritted her teeth. "Where did these things come from?" Tara asked sharper than she'd intended to.

Jasper looked at her, "I bought Melody's from the store new, and yours I got from the second-hand shop."

"I mean where did we get the money?" Tara asked.

"The oven was actually free," Jasper smirked. "There's a little second-hand shop operating out of the basement of that church in the middle of town. United Church of Christ or somesuch. It's run by volunteers and apparently works on donations to help fund the food bank."

"No kidding?" Tara asked.

"Yeah, so I was looking around for some other clothes for Melody when I came across the oven."

Tara's eyes narrowed, apparently Melody had already asked Jasper to buy her clothes and he'd agreed. The thought bothered her since he hadn't asked Tara how she felt about supporting the girl like that. Yes... they may have taken on the responsibility of feeding her at this point, but Tara didn't feel like it was their responsibility to clothe her as well. Melody had clothes; they were just dirty and in need of patching.

Jasper continued oblivious, "It didn't have a price on it, so I took it up to one of the fellas sorting things. It was way too much so I put it back. After a few minutes he came up to me, we chatted, and I explained our situation. Then he just handed it to me and told me to take it free of charge."

"So did you find any nice clothes for me there?" Melody asked hopefully.

"I didn't want to be greedy," Jasper smiled at the girl.

"Oh," Melody frowned.

"I hope that nice man didn't get into any trouble for what he did," Tara interrupted.

"No. The guy was in charge of the charity there. His name was Pastor Richard or something like that."

"Oh, well that was very nice of him," Tara said while trying not to let the fact that her husband had just bought lacy underwear for the little girl in their kitchen continue to nag at her.

Melody, on the other hand, was smiling at Jasper and he was smiling back. Tara couldn't stand there in silence and watch any longer.

"What's the plan for tomorrow?" she asked Jasper.

"I don't think there is a plan for tomorrow," he shrugged looking back at his wife.

"I'd like us to go work on Rose's shed."

"We can't both go; someone needs to stay with Melody. She's still having a hard time getting around.

Tara frowned. "Then I'll go by myself."

"That's fine dear," Jasper said. "It would be nice to have you getting some of the work done for a change."

Tara's frown deepened. Who did he think was doing all the cooking and cleaning? Who was waiting on Melody? But, Tara didn't say anything. Instead, she nodded.

CHAPTER 8

The next morning Tara felt positively buoyant to be out of the house. It was a lovely winter day. The sun was shining and the temperature was only a little below freezing. And Tara was looking forward to getting her hands dirty.

When Tara got to Rose's house she went straight to the shed without knocking. After several hours of digging and sorting Tara had made quite a stack of things in the trash pile, some in the pile to sell, and had even located the canning jars and pressure canner. When Rose walked in Tara looked up feeling a little guilty digging through piles of Rose's things.

"Where's your husband? Isn't he supposed to be helping with the lifting?" Rose asked looking around.

"Nope just me today." Tara dusted her hands off as she moved away from the pile of what she could only assume were old car parts in a wooden crate.

"What's the point in marrying them if we don't make them do the heavy lifting, open jars... that sort of thing?" Rose smiled.

Tara picked some cobwebs off her coat. "I think it has something to do with companionship or something like that." She mumbled the last part under her breath.

Rose looked at her expectantly for a moment before she continued, "So where'd ya' shake him off at?"

"I left him at home, we have a houseguest that needs some looking after. She's probably making him peel her some grapes right now." Tara tried to shake the image from her mind. It wasn't that she didn't trust her husband, she just didn't like the way the little girl looked at him.

"I was wondering if there was some tart somewhere getting your blood boiling." Rose winked.

"What?" Tara asked startled. "Why would you think that?"

"Because that's what it always was for me," Rose shrugged. "So instead of working off your anger out here in the cold and getting nothin' but achin' muscles for your troubles why don't we go inside where it's warm and be catty instead?" Rose gestured toward the door.

"I wouldn't mind a break."

Once inside, Tara pulled her filthy outer layers off while Rose offered her a glass of vodka.

"No, thanks. I'll just have some tea, if that's not too much trouble."

"Suit yourself," Rose shook her head. "I'll make you some nice chamomile tea. I don't have any black tea."

Rose pulled a jar with a handwritten label out of the cabinet and carefully measured its contents into a mesh ball.

Rose paused. "Have you been to the market lately?" she asked.

Tara shook her head, but Rose continued without letting her actually reply, "There wasn't a bit of tea or coffee in the whole store." Rose pursed her lips then continued. "Couldn't get chocolate chips to make some cookies neither. Not even one chocolate bar in the whole place. When I talked to the fella' behind the counter he told me he couldn't get any in." Rose snorted. "Empty spots all over the store."

Tara shrugged, "I didn't notice. We went to the bulk store. Haven't had any money for the usual stuff lately. It's been all rice and beans for us."

"I guess it could be a demand problem," Rose frowned, "but I doubt it." Rose poured tea from the pot into two dainty cups and pushed one across the table to Tara, then watched her expectantly.

"So are we gonna talk about the bitch or do I have to torture it out of ya'?" Rose asked in as polite a tone as Tara had probably ever heard. It was so at odds with the sentence that she couldn't help smiling.

"Her name's Melody. She's young, skinny, gorgeous, and doesn't have a problem with the idea of stealing other women's husbands," Tara admitted gripping some strands of her own hair tightly.

"Is she stealing your husband?" Rose asked primly.

Tara twisted the hair between her fingers. "I don't know." Tara's eyes traced the rim of her teacup. "She hasn't done anything blatant, like throw herself into his arms in front of me." Tara sighed, "It's just lots of little things, too vague for me to describe, that make me not trust her."

Rose nodded for Tara to continue.

"She's nasty to me, but the moment my husband is around she's all southern sugar, sweet as can be," Tara grumbled.

"So what's she even doing at your house? She a relative of yours?"

"My husband brought her home one day like a little lost dog. Her feet are all torn up so she can barely walk. She's a down-on-her-luck widow with a sad story who isn't going anywhere until she's healed up. I'm afraid that by then Jasper will want to keep her."

"So all you gotta' do is get her feeling better and she'll be out of your hair?"

"Yeah, I wish I had something that would speed this crap up," Tara admitted. She was starting to wish she'd chosen the vodka.

Rose smiled. "Just a minute, honey," Rose motioned for her to stay put as she slid her chair back and disappeared through the doorway. After a few minutes she returned holding a small jar with a handwritten label. She set it on the table in front of Tara.

"What is it?" Tara asked as she picked it up and twisted the lid off. Inside was a green salve with a peculiar and slightly unpleasant odor.

"Comfrey salve; it's one of the best wound healers out there. It should get her back on her feet, literally."

"No kidding? Where do you get this stuff?" Tara asked as she screwed the lid back onto the jar.

"I've been making it since just after my youngest was born."

"Is it a family recipe? Can you teach it to me?"

"It's not a family recipe. It's just a little something I picked up studying plant medicine over the years."

"I thought that stuff was old wives tales and snake oil."

"There's a little of that," Rose nodded. "You can't underestimate the placebo effect, but I've seen enough to believe in it." Rose took a sip of her tea. "Besides, it's a hell of a lot cheaper than goin' to the doctor."

Tara nodded. "That sounds like something I need to know more about."

"Really?" Rose seemed surprised. "I thought to you it was old wives tales and snake oil. Just another lost relic from my generation to you kids. Not like a doctor and his miracle pills."

Tara shrugged, "Snake oil or not, we can barely afford dinner. Heaven help us if someone gets sick."

"Follow me, honey," Rose gestured toward the doorway.

Tara followed Rose through the tidy living room past the door of a small bedroom decorated in a bright cheery yellow. Then, slowly Tara helped Rose up a set of stairs that groaned about being pressed into service after so many years. After the first few it was apparent they needed to be swept badly.

"Excuse the dust. I don't come up here anymore," Rose apologized.

"Don't worry about it, I wouldn't expect you to," Tara assured her as they reached the top of the staircase and found themselves in an open sitting area with only one door off to the side of it. The curtains were drawn so the space was dark and musty.

Rose turned the old glass doorknob that led them into a small office. At first glance it looked like it belonged to a stuffy college professor. There was dark paneling on the walls, green plaid curtains, and a large dark-stained desk with a leather chair. On the desk were a carved wooden pipe and a set of heavy, square-framed reading glasses.

Everything matched except one corner where a small table with a ladder-backed chair was sitting on a pink rug. Everything in that space was covered in lace or ruffles, except in the middle of the table where a rectangular cozy had impressively managed both lace and ruffles. And all of it was unapologetically pink. Next to the desk was a bookcase painted a pale pink with roses stenciled down the side, it was full of a combination of reference books and trashy romance novels.

"Well that looks out of place," Tara smiled at Rose.

Rose's face took on an impish expression. "I know dear. Garish ain't it."

"I assume this is your desk?"

"It gave my husband fits to have it in his study," Rose smirked while she pulled books off the shelf.

Tara lifted the corner of the pink frilly cozy on the desk to find an old typewriter.

"It's been a while since you used this space I'm guessing?" Tara pointed at the machine.

"I basically quit coming up here when my husband died." Rose put her fingers to her lips while she smiled as if she was remembering something she shouldn't say, but from Tara's experience probably would anyway.

"I told my husband I was writing a romance novel."

"You were?" Tara shouldn't have been surprised. If Rose had written it, it was probably banned.

"Goodness! No, girl. I would just wander in here when he was using the phone. I'd bang out nonsense just to make noise with the thing. Do you have any idea how hard it is to talk over a typewriter?"

"We had an old electric word processor when I was young, but computers have been mainstream most of my life," Tara admitted. "We never had a typewriter."

"My husband hated the sound of the thing. He used to yell that it was too loud to think over," Rose chuckled.

"Weren't you afraid he was going to ask to read what you'd been working on?" Tara fingered the keys on the machine.

"My husband would never have lowered himself," Rose shrugged. "That's why I told him it was a romance novel."

Tara grinned imagining tiny little Rose banging out nonsense in a steady rhythm near her red-faced husband.

"Would you grab that stack of books there," Rose gestured to the pile she'd made on the corner of the table.

Tara picked up the books and offered Rose her arm as they headed down the stairs. Once they were in the kitchen Tara set the books on the table and helped Rose sit while she caught her breath.

Rose pushed the stack towards Tara, "There you are, honey. That'll get you started."

Most of the books were old, but a couple of them were newer paperbacks. There was one about botany, one local plant identification guide, a wild food guide, several books on herbal medicine, a family medical manual from the nineteen-sixties, and an old physician's manual from the early twentieth century that looked like it was held together by wishful thinking. The most interesting book of the bunch, however, was a thick black ledger with a red spine and corners. Tara picked it up with great care.

"Those are my notes," Rose beamed proudly as Tara let the book's pages fall open in front of her.

Inside was page after page of small neat handwriting.

"A lot of what's in there are the remedies I've tried that I picked up here and there. Some work, some don't. It's all in the notes."

Tara smiled as she started reading, "February second nineteen fifty-six, L presents with diarrhea, suspect nervous stomach, just started new job. Gave half teaspoon blackberry root tincture twice per hour until diarrhea subsides. Recommended valerian tea drunk freely. L came back to report no recurrence after second dose."

Rose nodded, "He was a nervous little man." But she left it at that.

As Tara fanned quickly through the pages she found magazine clippings, photos, scraps of paper, typed notes, and even a few pressed flowers and leaves.

"It's not very organized," Rose apologized, "but, I'm sure you can make your way through it."

Tara found herself literally speechless for a few moments. How could someone choose to part with something so personal? "The book is beautiful and I can't wait to start reading it," she paused, "but are you sure you want to give this to me?"

Rose waved away her protest, "I don't use any of these anymore. Most all I need to know I've memorized and, frankly at my age, anything I don't remember probably isn't gonna help me anyway."

Tara thanked her again. The books would definitely keep her busy. Life without a television, computer, or radio was getting boring.

The idea of Melody leaving entertained Tara as she drove into town to Alex and Kate's house where she found Kate playing on the living room floor with her daughter when Tara rang the doorbell.

"Hey darlin', come on in. To what do I owe the honor?" Kate asked as Tara hung up her coat.

"Just needed to get some laundry done and a shower if you don't mind."

"Not a problem, come on in, take your clothes off, make yourself comfy," Kate smiled, gesturing broadly behind her.

After her shower, Tara sat across the table from Kate while her hostess poured them both a hot cup of coffee. Kylie was on the floor sorting pans noisily out of the cabinet while her mother smiled at her.

"Still having a problem with the water?" Kate asked. "If it's the well I know a guy who may be able to get in and look at it relatively cheap."

Tara shook her head. She still wasn't ready to tell Kate they didn't have electricity, she was too ashamed, but she was surprised that Pete hadn't already.

"No, I know what the problem is. We just don't have the money to fix it yet," Tara sighed. It wasn't a lie, but it wasn't exactly the truth either.

"I know the feeling," Kate echoed her sigh. "I told Alex that if the price of gas goes any higher he's going to have to be a cop by day and use that uniform to be a stripper by night."

Tara snorted mid-sip. That wasn't what she expected Kate to say, though by this point she really should.

"We're willing to kick in a little for the water bill," Tara offered. "We're here almost every day."

"Nonsense," Kate waved her hand like the statement was a mosquito.

"Me today, Jasper was yesterday. We owe you something."

Kate frowned, "Jasper wasn't here yesterday."

"He came to town for a shower. I just assumed he came here." Tara did her best to keep her face neutral while she struggled to figure out where he might have gone. He'd been acting so weird.

Kate was silent and glanced at her over the rim of her coffee cup. Silence wasn't normal for Kate. Tara shifted uneasily, but waited for her to speak. If she could wait out Pete she could definitely wait out Kate.

"I'm sure he headed over to Pete's to grab a shower," Kate smiled reassuringly.

It was Tara's turn to frown. There was absolutely no way Jasper went to Pete's house for a shower.

"Hey have you stopped out to see Pete lately?" Kate was changing the subject.

"Nope," Tara shook her head. She didn't want to tell Kate she wasn't even supposed to talk to Pete.

"Really?" Kate asked while she refilled her cup.

"Really."

"Why?"

"I don't really know Pete," Tara shrugged.

"Once you get past how blunt he can be, Pete's a great guy; heart of gold really."

Tara leaned in, "So what's his story?" She wasn't sure it

really mattered since she wasn't allowed to talk to him anyway, but as long as it kept the conversation away from Jasper's accusations Tara was happy. If Tara mentioned it, there was no way that wouldn't get back to Pete. Tara blushed just thinking about it. It wasn't that Pete wasn't a good-looking guy; Tara just didn't want anyone to believe that she was that kind of woman.

Kate bit her lip, "I wish I knew for sure."

"You don't know Pete's story?" Tara was confused.

"He doesn't talk about himself much, and when I question him he's evasive; like he's got some big secret or something."

"Is he a murderer, or a mafia informant, or something?" Tara smirked, "Maybe ex-KGB?"

"No," Kate rolled her eyes. "Alex knows, but he never told me about it."

"Huh," Tara was surprised. Alex and Kate seemed like one of those perfect couples. It seemed impossible that he would keep secrets from her.

Kate shook her head. "It's not like I'm surprised. They've been together a lot longer than Alex and I have."

"But you have some idea?" Tara asked intrigued.

"Of course. I thought it was kind of obvious," Kate winked.

"What's obvious?"

"Seriously?" Kate prodded Tara.

Tara shook her head. She had no idea what Kate was getting at.

Kate leaned in and looked back and forth like she was being watched. "He's gay."

"Okay?" Tara was confused. "Why would that be a secret?"

Kate sighed, "I forgot you came here from the city. Tiny towns like this aren't as progressive about that sort of thing. Pete works on a crew of all men for a good-ole-boy. In a job like that he'd have to keep that sort of thing to himself."

"Are you saying he'd lose his job if he was honest about that?"

"At least, but he's just as likely to get his ass beat."

"How awful," Tara shook her head.

"Obviously we need to keep this between you and me," Kate

told her.

"Does Jasper know already?" Tara asked.

"No and I think it's Pete's place to tell him. You know how weird men can be about that sort of thing."

Tara nodded. If Jasper knew Pete was gay that would save her a bunch of trouble. He couldn't accuse her of having an affair with a gay man. "Are you sure that's his secret?" It really seemed too good to be true.

"Have you ever seen him with a woman, or dating, or anything like that?" Kate asked.

Tara thought about it before she answered, "No, but I've only known him for a couple of months."

Kate leaned back and crossed her arms. "I've known him for a couple of years and I'll tell you, I've never seen him with a woman. He does disappear for a couple of days every now and again. I always assumed that's when the loneliness gets to be too much for him and he heads into the city to have a fling." Kate smiled. "Kinda' romantic if you think about it."

"Why would he tell Alex?" Tara asked.

"He'd have to. He and Alex were roommates. You should have seen them play house. It wasn't right over there. They were such a cute couple that I sometimes felt like the third wheel when Alex and I first started dating."

"So," Tara paused confused, "Alex is bi-sexual?"

"No," Kate chuckled. "I thought that too; turns out he's just very secure."

"Oh," Tara nodded.

"I always imagined that Pete sat Alex down over a candlelit dinner and professed his feelings," Kate remarked, offering Tara more coffee which she waved away.

"What? Why?"

"Are you kidding?" Kate bit her lip. "Alex is gorgeous. Of course Pete has the hots for him."

"Do you really…" Tara began.

"Shhh, don't interrupt my fantasy. Those two are both hot!" Kate winked.

Tara burst out laughing. Kate was smiling and pretending to

watch some sort of lewd show inside her head, or maybe not pretending; Tara never knew with Kate. Tara's giggles were finally winding down when she heard the buzz of the dryer telling her the laundry was done, and it was time for her to head home.

The first thing Tara did when she got home was attend to Melody's feet. Jasper had been reading a story out loud to her when Tara arrived. Thankfully with Jasper there Melody didn't complain about the comfrey salve, she just wrinkled her nose when she smelled the stuff.

Tara was too antsy to sit in the living room listening to Jasper read so she slipped away into the bedroom with her books. It was a little overwhelming to have so much information at once, so she laid out the books to decide where to start.

She wanted to start with Rose's ledger, but she realized it would be a little like saving dessert for last. In a world that had been denying her both big and little pleasures for so long the book itself was one. Tara picked it up and opened the pages randomly. Inside was a bookmark made out of a photograph of some moldy food. She smiled to herself. That was something Tara liked about old books, sometimes people used the craziest things as bookmarks.

She put the ledger down, and then started thumbing through the other books randomly trying to figure out where to start. She wrote off the old physician's manual after she read that some of the treatments included arsenic and mercury. The early sixties medical manual was basically like an encyclopedia of diseases and medical procedures, even though it was very outdated it might be useful. The herb books talked a lot about plant parts and dosages, but the plants they talked about might as well have been in hieroglyphs instead of just Latin because she didn't know what most of them were. There were a few line drawings but most of the plants didn't even have that. The botany book was very technical dry reading. The first paragraph she read was about the difference between a rhizome and a root. It was going to be hard to get excited about. At least the identification manual had good pictures, but to say that the descriptions were hard to understand was an understatement. It only took a few moments for Tara to make the connection between the two. The botany book was to understand the terms used in the descriptions of the plant identification guide. How else would she know what ovate-lanceolate leaves, acuminate at the apex with narrow margined petioles, decurrent on the stem was supposed to mean?

Jasper walked in while she was switching back and forth between the two.

"What's that stuff?" he yawned, gesturing to the pile of books on the bed.

"The books I need to become an herbalist." Tara gathered them up to put away on the top of the dresser.

"Why?" Jasper asked as he stripped down to his long underwear and crawled under the blankets.

"That stuff that Rose gave me for Melody's feet is supposed to help her heal faster. What if I knew how to do that sort of thing myself? Tell me that wouldn't be really useful," Tara said sliding under the blankets and blowing out the light. The pungent smell of smoke filled the bedroom briefly.

"Whatever you want to do with your time is fine I suppose," Jasper frowned, settling himself in comfortably. "Just don't let it get in the way of looking for a job."

CHAPTER 9

In the morning when the alarm clock went off Tara didn't move. Jasper was leaving before daylight on a handyman job to install some fences, which Tara thought that was an odd thing to do when the ground was frozen, but she wasn't going to argue with someone paying them. If that was what he was really doing.

She wasn't entirely sure that he was being honest about where he was going, but she didn't want to be that person. She wasn't going to question him or follow him. Tara had been up half the night listening to Jasper breathing while thinking about where he could have gone to take a shower. It bothered her more than she wanted to admit because she couldn't think of anywhere he could have gone other than Kate or Pete's house. He couldn't have rented a room and it wasn't like there were homeless shelters or truck stops around.

"Tara?"

She didn't move. He would want her to pack him a lunch and help him get his things together and she didn't want any part of that. She felt indefinably angry with him, but she couldn't put her finger on any actual transgression. But the nagging seed was planted. What if he was seeing another woman?

After the front door shut and the truck backed out of the driveway Tara slid out of bed and got dressed into long underwear, some jeans, a gray flannel, and a cream pullover sweater. Maybe it was silly. She and Jasper was still newlywed, but what if there was a toilet, and a shower, and a hot meal involved? Tara wondered if even she would be unfaithful for that. Probably not, but she could see the appeal.

Tara grabbed the botany book that Rose gave her off the shelf. She might as well occupy her mind before she made herself crazy, so she lay down in bed and read in the flickering light of the single candle.

Tara realized she'd fallen back to sleep when the bedroom door creaked open.

"Ya' awake?" Melody whispered.

Nope! Tara wasn't ready to deal with Melody this early in the morning so she decided to lay still and ignore her; it had worked with Jasper after all. Hopefully the girl would go away and make her own breakfast.

Footsteps padded lightly across the carpet. The weight of the girl's hand sunk into the mattress as something slid across the floor. A creak followed by a sharp intake of breath. What the hell was this girl doing?

Paper crackled.

Tara flung the blanket back and bounded out of bed. Melody was crouched on the floor at the foot of the bed with Tara's box open in front of her. In her hands was the envelope of cash that Jasper had given Tara.

"What in the hell do you think you're doing?" Tara demanded as she snatched the envelope from the girl's fingers.

"I... it —," Melody stammered.

"It looks like you're trying to steal from us." Tara crossed her arms with the envelope tight in her fist."

"What? How dare you!" Melody squealed.

"How dare I? You're the one stealing from me," Tara spat.

"I wasn't stealing. I thought I heard someone in here. I was afraid someone had taken your money. I was just checking to see if it was safe," Melody lilted.

"Right. How dumb do you think I am? Of course I was in here. This is my room."

"I didn't mean just now. I meant before. See for yourself," Melody shrugged.

The flap wasn't sealed so Tara flipped it open and pulled out the cash. To her shock she was holding five one-dollar bills.

"Where's my money?" Tara demanded throwing the envelope on the bed splaying the dollars across the bedspread.

"I don't have your money!" Melody shouted.

Tara stormed into the living room. Melody's bag was leaning against the couch. Tara snatched it up and flung the contents out onto the cushions with several quick snaps.

"Don't touch my stuff you lunatic," Melody screamed snatching at the things that had fallen onto the floor.

Tara ignored her. She had unzipped the pockets and was shaking the bag upside down.

"Give me back my bag, bitch!" Melody shouted, snatching at the bag. Tara pushed her arms away, but she wasn't finding any cash. Had the girl already spent it? How could she do that? Someone was always with her.

SMACK! The sound startled Tara more than the blow.

"Give me back my goddamn bag!" the girl shrieked. The next blow connected open-handed with Tara's cheek.

Tara dropped the bag and snapped her head towards the girl. This time Melody's fist connected with Tara's lip and she tasted blood.

Breathe, Tara commanded herself.

Melody snatched up her bag and stood in front of Tara panting and clutching it, like Tara had just tried to pull the head off Melody's teddy bear. Tara half expected the girl to yell that she was going to tell her mommy.

Instead she screamed, "I didn't steal your goddamn money ya' stupid bitch!"

"Whatever," Tara's mind swirled round and round. Was she wrong? Melody didn't seem to have the money with her, but she had to have taken it didn't she? "I want you out of here by the time I get back." Tara snatched her coat off the hook by the door and stuffed her feet into her boots.

Melody let out a snort as Tara slammed the door behind her. Tara couldn't be there, she didn't know what would happen if she didn't leave. She wasn't even sure if she hit the girl back that it wouldn't be assaulting a minor. Tara walked briskly down the driveway shaking inside and out, but she barely felt the cold over the heat of her anger.

Snow crunched underfoot with every step down the gravel road they lived on. Fortunately it was only about an inch deep making the walk pretty easy. By the time she reached town Tara was cold all the way through. When she looked up she realized she was on Main Street. She took a deep breath. Part of her wanted to go sit in Kate's kitchen, but the rest of her didn't want to air all of her dirty laundry. Instead, Tara settled on the library. It was right here after all. Maybe she could do some research about keeping chickens even if her money was missing.

The librarian looked up to the electronic beep while Tara stomped the snow off her boots on the mat. His smile faded as soon as it reached his lips.

"Are you some kind of street fighter?" he asked louder than Tara expected.

"What?" Tara asked startled.

"Every time I see you, you look like you've gone a couple of rounds. I'm not sure if you won or lost." He gestured towards her face.

Tara had forgotten her split lip, it was numb from the cold. Tara put her hand over her mouth.

"Do you have somewhere I can clean up?" she asked.

"Yeah, bathroom's through the door marked private. Then turn left."

"Thanks," Tara replied as she hurried away.

In the mirror it looked worse then she realized. There was a line of blood down her chin and spots on her sweater. She cleaned up the best she could, but it wouldn't come out; leaving brown spots on the chest of her cream sweater. At least her lip had already scabbed over.

"Are you sure you're okay?" The librarian asked when she walked back to the desk.

Tara wasn't sure if she should stay. She was embarrassed and didn't want to answer any questions. That's why she was here instead of with Kate.

"I can call the cops for you if you need."

Better stay, she decided, *or he might call the cops.* "Nope, I just did something stupid and got hurt." Tara smiled then winced as she tasted blood again.

He looked like he was going to argue, but instead asked, "So what are you looking for today?"

"I'm looking for books on chickens."

"Chickens?"

"Yup chickens," she nodded. "I want to raise some chickens."

The librarian leaned back in his chair. "Do you need help?"

"Nope. I remember seeing some in the section I was in last time."

"Well," he stood as she walked past his desk, "let me know if you find something worth crowing about."

Tara groaned.

He smiled before continuing. "I wish you the best of cluck."

"Thanks," she muttered while he chuckled to himself.

Tara took her time perusing the shelves, she had no intention of getting home before Jasper. Hopefully Melody would be gone with no explanation and Tara wouldn't have to catch hell. Tara savored the thought.

She ran her fingers over the spines of the books on the shelf. Some were old and rough with tape, others were new glossy paperbacks. Tara took her time flipping through them. Finally she picked one and moved to the heavy table surround by metal chairs that had probably been sitting there since the sixties. She read in silence until she started worrying about losing daylight. It would take her hours to walk home.

When Tara walked back to the front desk the librarian looked up from his phone.

"You were so quiet I was worried you'd been ab-cluck-ted," he grinned.

"That's awful."

"Yeah I guess I really laid an egg with that one."

Tara rubbed her face. "Were you thinking of those the whole time I was here?"

"It's boring here," he shrugged.

"Goodnight," she waved heading for the door.

"You too chicken to keep talking to me?" he baited her.

"Goodnight," she called over her shoulder as she pushed the door open. Once she was outside she smiled, he seemed like quite the character.

The snow had gotten deeper during the day. Several inches had accumulated, making Tara's muscles burn after walking less than a mile. When a horn honked Tara stepped off the side of the road and slipped into the ditch. A door opened while Tara floundered to right herself. The snow in the ditch was considerably deeper than what was on the road.

"What are you doing out here?" Jasper asked from the road.

Tara opened her mouth to speak, but she closed it again. She didn't know what to say.

"I was on my way to get you anyway. I've been building fence all day for Mister White. His wife invited us to an early holiday dinner tonight and I was coming to pick you up." He watched as she wiped her hands on her coat, and dusted the snow off her jeans before it could melt and soak her to the skin.

"Early holiday dinner?" Tara asked.

"It's the twenty-third," Jasper reminded her. "It's nearly Christmas."

"I'd almost forgotten. It's seems so weird since the town didn't put up any decorations." Tara looked around at the dark streets devoid of Christmas lights.

"Everyone's broke," Jasper shrugged, "None of that explains why you're out here."

"I was on my way home. I just needed to get out of the house."

"Were you visiting him?" Jasper's voice was as cold as the cab of the truck.

"Who?"

"Don't play dumb with me. Were you at Pete's house?"

"I was at the library all day reading about chickens," she explained as she slipped her seat belt on.

"Why is it always chickens when you're with Pete? Is it some kind of little inside joke about his cock?"

Tara thought that was clever, but Jasper wasn't joking. "I swear I wasn't with Pete. I haven't seen him since the day he brought us the kerosene. I was at the library. You can ask the librarian."

"Don't think I won't," he snapped.

At least she was about to meet the people he was working for all day so he must have been telling her the truth that morning. Tara felt momentarily guilty for having thought ill of him, but it was quickly replaced by the irritation that he'd accused her of what she'd only suspected from him.

Streetlights flooded the cab in waves as they headed through town in a silence that was painful. A few minutes outside of town Jasper pulled into the driveway of a Victorian-style farmhouse. The lights cast squares on the snow all around the porch, and in the front window was a brightly-lit Christmas tree. As they got out of the truck a motion-activated light flooded the lawn with a blinding white gleam that reflected off the snow. Tara was so used to night-time gloom that it seemed un-earthly.

As they approached the back door it was flung open by a middle-aged woman with short dark hair wearing a green dress and a gaily printed apron.

"Come on in. I didn't expect you folks so soon. Dinner's almost ready," Missus White called out to them. As they walked in past her Tara wished she had gone home to change into something not sprinkled with blood.

The house itself was large and overly-decorated. Garlands and baubles mixed with the faux-rustic that could only be found in a magazine.

Mister White greeted them just inside the door where he introduced them as Bob and Sharon. They were both comfortably middle-aged and while Sharon looked like she spent a fair amount of time at the gym, Bob was round and soft with a face that reminded Tara very much of a bullfrog. Sharon led them to a heavy wooden table that had been carefully aged.

As they were seated, Sharon turned to Tara. "So, Jasper tells me you two were thinking about starting a farm." Then she filled Tara's glass nearly to the brim with wine.

Tara smiled her warmest smile and tried to ignore the taste of blood in her mouth, "I'm not sure about a farm, but we were thinking of getting some chickens in the spring." Tara emphasized the word chicken just to watch Jasper scowl.

Bob chuckled. "Everyone has to start somewhere. Besides, chickens are the gateway animal. Once you have chickens it will lead to rabbits, goats, sheep, horses, cows, geese, and a whole host of others." Bob paused to smile at his wife who had just re-appeared with plates that she'd already made up for Tara and Jasper. "We've been meaning to start a farm for a great many years. I'm a broker by trade, we just moved into this area last month. There's a lot of real estate hitting the market around here and it's ripe for folks like us to make a move. Made a real good deal on this house, too, it was a foreclosure."

He'd said the sentences with a smile as if he'd said something nice, but Tara couldn't help but wonder if he realized he'd just skimmed over the fact that locals were losing everything.

Tara concentrated on keeping the smile firmly on her face while she continued, "What we're doing may expand, but for now we're just getting some chickens, and maybe we'll put in a garden."

"Jasper here told us you are the kind of folks that believe in putting something away for a rainy day. That's what we're doing too," Bob said spearing a piece of steak off the plate his wife had just set down in front of him. "That's what we need all the fence for. I had an awful lot invested in the markets and I saw the need to diversify into tangibles. I'm betting on a very nice livestock market in the near future." Bob leaned forward on his elbows which rested easily on the table. "Now's the time to be getting out of the markets and dollar wherever possible," Bob punctuated with a nod of his head and flourish of his fork.

"What do you mean?" Jasper leaned forward, mirroring Bob.

"The writing is on the wall," Bob shrugged as his wife poured herself what Tara thought might be her second glass of wine. She'd slugged the first down like water after crossing the desert. "I give it less than six months before the dollar isn't worth the paper it's printed on. Haven't you heard we just started an economic war with Russia and China."

"I'm sorry. Actually I don't follow politics."

"Don't get me wrong," Bob continued as if Jasper hadn't spoken, "this country has been spiraling around the drain for years at this point, but now it's getting urgent. Look at all those un-employed folks, guys on welfare, snap, or whatever it is they call food assistance nowadays. I mean, I believe that there are a lot of lazy people, but even I can't imagine that many men don't want to work even with so many millennials in the work force."

Jasper and Tara stared at each other unsure of what to say to that many insults all in one sentence.

Sharon poured another glass of wine and offered Tara a top up. Tara waved her away, but the woman poured wine into the cup until it dribbled down the sides. Maybe Sharon had had more than two glasses already.

Bob continued without pausing to pay attention to his wife's actions, "That's why people like us need to start investing in the things that matter." This time when he paused he looked back and forth between Tara and Jasper like he expected them to know the answer. Jasper nodded, which appeared to be enough interaction.

"Gold, guns, ammo, food, land, and livestock," Bob counted things off on his fingers.

The hair on the back of Tara's neck prickled. "What sort of livestock are you intending to raise?" Tara asked desperate to change the subject to something that sounded less crazy.

"Mostly cattle," Bob said waving his wife forward to refill his glass which she did with a great deal of concentration. "But really I'm branching out in all directions to start. I've got several incubators full of eggs that I bought off a nice farm. Had them shipped in from the coast. I've had agents going around to the livestock auctions for me. The first of the animals will be arriving around the end of the week." Bob boasted with a smile.

Tara waved Sharon away from her glass again as she hadn't touched it yet, but Sharon didn't appear to notice. "What breed of cattle are you planning on?" Tara asked as she held her hand over the top of her glass to keep Sharon from trying to pour any more in.

"Not sure yet, all kinds." Bob's smile never left his face.

"Beef or dairy?" Tara asked expectantly.

"Aren't they all made of beef?" Sharon slurred. She and Bob burst out laughing.

"What do you mean little lady?" Bob asked.

Tara paused, "Most livestock are bred for a specific purpose. A beef cow would have a lot of muscle, but may produce an inferior quantity or quality of milk as compared to a milk cow."

"Well who the hell knew," Bob shrugged. "I learned something today. What about chickens? I thought they were all for eating and making eggs, are they specialized too?"

"Actually," Tara replied, "they are specialized. You have bantams, light breeds, or heavy breeds that can be either egg breeds, meat breeds, or dual purpose birds."

"I got a bunch of white birds that looked tasty. They're called Cornish Cross or something like that. It's a bunch of light brown eggs. Brown eggs make great farm chickens right?" Bob asked.

"The Cornish Cross is specifically a meat bird. From what I've read they grow to butchering weight really quickly, but tend towards health problems like heart attacks and the inability to stand up under their own weight. It's one of the breeds I made up my mind not to raise." Tara smiled at Jasper who was now watching her open-mouthed. Now maybe the bastard would believe what she was doing all day.

"Well how about that," Bob looked at his wife who swayed in her chair. Bob raised his glass to his wife like a salute, and then he turned back to Tara. "Young lady, that is a good deal of help to me. I need to get some more birds. What would you recommend?"

"If you're looking for some good dual-purpose birds I'd recommend the Barred Rock or Buff Orphington. I've read a few blurbs about them that seem interesting. I was thinking about starting there myself."

"Looks like I've got a lot more to learn than I thought I did," Bob marveled at her. "I better get on that before everything comes apart at the seams."

Sharon smiled in their direction. "Ish' going to happen shoon' ya' know. We pay tenshen'. We gots' lots bags of food and thosh' big cans and the freesh' dried."

Tara smiled indulgingly at her, unsure what she was on about.

"We gots' everythin' we need. Lots people gone die shoon," Sharon nodded gravely, "But not ush', we gots' what we need. We even got seeds."

"Really?" Jasper smiled, nodding.

"We gots wheat, corn, beansh, and all 'shorts of other thingsh.

"Do you farm?" Jasper asked.

Tara was glad he'd been able to ask a question because she wasn't entirely sure what the woman was saying.

"No, but how hard can it be?" Sharon smiled and burped. "S'cuze me. We has' what we need."

Back in the truck Jasper looked at Tara. "I'm sorry."

"For what?" In Tara's opinion Jasper had an awful lot to apologize for. She needed him to narrow it down.

"Those two were whackjobs. I'm sorry if you were uncomfortable there."

"Uncomfortable doesn't even start to cover how I felt about that dinner. But hey, a drunk and a raving lunatic, it was like going home for the holidays," Tara smirked.

"You don't ever have to go back there with me. I'll be finished with the fences before the end of the year, then we can forget about them and they can hide in their bunker with their beans and bullets waiting for the world to end."

"Maybe they'll need a farmhand?" Tara smiled.

"Oh hell no, I don't do crazy. I'd be afraid they would want me to drink some poison punch," Jasper said shaking his head.

"I wonder if Bob's right about the markets, I mean he was a stockbroker." Tara shrugged, but in the dark Jasper probably didn't see it.

"Oh come on now, don't let them suck you into their madness. That's the problem with delusional people, they can sound sane," Jasper chided.

"But look at the job market, there's nothing out there."

"I think that's a local problem," Jasper argued. "I think if we'd just got back to the city we'd be doing a lot better."

"I don't know," Tara grumbled. "At least here we have some place to live when we can't find work. In the city we might end up homeless living on the streets. I don't think my mom would be willing to help us out again."

"Can't you see the cycle that leaves us in? We don't leave here because we can't find work, but there's no work in the area so we're never going to leave."

"I don't know," Tara admitted. "I'm scared to leave here. At least we can have chickens and a garden and stuff. If we go to the city and there's still no jobs what do we do?"

It was a familiar debate at this point and they volleyed it back and forth without either of them making any progress as usual.

When they arrived home Melody met them on the porch.

"Damnit," Tara muttered under her breath.

"Where have y'all been all day?" she asked looking suspiciously back and forth between Tara and Jasper.

"We went to dinner," Jasper patted her shoulder.

"To dinner?" Melody nearly whined.

Tara smirked. The girl had no way of knowing that she hadn't talked to Jasper about what happened.

"Yeah, we got invited to a holiday meal at the house of the man I spent the day working for today." Jasper patted her on the shoulder again. "Move; you're letting all the heat out."

Melody stepped out of the doorway to let them into the house, but glared at Tara.

"Why didn't ya' invite me along too?" Melody asked Jasper sweetly.

"I can't just invite you to someone's house for dinner. They invited me and my wife, that's all. It wasn't anything personal. Besides they were weird. You should be happy you didn't have to go there."

"What did ya' eat?" Melody ventured.

Tara smiled slightly. She didn't want to taste blood in front of Melody. "Steak, potatoes, corn on the cob, a semi-sweet red wine, and cheesecake for dessert."

Melody's eye's narrowed. "So what are we gonna' do for Christmas?"

"Nothing," Jasper shrugged. "There's no point, we don't have anything.

"Can't we at least have a tree?" Melody asked.

"For what?" Jasper asked with irritation. "We don't have anything to decorate it with. No power to light it. Nothing to put under it. I don't see the point."

"It just don't feel right not to have at least a —," Melody started.

"I said no!" Jasper burst out sharply, striding into the bedroom.

Tara followed him leaving a shocked-looking Melody in the living room.

While Jasper was undressing for bed Tara hazarded to talk to him. "Do you think it's safe for you to go back and build more fence for that man?"

"That man," Jasper said throwing his pants into the corner, "is off in the head, but he's got a lot of money. I'd like to have some of it so I'm going to keep building fences for him. It's not like money is coming into this house any other way."

"What?" Tara was startled by his tone.

"Don't act like you've done a single thing to contribute to this household in over a month."

"I'm looking for a job," Tara protested

"I don't call what you're doing looking for a job. All you've been doing is sitting around on your ass expecting me to take care of you. So don't you dare judge me or what I do to bring money into this house."

"I didn't mean anything —," Tara began.

"Of course, you never mean anything."

"I'm sorry," Tara whispered.

"You should be," Jasper scowled before snuffing out the light.

Tara listened to Jasper breathing in the dark beside her.

"Jasper?"

"What?" he snapped.

"Don't you even want to know what happened to my lip?"

"I don't care."

CHAPTER 10

When Tara woke up she could hear Jasper and Melody laughing in the living room. At least he was in a better mood. It had shocked her the night before when he'd gotten short with both of them. She was used to him being mad at her, but him lashing out at someone else wasn't like him at all.

Tara shivered her way into a pair of jeans, a t-shirt, and sweater to go out and join them. Maybe they had breakfast ready.

When the bedroom door creaked open Jasper and Melody went silent.

Crap, Tara sighed. *Melody must have told him some version of what happened the day before.* There was no way she could deal with this crap today.

"I was thinking of running to Alex and Kate's house today to grab a shower. Does anyone want to go?" Tara hadn't really planned on going anywhere, but now she didn't want to stay here.

"Do you really think you should go bug them on Christmas Eve?" Jasper asked without looking at her.

"Christmas Eve or not I still need a shower." Tara ran her hands through her hair to express how much it needed to be washed. "Does anyone want to come?"

Melody smiled sweetly and shook her head.

"You go on ahead," Jasper shrugged. "Hopefully they'll be home." He paused and leaned forward. "If they aren't home where are you going to go?"

"I can stop over at Rose's."

"You could start there. She's probably home," Jasper suggested.

"I don't want to tell her about all of this." Tara gestured

around the room. She wasn't ready to tell Rose about her circumstances, but more than that she didn't want to talk about Melody today. Rose would ask. Rose was like that. The problem was Tara felt guilty about what had happened the day before. She wasn't sure if she had over-reacted.

"I'm sure old Rose wouldn't..." Jasper was telling her.

Tara didn't stay to listen. She had already snatched her coat off the hook and was closing the door behind her before he could finish his sentence.

"Hey honey," Kate greeted Tara without enthusiasm as she stepped back out of the doorway to let Tara into the house.

"Merry Christmas," Tara nodded, but she noted the tree in the corner was dark and the always-tidy house looked disheveled.

"Oh right, merry and all that crap," Kate grumbled.

"Is everything okay? Am I here at a bad time? I can go." Tara turned to reach for the door she had just shut behind herself.

"No," Kate held up her hand to stop Tara. "Sorry. We just got some bad news."

"Is Alex okay?" Tara felt a twist of panic.

"He's fine," Kate soothed. "He's in the bedroom sleeping. He worked a double shift last night." Kate led Tara into the kitchen where she was shoving cookbooks into a box. "Turns out that paying your rent doesn't insure that you landlord won't sell your house out from under you."

"Can he do that?" Tara was shocked.

"No, and yes. Turns out he can do whatever he wants when you can't afford a lawyer and the bank can. Technically we have sixty days to vacate, but I'm not going to stop the new owners from moving in. We're going to go stay with my mother until we can find a new place," Kate shrugged.

"Does she live in town?" Tara asked.

"Nope, about an hour from here."

"I don't even know what to say."

"Exactly," Kate nodded.

"Well, I feel like a heel now," Tara paused. "But can I use your shower?"

"Go ahead," Kate sighed. "Use it while we have it, but you might want to get something set up with Pete if you aren't going to get your well fixed in the next week or two."

Tara ignored the comment about showering at Pete's house. "Is that when you're moving?"

"Not a clue. It'll depend on when Alex can get his uncle's box truck."

Tara got a quick shower, refilled the water jugs, and spent the next few hours helping Kate pack her breakables that needed special wrapping. When she couldn't put it off any longer she headed back home.

"What took so long?" Jasper demanded when she walked back into the house.

"I was helping Kate pack. They got evicted." Tara spoke matter-of-factly, sniffing the air. It smelled really good in the house.

"Shit," he muttered. "Them too? Where they moving to?"

"In with her mother; about an hour away..." Tara paused, "Them too? Who else is moving?"

"Didn't I tell you Rose put her house on the market yesterday? She found a buyer for her antiques. A guy should be coming in a few days and basically cleaning out her house. She called me to come help her move some boxes around."

Tara was shocked. "I knew Rose was going to sell her house, but I didn't expect it to go on the market so soon. It sounds like it's going to end up pretty lonely around here."

"Yeah," Melody nodded. "I'm gonna have to leave y'all too."

"Not yet?" Jasper looked concerned.

"Not yet," she assured him. "I was thinking about waiting for it to warm up a bit. So, maybe spring?"

How much bad news could one person get in a day? Tara

took a deep breath.

"Good. I didn't want to worry about you out on the road in this terrible cold," Jasper smiled at Melody and she smiled back blushing.

"I thought I was delirious for a while there," Tara interrupted, "but is that stew on the stove."

"Oh that," Jasper smiled. "Do you remember when we got the free oven from the United Church of Christ?"

"Yeah?"

"I guess they remembered us. The pastor and some young guy dropped by."

"They brought us food!" Melody nearly shouted. "Two big boxes of it. They prayed for us and took up personal donations from the parishioners."

"Pastor Richard asked us to stop by next Sunday if we can get into town."

"What did you tell him?" Tara asked horrified. She didn't want to imagine facing a whole room full of people who pitied her.

"I told him that gas is tight, but we'd try to attend if we can," Jasper smiled.

Melody squealed. "That would be wonderful. I haven't been since I was back in Texas."

Tara shook herself, "That's wonderful dear. What was in the boxes?"

"Sugar, flour, soups, stews, cereal, powdered milk, canned vegetables, and all kinds of other things. We'll be eating good," Jasper smiled.

"For a few weeks at least," Tara agreed.

"Finally," Melody added.

A look of irritation crossed Jasper's face. "What?"

"Nothing personal," Melody added hastily, "but the food's been pretty awful."

"I've been doing my best." Jasper looked hurt.

"Oh I know that, and I know ya'd buy more food if ya' could," Melody soothed. "I know how hard ya' try," Melody placed her hand on his arm.

Tara's heart fluttered in her chest like a wounded bird when Jasper smiled back at Melody.

"Merry friggin' Christmas," she grumbled, but nobody was paying attention to her anyway.

CHAPTER 11

The first week of the New Year was so blustery cold they'd had to keep the heater turned up. Tara was afraid of how fast this was emptying the kerosene.

Jasper had gone out that morning to pick up his pay from the White's and hopefully refill the kerosene containers again. But, just after noon he stormed back into the house slamming the door behind him. This did not bode well.

"You would not believe what just happened," he announced.

"Try me," Tara offered, "There's not much I'd have a hard time believing at this point."

"When I asked for my pay, Mister White told me he couldn't offer me anything as useless as money."

Tara stared at him. "What did he pay you in?"

"Nothing. He told me to come back tomorrow to collect my pay."

"Can I go with ya' when ya' do?" Melody asked. "I've been so bored here."

Jasper looked at her confused for a moment before his face softened. "Yeah I suppose. We'll only be there for a minute."

"I don't mind. I like to do things quick," The girl smiled suggestively.

What the hell did that mean? Tara frowned. "So do we have a plan to get kerosene?"

"No we don't have a plan. I was expecting to get paid."

Of course not, she thought to herself. "I don't think we have more than two days' worth. "Tara shook her head. "Not at the rate we're going through it anyway."

"What the hell do you want me to do about it?" Jasper demanded.

"I don't know. I don't know what to do either."

"Here's a thought… Why don't you get your fat ass out there and bring home some money too?" Jasper demanded.

Tara stared at him in shock then spun on her heel and grabbed her coat.

"Leave the goddamn truck where it is," he yelled after her.

Tara threw her keys back over her shoulder on the porch and stormed off towards town.

The road was slick and once Tara reached town the snow on it was basically mud. On one corner several men huddled around a lighted barrel, Tara hurried towards them.

"Hi. Do you mind if I join you?" she asked.

All three men looked at her. The youngest was a red-headed boy who looked like he should have been in school instead of standing on the street. The next man was around her age, and the eldest looked old enough to be her father. He was crowned with unruly gray hair and had a coughing fit before taking a long drag off an unmarked bottle. The youngest man shuffled over to make room for her.

"I'm sorry. I'm frozen through. I'm afraid my fingers will snap off like icicles if I try to shake anyone's hand." She rubbed her hands together and huddled as close to the barrel as she dared without physically setting herself on fire.

"Where you from?" the boy asked her.

"I live a little ways outside of town. I just walked in," she smiled. At least the boy was trying to be friendly the other two barely acknowledged she was standing there.

"Why?" he asked

"I'm running out of kerosene and needed to see if there was something I could do to bring in some cash around here today." Tara chose to leave out the detail of Jasper's behavior.

The older two looked at each other while the boy rubbed the back of his neck.

"If there was work we wouldn't be standing here," the boy shrugged.

"I'm sure she's got skills you ain't got," the older man teased.

"Like what?" the boy demanded.

"I'd pay her for a bang if I had any money. I wouldn't pay you." The old man laughed.

Tara stared at him shocked. "I'm sorry I bothered you guys, I gotta' go," she told him quickly.

"Don't pay him any mind," the man her age told her, "he's drunk."

"He's like that sober too." The boy looked away like he was embarrassed.

Tara hesitated.

"No sense in you wandering around out here freezing to death. Stand by the fire. It'll keep you warm." The man her age reached down behind him and handed her a piece of cardboard. "You can use my sign if you want."

She took it. It said, "Help, desperate for work. Need to feed my family."

"Close enough," Tara nodded, "Thank you."

In the six hours that Tara stood on the corner several men stopped and offered her a choice of positions in their bed which she declined, but nobody offered her any work.

"Crap," Tara leaned over the barrel again throwing some wood scraps in. The older man had gone off to a shelter for the night, but the other two continued to stand on the corner with her.

"I know," the boy, whose name she had discovered was Mark, said, "I do this every day."

"Really?" she asked.

"Yeah," he shrugged. "I sometimes get a handout, or some little job every couple of days."

Tara nodded unsure what to say.

"Have you had a good meal today?" the man her age asked. She'd learned his name was Daniel and he had a wife and three kids.

"I had a breakfast of oatmeal."

"You wanna' go down to the church with us? They lay out a hot meal every night about this time."

"I suppose," Tara nodded. It was, in fact, night. Tara wasn't sure how she was going to make it home. It was bitterly cold and she didn't even have a light, but she couldn't leave earlier, she didn't want to show up empty-handed.

While the men gathered their signs and some folding stools, Jasper's truck roared to a stop at the corner.

"Get in the truck," he yelled out the window to Tara.

Daniel stepped forward and crossed his arms, "Lady's not a whore."

"I'm not so sure about that," Jasper hissed.

"It's okay," Tara assured Daniel, "he's my husband."

"Are you going to be okay with him?" Mark asked her. "We can take you to the church. They'll give a safe place if you need it." He took a deep breath and gestured to her face. "Was it him that did that to your lip?"

Tara brushed her fingers across the peeling skin of her split lip. It was nearly healed, but there was still a scab. She couldn't blame the boy for asking, Jasper looked like he'd been chewing on a mouthful of lemons.

"Nope, I just did something stupid and hurt myself. I'll be fine," she nodded.

"We're here most days," Daniel mentioned gravely.

"Thanks for the place to sit and the use of your sign," Tara called back as she climbed in the truck. Both men stood shoulder to shoulder watching Jasper.

Jasper sped off without even letting her buckle her seatbelt.

"What in the hell is wrong with you. I've been all over town looking for you. I went to the library, the industrial park, Kate's house... Nobody had seen you."

Tara noted that he didn't say he'd been to Pete's.

"And there you are standing on some street corner like a whore."

Tara took a deep breath, "I was looking for legitimate work, like you."

"But you don't have any skills," Jasper snapped. "Who the hell is going to hire you to do something?"

Tara frowned. "I did a lot of babysitting in my youth. I know how to clean a house. I could split wood, cook meals, or bathe little old ladies."

"Were you offered any jobs like that?" Jasper asked.

"No."

"Were you offered any jobs at all?" Jasper sounded smug this time.

"Yes."

"What was it?"

"You know what it was," Tara sighed while they headed home.

In the morning Melody helped herself to Tara's nicest clothes, and stood in front of the mirror preening like she was going out on a date. Jasper and Melody's "quick trip" took hours. They had taken all but one of the kerosene containers with them so Tara assured herself that they were just looking for someplace to fill them.

Tara eventually decided to take advantage of the quiet to study. She'd gotten the basics of plant anatomy down and had moved on to the plant identification guides. While she looked at the glossy photographs she tried to shuffle through her memory. It was strange. Some of the plants seemed vaguely familiar, but she couldn't be sure what she'd seen before and what she hadn't. It was amazing how little she noticed. Everything outside that was green had always just been classified as lawn or trees inside her head. In reality, there was a hidden world under her feet that she'd spent years walking over without ever knowing its value. At least she remembered seeing dandelions before. Tara had become so engrossed she didn't notice the truck on the driveway until the front door opened.

"Tara, we're back," Jasper called.

"We have a surprise," Melody announced, "Ya gotta' come out and see it."

Tara groaned inwardly and rolled her eyes, "I'm coming, just a minute." Tara put her marker in the book and set it down on the bed. When she reached the living room Melody was standing there with her hands clasped.

"You'll never guess!" she trilled

"I'm sure I won't," Tara answered unenthusiastically.

Tara followed Melody onto the porch. In the front yard was a black goat with brown floppy ears serenely picking at the dry grass.

"Surprised?" Jasper asked.

"Shocked, is more the word I would use," Tara replied, slowly approaching the animal. It looked up at her and burped sweetly.

"You don't like it?" Jasper frowned.

"That's a goat." Tara stared pointedly at the beast.

"Man," he said doing a double take at it, "I got cheated. I thought it was a little cow."

"Why is there a goat in our yard?"

"I thought you wanted to be self-sufficient or whatever?" Jasper shrugged.

"We were getting chickens," Tara reminded him. "That's not a chicken."

"Yeah, but I got you a goat." Jasper pointed at the animal that had stopped eating to stare at them.

Tara sighed, "We didn't even discuss a goat. I thought we were going to get chickens."

Jasper covered his face with his hand for a moment, "Now, you're mad because I did what you wanted and got a goat so we could be more self-sufficient? Not only just a goat, but a way to feed it for the rest of the winter." He pointed to the truck. On the back, tied down, was an impressive pile of hay bales and a pile of grain sacks.

"Mister White must have paid you very well if you were able to buy all that with it." Tara gestured.

"Oh no," Melody assured her, "the goat and its food are his pay. He was offered that or some silver quarters. I chose the goat because I thought she was cute as a button."

"This is Melody's goat?" Tara asked confused.

"What would I do with a goat in Chicago?" Melody asked.

"No, it's our goat," Jasper assured her.

"What exactly are we supposed to do with a goat? Are we going to eat her?" Tara asked.

"No, she's a dairy goat, a Nubian or something like that."

"Her name's Greta, and y'all'll be milking her," Melody goaded her.

"You do know that they have to have a kid for that," Tara remined them.

"Surprise! She's pregnant!" Melody squealed. "She's due in a month."

Tara took several deep breaths. "We don't have a barn and I don't know how to take care of a pregnant goat."

Jasper looked briefly uncomfortable. "I didn't know. After the other evening at the White's I thought you knew all that stuff."

"I'd spent that day at the library reading about chickens. All I know about goats is that they are similar to sheep."

"Well, do you know anything about sheep?" he asked.

"No, we hadn't discussed raising sheep!" she exclaimed. "Or goats, or anything other than chickens! Where are we going to put her?"

"Can't you just leave her outside like a cat?" Melody asked.

"Cat's get left outside in the winter because they know how to seek shelter in things like barns and under houses. Do you think the goat is going to crawl under the house to keep warm tonight?" Tara asked.

"Well," Jasper said to Melody, "she's a lot less excited or grateful than I thought she'd be."

Tara looked heavenward for a moment. "Where are we going to put the feed? The hay?" she asked. "Why didn't you just take the silver? We could sell that. We need kerosene, not a goat."

"We can put the feed in the shed and stack the hay outside, don't haystacks normally get left outside?" Jasper chose to ignore Tara's comment about the silver.

"I don't think you can just stack square bales outside. They at least need to be under a tarp." Tara took a deep breath. "Let's get this unloaded and then I'll head over to Rose's. There's some lumber there. Maybe we can slap something together to keep the goat out of the wind tonight. We can worry about the hay later."

Half an hour later, Tara was pulling the truck around the side of Rose's yard so that she could throw the stacks of lumber on it. At least the physical work allowed her to burn off some of her irritation and clear her head. By the time the job was done she felt calmer.

Tara decided she'd better stop in and say hi to Rose.

"That's was pretty impressive dear," Rose remarked as she opened the door. "I don't know a fella who coulda' gotten that loaded any faster, or louder."

Tara grimaced, "Sorry about that, I was pretty angry when I got here. I'd have come to the door first, but I would have been rotten company."

"Are you gonna' be more pleasant company now?" Rose asked stepping out of the doorway to let her inside.

"Yeah, I think so," Tara smiled, but when she stepped into the kitchen her smile vanished. The room was full of stacks of newspaper and packing boxes. One box on the table was half-full of glassware carefully wrapped in the newsprint.

"Did the house sell already?" Tara asked concerned

"No, but I've got a lot of interest. Now I'm just haggling over prices," Rose admitted. "Bunch of city folks, they make enough money to pay what I'm asking, but they think that I'm old and feeble so I'm just gonna' give the place to them."

"Hold out for the best price you can."

"Of course, how else am I gonna' afford to pay the strippers, and buy my booze," Rose winked. "Now dear, what can I get you to drink? I've got water, herbal tea, and tequila."

"I'll take a shot of tea, thanks."

"Nothing stronger than that on a cold day like today?" Rose asked.

"No thanks. I'm plenty warm from all my work."

"What brought you over here all hopping mad in the first

place?" Rose asked putting the kettle on the stove.

"Greta."

"Who?"

"A goat."

"A what?"

"A goat. A black and brown Nubian."

"A milk goat? We use to have a sweet little nanny named Daisy when I was younger. I don't remember what breed she was," Rose said, looking thoughtful. "She gave a lot of milk though. Why are you mad about a goat?"

"It's not really about the goat," Tara admitted

"So what is it about?" Rose asked, leaning forward on the table to keep the box from sitting between them while they talked.

Tara moved the box carefully to one side. "My husband decided to get a goat without me. When he got paid he was given the choice between money or a goat. Melody wanted to get the goat. Jasper knew we needed the money, but he picked the goat instead to make her happy and I don't like it."

"Why?" Rose asked.

Tara suddenly felt self-conscious about having to justify her feelings. Was she wrong? Was her annoyance unwarranted? Tara had been sure that Rose would understand. "I just don't like them making decisions together about our future as if Melody is part of it and I'm not."

"So basically, you think they're having an affair?" Rose asked.

"What?" That wasn't exactly what Tara had said.

The tea kettle started to grumble just before the boil and Rose shuffled over to grab a potholder and pull it off the burner. Then she dug some lose tea out of a jar and put it into the tea ball. She placed this in a cup in front of Tara and poured the hot water over it. The scent of apples flooded over her, meaning it was chamomile.

Rose set the kettle back on the stove. "I'm not trying to be unkind honey. It's just that I've found over the years that if it seems like they are having an affair, they normally are."

"Affairs are for couples who don't care about each other. Jasper and I are still newlyweds. We've been together less than a year, and we got married because we love each other. I have a hard time believing he'd cheat already."

"Then," Rose paused briefly, "why are you jealous?"

By the time darkness fell they had a very basic building that could be described more as a stall than a shed. It had no roof, and no walls above five feet. The door was a sheet of wood with nails in it tied in place on the front until they could come up with something more permanent. Thankfully that night the weather was fine and stayed above forty degrees. It wasn't even freezing. Tara didn't re-fill the heater that evening. She wanted to leave it off until they really needed it.

By the end of the second day they had walls that went all the way up and a proper door that opened and closed with a wooden latch. It wasn't surprising when Melody had an excuse not to help them both days. She claimed she wasn't feeling well and needed to rest. Tara didn't care that Melody didn't help. It felt good to reconnect with Jasper without the girl in the way. Maybe the goat wasn't such a bad thing after all. By noon Tara's coat was hanging over the porch railing. It felt like spring wanted to come early and they reveled in the sensation.

Tara woke in total darkness that night to a scream. When she sat up the air that hit her skin was so cold she gasped. The temperature had dropped drastically, and the sound that made her scalp prickle came again, it was a scream, but it wasn't human.

Tara scrambled out of bed, unsure what she was listening to. After hearing it twice more she realized it was the goat. The sound fell into an insistent wailing.

Tara snatched at the blankets, "Jasper, something's wrong!"

"Wha...?" he mumbled trying to pull more blankets over himself.

"Get up!" Tara insisted, "You need to light the stove the temperature dropped. It's freezing in here."

"What's that noise?" Jasper asked shaking himself out of his dreaming haze.

"I think that's our goat," Tara stammered as she dragged on a layer of long underwear under the skirt of her nightgown. Then she pulled on some socks and her boots. A sweater went on next, but she was in a hurry so she grabbed the candle and scrambled out the door. There was a light coating of ice on the porch that caused her to fall hard on her knees and one hand. Tara gritted her teeth, got up, and moved more slowly off the porch. The candle in her hands shook as she tried to light a match. The wind wouldn't cooperate, snuffing it out as soon as she could get it lit.

Blindly she groped through the darkness following the sounds of distress. The air that filled her lungs was so cold it hurt to breathe. A pattering sound told her sleet was falling lazily onto the ice. As Tara got closer the screaming dropped from a howl to what she Tara could only describe as crying. After fumbling several moments with the unfamiliar latch in the dark, Tara stepped inside the small room. Ice was crusted on the ground inside. It crackled as she moved and Greta had fallen silent except for the gritting of her teeth. Tara tried lighting the candle again, this time she succeeded. In the dim glow it was hard to understand what she was seeing. Greta lay on her side, quiet and shaking, and at her rear end was a small black and white pile. Tara bent closer and was able to discern small limbs and translucent hooves. The eyes didn't look right and a tiny tongue protruded from the side of its mouth. Steam rose from it, but otherwise there wasn't a whisper of movement.

Tara reached down and pulled it gently away from Greta. It was warm and slippery, but premature. The baby didn't even properly have fur. Tara set it in the corner to get it out of the way as her stomach flopped in revulsion; the poor thing was obviously beyond her help.

Turning her attentions to Greta, Tara got scared. Ice was

crusted in her wet fur, she was shaking, gritting her teeth and she looked too tired to move. Tara didn't have a thermometer so she stuck her fingers inside the goat's mouth. It didn't feel very warm.

"We need to get you inside love," she soothed. "Can you walk?" Tara asked pulling at the goat, trying to get her to her feet. After some straining and shuffling all four of the goat's legs were underneath her, but, when Tara urged the animal forward she tumbled back down onto the ground.

"You're not going to give up and die on me!" Tara ordered the goat sternly as she blew out the candle and slipped her sweater off. She slid it around the goat's ribcage and grabbed hold of the sleeves using it to help pull her back up to her feet and walk her forward. The trip towards the house in the dark over the crackling grass was slow and physically demanding. Twice, Greta's back legs gave way completely and they both tumbled to the ground. When they finally reached the porch Tara got above her and lifted her up the steps holding tightly to the arms of the sweater while the goat scrambled uselessly against the floor.

"What are you doing?" Jasper demanded as he crossed the porch. "You're going to catch your death out here without your coat," he chided Tara as he threw her coat over her shoulders.

Tara realized she had stopped feeling cold about halfway across the yard.

"We have to get her inside, she's going to die," Tara managed to say, pointing to the goat lying on the porch.

"Oh hell," Jasper mumbled, "What's wrong with her?"

"She just miscarried, and I think she's hypothermic. We have to get her inside or your weeks' worth of work is going to die."

"I don't want a goat in the house, that's nasty," Melody complained from the doorway where she'd stuck her head out to see what was going on.

"Get inside and stop letting the cold in," Jasper scolded.

Tara locked eyes with Jasper, he was obviously torn. Livestock doesn't belong in the house, but the goat was obviously dying. Hopefully he'd see there wasn't really a choice.

"Help me pick her up," he said grabbing hold of the sleeves of the sweater. Tara hooked her hands under the goat's knees and they both lifted Greta into the house, laying her on the rug next to the heater. Greta gritted her teeth and stared at them wide-eyed, but made no other movements.

"That goat can't sleep with me in the living room," Melody groaned.

"Where do you suggest we put the goat?" Tara asked instantly irritated.

"Put it in your room," Melody whined. "I don't want it to attack me in the night."

"Why would it attack you?" Tara asked confused.

"I don't know. Why wouldn't it? Ya' admitted that ya' don't know much about goats neither," Melody reminded her.

"We can't put it in the bedroom It's too cold in there, and it's carpeted. She still hasn't expelled the afterbirth, and I don't have the water to clean the carpet. It's easier to clean the linoleum." Tara was losing her patience with the girl.

"That's fine, but I'm not sleeping in here."

Tara ignored the girl as she walked into Tara's room and closed the door. Jasper could deal with that. Tara had a goat to deal with. She started a kettle of water warming on the stove and dug through the cabinet until she found the bottle of molasses. When the water was warm, but not boiling, she poured it into a bowl and mixed in a generous amount of molasses. Then she set it in front of the goat.

"Why are you doing that?" Jasper asked.

"She needs fluids, energy, and to warm up." Tara smiled when the goat began to suck up the water. "Think of it as giving her some coffee to take the chill off."

Jasper and Tara sat back on the couch watching the goat grit her teeth and occasionally lift her head until she expelled the afterbirth about an hour later. Tara did her best to clean up the mess, then scrubbed it with ice and threw some sawdust down to sweep later. She didn't have much water to waste.

"I'm sorry, but I need to get some sleep. If you're going to sit up with the goat that's fine, but I'm not going to sleep in the same room as a goat."

"Where are you going?" Tara frowned.

"I'm going to sleep on the floor in the bedroom," he explained flatly, picking up the sleeping bag that they had been using as a cover for Melody on the couch. "Sorry."

"I'm not really comfortable with that." Tara fidgeted the words coming out barely above a whisper.

Jasper looked shocked for a moment, before his brow furrowed. "Why is that exactly?"

"I don't know, I'm just not comfortable with that," Tara repeated. What if they were actually having an affair? She didn't want them sharing a room.

"You'll be fine, because I'm not comfortable with this," he said gesturing to the goat; who had its head back in the bowl of molasses water.

"But you brought the goat," Tara reminded him.

"Yeah, but I never imagined you'd have her in the house."

"I'm saving her life," Tara spoke carefully through gritted teeth.

"And that's why I'm fine with the fact that she's in the house, but I don't think you can reasonably force me to sleep in the same room with her. You can join me on the floor in the other room," he said gesturing toward the closed bedroom door.

"Someone needs to watch over the poor thing. Do you want to wake up to a dead goat or a burning house?" Tara asked.

"Suit yourself, I'm too tired to do this with you right now. I'm going to go lay down. Goodnight."

Tara watched him walk into the bedroom and close the door, which was followed by some murmuring that Tara couldn't hear. Tara crossed her arms and sat down on the couch.

"Men," Tara grumbled to Greta.

"Meh," Greta bleated softly.

"My thoughts exactly," Tara agreed.

CHAPTER 12

Tara woke to a tapping noise in the morning. She brushed her face because something tickled her nose. After a moment the tapping started again and something pulled her hair sharply. Tara jolted wide awake face to face with Greta who burped calmly and began chewing some cud.

The tapping started again, louder this time.

"Just a minute," Tara called as she pulled herself free from the blankets and shoved the goat away so that she could answer the door.

"I'm glad I caught you awake." Tara's mother breezed into the house pushing past Tara so that Tara had to stumble back a step. Silvia was a very short woman, a little heavy, but always remarkably well groomed. Her dyed blonde hair was an elaborately-styled pixie cut, and she wore a suede leather coat and shiny boots with a chunky heel.

Stopping mid-step, Silvia grabbed Tara's arm, "What is that?"

Tara smiled, "It's a goat, Mother."

"What the hell is it doing in the house?" Silvia demanded. "Is this what you do when someone does you a favor?"

As if on cue the goat lifted its tail and dropped dozens of perfectly round pellets on the floor. Silvia gasped, and then covered her mouth with her hand. Tara ignored her and grabbed the broom to sweep up the dry berries while her mother sputtered angrily.

"Well," Silvia regained her composure. "I felt really bad about what I was coming here to tell you until just one moment ago."

"What's that?" Tara asked.

"We've been evicted," her mother said pursing her lips into

an angry pucker.

"We've what?" Tara asked.

"Things have been a bit difficult since your father's insurance money ran out. I stopped in a while ago to ask for money from you, since you've been freeloading. But Jasper told me you don't have any money coming in at all, so you couldn't contribute to your upkeep."

Jasper knew? Why didn't he mention it to her? "What are you going to do?" Tara asked, feeling as if she'd been slapped in the face and punched in the stomach simultaneously.

"My brother in California makes a very decent living and he agreed to get me out there and take me in. I'm going to sell what I can and get out of here."

"Have you told Eric and Cheryl yet?" Tara asked. Eric was her younger brother whose house they were staying in, and the family favorite. Cheryl was her older sister who had married young. Nobody had heard from her in at least five years.

"Eric will be joining me after he finishes up his semester of collage, and you know I haven't talked to Cheryl since she moved," Silvia huffed.

"How long do we have?" Tara asked.

"About that…" Silvia began.

"How long?"

"Well, I've had my lawyer working on this to see if he could do anything," Silvia insisted.

"You mean that ambulance chasing boyfriend of yours?"

"That was uncalled for." Silvia stepped forward and Tara had a passing fear she was going to get slapped for her sass, but she wasn't a child anymore and Silvia no longer towered over her.

"How long?" Tara asked her mother more sternly this time.

"Two weeks." Silvia pulled her gloves out of her pocket and stuffed her hands in them.

"Two weeks? That doesn't sound right. How long have you known?"

Silvia shrugged, "I thought my lawyer would be able to get it taken care of."

"For some reason you don't know that Ray, the clientless

lawyer, wouldn't be able to handle this? You never thought to warn me? What are we going to do?" Tara asked trailing off as the shock of it started to set in.

"That's not really my problem," Silvia raised one perfectly penciled brow, "but I'd suggest doing something with that goat when you do. Nobody's going to let you keep that in a house."

Jasper wandered out into the living room scratching his stomach. "Good morning, Silvia. I thought I heard voices out here. Was afraid my wife was talking to the goat until she got an answer."

"Good morning, young man," Silvia sneered.

"It's Jasper, I know you remember," Jasper told her darkly.

"It's not really important. I was just on my way out," Tara's mother huffed, glaring at the goat once more before she strode out the door.

"To what did we owe the unexpected pleasure of her company?" Jasper asked sarcastically.

Tara pulled out a chair and sat down hard before she could answer him. "We're being evicted."

"She can't do that!"

Jasper turned to go after Silvia but Tara grabbed his hand. "She's not, it's the bank. Mother didn't keep up with the payments. She told me you knew."

Jasper sat down in the chair across from Tara at the table, "You know that vindictive crone is a liar. So what do we do now?"

"I don't know. I was just wondering that myself," Tara admitted wringing her hands.

"Wondering what?" Melody drawled as she yawned and stretched. "Ew! It's peeing on the floor!" she squealed.

Tara sighed and led the goat out of the house back to the stall, where she put her now ruined sweater on the goat. One of the sleeves had come partially off and started to unravel on the way into the house with it last night. Tara promised Greta she would check on her in a couple of hours. Greta gave no indication that she cared.

"So your mom is just throwing us out?" Melody asked when

Tara walked back in.

"Yes she's throwing me and Jasper out. So, it looks like you won't be staying until the weather gets warm," Tara shrugged.

Jasper's eyes darted to Melody and he shifted in his seat, "I haven't gotten up the money for a bus ticket to Chicago yet."

"You've been putting aside money to pay bus fare for her?" Tara asked

"Yeah, is that a problem?" he challenged.

"No," Tara answered startled, "I just wish you'd told me is all." But it was a problem. It was a big problem. He was going to buy a bus ticket for Melody, but they hadn't even gotten Kerosene yet? Where were the man's priorities?

"Good." Jasper's answer was a warning.

"Ya' know what I think," Melody said catching Jasper's eye. "I think y'all should come with me to Chicago."

"No, we're not doing that," Tara replied quickly. She paused and looked up, "Sorry. I mean, thanks for the offer, but we don't have anywhere to go in Chicago. I don't think we should."

"Y'all can stay with my great auntie too," Melody smiled in a way that Tara could tell was meant to appeal to Jasper.

"It costs a lot more to live in the city than it does out here and we can't even make it out here." Tara was beginning to feel panic rising up through her chest like creeping heartburn. Her breath quickened.

Jasper laid a hand on Tara's arm in a way that was meant to imply that she should quit talking. "We'll take some time to think about things before we make a decision." He glanced at Melody, then back to Tara, "but, I'd like you to be open-minded about whatever we talk about."

Tara stared at Jasper as a mix of emotions flickered around inside her. After a few deep breaths she settled on hurt. Why would he even consider Melody's request? They didn't know anyone there; they would be worse off in Chicago than they were here. At least here, they still had friends.

"Melody and I will fix breakfast," Jasper said clearing his throat. "The goat needs milking doesn't it?"

"What?" Tara asked, shaking herself mentally.

"The goat," he said impatiently, "it had a baby last night. That means it needs to be milked this morning doesn't it?"

Tara stared at him for a moment. "Why is milking this goat my problem?" she asked irritated.

"It's your goat ain't it?" Melody asked bluntly.

It seemed to Tara that this was less about the goat and more about getting her outside so they could talk alone. Tara picked a pot out of the cabinet, snatched her coat off the hook, and stormed outside to deal with the goat.

Tara led Greta slowly out of the pen and tied her securely to the porch railing. Greta was moving easier today, but when Tara bent down to look at the udders she noticed there was still some ropey mucus and blood on the goat's backside. The goat eyed Tara nervously, burped, and shifted her hindquarters away.

Uncertainly, Tara reached underneath the goat and gently touched one of Greta's udders. She had no idea what she was doing. Greta struggled and stomped flipping the pot that Tara had placed there moments ago, and sidestepped around to glare at Tara with her oddly frog-like pupils.

"Oh Greta, why can't you take it easy on me?" Tara implored. "I've never done this before and we're going to have to work together to get through this."

Tara pushed Greta up against the house and leaned against her to stop her from going anywhere. Then she reached out and wrapped her thumb and first finger around the base of the teat. This resulted in even more dramatic dancing, kicking, and bucking during which Tara was knocked off her feet. Greta was obviously not interested in a truce.

Tara stood up and took a couple of deep breaths. There was no point in getting angry with the goat. Tara rubbed her face with both hands and decided that she needed to work smarter. A moment later Tara was back with a bucket of feed from the shed. Greta's ears swiveled and she strained against the rope that held her to the porch.

"How about I make you a deal," Tara spoke softly, rattling the feed in the bucket. "I give you this and you stop kicking me."

The goat strained against the rope again and cried, "Maaah!"

"I thought so," Tara smiled, setting the bucket on the porch in front of Greta. She watched until the goat seemed lost in its greedy euphoria then she slid forward to attempt again.

Wrapping her fingers around the teat produced only a little half-hearted dancing and Tara was able to hold the goat easily this time. When Tara wrapped the other fingers downward she was surprised when nothing came out. Several more tries only set the goat to grumbling, but didn't produce the stream of milk she was expecting.

"I think you're broken," Tara mumbled to the goat as she gently removed what looked like yellowish scabs from the end of the teats. When she tried again Tara was startled when a thick, sticky, yellowish ooze pooled out slowly from the end of the teat and dropped into the pan. When she squeezed again more came out, and the other teat produced the same.

"Your milk's gone bad honey," Tara informed the goat as she pulled the pot out to look at what was in it. Surely this isn't what goat milk was supposed to look like. She closed her eyes and tried to think of everything she'd read about milking, which was next to nothing.

"Colostrum?" she wondered, eyeing the substance in the container. It had been mentioned as first milk, but nothing had described it. She had assumed that it looked like milk. She sure hoped that was what it was and not some sort of infection.

Tara set the pot back under the goat and continued stripping the thick custard-like substance until she had a pool of it at the bottom. It was only a little thinner by the time she was through. But it still looked truly disgusting.

When Tara walked back into the kitchen Jasper was stirring a pot of oatmeal on the stovetop and a quiet conversation between the two came to an abrupt end. Melody silently cut Tara into tiny pieces with her eyes and Jasper cleared his throat.

"So, do we get some fresh goat milk with breakfast?" he asked.

"Help yourself to whatever that is," Tara sighed, setting the pot on the counter between Jasper and Melody. She noted with irritation that Melody had to step back to give her enough room to do so.

"That's nasty! What is that?" Melody demanded stepping back again and covering her mouth with her hand as if she was going to throw up.

"It's what came out of the goat this morning. I'm assuming it's colostrum," Tara shrugged.

"Yuck, get it out of here!" Melody shoved the pot down the counter.

"How about you clean out the pot." Tara shoved it back. "You picked out the goat after all."

The silence that followed Tara's statement was full of glances between Jasper and Melody. Tara didn't care. She didn't even care that she was being mean to the girl. They could both go to hell right now as far as she was concerned.

Jasper looked away, and then walked off to set the table. He looked up with a stack of bowls in his hands. "Tara, honey, get that stuff cleaned up and out of here," he gestured to the pot on the counter.

Of all the things she expected to happen this wasn't one of them. He'd spoken to her calmly, and she didn't know how to react to that. It took the wind out of her sails. Instead of saying anything Tara grabbed the scraper she kept next to the trash can and took the pot outside.

A whispered conversation started the moment she walked out the door. She didn't want to hear what they were saying so she chose to sit on the step for a few minutes, but the lump in her throat was hard to swallow.

The next day Tara headed into town to do some laundry, get a shower, but mostly just to get out of the house. She was starting to feel like an unwelcome intruder in her own home. The rest of the last evening had been punctuated by whispering that Tara assumed had something to do with going to Chicago.

Just the fact that Melody and Jasper seemed like they were planning to go with or without her approval was enough to make Tara balk. Didn't her opinion matter at all?

She was turning onto the street that Alex and Kate lived on before she even knew it. Parked in front of the house was Pete's truck loaded with packing boxes and a small box truck that Alex and Pete were steering the washing machine into.

"Well, laundry's out," she mumbled to herself as she put the blinker on and pulled to a stop at the curb. Pete was here so she wasn't supposed to be, but Tara didn't care. It would serve Jasper right if she hung out with Pete today.

"Heya honey," Kate waved from the porch with Kylie on her hip in a pink coat so puffy that the child looked like a little balloon.

"Hey, I was just stopping out to use your shower. Sorry if it's not a good time."

"No, it's fine," Kate reassured her, gesturing into the house. "Just make your way around the boxes."

When Tara joined them later she helped pack boxes into the back of the truck with everyone else.

"You've been awfully quiet," Kate remarked, handing her a box labeled, "kitchen misc."

"I'm sorry," Tara admitted, "I've got a lot on my mind. We just got evicted too."

Kate looked shocked momentarily. "I guess I shouldn't have put it past your mom."

"It wasn't her, it was the bank," Tara said deeply ashamed. "Apparently nobody has been paying the bills."

In a quick movement Kate slid the box out of Tara's hand and set it on the top of a pile behind her. Before Tara could even protest Kate was holding her in a tight hug.

"Where are you guys gonna' go?"

"We'll figure something out," Tara assured her. Though she hadn't a clue what they were going to do.

"What's with the strange girly bonding moment instead of working?" Alex asked as he came in the front door and started taking the boxes off the dining table so that he could free it up to carry it out.

"They're out on their asses, too," Kate informed him, still not letting go of what was now an uncomfortably long, awkward hug.

Pete stood in the doorway. "What's the plan?" he asked.

"Table's next," Alex instructed.

Pete shook his head. "No. I meant what's the plan, Tara? Where are you guys going?"

"Jasper wants to go to Chicago," Tara confessed, unable to hide her irritation.

"What's in Chicago?" Pete asked looking confused.

"Melody's great aunt's place."

"Who's Melody?" It was Kate's turn to look confused.

How did they not know who she was? Didn't Jasper drag her out of the house to shower twice a week? Tara had just assumed they were coming here.

"Melody is our houseguest. Jasper picked her up on the side of the road. She's been staying with us for way too long," Tara answered Kate, too emotionally exhausted to try to keep it to herself.

"You have some random woman staying with you and your husband?" Kate said shaking her head in disbelief. "Why don't I know this? Am I the only one that didn't know this?" she asked shooting an accusatory look back and forth between Pete and Alex.

"No, this is news to me," Alex assured her.

Kate nodded. "So back to this Chicago thing. You guys are just going to pack up and leave?"

"I don't know. I told him that I don't really want to go," Tara sighed sitting down onto a stack of cartons marked, "books."

"Actually," Alex hesitated, "it might be a great idea."

"How's that?" Pete asked surprised.

"I'm not saying I want you guys gone, it's just that I've been hearing a lot about the cities on the news lately," Alex pointed out as he picked something out from under the end of his fingernail. "As a cop I can tell you that things are getting rougher around here every day. Did you know that just this week the chief told us that we won't be involved in clearing out evictions anymore? He said the number we went to last week was ridiculous. He said that we are servants of the community, not enforcers for some banks." Alex shifted. "Not to mention crime is way up. There was a mugging two nights ago. An actual mugging… here. There's been a rash of home invasions, someone held up the gas station, and metal is being stolen at an alarming rate."

"Metal?" Tara asked.

"You know, copper pipes, aluminum rims, that sort of thing. Besides, I'd say ten percent of the town can't afford to keep their power on and their water running," Alex complained.

Pete looked at Tara with pity or to offer comfort, she couldn't tell.

Alex continued. "There's people crapping in buckets and trying to build fires inside to keep warm. Two houses have burned down in the last week."

"We're off topic here," Pete stopped him. "What does this have to do with Chicago?"

"They might be safer in Chicago," Alex finished.

Pete shook his head. "How's that? If our small town haven is a festering pool of crime and poverty just imagine what the city must be like."

"Do you even watch the news?" Alex asked.

"I don't particularly like being lied to, why?"

"According to the news the cities are doing a lot better than the countryside. They are adding new jobs every day and aren't seeing the same shortages and price gouging we're seeing here. According to an address the president gave it has something to do with a terrorist attack on a major fuel supply line. They are concentrating on getting supplies into the cities because you can move more goods to more people with a lot less gas."

"You don't actually believe that, do ya' buddy?" Pete asked, looking surprised.

Tara sensed that things were about to get tense and she didn't want to see them fight about her situation.

"I'm going to have to get going guys," she interrupted.

"Not a problem." Kate rushed over to give her another crushing hug. "Please don't be a stranger. We're going to be just thirty minutes from here, and you have our numbers."

"Of course." Tara slipped out the door breathing a sigh of relief as she started towards the truck. The door opened again quickly behind her, but she didn't turn around.

"Hey!" Pete called jogging to catch up with Tara.

"What's up?" Tara asked as he stopped in front of her.

"Just wanted to let you know that you guys can stop into my house for the use of my water. I know I'm a little harder to catch at home, but after seven I'm normally there."

"Thanks," she nodded. "I came into town with my laundry to do, too. I can come back out with it maybe tomorrow."

"Seems silly to make a second trip," he said, "unless you need something else in town."

"Nope, just can't afford the laundromat," Tara admitted.

Pete reached into his pocket and pulled out his wallet. "Here's five dollars, don't waste the gas." He took her hand and pressed the money into it.

Tara held the money back out towards him. "I can't accept your money." Tara felt panicky.

"I don't want you to pay me back," he sighed. "It'll nearly cost you that much in gas to come back into town again. Please just accept it. That way, it's one less thing to worry about." He offered his most reassuring smile.

Tara sighed. "You're not taking no for an answer are you?" she asked.

"Nope." He tipped his hat at her and turned around to hop into the back of the van to re-arrange a couple of the boxes.

Sitting in a stiff chair, Tara tried not to doze to the sound of the machines at the laundromat. Above her a florescent light flickered and buzzed and an older gentleman was taking great care to precisely fold his boxer shorts at the room's only table. A young woman with a baby worn in a sling across her chest was sitting in another chair reading some sort of fashion magazine.

Tara sighed. The events of the day were parading through her head. Round and round her thoughts tumbled. She didn't want to go with Melody, but she didn't know what they were going to do with themselves. Twenty minutes of this had her feeling agitated so she got up and walked over to read the bulletin board just to keep her mind occupied. Mister boxer shorts had taken off without her noticing.

"Don't move, this is a knife," whispered a woman's voice while something cold touched Tara's neck. Tara's mind reeled, her breath caught, and hot panic spread through her body like spilled coffee. Tara was staring at an ad selling a Shetland pony, and she didn't know why her brain counted that as important.

"Now, turn around slowly," the woman rasped.

Tara's feet screamed in protest and she was afraid she was actually going to fall down instead of turning around.

The woman stepped back from her and Tara saw it was the sweet-looking little blonde with the baby on her chest. The baby squirmed and gave a little grunt.

"Give me all your money!" the young mother commanded.

Tara willed her hands to move but she was frozen.

"Empty your god-damn pockets," the woman demanded spraying little flecks of spit in her anger. The baby began to wiggle and fuss.

Tara dug the change from her pocket and held it out trembling.

"Turn your fucking pockets out!" The mom breathed heavily while she snatched the money from Tara's outstretched hand.

Tara turned out her pockets to show her that she didn't have anything.

"Throw the purse over here."

Tara complied immediately. The woman went through the purse one-handed, glancing in occasionally. When the wallet produced nothing she threw it and dug through the purse's pockets. Then she threw Tara's purse to the ground in frustration.

"Put your hands up and don't try anything!" The blonde mother nearly shrieked, beginning to look panicky. Tara did so immediately while the woman lunged forward.

Tara's breath caught, but the knife didn't strike her. The woman began patting her down. She slid her hands quickly under Tara's shirt and pulled at the wire of her bra, sliding her fingers just along the bottom of the cups. Tara's mind raced, but the woman had already moved down to the waistband of her jeans. She stepped back.

"Take off the ring!" The woman gestured the knife in little circles in the air in the direction of Tara's left hand.

Slowly Tara lowered her arms and grasped the ring with her right hand.

"Give it to me or I'll cut your goddamn finger off."

Tara pulled the ring from her finger and the young woman snatched it as the door dinged. A tired looking woman with a couple of big bags of laundry and five children in tow walked in. The knife disappeared quickly and the sweet-looking little maniac turned and strolled out the door as if nothing had happened.

Tara let out a ragged breath with a little sob at the end of it and she slid to the floor. She had no idea how long she sat there with her knees to her chest and her head down on her arms rocking slowly.

The tired woman called out in a slightly gravelly voice as if she had a three-pack-a-day cigarette habit. "You okay honey?"

Five small children were looking at Tara owlishly.

"Fine," Tara assured her, rising slowly and dusting off her bottom.

She pulled her clothes out of the dryer and stuffed them in the laundry bag she brought them in. Then Tara hurried to the truck, happy that she had parked under a street light. She locked the door the moment she was in and leaned across to make sure the passenger door was also secure before she started the engine.

The whole way home she was thinking about what had happened and Alex's assurances of being safer in the city.

Inside, the house was dark and cold. As cold as it was outside. Fear briefly gripped her until she heard the sound of Melody snoring lightly on the couch. Tara was afraid they'd left.

Tara struck a match and looked around until she found the lamp on the table. The kerosene heater was sitting in the middle of the room and the indicator showed it was empty. Tara searched the containers on the porch, but just as she'd feared they were all empty. Tara went to the small roofless stall that Greta waited in. In the lamplight it seemed ominously full of shadows.

Her breath came out in plumes while the goat munched quietly and Tara warmed her hands. Greta's dancing was short-lived allowing Tara to strip out more yellowish liquid. Thankfully it was not as thick as the first time.

Back in the house she slipped quietly into bed and hesitated before she blew out the lamp. The moonlight made the pools of darkness in the room seem frightening. It was a long time before sleep took Tara.

CHAPTER 13

Tara wiped Greta's udders with a warm washcloth while the goat strained to inhale the entire contents of the feed bucket as fast as possible.

Tara hadn't slept very well. Sleep had been nothing but prickly cold air and nightmares. So she'd crept out to milk the goat before the others were even out of bed.

After squirting the first streams of milky substance onto the ground Tara leaned against Greta's side and took a few deep breaths. The rhythmic pings of milk in the bucket were a background harmony to thoughts that were all jumbled up.

Jasper wandered out of the bedroom while Tara scalded the milking equipment. Now that they were milking the goat they were running out of water faster than before, they were going to have to get more soon.

Jasper leaned against the counter watching her. He was wearing his coat with a stocking cap, and was blowing into his hands to warm them.

"Tara?"

"What?"

"Where the hell is your wedding ring?"

Tara stared at her hand. Her wedding ring was gone. What happened the night before wasn't just a nightmare.

"A woman with a knife wearing a baby at the laundromat took it." Tara took a deep breath as a fresh wave of fear trickled through her thinking about the knife on her skin.

"A what, did what?" Jasper crossed his arms.

"I was robbed, by a woman with a knife wearing a baby." Tara rubbed the place where the ring was supposed to be. Its absence made her skin prickle.

"That's stupid even for you," Jasper growled.

"What?" Tara was startled.

"Where's your ring?"

"I told you what happened to my ring. Speaking of which, we should probably make a police report," Tara frowned.

"Holy shit. How far are you going to go with this? We're not going to make a police report when you and I both know that ring is probably on Pete's bedside table."

Tara stared at him blankly. "No matter what happens to me. No matter what I go through, it all circles back to me having an affair. I end up in an angry mob, so I must be screwing someone else. I get mugged. A woman holds a knife to my throat." Tara ran her finger angrily across her throat. "That means I must be screwing someone else." Tara threw her hands in the air. "What is your malfunction?"

"You're acting like a lunatic," Jasper whispered.

"Am I?" Tara picked up a pot holder from the counter and hurled it across the room. "How about now?"

"I'm sick of your bullshit," Jasper slammed his fist on the counter. Melody jumped on the couch but didn't sit up.

Tara wondered how long she'd been awake listening to this.

"We're going to Chicago. It's final," Jasper told her slowly.

"What does this have to do with Chicago?" Tara demanded.

"If you got mugged by a woman with a baby and caught in a riot, I think it's time to leave this shithole," Jasper frowned. "We need to go somewhere we can build a real life. Somewhere we can have a blank slate and a fresh start."

"Don't I get a say?" Tara demanded.

"Sure, when you're not so hysterical. Then you'll see that I'm right."

"But —."

Jasper put a hand on her mouth. "I'm not listening to this until you calm down and think rationally."

Tara wanted to bite him, but that would not have proved how rational she could be. Instead she took a deep breath and grabbed her coat off the hook.

"You're not running away again! I need the damn truck today!"

Tara threw her keys into the house so he wouldn't follow her out the door and then stormed outside.

When Tara knocked on Rose's door she could hear some loud trumpet music from inside. She had to knock three different times before the door opened. When it did, Rose did a shuffling little dance that made Tara smile in spite of herself. A big-band song was roaring out of the radio.

"What's the celebration?" Tara asked as Rose danced back to let her in.

"What honey?" Rose yelled. She shook her head pointing to her ear then shuffled her dance across the floor to the radio where she turned the knob until the music was barely a whisper.

"I asked what you were celebrating," Tara repeated, shutting the door behind her as she came in. It was so nice and warm here.

"The house sold. Cash… Well above market value."

"Wow. Imagine how many g-strings you can stuff now," Tara giggled.

"Why do you think I'm celebrating?" Rose winked.

The room around them was nearly bare, with only a small radio sitting on a folding table. Even the pictures were off the walls leaving discolored marks on the wallpaper. As Tara followed Rose into the kitchen she noticed the shelves were nearly bare and in the middle of the room was a folding table with two chairs.

"This looks so wrong. Do you have everything stored already?" Tara asked.

"Not at all. The antique store came out and finished the clean-out. I sold all them old things. I don't need 'em anyway. I'm moving to a tiny little place right off the beach in Florida where the men all parade up and down in them itty-bitty little swimsuits." Rose winked. "Oh by the way," she slid her lard tin out of the top box of a stack in the corner of the kitchen. Out of this she pulled a pink envelope. "This is for you and your husband. He helped set up the deal and I told him I'd give him a cut."

"He never said anything to me about that." Tara was confused. Normally he crowed about any money he brought in. Maybe he guessed, correctly, that she wouldn't have approved of this.

"Didn't he?" Rose's eyebrows shot up. "This is your portion." She shook the envelope at Tara.

"We can't accept this," Tara demurred when Rose set the envelope on the table.

"You damn well can. He and I made a deal. I don't want anyone to say I don't keep my end of a fair bargain." Rose crossed her arms in front of her chest. "Do you want to explain to him why you don't have the money?"

Tara thought about this for a moment. "I guess I'd better take it." She stuffed the envelope in the pocket of her coat, but she felt wrong putting it there.

"So what brought you over here today?" Rose asked, pulling a bottle of whiskey and two paper cups off the counter.

Tara held up her hand, "Water for me thanks."

Sighing, Rose poured one glass of whiskey and one of water then set them on the table. "Your face looks like you have a novel worth of stuff to say."

"We're going to Chicago with Melody." Tara took a deep breath before she plunged through the events of the past couple of weeks and ended with her mugging at the laundromat the night before.

"Why are you agreeing to go with them to Chicago?" Rose asked. She looked like she smelled something awful.

"Because," Tara struggled looking for some way to explain her motivation. Instead she just slumped deflated in the chair.

"I see," Rose took a long drink of her whiskey.

"My friend Alex told me that he heard the cities were safer than here; full of jobs, too. I guess it's not a bad idea," Tara stammered.

"What a load of crap," Rose shook her head.

Tara stared at her, shocked.

"You don't want to go with your husband and his little girlfriend to Chicago and you know it." Rose drank down the last of her whiskey and stared at the empty cup.

"I don't know what else to do. I don't know where to go. Besides, his heart is set on it." Tara sighed; too agitated to stay in her chair so she paced across the empty kitchen and back.

"Are you afraid that if you say no he'll go without you?" Rose leaned back looking at her.

"No," Tara shook her head. "Maybe. I don't know. I don't think so." Tara used her free hand to tug on the ends of her hair. "He wouldn't just leave me here."

"If he would, you'd be better off. You know that right?" Rose shrugged. "If they go, leave them to it. You shouldn't have to go through that. I worry for you, dear."

Tara's eyes welled up. "I should go," Tara spoke quickly. "There's a lot of things that need to get done. We have to pack and all that. One way or the other we can't stay where we are."

"Sure honey," Rose smiled, "I got you a little something. It came in the mail yesterday." Rose pointed to a large box on the counter.

"What is it?" Tara asked startled. Why would someone get her a present?

"It's re-usable canning jar lids. There's a company that makes these plastic lids that you use with a rubber gasket. They had a lot of good reviews and I thought it might be a nice way for me to say thank you about the shed that you kids got out of here for me. Jasper was by loading up all the stuff you were keeping and I noticed he got all the canning stuff. While I was at it I ordered a couple of overpressure plugs for the canner."

Tara opened the box and inside was bags of white plastic discs and sleeves of flat rubber rings. There were too many to count.

"Oh my gosh, how many are there?" Tara asked startled.

"About a thousand lids and two-thousand rings," Rose smiled. "I thought that would keep you for a good long time."

"This is all too much," Tara shook her head.

"You've been a good friend to me," Rose smiled.

Tara threw her arms around her friend's frail body. "I'll miss you. Please take care of yourself." Tara's eyes began to fill with tears again.

"You too honey," Rose smiled. "Just remember you're a grown woman and you go where you want to go."

"I will," Tara smiled sadly, picked up the box, and carried it out Rose's back door.

The box was awkward and heavy; by the time she got back to the house she was glad for the chance to set it down. Jasper and Melody were huddled together under a blanket on the couch. He was reading a book out loud to her.

"What's that?" Melody called looking at the box Tara had just set on the counter.

"I stopped over at Rose's. Her house sold and she's going to be leaving soon. She gave me a present. It's just canning lids and a couple of overpressure plugs for the canner."

"That seems like a dumb gift," Melody shrugged.

Tara put her hands in her pockets to warm them and the envelope crackled. "Oh yeah." Tara pulled the envelope out. "Jasper, she said this is your money for the antiques deal," Tara huffed.

"What deal?" he asked getting off the couch and taking the envelope.

"She said you helped her set up a deal with the antiques place and she owed you a cut."

Jasper opened the envelope while shaking his head. "I wasn't part of any..." Jasper stopped. "This is nearly a thousand dollars."

"Really?" Melody squealed.

"You weren't what?" Tara asked stepping towards him and the envelope.

"Nothing."

"You weren't what?" Tara asked again. "If that's not our money and she owes someone else we need to give it back."

"I forgot. The antiques deal. Yeah I mentioned that to you, didn't I Melody?" Jasper was counting the money again.

"I remember," Melody nodded putting her hand on the envelope.

"We're leaving ladies," Jasper smiled. It's time to find some Kerosene and stock up on groceries.

They drove to every gas station in town, but not one had any kerosene. Then to the feed store, then the hardware store; still nothing.

While they were sitting in the parking lot of the hardware store Tara leaned against the side of the truck. Jasper was calling the gas stations in the surrounding towns.

"Do you know who might have some kerosene?" he demanded. Then he hung up and tossed the phone into the front seat without saying goodbye.

Melody picked the phone up and turned it over while she sat in middle of the bench seat, "No luck?"

"Nobody's got any. Nobody knows when anyone will get any."

"That sucks," Melody scooted into the driver's seat and leaned out the window to look at Jasper. "Didn't y'all say that some guy gave that to you? Maybe he has some more."

Jasper shot a nasty look at Tara as if it had been her suggestion to go see Pete. She looked away.

"No, we can't do that right now," Jasper sighed. "Maybe we should just go get some food."

Jasper was staring at Tara. She shrugged. What did it matter anyway? They were leaving in a matter of days. What were a few more days without Kerosene? What were a few more days of eating just rice? Tara didn't want to spend the money.

Tara tried to call Rose and let her know the she'd had made a mistake, but Jasper had denied her the phone and insisted that they had a deal; but Tara knew he was lying.

When they arrived at the market there were only a few cars

in the parking lot, one of which was up on blocks.

"Do you think they're even open?" Tara asked looking at Jasper past Melody who was seated between them.

"They're open. Stop it, I've told you for the last time this is our money and I don't want to hear one more word about it."

Tara slid out of the truck and followed Jasper and the girl into the store. What she saw nearly took her breath away. Only a few of the store's lights were on, just enough to not bump into shelves. In the gloom she could see that more than half of the shelves were empty. Where there was actual food, prices were written on pieces of paper taped to the shelf. The numbers had been scribbled out multiple times going up by several dollars at a time. There weren't any shopping carts and only a few people drifted among the aisles like ghosts carrying a couple of items and looking nervously at one another.

Jasper walked boldly through the store cussing because everything they were looking for seemed to be sold out.

"Damnit, I really wanted some bacon," he grumbled as they stood in front of an empty freezer section.

"Me too," Melody smiled putting her hands on her stomach, "I'm really craving it."

Jasper glared at Melody.

At least the girl was starting to get on his nerves too. Tara sighed.

"Maybe we should focus less on what we want and more on what they actually have on the shelves?" Tara suggested as she leaned against the empty freezer bin behind her.

"Like what?" Jasper shot back.

"We won't know until we look," Tara sighed.

Jasper and Melody snaked their way through the shelves rejecting pickled pig's feet, pimentos, and croutons. Tara just followed. She was apathetic about the whole mess.

"This is ridiculous," Jasper spat.

"What?" Melody asked squinting to read what was in his hands in the low light.

"They want seventeen dollars for a pound of pinto beans!"

"Is that bad?" Melody asked.

"Are you kidding, it's disgraceful."

Tara stopped listening while Jasper continued to debate the cost of various dried beans with Melody. She leaned against the empty endcap, poking a plastic package on the floor with the toe of her boot until she heard something hit a shelf across the aisle from them. She snapped her attention towards two young men. The one who hit the shelf was clutching a can under his arm. The other man had obviously pushed him.

"I had it first," the man with the can insisted.

"I need that formula," the other held his hand out. "Give it to me."

"Guys?" Tara hissed to Jasper and Melody, but Jasper was complaining so loudly that Tara was pretty sure he didn't hear her. She didn't dare look away from what was happening to see if he did.

"This is mine," the first man covered the lid of the can with his hand.

"I will fucking kill you if you don't give me that goddamn can!" the second man shouted.

"Fuck you," man number one spit at the man threatening him then turned and stormed towards Tara, away from the other father behind him while he clutched the can of formula under his arm.

A woman screamed. Tara didn't see her, but she saw what the woman saw. The first man pulled a gun out of his coat and aimed it at the man coming towards Tara.

The world slowed down and her heart sped up. If the man shot; if he missed the man with the can, they were in the line of fire.

Tara stumbled a step backwards. The gunman was shouting something to the man with the can, who was now frozen in place. Tara didn't hear it. It didn't register as anything but an animalistic howl. Maybe that's all it was.

"Get down," Tara hissed behind her and she attempted to fall to her knees, but an arm caught her around her waist from behind and lifted her flailing into the air. A second arm pulled tight across her shoulders and neck straitening her back and choking her slightly.

Tara didn't scream. She didn't want to scare the gunman. She was fully exposed. She twisted her head to see behind her. It was Jasper. He held her tightly in place trying to make himself as small as possible. Melody was pressed against his back. Tara was their human shield. She didn't dare struggle, but it was as if the air had disappeared from her lungs. Not like she'd stopped breathing, it just wasn't there anymore.

Tara turned her face back to the scene in front of them as the gunman approached the man who was still holding the can, and the gun was leveled shaking at his head.

Then... nothing.

Tara was afraid for a moment that she'd been shot, but there was no loud sound. She could smell leather and soap. After a second Tara realized what she was looking at in the low light. It was the back of a man's neck. He had dark hair and a navy blue collar. His shoulders were squared and he stood tall in front of her. His hand reached back and touched her right hip as if making sure she was squarely behind him. The point of contact burned in her mind like an electric shock.

"Give me the goddamn can!" a man shouted.

The sound had been turned back on in her head. People whimpered and cried around them. Melody was crying and Jasper's breathing was ragged. The man in front of her breathed slowly. He was a wall; as unyielding as a force of nature.

A grunt, a man running... Melody collapsed behind them. Jasper dragged Tara backwards as she clawed at the hand on her neck. Suddenly he released her and shoved her forward against the man in front of her. The man had turned towards her and now caught her before she could fall.

"Tara?"

She stared at him without understanding for a moment.

"Pete?"

"Are you okay?"

He held her at arm's length as she swayed and put her hand to her throat. She nodded before looking at Jasper who was trying to gather Melody off the floor.

"Is she okay?" Tara rasped.

"Does she look okay?" Jasper barked, pulling the girl onto his lap; cradling her like an infant.

Tara swallowed twice. It felt like she had a rock stuck in her throat. Pete let go of her and she wandered a few steps away and sat down on the floor.

Pete stayed still, watching Jasper and Melody.

"Is the child okay?" he asked.

Tara realized the girl's eyes were open.

"I'm not a child," Melody purred, sliding off of Jasper's lap.

Jasper stood and dusted off his bottom while Melody approached Pete.

"My name's Melody," she drawled stepping into Pete's personal space.

Pete stepped back, "Pete," He didn't offer her a handshake; he just took another step back.

"Pete?" Jasper seemed surprised to see him. He stepped between Melody and Pete as if Pete was a bear who might eat her.

Pete watched him like he was some sort of tiny yapping dog. He wasn't afraid of him, but he seemed weary of the man.

When Pete didn't say anything to Jasper, he pressed on. "Pete, you're just the man we were going to find today."

Pete's eyebrows shot up, but he continued to say nothing.

Tara looked around as people started drifting through the aisles again, like some lunatic hadn't just run through the store with a gun. What was wrong with these people? What was wrong with Jasper?

"We'll be leaving in a few days. We're headed to Chicago," Jasper smiled at him.

Pete nodded. "I know. Tara told me."

Jasper glared at Tara. "Did she?"

It wasn't a question and Pete didn't answer. Tara put her head down in her hands. She was too upset for this nonsense, accusations and small talk. She rocked gently back and forth while Jasper made plans with Pete to come pick up his heater and maybe the goat if Jasper couldn't sell it in the next couple of days.

"Are you sure you're okay?"

Tara looked up at Pete who stood over her.

"Yeah," she mumbled.

Pete offered her a hand up off the ground, but Tara ignored it and pulled herself to her feet. She was distinctly aware of Jasper and Melody watching her.

They left the store without buying a single thing and Tara trailed after Jasper and Melody like she was on autopilot. They were undressing for bed before Tara really felt like she was living in the present again.

"Jasper," Tara watched him push his way under the blanket. She felt like she had a weight on her chest that made it hard to breathe.

"What?"

"You used me as a human shield."

"What the hell are you talking about?" he demanded bunching the blankets up by his face.

"You held me in front of you when that man was pointing a gun at us."

"Are you crazy? I was protecting you," he muttered.

"How does holding me in front of you protect me?" Tara demanded. She wanted to yell but the weight on her chest was too heavy to get enough air to yell.

"You were going to run like an idiot. I didn't want that guy to shoot you."

"I wasn't," Tara protested.

"Yes you were! You do stupid stuff like that all the time. You were lucky that I was there to protect you," Jasper assured her.

Tara said nothing. How was she supposed to argue when she felt like she was being strangled? She guessed she must have done something stupid, she always seemed to.

CHAPTER 14

The next few days were a blur of packing and preparations. It was amazing how fast the days leading up to leaving went by. Kind of like a dreaded medical procedure or a test in school.

The morning of the trip Tara woke suddenly before the sun was up terrified with a terrible stomach ache. Shaking, she felt around on the top of the nightstand for the lighter. Once a candle was burning she concentrated on taking a couple of slow, deep breaths before creeping into the living room where she slipped on her coat and walked barefoot onto the porch. The stinging cold took her mind off the panic, and the cool breeze felt nice on her flushed cheeks. She gulped deep breaths of air that smelled sharp and metallic like it would snow soon.

Once she was back inside, Tara lay down in bed and tried to clear her mind so she could go back to sleep. Unfortunately her mind was full of all the things they needed to do that day, all her fears, and everything she was going to miss.

As the first slivers of gray light slid silently into the room through the window panes she gave up on the pretense of sleep.

Since they were going to be confined in a car all day and she already felt queasy, Tara chose her outfit with great care. After staring at the contents of her dresser for some time she finally settled on a set of gray long underwear. The top and bottom were both the soft, smooth kind that would make her feel like she was wearing pajamas. Over this she put on a sleeveless linen dress that ended just below the knee and was the color of faded goldenrods. To add another layer of warmth in the cold house she put on her favorite wool sweater, it was a plain brown pullover with a low shawl collar. After that she pulled on the red and gray socks she'd knitted; they admittedly didn't match her outfit, but there was a certain comfort in the warm bulk of hand-knit socks. She needed that this morning.

When she pulled her black leather boots out from under the side of the bed Tara decided she would give them a good coat of waterproofing polish because it was better to be safe than sorry. When she thought of how far Melody had walked she shuddered. What if the truck broke down? What if they ran out of gas? What if someone hijacked the truck in some desperate small town between here and Chicago? Having to walk for miles in wet socks didn't appeal to her.

By the time she was lacing her boots the others were beginning to stir. After they were up there was an air of excitement in the house. Tara wasn't excited. She didn't want to go to Chicago, but now wasn't the time to argue the point.

Breakfast was simple, consisting of a can of peaches and a can of pears mixed together because most of the cooking pots were already packed in boxes sitting around the kitchen.

The unmistakable rumble of a truck in the driveway made Tara hurry to the window. It meant Pete was there to pick up Greta. Jasper frowned as she went out the door, but Tara met Pete on the porch anyway.

"Excited about the big day?" Pete asked.

"Sure," Tara lied without looking up at him. "Greta needs milking this morning in about an hour. If you want me to show you how I can."

"Nope, it's fine. I used to milk cows as a kid. I'm sure I can figure it out," he assured her.

"Okay, just remember a scoop of feed will normally calm her right down, no matter what you need to do."

Pete watched Tara as she stood and fidgeted. "So, you guys are really going to do this?" he asked.

Tara looked at him, relieved he didn't expect her to be happy about it. "Not a lot of options at this point," she shrugged.

"There's always options, especially ones that don't involve going to Chicago like this," Pete frowned.

"I don't see any —."

"Hey there," Melody called cheerfully, cutting Tara off mid-sentence as she slunk out the door. "Jasper said he'd be out to help y'all load the feed and hay in a few minutes," she directed her attention to Pete, her accent getting thicker and more syrupy with every word. She didn't stop advancing on him till she was in his personal space again.

"Okay," he said politely as he took a step away from her.

Melody looked him blatantly up and down. Her appraisal made him blush slightly. "You clean up real nice." She grabbed a hand that he hadn't offered to her. "Seems a shame that we weren't introduced before the other day."

Pete cleared his throat loudly and shook his hand free from her grasp. "Tara, if you could show me where the hay's stacked I'll get started there."

Tara couldn't help smiling. "Right this way," she pointed around the side of the house. "If you want you can back your truck around the side."

"Sounds great." He retreated quickly while Tara started around the side of the house. Melody frowned and went back inside. Tara noted she was watching from the window.

"What's wrong with Melody?" Pete asked quietly before looking up at the window.

Tara shrugged slowly, reluctant to say more.

"Are you sure you want to travel to Chicago with that woman?" he asked.

"You mean me and my husband with such a young and beautiful girl?"

Pete's brow furrowed. "I wouldn't go that far," he replied, squinting back towards the house. He turned back to Tara, "What I meant is she seems awful. I'm not sure I would trust her if I were you."

"Tell me why it's so obvious to you, but not my husband," Tara sighed.

"I'm sorry," he shrugged. "I guess I don't think about women the same way that a lot of men do."

Of course Melody's charms wouldn't work on Pete! Tara smiled slightly at the thought. She had forgotten. Melody had nothing Pete would be interested in.

"Let me help with that," Jasper called out as he came around the side of the house.

While the boys worked, Tara took the opportunity to escape Jasper's dirty looks and say goodbye to Greta.

Greta hopped to her feet when Tara opened the door, and snuffled greedily at her hands. "I'm going to miss you," Tara rubbed the goat under the chin until Greta leaned away to scratch her side with one of her horns. With a leash clipped to the goat's collar, Tara led her out of the pen. When Greta caught sight of the feed sacks being loaded she began to struggle as she attempted to pull Tara across the yard. She reminded Tara of a dog who would do anything for a treat.

After Pete's heater, empty kerosene containers, and all the feed sacks were on the truck; Greta was loaded carefully.

Jasper grabbed Pete's hand in a firm handshake, "Thanks for everything you've done for us. We'll never forget it, or you. We'll call when we get settled," Jasper promised.

Tara knew that was a lie. In all likelihood they would never see or speak to Pete again.

"Not a problem, good luck in Chicago," Pete smiled, glancing at Tara before returning to Jasper.

"I can't thank y'all enough for the heater and taking the goat." The way Melody said it was suggestive of things that had nothing to do with heaters or livestock. Then the girl leaned in to give him a hug. Pete turned his face away from her and did his best to move back as she attempted to press every inch of herself against him. Jasper's face momentarily scrunched in rage.

As Pete stepped back out of Melody's reach Tara did her best to catch his eye. When she did, she gave him a sad smile. "Thanks for everything." It seemed inadequate given what he'd done for her the other day, but she didn't dare talk about it in front of Jasper. The fact that Jasper hadn't blown up about it yet was a small miracle and she didn't want to press her luck. She'd be stuck in a truck with him until Chicago.

"Oh, and help yourself to anything that's left here tomorrow. There's canning supplies in the shed, lumber, and a few other things we won't have room for."

"I might have to take you up on that," Pete smiled, tipping

his hat to her.

"I'll miss you guys," he called as he got into his truck. While they called some final goodbyes Tara was surprised at how sad she felt as she watched him drive away for the last time.

After Pete left, the house seemed strangely quiet. Melody and Jasper had been chatting happily all morning and now they moved about quietly mostly avoiding each other. Tara and Jasper carried things to the truck while Melody watched.

Tara was carrying some boxed dishes to the truck when a hushed conversation between the two came to an abrupt stop.

Unable to take the exclusion anymore Tara turned to Jasper. "What's going on?" she demanded, "Is there a problem?"

Jasper began to vigorously shake his head while Melody turned to her and smiled.

"I was just telling your husband here," Melody gestured to Jasper whose eyes were now wide with panic, "that I'm pregnant. We're going to have a baby. He thought I shouldn't tell you now, but I thought you had the right to know before we went all the way to Chicago."

For Tara the moment was like being at that point on a roller coaster when you teeter on the top of the hill with gravity beginning its pull to make you fall fast. Her legs felt like jelly and she fell down hard over a rock that she had backed up into without even realizing she was going anywhere. The box she'd been holding was laying on the ground with a split in the side and broken pieces of dishes rattling out.

"Honey," Jasper said stepping forward.

"No." Tara scrambled to her feet.

"We need to talk." He continued to advance towards her.

Tara turned and fled around the corner of the house. By the time she noticed where she was, she was standing just inside the woods line. Her mind was swimming as she studied the bark of the tree in front of her, afraid she was going to be sick into the leaves at its base.

The crunching of leaves made her look up. Jasper stopped under the heat of her gaze and jammed his hands into his pockets.

"I wanted to start by saying I'm sorry," he stammered.

"You got her pregnant?" Tara demanded. "When? Why? How could you do this to me?"

"I made a mistake. I'm sorry. I've been so lonely and since we haven't…" Jasper paused looking around as if the word he wanted was written on one of the trees, "been intimate."

"We made that decision together!" Tara shouted. "If I remember correctly it was specifically to avoid this particular situation. We decided we couldn't raise a child without any money and that it was the last thing we would need. It's not like we've abstained from everything."

"I know, but that's just left me more frustrated, it probably would have been better if you weren't laying hands on me at all. I've craved the intimacy of the actual act. I had a moment of weakness. I don't know what I was thinking, she was there and one thing led to another."

"How could you?" Tara demanded. She didn't know what else to say.

"How could I?" he asked, anger overriding his guilt. "With the way you've been acting."

"You're not making this my fault!" Tara yelled spitting the taste of bile out of her mouth. "You don't see me whoring around."

"Your lover just picked up your goat and tried to seduce the mother of my child!" Jasper barked.

"He's not my lover." Tara shouted. "I can assure you I'm not his type." Jasper didn't deserve to know Pete's secret. Pete, after all, hadn't betrayed her. Jasper had.

"So you tried and I'm supposed to believe you're innocent because he didn't want your pathetic ass."

"It's not like that. Nothing happened. I never tried to make anything happen. Oh and go screw yourself. We're talking about you getting that little girl pregnant." Tara crossed her arms and glared. She wasn't going to let him worm out of what had happened by shifting the blame like he always did. Not this time.

Jasper's fists clenched and his jaw worked like he was

chewing on whatever nonsense he was about to spit out.

"Do you think I planned to get her pregnant? That was an accident." Jasper growled.

"Well that makes it all better then. I didn't realize that you were only planning to have an affair and not start a family with another woman."

"So I'm not perfect," Jasper flung his arms out dramatically. "You're no goddamn prize yourself."

"Go to Hell!" Tara's voice was ice.

"You think I didn't think about what a mistake our marriage was every day? I knew you were shy, but I didn't realize you were such a loser; and stupid too. I don't think you've done a single thing right since our wedding. I've done everything I can to take care of you." Jasper pointed his finger at her as he continued, "But you haven't done a single thing to contribute. You're useless. You're nothing without me and you wouldn't last five minutes in the real world."

"I can do one thing right," Tara crossed her arms and stared at him.

"Bullshit," he countered.

"I can tell you and your little whore to get the hell out of my life."

Jasper smirked. "You don't have money, food, or even somewhere to go without me. The only reason our friends tolerated you was that they wanted to see me. You said yourself you threw your ugly ass at Pete and he turned you down."

She couldn't take this crap any longer so she stormed past him to leave.

Jasper followed her as she went around the house past where Melody was standing in the front yard. The child had heard everything they'd been saying.

"You don't want to come along to Chicago anymore?" Melody smirked. "We might need a nanny after we get settled." Then Melody laughed.

It was a damn good thing for the girl's sake that she was pregnant because every fiber of Tara's being screamed that she should go punch the girl in her disgusting mouth.

"Hey, I'm not a monster." Jasper looked at his wife. "I'll still drop you off in Chicago if you want to give it a try. You're not going to make any money here."

Tara squared her shoulders towards him. "I'd rather starve to death slowly than go anywhere with you."

"I hope you get a chance to do that," Melody grinned.

Tara turned to storm off towards the gravel road.

"Seriously," Jasper called after her. "If you're not back here by the time we leave I have no problem leaving your ungrateful ass here."

"That's good, because I don't ever want to see you again." Tara hissed.

He stepped into her path, forcing her to stop. He stared at her with an angry intensity. "I don't think you understand the position you're in. You have nothing if you stay here."

When she went to push past him he grabbed her arm with crushing force to stop her from walking away again. "You don't walk away from me. I didn't plan this, and I don't think you understand how nice it is for us to offer to take you somewhere better in the circumstances..."

"Don't patronize me," Tara interrupted, twisting her arm free of his grasp. "I don't need you, and you can shove your offer up your ass."

Tara tied her coat tight against the wind and took off down the driveway and onto the road. The first few hundred feet she was ready to break into a sprint. She never knew what Jasper was going to do when he got angry.

The gravel crunched under her feet, but other than that, she only heard the wind in the branches and silence. After about a mile Tara realized that she was still listening, waiting to hear the truck tires, waiting for Jasper to come after her. Hot tears ran in trails down her chilled cheek, but she didn't stop until she saw the Penderton's mailbox.

When she knocked on the front door it rattled and Tara felt a little panicky because she didn't know if Rose was even here. To her great relief Rose came to the door with a warm smile that faded quickly when she saw Tara's tear-stained cheeks.

"I thought you kids were leaving for Chicago today, but I can only assume you didn't walk five miles in the cold, alone, because you wanted to say goodbye." Rose smiled comfortingly

Tara shook her head and followed Rose inside, closing the door behind her. "I'm sorry, I wasn't really thinking about where I was going and I found myself here. Honestly I'm not sure where else to go."

"Let me put the kettle on." Rose dug it out of the top of a cardboard box on the kitchen counter. Tara stopped in the doorway.

"How long before you take off for Florida," Tara asked slowly, the kitchen was so empty that her words echoed.

"We'll have plenty of time to talk about that later, dear." Rose filled the kettle with water and turned on the stove. "What brings you here? Cold feet about making the trip?"

Tara broke down. She related all the details to Rose slowly with a lot of sniffling. Rose listened quietly, nodding sympathetically until they were interrupted by the whistling of the kettle which Rose frowned and turned off. She left it sitting on the top of the stove and reached into the top of the same box she'd pulled the kettle out of and produced two glasses and a bottle of bourbon.

"Drink this down, it'll help," Rose said, setting the glass in front of Tara.

"What do I do now?" Tara sobbed.

"Tonight you stay here of course. Men gotta' go and complicate everything. You did the right thing child," Rose patted Tara's hand. "Well, almost," Rose formed her hand into a claw to demonstrate, "I'd have scratched the little bitch's eyes out."

Tara smiled between sniffles. "I don't doubt that for a second," Tara assured her.

"So when do you leave?" Tara asked.

"My flight leaves in the morning two days from now." Rose smiled sadly.

"Oh?" Tara hadn't expected it to be so soon.

"I can reschedule. I have enough money to stay in a hotel if you need me here. Do you have somewhere to go?"

"No, but it's not a problem, I'll be fine." Tara fidgeted. It was a lie. She wouldn't be fine. She didn't have anywhere to go. When Rose left she would be sleeping on the streets. She didn't have anyone she was close enough to go stay with.

Rose studied Tara's face for a moment. "I may have a very appropriate solution for you," Rose smiled. The old woman got up from her chair and shuffled into the living room where she started digging through a box labeled, "Important Papers."

Tara watched from the doorway, waiting patiently for the mystery to unfold as Rose pulled out file folders and stacks of envelopes with no explanation

"Gotcha!" Rose exclaimed holding up a battered manila envelope with some sort of stain on the corner. When she bent the clasp both metal arms fell off on the floor. "I was saving this as an unpleasant surprise for the boys to fight over in probate court, but," she said handing the envelope to Tara, "I think you can make much better use of it."

Inside the envelope was a deed and a black and white photograph of a small cabin. "Why didn't you sell this when you sold your house?" Tara asked, setting both down on the folding table.

"The cabin was my husband's," Rose looked at the picture solemnly. "It was his hunting cabin, and I've spent so many years pretending it didn't exist that I didn't want to deal with it now," she admitted.

"What's so bad about a hunting cabin?" Tara asked confused.

"The man never fired a weapon in his life," Rose admitted to her, pouring another glass of bourbon. "You're the first person I've ever told this to, but, it's where he took his mistresses."

Stunned, Tara watched Rose quietly while the morning's events raced around in her head. She couldn't imagine letting it go on for years knowing about it. That thought made her feel sick for Rose and what she must have gone through.

"How could you stand knowing that he had mistresses?" Tara asked quietly.

"I had a few misters," Rose winked. "One fellow was quite

dear to me," she admitted smiling slightly while her eyes looked beyond the kitchen into the past. "He was dumb, but boy was he handsome, and he sure knew how to make a lady's toes curl."

"You are full of surprises," Tara admitted shaking her head.

"Don't judge honey, sometimes that's the best way to deal with life's little heartaches. You should consider it. Do you know any attractive single men in the area?" Rose teased.

"Sure, but I hear he's gay," Tara chuckled.

"That won't do you no good at all," Rose admonished.

"I know, but, that's not really what I'm looking for at the moment," Tara admitted letting her tone become more serious. "I just want to be alone."

"That's not gonna' get your mind off things," Rose shook her head.

"I'd rather just face it and keep going instead of trying to find ways to pretend it didn't happen," Tara shrugged.

"Suit yourself, but that won't help you get someone curling them toes for ya'."

"It's okay," Tara shrugged.

Rose looked at her with narrowed eyes, and then relented. "Suit yourself. Anyway I want you to have that cabin. I'll call my lawyer in a little bit and see if we can get him to draw me up a quit claim."

"What's that?" Tara asked.

"Just what it sounds like. We put another name on the deed and then I quit my claim. They're really fast and easy. It's what's normally used when money doesn't change hands but property does."

"You're just giving this to me?" Tara asked surprised, "I can have it just like that?"

"Yeah honey, but don't get too excited. It's in rough shape. It's sat empty for quite a number of years now. Besides, it wasn't ever much to begin with. It's a one-room cabin that doesn't have electricity or indoor plumbing," Rose warned. "Just a little hand-pumped well."

"If it has water available right there, then I'm already better off than I was before," Tara admitted pushing her hair back out of her face and smiling.

As the sun came up on the morning of Rose's trip Tara sat in awe of the deed sitting on the table with her name on it. Rose's lawyer had helped speed things along. They'd been in to see the county clerk and now, that fast, it was her place. The funny thing was she still hadn't laid eyes on the property. At least now she knew where it was and was surprised to learn that it also had ten acres of woodland.

Rose walked in and sat down at the table. "Honey, the phone's gonna' be shut off this afternoon and if you're gonna' call that friend of yours, you better do it soon."

Tara nodded at her distractedly. The moving company had been by just a couple of hours before and loaded up all the boxes of Rose's things that Tara had put by the door. The morning felt surreal.

Tara hesitated before dialing Pete's number, she didn't know why but she felt ashamed of what she was going to have to tell him. Taking a deep breath she punched in the numbers, there was no going back now. Pete answered on the third ring.

"Hello?"

"Hey Pete, it's me Tara."

"Sorry, I didn't recognize the number you're calling from. How'd it go? Did you make it safe to Chicago?"

Tara sat quietly for a moment. "I didn't go," she admitted, barely above a whisper.

"I didn't quite catch that. Is everything okay?"

"No, I didn't go to Chicago."

"Oh, is this temporary, or did you guys find a place to stay," he asked brightening.

Tara took a shaky breath and told him what had happened. When she'd finished the phone was silent for quite a while.

"Pete?" she asked.

"That slimy bastard," he swore, "Then they just took off?"

"As far as I know, I haven't been back to the house. Actually,

I called to ask you for a favor. Is there any way you can help me move my things out of there this evening?"

"Where are you going to go?" he asked solemnly.

"A friend of mine gave me a little cabin, she said it's a handyman special, but it's mine and I'm pretty excited about having a place," Tara smiled across the table at Rose.

"I get off work at around three. Where do you want me to meet you?"

Tara thought about it for a bit. "I'm probably going to go over and start packing in a little bit. You can just meet me out there."

"If you want to wait, I can give you a ride. I don't mind helping you pack." Pete offered.

"No thanks, I just want to get this done and over with, and," she admitted. "I'm afraid I may get a little emotional, so, I'd rather do this alone."

"It's okay to be emotional about something like this. I'm not going to judge you for that," he replied sincerely.

"I really appreciate that," Tara told him, and she meant it, "but, I'd still rather do this alone."

The rest of the morning was a flurry. Rose was hurrying around making absolutely sure everything was tidy and in order. She re-dusted the windowsills, re-swept all the floors and in general spent time straitening folding chairs. Tara was moping around; helping to the best of her ability, but she didn't want to think about the fact that, in less than an hour, she would see Rose for what would probably be the last time.

Rose fussed about, telling her to take all the cleaning supplies over to the cabin, because she was going to need them, and to get all the planters loaded into her friend's truck. They were full of medicinal herbs that she'd find useful. Tara was even ordered to dig up a few thick roots out of one of the front flower beds. She was told to plant them somewhere near the cabin, but not where she ever wanted anything else to go. Once planted these comfrey roots would be darn near impossible to get rid of.

When Rose's taxi pulled up to the front of the house Tara did her best to be strong, but after a few moments of lip quivering she burst into tears.

"Honey, if you need me to stay, I can cancel my flight," Rose assured her, gathering her into a hug.

Tara shook her head no against Rose's shoulder, "I can't ask you to do that."

"Honey, you didn't ask, but I can be there if you need me," Rose smiled patting Tara's cheek.

"No," Tara wiped her tears and sniffed loudly, she didn't want Rose stuck in the cabin, what if it was cold? "No. There are un-paid strippers, un-drunk drinks, and un-played slot machines waiting for you. You shouldn't disappoint them," Tara forced a smile.

"Sweetheart," Rose said squeezing her arm, "If you need anything I'm a phone call away."

"Thanks. I'll miss you, but go have the time of your life," Tara told Rose, bending down to pull her in for one last hug before helping her into the car and putting her carry-on in the trunk.

The moment the car had disappeared around the bend Tara sat down hard on the driveway. Curling her arms tight around herself, she remained unmoving for quite some time until the cold seeped through her legs and bottom chilling her to the bone. With teeth chattering, she dusted herself off, picked up the cleaning supplies from the porch where they'd been left, and walked away from Rose's locked and darkened house.

When Tara reached the top of the driveway at the cottage, it was a shock to realize that it used to be her home. The rooms were all dark and the door stood slightly ajar as if the place was the sight of a break-in.

Taking a shaking breath, she straitened her spine and pushed the door open with the toe of her boot. As she surveyed the room she realized that the similarity to a burglary didn't end at the door. The place looked like it had been ransacked. Drawers stood open, cabinets showed their bare shelves like ribs through the open doors. The entertainment center stood empty, leaving shapes in the dust that defined where the TV, DVD player, and stereo had been. The cushion covers had even been stripped from the couch, which didn't make sense until she realized they probably were used as makeshift packing containers.

Tara didn't know why the state of the house surprised her. She knew that Jasper and Melody would need supplies to start their new life together. But, a part of her never expected them to take the pieces of the life she and Jasper had already built if she was staying here. It felt like a further betrayal, adding insult to injury.

In the kitchen she scanned the mostly empty countertop. The toaster sat alone, the microwave and blender were missing. Going through the cabinets proved that they hadn't missed a dish, pot, or pan. Tara feared they hadn't left anything for her. After searching the area thoroughly she managed to find only a couple of dish towels, her enamel dishpan, and a large wooden spoon. She turned the spoon over in her hand suddenly sad that she and Jasper hadn't lived together long enough to have more than the basic necessities. Tara tucked her things into the dishpan and set them next to the door to wait for Pete.

In the living area she rolled the rug up from the floor and took the two books that had been left behind: A poetry book and Rose's canning book. Jasper had always been fond of fiction so there weren't any novels left. Next to the couch she found her knitting basket kicked over with its contents splayed across the floor. The bracket of the oil lamp still hung on the wall, but the lamp itself was nowhere to be seen. She lifted it off the nail and set it along with the other things by the door.

In the bathroom the shelves were almost entirely bare. The towels, soap, shampoo, and toothpaste were all gone. The only things left were her toothbrush and her grandfather's safety razor in its black case. At least they'd shown her that courtesy.

In the sink was a mass of ashes and scorch marks. They had burned something. Tara's eyes flew open when she thought of

Rose's journal.

Tara paused outside the closed bedroom door. She didn't want to think about what Jasper had done, probably in their bed. Unwelcomed images started creeping around inside her head, and she felt briefly like she was going to be sick. Tara shook her head as if to physically loosen the image, but it held on like a tick.

Inside the room the first thing she noticed was that the bed had been stripped leaving the mattress exposed, the pillows and blankets were all gone. Jasper's dresser was missing; only some dust bunnies and a toothpick marked the place that it had stood. Her dresser drawers all stood open and empty except for one. On top of the dresser were all of the herbalism books Rose had given her including the ledger.

"At least some things are sacred," she mumbled under her breath. When she opened the only drawer to inspect the contents she realized her original assessment was incorrect. Her special lingerie was most definitely missing. Her camisoles, garter belt, stockings, all were gone. For an angry moment Tara wondered which one of them would have taken those things, but she realized it didn't much matter anymore. It didn't stop her from feeling queasy about the idea of Melody wearing them for Jasper. She sighed; at least she had her own panties and bras. Tara probably wouldn't still have the bras if Melody could have filled them out.

Under the bed, to her relief, Tara found her wooden box. Had they forgotten it, or had Jasper simply spared her its removal? When she pulled it out from under the bed, she quickly checked the contents. Obviously they hadn't forgotten about it. The envelope of money was gone. Even if it was only five dollars it would have been better than nothing. Besides that her childhood photos were missing. Tara gasped when she thought of the ashes in the sink. Tara started to cry again. Her cherished pictures of her favorite aunt and her grandparents now only lived inside her head.

She removed her sewing box. Beneath it her journals were untouched. Setting the stack of journals on the bed, she opened up the oldest one. It was a small book with badly worn cardboard covers featuring a kitten and a ladybug. Inside the entries were written in swollen optimistic cursive in inks all colors of the rainbow. Each one describing, with some intensity, her series of pre-teen crushes, the interesting gossip from school, or the unfairness of life. Most of it seemed pretty insignificant when compared to the concerns of her adult life, but she remembered with some embarrassment that some of these things caused her to sulk in her bedroom for hours playing loud, sad music.

All of the journals were full except the one her mother had given her at graduation. It was a thick, old leather volume inscribed on the inside cover, "To my darling father, for your future dreams – Love J. Jenkins." Her mother had purchased it at a yard sale because it was, as her mother put it, "charming." The fact that it was completely blank had always struck Tara as sad so she'd never used it.

After a few seconds of hesitation Tara decided to put the journals back in, after all she would need toilet paper and fire starters.

She pulled her underwear out of the drawers and added them and the sewing box to the wooden chest. She fetched her things from the bathroom, stirring the ashes briefly. Her burnt memories clung to her fingers, but there was nothing left to save. Tara put her toothbrush, razor, and her books from Rose into the box before closing it up.

Before she walked out of the room she wiped her fingers on the mattress leaving a black smear on Jasper's side of the bed. It seemed appropriate.

When she carried her box to the stack next to the door she was terribly discouraged. Everything she had from her life in that house would fit into a wooden trunk, a basket, and a dishpan.

Tara headed out to the shed to check if the boxes were still inside. To her relief all of the canning supplies, including her lids, were still sitting in a pile. "At least that's something," she mumbled to herself. She didn't get a chance to search further because she heard the familiar rumble of Pete's truck in the driveway. He was early.

Pete was covered in black grime when he climbed out. "Excuse how filthy I am," he gestured his hand down over the front of his clothes. "I came strait here from work. I didn't want to leave you waiting in the cold longer than necessary."

"It's okay," Tara shrugged, "This winter I've gotten pretty used to the cold."

Pete frowned, "I was afraid that you guys hadn't kept the heater filled."

"We did okay until just before they left," she smiled. "Thanks for loaning it to us."

"Are you going to be all right?" he asked solemnly.

Tara tried to keep a smile on her face, but just being asked made her eyes go watery. Her voice shook when she answered, "Don't really have a choice." Tara sniffed a couple of times and wiped her hands across her eyes; taking a couple of deep breaths to steady herself.

"It's okay to be upset." Pete made no move towards her to comfort her, which Tara appreciated under the circumstances.

"I know, but," she sighed, "he doesn't deserve my tears at this point."

Pete smiled sadly, "I agree."

It took less than an hour to get Tara's mattress, dresser, her few belongings, and all the canning supplies loaded onto the truck. As a nice surprise Pete found the oil lamp and the camping oven sitting on the back porch, though neither of them had any idea why they were there. Holding her frozen hands in front of the truck's heater vents, Tara tried to relax as they headed to her new home.

CHAPTER 15

When they reached the base of the driveway it was exactly as Rose had described; winding, rough, and in need of maintenance. It was a good thing Pete had a truck; a car would have been torn apart on the uneven stretch of gravel. At least Tara assumed there was gravel. They were following a path through the trees, but it was so covered in dead weeds that they went up at a snail's pace. It left Tara holding her breath to see if the cabin was still standing for an agonizingly long time.

At the top of the hill they reached a clearing that might at one time have been a yard, but was now only where the trees were smaller than those surrounding them. The cabin itself was barely more than a shack. It had a covered porch, a tin roof, and weathered clapboard siding. Tara's first observation was that it would need painting, what little she could see of it. There was a tight layer of brush consuming the house.

Tara slid slowly out of the truck into knee-deep grass so dry it crackled.

"I want to start by finding the pump. Rose said it was in the front yard. And I can only imagine that this place will need a good scrub," she said looking back over her shoulder at Pete, who was beginning to wade forward carefully.

After several minutes of searching Tara found a cheerfully red pump mostly hidden in a bush ten feet from the front door. She grabbed the end of the handle and attempted to push it downwards, but it stayed stubbornly and solidly in place. It might as well have been a statue.

"Let me a have a look at it," Pete offered, pushing his way through the yard stopping only briefly to untangle himself from some sort of thorn bush. "Actually I'm surprised how nice this is," he remarked after examining it carefully. "There's a little rust, but I think with some oil and some light cleaning it'll work good as new. I've got some oil in the truck. We'll see what I can do with it. I can't guarantee the seals will still be good, but we'll keep our fingers crossed."

Tara left him to work on the pump while she headed toward the cabin. Gingerly, she walked up the front steps and across the porch; thankful that it seemed pretty solid. Once she was there Tara pulled the key from her coat pocket and unlocked the front door.

It took a couple of minutes before her eyes adjusted to the gloom. All the windows were nearly covered with vines and bushes, making it darker than she expected for early afternoon. The air was thick and musty and everything had a slightly blurry quality from the layers of dust and grime. Spider webs hung thick and ropelike as only dust and time can make them.

The interior was one open room. Along one wall was a short, rusty woodstove with round cooktop lids. In the corner was a small, white enamel-topped table with a drawer on the side. Next to this was a Hoosier cabinet painted white that matched the table with the same enamel work surface.

On the opposite side of the room from the stove was an old bed frame. It didn't have a mattress, but the frame was strung with crisscrossing ropes that were broken and hanging loosely to the floor in one corner. Under the bed was a small, bulbous white crock with a lid and a handle on the side like an enormous mug. Tara hoped desperately that it was clean.

Above the bed was a set of shelves, the only thing on them was a black and white photo of a smiling woman who looked like it could have been Rose when she was young. Tara couldn't help wondering if it was there out of a strange sense of loyalty or as some sort of insult. Making Rose watch.

At the back of the room was a door. Tara crossed the room to open it, but the sensation of getting there was revolting. So many threads, invisible in the gloom, stuck to her face and hair as she passed that she couldn't help but brush at herself urgently imagining all the big spiders that must be crawling all over her. The door itself was stiff, but eventually yielded with a squeak, followed by a groan.

This opened onto a screened-in sleeping porch that she hadn't noticed from the front of the house through all the brush. Unlatching the door, she wandered carefully around the yard. The back was as overgrown as the front. A small shed stood next to a rusty heap that appeared to be a refuse pile. A stone path led past it down to an outhouse with a moon cut out of the door. Thoughts of the things that were living in the little outhouse skittered through her brain and she grimaced.

"There you are," Pete called causing Tara to jump. "You have running water, sort of anyway." Pete held up a bucket that sloshed.

"Sort of?" she asked.

"You have to pump it and carry it into the house, but at least it's available," he shrugged.

"After carrying and rationing water from town, a pump in the yard seems like a dream come true." Tara assured him.

Pete looked around and smiled, "It's a nice little place out here."

"Probably will be when it's cleaned up," she admitted.

"How about I stick around for a while tonight and give you a hand?" Pete offered.

"It's fine. You don't have to. I'm sure you have more important things to do," she replied quickly. "If you just want to drop my stuff on the porch I'll take it in when I'm done cleaning."

"At least let me get your windows uncovered so you can see what you're doing. I have a saw in the truck," he gestured toward his vehicle.

"Is there anything you don't have?" she asked raising an eyebrow.

"Of course," he shifted uncomfortably, "but, I like to be prepared."

"Boy Scout?" she asked.

"No." He offered her no other information. When he came back from the truck a few moments later he had a small pile of stuff in his arms. Once he'd set it on the porch he offered Tara an olive drab bandana.

"You don't want to breathe that stuff in."

Tara shook her head no before tying the bandana around her face covering her nose and mouth.

It didn't take long for Pete to let the daylight into the room. Then he busied himself with the stove, cleaning it out thoroughly and oiling the hinges. After that was accomplished he removed the stovepipe that was connected to the wall and took it outside to clean.

Once inside, Tara spent hours cleaning the old grime and making a few nice discoveries. In the drawer of the table were two each of knives, forks, and spoons. In the cabinet were a set of two each of white enamelware plates and bowls, the kind she normally associated with camping trips. They were accented with black rims, but the cups were different colors.

Before Pete was back inside she had to clean and fill the hanging lamp that she'd found in the middle of the room. Thankfully the bottle of lamp oil had been on a shelf in the shed and she'd had the good sense to pack it when she was getting the canning jars. Once the lamplight filled the room with the cozy glow that she'd become accustomed to, she began carrying in her things from the truck; Pete hurried to help her.

"I'm sorry I kept you here so late. Once I've unloaded you can head home. Nothing more that can be done in the dark anyway."

"You don't think I'm going to leave you out here?" he asked as they carried her mattress in and set in on the floor next to the bed frame.

"It's my house," she answered him, confused.

"This may be your house, but the chimney needs to be cleaned before you can light a fire. It's anybody's guess what may be living up there. You don't have any food. You don't even have a blanket," he told her matter-of-factly. "I can't in good conscious leave you here, so I must insist you stay at my place tonight. We'll get some dinner and you can have a hot shower and wash your clothes."

Tara thought briefly of disagreeing, but she wanted a hot

shower and warm couch more than she cared to think about. "Okay, you convinced me," she relented with a tired shrug.

"Good," he smiled, "I didn't want to have to resort to force. We'll see what supplies we can find for you in the morning. It's best to stick close to home after dark."

"What do you mean?" she asked him confused.

Pete shook his head. "The neighborhood's been getting a little... rough."

Less than ten minutes later they were pulling into the city limits. The street lights were out and on several corners people stood around lighted barrels drinking out of bottles that they passed back and forth. Tara recognized Mark and Daniel and waved as she passed. Some of the homes had boards on the windows. Dotted amongst these were smoldering wrecks of brick and boards.

"What happened?" Tara asked

"Do you remember when Alex told us that the police force had stopped doing the bank's evictions?"

Tara nodded.

"Well, the banks have been hiring their own private enforcers to carry out the evictions and they are a lot less kind about it than the local sheriff had been. I heard an older couple died after they were dragged from their homes by those thugs and left out in the cold. A couple of the local churches are running soup kitchens and basically letting people sleep in pews for the night. Problem is there are too many people who need right now, and not enough with extra supplies to spare." Pete looked momentarily embarrassed. "I've been giving a small donation every week to the United Church of Christ."

"Every little bit helps I'm sure."

"More people's lights go off every day. In the poorer section of town most streets are dark. Half the houses sit empty and the banks order them boarded up or burned down to keep from having squatters."

"Why would they burn a house?"

"To make a point," Pete huffed.

As they were climbing out of the truck in the garage at Pete's house, it struck Tara how truly bone tired she was. Pete offered to make dinner while she got cleaned up.

Tara slipped into the bathroom with the towel Pete had given her from the hall closet and a pair of his pajamas for her to change into. While she looked at them on the top of the pile, it really sunk in how little she owned now. She didn't even own pajamas anymore. Tara frowned when she thought about it. Melody didn't even like her clothes. Taking them all had to be spite. She wasn't sure what Melody had to be angry about; she'd won after all.

Just a few moments later Tara drank in the bliss as cascades of hot water washed the cold ache out of her bones and the day's dirt swirled down the drain.

"Just set your clothes on top of the washer, I'll start a load after dinner," Pete gestured to the small laundry room off the kitchen. Pete was still in his work clothes standing over the stove stirring a pot that smelled heavenly. On the counter were two bowls and a plate of grilled cheese sandwiches all cut in half nicely.

He ladled soup into one of the bowls and handed it to her. "Make yourself comfy in the living room, I'm going to get cleaned up before I eat." He switched off the burner and headed off down the hall towards the bathroom, untucking his shirt.

The living room screamed bachelor. There were no knick-knacks, unnecessary furniture, or even a rug. The coffee table was stained and looked as if it had come from a second-hand store, and the matching couch and loveseat were both threadbare with an upholstery pattern that suggested they were at least ten years old. There was, however, a very nice entertainment center with a television that surprised Tara with its size. On the couch a sheet had been carefully tucked around

the cushions and a folded blanket was sitting on top of the
pillow at one end.

Tara ate quickly; she hadn't realized how hungry she was
until she'd finished off a bowl of soup and two whole
sandwiches. She set the bowl next to the sink. She'd wash it in
the morning. She was too tired to think. Tara walked into the
living room and dropped onto the couch disappearing under the
blanket.

Pete walked into the room with a bowl of soup and a plate at
that point, but she lost the struggle to keep her eyes open before
he had a chance to sit down.

CHAPTER 16

The smell of bacon woke Tara in the morning. She could hear the sizzle and pop from where she lay on the couch and she could have sworn she was still dreaming. Her mouth watered. She hadn't had bacon in months.

"Good morning," Pete smiled when she walked in. He was already dressed; wearing jeans, a long sleeve flannel, and some heavy work boots.

Tara yawned, "I didn't mean to sleep in."

"Not a big deal, you seemed like you needed it," he nodded as he scraped the bacon out of the cast iron pan on the stove. Into the bacon grease he cracked a few eggs.

"Can I do anything to help?" Tara asked.

"No. I think I've got this, but I left your clothes folded in the living room on the loveseat. If you want to get going right after breakfast we can get some of your errands done."

"I couldn't ask you to do that," Tara insisted, "I don't want to make you late for work."

"You're not. I took the day off."

"Thanks," she smiled.

"Not a problem."

After breakfast Pete insisted that they needed to start by loading the truck.

"With what?" Tara asked. She didn't have anything here.

"A fair few things. It'll probably take more than one trip," he admitted.

Tara looked at him confused. Pete didn't elaborate; he simply asked her to wait for him while he unlocked the basement door and headed downstairs. Tara felt suddenly uneasy, why was the basement door locked? He seemed like a nice guy, but how much did she really know about Pete? A few moments later he came back up carrying a chimney brush and a bottle of stove black, both looked brand new.

Going back down the stairs again he came back up more slowly this time with a wooden barrel on a hand truck. It was about the same size as a metal beer keg, and he struggled with the weight. He maneuvered it through the door to the garage and rolled it off next to the back of the truck with a grunt. Then he headed back down the stairs and repeated the process with two more barrels. Tara offered to help, but he asked her not to saying that he didn't want her to accidently get hurt.

Tara stood at the top of the steps at the open basement door and tried to peek down. There wasn't much to see; only scattered piles of boxes, everything else was outside her view. Nobody screamed for help, that was something.

As she stood in the doorway of the kitchen, Tara watched Pete take down a metal ramp off the wall of the garage and fit it carefully into a couple of grooves in the tailgate of his truck.

He gave no indication that he was going to tell her what the barrels contained. Curiosity overcame her and she asked, "So, what's in the barrels?"

"This one," Pete explained to her walking it to the base of the ramp, "is rice. The one over there is beans, and the one beyond that is flour."

"Okay, let's forget for a second that you have barrels of food in your basement… why are you putting it on the truck?"

Pete looked at her. "Because I'm giving it to you. You don't have any food out there."

"You're just going to give me barrels of food?" Tara asked surprised.

"Yeah, I don't want you to starve; and the stores are having some supply issues right now. Even if you could get in to buy food there may or may not be any available, as you know."

"Okay," Tara nodded. "So, why do you have barrels of food in your basement?"

Pete sighed, "I read, and I also read between the lines. The economy took a dive and I turned my savings into food, and some useful tools. I figured if things got worse I could eat food, but not money. I also assumed, rightly so at this point, that my money would buy me less and less with time."

"So you keep your basement door locked because —."

"Because," he interrupted, "my life savings are down there and I would appreciate if you don't tell anyone. I'm trusting you."

Pete let her help him get the barrels up the ramp, but once on the truck they left them laying on their side; tying them down tight. Pete didn't want them to be obvious to anyone who might see the truck.

After that, Tara was helpless to do much more than watch the flurry of activity that was Pete. He carried up two smaller barrels; one containing sugar and one containing salt.

"How could one person need that much salt?" Tara asked following him to the truck.

"Have you ever done any pickling or curing?" he asked.

"No," Tara admitted

"That's how," he assured her rolling it into place on the back of the truck.

Next came a couple of towels, a coil of rope, a kitchen knife, a cast iron skillet, a cast iron dutch oven, a gray wool blanket, a pillow, a box of matches, a couple of bars of soap, some toothpaste, and a few old sheet sets, all of which Pete packed inside a large metal washtub. It was pretty much everything that would fit on the back of the truck.

"We'll have to come back later this afternoon for Greta and her food."

"You still have Greta?" Tara asked elated. "I thought you would have sold her by now."

"How did you not hear her when I let her out this morning?" Pete shook his head.

"I must have slept like a rock," Tara shrugged.

"I suppose, but I'm still surprised that you didn't hear her."

"How have you kept her safe in town?" Tara asked peeking out through one of the blinds to watch the people walking. It was amazing how many people were out walking.

"I close her into the mud room during the day when I'm gone. Normally overnight, too. She gets some exercise in the yard only when I'm here and awake.

All the back and forth chores took them the rest of the morning. First, they dropped off the load they had on the truck. Then they went to Rose's to pick up the planters, which put Tara instantly in a bad mood because the place felt wrong without Rose. After that they went back to Tara's old house and loaded up all the wood; tearing down Greta's old stall and, strangely, Pete insisted on bringing the freezer. Tara didn't bother to argue.

When they had all that unloaded and sitting beside the shed under a tree, Pete pulled his chainsaw and an axe out of the back seat of the truck. He spent the next couple of hours helping Tara get a handle on the task of cutting and splitting wood. There were plenty of dead limbs and downed trees lying around to keep her in wood for the rest of the winter. Pete regretted that he couldn't leave his chainsaw with her, but he was willing to leave her a large handsaw and an axe to use until she got some tools of her own.

After they had a reasonable stack of wood, Pete backed the truck up to the porch roof and carefully made his way to the top of the chimney with the brush in hand. Tara opened the clean-out at the bottom and scooped out piles of creosote, bird's nests, and even some bones into an unsightly pile at the base. After a few more passes they deemed it clean enough to light the first fire.

Inside they took a heavy brush to the stove and carefully covered it with stove black. When Tara finally opened the door to set the fire she breathed in the smell of old ash and iron, it was a distinct smell that she hadn't found anywhere else. For a moment she was back home as a child poking the sticks into a pile and stacking the larger logs around them waiting to be able to hold her hands to the woodstove, the only kind of heat that had ever warmed her through on a blustery winter day.

Today her numb fingers fumbled with the fire starting sticks that Pete had cut little curly shavings out of with his knife. After she'd stacked a reasonable pile of dry grass and twigs on the bottom she put some slightly larger pieces above them and pulled the draft open. It took her less than ten minutes before she had the flames crackling among the branches strong enough that she could shut the door.

"I'm going to head back and get the goat while you get the fire established." Pete headed for the door.

"Sounds good," Tara called. "I'll see you in a few."

Tara headed outside to see if she could figure out a good place to put the goat for the time being. The shed seemed like a pretty good place to start. When Tara tried the door, she was surprised to find it locked. She headed back inside to grab the key off the peg by the door where she'd hung it so she wouldn't lose it. Before she went back out she checked the fire. It was ready for some slightly bigger logs, so she dropped a couple on and closed the draft slightly. The chill was starting to disappear from the air.

Luckily, the front door key was also the shed key. Tara had been worried when she put it in the slot, but it had turned without difficulty. The windows were covered with grime and in the fading daylight all she could see in front of her was an inky gloom.

Tara sighed and headed back into the house, lit the lamp, and brought it back out with her. The shed was even dirtier than the inside of the cabin had been. The dust was thicker and it had an unpleasant smell that she couldn't place. It was about half the size of the cabin in Tara's estimation, which had been hard to tell from the outside because it was as completely consumed by the encroaching forest as her new home was. As she swept the lamp from side to side she could see that the place boasted a small collection of tools; a hammer, hatchet, pliers, and shovel were out in the open.

On the wall was a shelf full of jars. She looked closer at them, giving them a quick wipe, and saw they were all full of nails, screws, hinges, and bits of other hardware.

Stacked near the door were several more buckets, and against the back wall were some big crocks and really large glass jars that Tara recognized as carboys only because of their stoppers with airlocks made of glass. Cloudy dark liquid sat in one of them.

Tara realized she couldn't put the goat in here with this stuff so she hurriedly began carrying things out to stack them next to the shed. She set aside a nice enamel kettle that looked like it used to have a coffee percolator in it, but that was long since missing. Now it just seemed an excellent way of heating water. It didn't take long for Tara to become filthy with dirt thick on her clothes and skin. While she was sweeping down the walls she heard the truck coming slowly up the driveway with a bawling goat. Tara smiled. The goat was, by far, the louder of the two.

Tara met Pete on the driveway and he shook his head when he saw her. "How did you get so filthy so quick?" Pete asked looking impressed.

"Figured the shed would be a good place for Greta, but I needed to clean it out first. There wasn't a lot inside so I'm nearly done."

"I guess it's a good thing you have running water," Pete sighed.

"Just let me finish sweeping the place out and we can get Greta put up for the night," Tara told him, heading back out to the shed while Pete began unloading the hay and stacking it in front of the shed.

It wasn't long before Tara was comfortably situated on an upside down bucket with a pail of grain in front of Greta and another bucket under her. Pete leaned on the wall by the door while Tara relaxed into the rhythm of the milking.

"I think you could make this work as a goat shed and a regular shed with a dividing wall down the middle," Pete mused, looking around. "You should consider it. That way you can get all that stuff outside back under the cover of a roof. It would also give you somewhere to store her feed sacks since you can't have them in here with her."

"The old door off the other shed could probably be framed right into the side wall over there," Pete gestured as he walked toward the back of the building

"I sure hope so," Tara admitted. "I'm not sure what else I can do."

Tara carried all but the feed bucket out of the shed. Inside the cabin, Tara poured the milk into a glass quart jar; straining it through a dish towel, and then set it on the back porch.

It was already warm enough inside that Tara could take her coat off. She shut down the damper to keep from burning through the wood too fast.

"Thanks for all your help today."

"Not quite done yet," Pete pointed out, getting the coil of rope out of the washtub they had set just inside the door. "Still need to get your bed restrung."

Neither of them had ever strung a rope bed before, but they did the best they could paying careful attention to the way the old rope was knotted on. Pete helped her pull it taught to keep the mattress from sagging. When it was done she had her mattress on the bed frame made up nicely with some old sheets with tiny yellow flowers and a heavy gray wool blanket.

"If you don't need anything else I think I'm going to head out."

Tara wanted to ask him to stay. She wanted to tell him she was scared; she was going to struggle with all the work that was going to need to be done, and that she didn't know how she could be out here all alone. Instead she gave him a thin smile and said, "Nope, I can't think of anything that I can't manage."

"Take care of yourself," Pete offered as he put his coat on at the door and slipped out before Tara even thought to ask when she would see him again. That was that.

Wanting nothing more than to crawl between the covers for a while and maybe cry herself to sleep, Tara grabbed the kettle and carried it out into the yard to fill it with water to warm on the stove.

While the water was warming she busied herself for fear that if she sat down she'd fall asleep strait away. She rolled the rug out in the middle of the room, put the books away on the shelves above the bed, and in general neatly arrange the cabin to her liking. It wasn't like she had a lot of things that needed to be put away.

When the water was ready, Tara poured it in the dishpan and re-filled the kettle again from the pump so that she'd be able to rinse herself. Stripping down next to the stove, Tara scrubbed her body as clean as she could manage then kneeled in front of the dishpan; scrubbing her hair in the soapy water. When she was done the water was the same dark gray as the blanket on the bed, she cringed and carried it to the front door and flung it far out into the night. She instantly regretted leaving the fire and shivered violently as she hurried back to her place next to the stove. She refilled the pan with the lukewarm water to clean off her body one last time, and then did her best to rinse her hair. After she'd toweled off she slipped on a clean pair of panties, fed a few logs into the fire and crawled between the sheets. She'd deal with her filthy clothes in the morning. Outside the snow fell gently, but she didn't notice.

CHAPTER 17

When Tara opened her eyes she was momentarily confused. The dream didn't want to let her go. She'd been sitting on a sofa watching TV, eating microwave popcorn out of the bag snuggled up with her husband. The reality of where she was gave her a shock. The first light of dawn was painting a light gloom on the room, which was starting to get cold.

She let her eyes go unfocused in the stillness for some time before she pulled the blanket over her head and let herself feel the ache and panic. She might need to stay like that forever because sitting in the gray light of morning all she could think of was Jasper, and where he must be with Melody by now.

Painted by her mind's eye she imagined Jasper waking up and reaching out for Melody. He would pull her close and kiss her closed eyelids as he'd often done to Tara when they were first dating. He'd hoist himself out of bed and flip on the light in a room made comfortable by the electric furnace. Jasper would pour himself a cup of coffee made by an electric coffee maker using a timer, and bring Melody a cup calling her sleeping beauty just like he use to do with Tara.

She didn't realize she was crying softly until her nose started to run. Curling up, she cried harder until she wasn't sure she could cry anymore.

The day was a struggle. Tara beat her clothes on the porch to get the dirt out like a rug. She didn't have time to wait for them to be washed and dried, so they were going to have to go without for now. Her very modern sensibilities rebelled at the idea, but it was the best she could do. As she got dressed Tara realized that she had never, in her entire life, imagined she would only have one set of clothing.

Breakfast consisted of some very flat things. They were

supposed to be pancakes, but that's not what happened at all. All five of them burnt. The well-seasoned cast iron helped, but it was still difficult to cook without grease. Before Tara headed out to milk Greta, she set a pot of beans soaking on the top of the stove.

When Tara walked in with the bucket of feed Greta rushed to her side, she knew the routine. Animals were so simple, much simpler than men. To keep Greta's interest all she had to do was have the food. Greta needed her, and didn't even care that she'd been given away. All was forgiven, thanks to food. At least she had no illusions about the nature of their relationship. It was simple and straightforward and Tara could never be misled by it.

When milking was complete Tara strained the milk and set it on the back porch in another jar. Then she headed back out to work on framing up a door on the side of the shed. A found claw hammer and the hand saw were her only tools for removing part of one stud. The measuring was done with her dressmakers tape, but inches are inches after all. By the time twilight was creeping in she had finished shimming the door and it opened and closed easily.

After the evening milking Tara sat down to study her herbals in the glow of lamplight, but she was too agitated. Her beans were done by now, so she scooped out a bowl and sweetened them slightly with sugar. While she ate she tried to figure out what to do with her evening. Sleeping wasn't an option. Her muscles ached, but her physical exhaustion didn't do anything to slow her racing mind. Jasper and Melody's new life was all that Tara thought about. This time of night they were probably sitting down to dinner, macaroni and cheese… or a burger. All Tara had was a bowl of flavorless beans and a glass of cold goat milk.

How was it fair that the people who broke hearts and hurt others were the ones who were rewarded? Tara's reward for being a faithful wife was to be sitting alone in the middle of the woods.

With dinner finished she left the pot of beans on the

screened-in back porch to stay cool and washed the dishes. With nothing to keep her mind occupied her agitation returned and she paced back and forth, angry and sniffling. She needed to be doing something or else she felt as if she may go crazy. Tara considered her situation for some time then pulled out a sheet with a gray plaid pattern. She pulled a stick out of the fire and let it cool then began taking some measurements to draw a pattern for a nightgown. If she had something to wear she would be able to wash her clothes. Tara decided on a simple shift.

The sheet was laying on the floor at her feet marked with dark lines for her to cut around, but she didn't have the confidence to do it tonight. She would go over all the measurements again and construct it in her head to make sure she wasn't forgetting any seam allowances. There wasn't any room to recut any pieces. That was the perfect thing for her to do in the dark while lying in bed.

The next morning crashed over her like a wave and Tara scrambled to her feet. The room was chilly. She was wearing only her long underwear; her dress and sweater draped nicely across the end of the bed. Thankfully it was already full daylight because her pounding heart began to slow as she recognized the small room she'd gone to bed in. The day was spent working on building a dividing wall in the shed to keep the goat confined to one side so that Tara could use the other side to put things away out of the weather. The evening was spent cutting the pieces that she would sew together painstakingly by hand to have a nightgown.

It didn't take long for one day to run into the next; the food, the routines; nearly everything was exactly the same day after day. During the daylight hours Tara used every minute she could spare to work. Once the sun went down she would sit by the light of the lamp and study, or sew, until exhaustion would let her sleep. The only variation being what kind of work she did during the day. She finished the shed, then she put everything away as neatly as she could, she split wood, did laundry, and began building a fence to keep Greta from losing her mind. She started with a small exercise yard so the goat could be out in the sunlight during the day. She was already planning larger rotating pastures around it, but it would take her ages to fence.

While scrubbing her clothes together in a tub Tara sat up panicky realizing that not only did she not know what day it was, she didn't know what week or even what month. She'd spent nearly the whole next day rocking back and forth while feeding logs into the fire. It was amazingly unsettling. During that time she wondered if enough time had passed for the baby to be born, but after a bit of deliberation she realized she could at least guess that it hadn't been that long yet because it was still winter. Jasper's baby wouldn't be born till early fall, summer would have to pass first. This realization calmed her for a time.

The sound of a log popping in the stove jarred Tara awake. Her eyes didn't adjust to the darkness, it was absolute. Sliding her hand slowly along the rough wall, understanding hit her all at once; at least she knew where she was. As she gasped in a deep shuddering breath she tried to remember who she was or why she was there, but it wouldn't really come to her; nothing that made sense anyway.

She knew her name, but who she actually was… that was a blur. The next breath was a struggle because her chest felt heavy, as if she was being crushed under the weight of every decision she'd ever made in her life; especially the one that brought her here. She was alone in the world, and she couldn't think of a reason that she existed. She was breathing and taking up space, but why? Her heart ached. Why did she toil forward every day when there wasn't any reason to? At this point she began to truly panic. She flung back the blanket and stuffed her feet into her boots, which she didn't bother to lace before she scrambled out in to the night. When the cold air hit her skin she gasped and inhaled deeply. Then she began pacing restlessly back and forth. She couldn't be here. Not like this. She needed to run until she found someone to say her name, till she met someone who cared that she was alive. Dark woods surrounded the cabin in all directions and she may have fled into the trees if it wasn't for the fear that gripped her. Would she ever come back if she stepped off into the unending darkness?

Tara forced herself to sit, but she couldn't be still. She rocked rhythmically, humming to herself to drown out the sound of her pounding heart. She didn't even notice that she'd started to cry until the drops landed cold on her chest. The fabric of her gray plaid nightgown wasn't nearly enough to keep her warm and she began to shiver violently. Moving quickly, Tara swept back into the house and grabbed her blanket then continued out through the back door. She couldn't be alone.

When she opened the door to the shed the smell of goat and manure reached her nose and it felt like a blessing. The sound of her sniffles made the goat mumble sleepily, allowing Tara to find her in the dark. Tara pulled all the clean hay out of the feeder and dropped it on the ground next to Greta where she settled in. Pressing her forehead against the goat's warm body Tara noticed she smelled like a dusty used blanket, but the sound of her breathing was soothing. Her rumen noises were regular, and she belched quietly.

"If only you could talk, we could actually be good friends. We could keep each other company. What do you think?" Tara asked soothingly as she combed her fingers through the goat's rough fur. Greta lay tensely until she seemed to reach the goaty conclusion that no food was forthcoming so she laid her head lightly on Tara's chest. That's how they slept till morning.

Tara's crisis of character didn't end with the dawn, but at

least in the day she found herself busy with all the demands of living, though she felt like a ghost. But it wasn't like the night. In the night she had time to think about the world and her place in it. The morning she'd gotten up with Greta she'd considered that it might be time to make a trip into town, but she realized she was too afraid. Some woman reeking of goat... would she be arrested when she arrived? What if things had gotten more dangerous? Eventually she talked herself out of the idea, but she knew she couldn't stay away forever.

CHAPTER 18

The rumbling mumble of thunder brought Tara out of her dream slowly, and she looked around in the dark wondering why. Her breath caught as lightning flashed; throwing exaggerated shadows cascading around the room and Tara felt a bubble of joy swell inside her. It was something she hadn't heard in months. She smiled as the first drops of rain pattered on the tin roof. She stared at the underside with its old nails poking down through. In the occasional flashes she couldn't stop thinking about how wonderful it was that it was warm enough for a thunderstorm.

Tara's thoughts turned immediately to the hope of a garden, obviously it was nearly spring. The last snow of the year probably hadn't fallen yet, but at least spring was letting her know that it was nearby, like an old friend. Overcome, tears glistened in her eyes. This must have been what spring felt like in the old days. Relief.

Outside the window the rain tickled the tree branches and the window panes wept softly as she drifted back to sleep.

The morning was warmer than usual, and Tara felt compelled to be outside. She'd been hiding away in the cabin too much lately; perpetually tired. She'd managed to sleep an entire day earlier in the week… or was it last week? She didn't know anymore.

The wind had a bite to it and Tara still needed her coat, but she left it hanging open comfortably. The brown clumps of grass were wet and the ground squelched with each step out to the shed.

After milking, Tara wandered aimlessly out into the yard. It smelled nice; earthy and alive. As she passed the corner of the house a flash of bright green caught her eye. Curious, Tara knelt down and parted some of the brush to have a peek. Near the ground were some tiny green plants. Green plants! She dropped to her knees to have a closer look, nearly oblivious to the cold water seeping into her clothes. The leaves were smooth and oval shaped with a pointed tip on long draping stems. Tara thought she recognized the plant, but she had to pick one of the long stems to be sure. It was tiny and the stem had a single line of hairs up the side that moved around the stem at each set of leaves, like an herbal Mohawk. This was definitely chickweed. She'd been reading about it for months. It was exciting to actually be able to start making some real world connections to the things she'd been learning.

Chickweed was edible. Tara pinched off a single leaf and placed it carefully in her mouth, then chewed slowly. She'd never tried eating wild plants before. Her mother had always told her not to eat plants, they could be poisonous. It wasn't at all what she expected. The leaf was juicy and tasted green, like fresh young spinach. Her mind raced through the possibilities. Finally she could eat something different. Beans, rice, and pancakes were getting old; really, really, old. Not that she wasn't thankful to have the food, but she wasn't sure she was eating as much as she should and was frankly feeling a bit out-of-sorts and tired lately. Maybe she was deficient in some vitamins.

Tara's initial caution fell away faster than it should have and she found herself stuffing handfuls of the stuff in her mouth. She needed more; surely there was more than the one little patch. It would make an excellent lunch, like the ghost of a salad. Amazingly the more she looked the more Tara found. The plants were all around the buildings and around the bases of trees. The stuff was creeping everywhere; it was wonderful she marveled.

While on her hands and knees under an old oak tree Tara heard a sound that made the hair on the back of her neck stand up, an engine, a fairly loud one. Thinking about it, she hadn't heard one in quite a while. Strangely, she hadn't even noticed when she stopped hearing them. That was worrisome to think about. Was she really that isolated?

As the sound of the motor grew louder, it become obvious it was on the road heading in her direction. When the engine slowed at the end of her driveway Tara retreated to the porch and stood frozen with her hand on the door, until she heard the crunch of gravel as it began climbing her driveway. Tara tore into the cabin with her heart hammering in her ears. Who was here? What did they want? Would this person hurt her? Panic swam around inside Tara's head when she realized she had nothing to bar the windows with. Locking the door wouldn't do any good when someone could just come in through the window.

Tara grabbed the kitchen knife out of the drawer and crouched by the front door, watching perfectly still from the edge of the window. She hoped the dim interior of the building would hide her. The place still looked abandoned. Maybe nobody would notice she was here.

A black vintage motorcycle idled carefully into the yard as Greta bleated hungrily at the stranger. Oh hell, with Greta out nobody would believe this place was abandoned. A man wearing a black helmet, blue jeans, and a torn leather coat dropped the kickstand and swung his leg over the bike. Tara held her breath. He seemed well-built and Tara immediately recalculated her odds of getting away unhurt. She'd bet anything that this man with broad shoulders was a lot stronger than her and she was definitely going to have to start out with and maintain the upper hand, but how? When he turned to look at the goat it was apparent that he was wearing a shotgun strapped to his back and Tara began to hyperventilate.

Tremors ran through her body as she gripped the handle of the knife. He couldn't know she was here or she'd never get the chance to use it.

The man unbuckled the helmet and set it on the seat of the motorcycle. Blind with fear Tara noted that his hair was a dark shade but mostly she was checking the thickness of his neck and thinking about where to strike.

"Tara?" the man called.

She dropped the knife, startled by her name.

"Tara?" he called again looking back and forth from the house to the shed and then down towards the outhouse. "You here?"

With shaking hands Tara scrambled with the door latch and flung it open, unable to believe her ears.

"Pete?" she called.

"There you are, I didn't mean to scare you," Pete smiled looking her up and down as if he couldn't believe she was really there.

"No, don't worry I wasn't," she shook her head.

"Then you are a liar or a fool," he stated matter-of-factly. Moving forward he smiled again. "I wasn't sure you were here, I didn't see the smoke until I was pretty close. The woods are definitely your friend. It doesn't make you less visible on the still days," he warned. "Oh, and that loud ass goat is a dead giveaway."

Confused, Tara cocked her head and stared at him. "I'm sorry what?"

"I would think you'd be more careful now."

"Why?" she asked cautiously.

His mouth dropped open slightly while he stared at her. "When was the last time you were in town?" Pete finally asked.

"With you," Tara shrugged, suddenly embarrassed, but she wasn't entirely sure what about.

"Well," his eyebrows furrowed while he chose his words. Then he shook his head. Opening his mouth again he looked at her apologetically, "I've been worried. I'm sorry I didn't make it out here to see you before this, but when everything started happening I had other plans. Eventually things fell through so I'm back now. I figured I should come out and check on you."

Tara took a step back confused, "What do you mean? What are you talking about?"

Pete stepped forward running his hands through his hair, as he took a deep breath he started again. "Things have changed," he said slowly.

Tara felt like she did when her mother told her that her favorite aunt had died in a car crash. "What do you mean changed?" Tara asked, still standing on the porch.

He shook his head, "I'm not even sure where to start."

"Okay, but is it really this bad?" she asked lowering herself down to sit on the steps.

Pete approached her cautiously, sitting down on the step next to her. "You know me. I'm kind of a pessimist. Crime has risen dramatically since the government cut everyone off."

Tara turned to him startled, "You mean no more food stamps?"

"No more food stamps, no more disability, no more welfare, no more social security, no money for police, no money for social workers," he paused while she took this in.

"How can they do that?" she demanded, "What are they telling everyone?"

"We're at war with Russia and the economic costs are high," he paused, "Or, it has something to do with a terrorist attack in the DC area, or the EU has imposed economic sanctions on us due to the drone strikes."

"I'm confused." Tara shook her head.

"We all are," Pete sighed, "There was some sort of media blackout for national security reasons. All the major news stations signed off weeks ago. They killed the internet, shut down the cell phone towers, well, someone did anyway. At this point we don't even know if we are at war. The only news we've had is from a ham radio operator just outside of town. And all he's been getting are rumors, the sanest of which I just shared with you."

"I wish I had some money," Tara sighed. "There's so much I need to get."

"You can use that stuff as toilet paper at this point," Pete shrugged. "Nobody around here accepts the US dollar anymore."

Tara's mouth dropped open, "What?"

"Our money went into some serious inflation, something to do with the stock market crash and the attack on our petro-dollar monopoly. Remember all the money creation that was being done during the recession? When we were no longer the petro-dollar, meaning the world didn't have to trade in our currency anymore, all that money came flooding back to our shores. Last time I checked a loaf of bread was several thousand dollars."

"What am I supposed to use?" Tara asked visibly shaken.

"Silver, gold, food, goods, or skills," he explained.

Tara stood up and paced off the porch, looking back at him slowly, her mind raced. "Isn't this a state of emergency? Is the National Guard and Red Cross and all of them handing out food and water and stuff?"

"I've heard rumors that they are active in the cities, but that's just rumors," he said quietly.

"But just a just a few weeks ago the news was saying that the cities were pulling out of the economic slump. They were encouraging people to move there because they needed an influx of workers."

Pete looked pained. "That wasn't a few weeks ago, that was a couple of months ago." Looking away he added, "Do you know how long I've been gone?"

Tara felt helpless and a bit panicky. That wasn't possible. She'd only had one period at the end of her first few days in the cabin. A messy affair that had cost her an entire pillowcase. Was she that malnourished? That stressed? At least she didn't have to worry about pregnancy. "What does time matter out here?" she told him dismissively.

His face was calm, as he replied, "It's been almost two months. It's nearly April."

Tara hiccuped a little sob, "How is that possible?" Tara couldn't help it as hot tears started trickling down her cheeks. She'd been out here alone for months, but it was such hell that it could have been years for all she knew. That was why she'd given such a conservative guess on the amount of time that had passed. She felt frozen outside of time itself. There had been days when she'd considered lying in bed until someone in the far distant future found her corpse. But Pete's arrival had shown her something she hadn't thought was possible. She'd been scared for her life. Her life still mattered. She still needed to live.

Pete sat in silence watching Tara's shoulders shudder, for at least ten minutes before he leaned in a little closer, "I'm sorry. I'm really uncomfortable. I don't know what you want me to say or do right now."

A choked laugh escaped Tara, "I don't know either."

"Good, so we're on the same page." Pete hesitated, "If you don't need me to help you with anything I should probably go."

"No," Tara shook her head, "take me with you."

"What do you mean?" Pete's eyes were wide with panic.

"I mean, take me to town. I can walk back home," she told him, drying her eyes.

"No, town's too dangerous. You'll be safer if nobody knows you're out here. Then nobody will come looking for you." He shook his head.

"Do you really believe nobody will come out here?" she asked. "If town's so scary what if something happens to you? What do I do when my food runs out? Do you expect me to lock myself in my cabin and starve? Besides, I need to see it. I need to, and if you won't take me to town, I'll go by myself. Into the unknown dangers, without a weapon, or anyone to help me."

"That's not fair." Pete grumbled, "I can't guarantee your safety in town."

"Will I be safer with you or all by myself?" she asked crossing her arms and looking at him pointedly.

"Fine," he huffed, getting up from the porch. "You want to go, let's go."

Tara was both thrilled and terrified, "I don't think I have anything to do any trading with. What sorts of things are they looking for in town?"

"Don't worry about it. I have some extras. We'll get you some basics if they're around." Pete headed for the bike and tied the gun's sheath under one of the saddlebags. "Do you have any pants you can wear?"

"You know I don't."

"Then tie that skirt up out of the way or tuck it into something," he gestured absently up and down her as if he wasn't sure or didn't care what she did with it.

Tara gathered the skirt up near her hips. Looking over cautiously she realized that Pete wasn't paying any attention to her. He was rearranging the bike's load to allow a passenger to ride comfortably. She tied the whole skirt into a big knot at her thigh so that it was now only long enough to cover her bottom.

Pete looked down at the knot. "Will it stay tied?" he asked.

"I think so."

"Good, have you ever been the passenger on a motorcycle before?"

"No actually."

He sighed. "Okay, you follow my lead. Don't fight the bike, don't lean out against me when we tip, its normal and part of the turning process. I don't want to eat it, that long underwear you're wearing is no match for pavement. Understand?" he asked throwing his leg over the bike.

Tara nodded

"Well, get on if you're going to," he instructed, pulling the bike upright. It seemed small for a motorcycle, and its tires reminded her more of a dirt bike now that she was really looking at it.

Tara slid one leg over the seat and was now a lot closer to Pete than she could ever remember being. Her thighs brushed his and she was suddenly very uncomfortable, and unsure of where to put her hands.

"You're going to want to hold on to me," he said sliding his helmet on. "Sorry I don't have another helmet. I'd give it to you, but I don't have any other eye protection."

"Not a problem," she murmured as the bike rumbled to life below her. Leaning forward she wrapped her arms around him slowly; trying to take everything in for fear that this wasn't real. She hadn't spoken to another human being in months nonetheless touched one.

Leaning in a little more as the bike started to idle down the driveway she noted he still smelled like leather and soap, but now there was a hint of wood smoke. As she wrapped her arms tighter, she was surprised by how solid he was. She honestly couldn't remember if they'd ever hugged before, she suspected they hadn't because he wasn't what she expected at all. A warm sensation tickled through her in a pleasant way when she realized that he smelled great and everyplace their bodies touched he was very firmly muscled.

Tara shook her head to dispel such foolishness. She was barking up the wrong tree. There couldn't have been a more wrong tree in the whole forest so there was no point in even starting to think that way.

It wasn't hard to shake those thoughts when Pete slowed down as they came into town. It really had changed. The most striking difference was the smell. The only scents Tara had ever associated with town were hot pavement and exhaust fumes, occasionally barbeque or chlorine. Now it was an evil-smelling mix of unwashed bodies, human waste, garbage, and manure; sweetened only slightly by the smell of wood smoke and cooking outdoors.

Besides the smell, it seemed everyone was outside. When Tara thought about that she sure hoped this wasn't everyone in the town. A plump woman with ashy skin hung laundry on a clothesline. A man emptied a bucket of what looked like urine into the gutter. Two men huddled over a fire stirring something in a pot. When they reached the center of town the church had its doors wide open and people who looked like bums milled about on the steps. As the motorcycle grumbled down Main Street Tara tried not to stare. Everyone they passed looked hungry, tired, or at least dirty. Pete stopped in front of what had, at one time in the town's distant past, been a bank.

Two men stood at the door, flanking it. The taller one with a shaved head stood with his arms crossed and an angry look on his face. A bandolier of bullets weighted across the front of his jacket and he wore an exceptionally large pistol on his hip. The shorter fellow looked a little younger and more weary than angry. He held a shotgun in both hands. The barrel pointed at the ground, but presumably ready to be pulled to attention at any moment.

The building was made of brick. The door was a heavy wood and the windows, one of which was already missing and boarded over, were covered by a heavy iron grating that was set into the masonry. Tara had driven past it more times than she could count and never really looked at it before. A large hand-painted sign that hung above the door, said simply, "Buy, Sell, Trade."

Pete dismounted and pulled his shotgun out of its sheath under the saddle bag. He broke the barrel and draped it over his arm in a swift movement. The men at the door didn't move. Pete walked towards them as if he were carefree and handed his shotgun to the taller fellow. Tara, on the other hand, was trying to make herself as small as possible while she untied her skirt and smoothed it down over her knees. Pete was shown through the door with a nod, but when Tara tried to follow him the big guy put his arm out across the doorway.

"I'm gonna need your weapons."

"I don't have any weapons," she answered quietly.

"Put your arms out. I'm going to have to search you," he replied gruffly.

Tara stared at him aghast, "You're going to touch me?"

"You wanna' go in or not lady?" the younger man asked.

"I don't know," Tara replied taking a step back.

"No funny business. I promise miss," the first guard soothed, "It's my job. Until Hannity trusts you, you get searched. Simple as that."

"He really won't try anything miss," the young guard snickered. "If you think this guy is big and tough, you should see his wife. She'd put an end to him real quick if she heard about him up here groping ladies."

Tara couldn't stop a smile, "fine." She stepped forward and held her arms out while the big guy quickly patted her around the waste, hips, and back. Then he stepped back and instructed her to run her hand between her breasts so that he could see there wasn't a gun there.

"Aren't you suppose to check my thighs too," she asked.

"He already did," the other guy grinned, "We watched you get off the motorcycle."

"Why would you be looking at me? I don't look dangerous," she asked confused.

"No," shotgun admitted, "but you have really nice legs." He nodded and looked at the taller guard who looked back at him with narrowed eyes.

"What have I told you? If you can't be polite, you can be quiet," the taller guard glowered. "I apologize if you were made uncomfortable in any way miss, you may enter." He held the door open. Pete waited just inside the door smirking.

CHAPTER 19

Inside, dust motes floated in the air and the room smelled like body odor, rusty metal, moth balls, and other things Tara couldn't identify. The room was full of tables and the walls were lined with shelves. The things piled near the door appeared to be mostly junk: balls of twine, chipped coffee cups, combs, and the like.

The entire wall to Tara's right could only be described as one long closet. Clothes were hanging on a bar, and stacked on the shelves above were hats, scarves, gloves, high heels, sneakers, and various other things. Along the entire left wall were tools of every variety and description.

Tara followed Pete towards the back of the room where her eyes focused on the three men at the long wooden counter about as far from the door as a person could get. As Pete and Tara got closer to the men the junk began to give way to cans of food, home canned jars of pickles, barrels, buckets, and even pillowcases of dried hulled corn, oats, and wheat. On the counter was a stack of cards saying things like, "1 block of cheese," and "1 quart of milk." Several baskets of eggs sat near the end of the counter.

Tara was avoiding looking at the most obvious thing in the room; the only man sitting. Maybe it was because he was watching her openly without apology. When she glanced at him he didn't look away and it made her uncomfortable, like he was at the top of the food chain and he knew it.

The men with him were standing on either end of the counter, both wearing pistols, but that was where their similarity ended. The one on the left was heavy with shockingly red hair. The one on her right looked like a typical blonde, high-school quarterback all the way down to his letterman's jacket.

Between them sat the lion with a winning smile, full of strait, shiny, white teeth. A salesman's smile. It only took a moment to realize his eyes were cunning. He'd been busy drinking in information about Tara since the moment she'd walked through the door. She figured it was time she appraised him back. His clothes were neat, neater than most, but they were work clothes. A red and black flannel shirt partially unbuttoned over a long-sleeved t-shirt, with the sleeves rolled up like he was going to go split some logs, instead of count change. His dark brown hair had veins of gray forming at the temples, and the depth of the lines around eyes and mouth are what made Tara guess he was in his middle or late forties. Honestly it was hard to tell. The man was reasonably handsome, and in fairly good shape, with only a slight thickness in the middle. A set of shoulder holsters flanked his chest and in them hung a pair of expensive-looking semi-automatic pistols that moved with each breath.

"It's good to see you, Pete!" the man called and his smile widened slightly as he turned his attention to Tara and thrust a large, calloused hand across the wooden counter. "Hannity, Jack Hannity," he introduced himself, "but I assure you nobody calls me Jack."

As Tara held out her hand he gingerly took her fingertips in his rough fingers, resting his thumb briefly across her knuckles he gave them a gentle squeeze. A lady's handshake.

"I'm Tara."

"Tara?" he asked inclining his head ever so slightly towards her as if he needed more information.

She paused a moment and considered giving him her maiden name, but since she was technically still married she opted for her legal name, "Hillcrest."

"It's nice to meet you Miz Hillcrest," he rubbed the back of his neck and stretched. "I don't mean to seem nosey," he flashed his brilliant smile, "but are you a local Miz Hillcrest?"

"Yes," she replied while she watched Pete lean against the counter, settling in. "Why do you ask?"

"Just because I don't like to seem nosey doesn't mean I'm not," Hannity shrugged. "A lot of people took off, a lot of others died, and a few are just passing through. I try to pay attention. I was just wondering why I hadn't seen you around town."

Tara watched him with suspicion which made him laugh, he could read her face like a book.

"Miz Hillcrest, I'm not trying to make a bad impression. I just like to keep track of what's going on in this town. Think of this building as a hub of sorts. I like to think it's my job to find you what you need. Just because it isn't on my shelves doesn't mean it's not available. If you need a blacksmith, I know an excellent fellow. A seamstress? I know one of those, too. Need to find something? I can keep an ear to the ground. Need to get rid of something? I might be able to find a taker." He smiled as he leaned across the counter on his elbow.

Pete rubbed the bridge of his nose and continued to watch the exchange. Tara found it unnerving how much watching Pete did. Turning back to Hannity she asked, "So, what do you get out of all this?"

He smiled a crooked smile. "That's the important question to ask someone isn't it? You're a smart one. What I get," he leaned closer, "is to watch this community's wheels keep turning a little while longer. I see needs get filled so we have less desperation and crime, but most importantly I get to know everything that's going on. At the end of the day that makes me sleep better. I have my fingers on this town's pulse so I see where she's heading."

"Are you the new mayor?" Tara asked

"Oh no," Hannity chuckled and shook his head, "I just have some respect in the community."

"Him, Farmer, and Pastor Richard are the most respected men in town," the football player uttered solemnly.

"A farmer?" Tara asked.

"Doctor Jim Farmer," Hannity corrected her, "He's a good guy, works on credit. He's normally over at the clinic if you ever need him for anything. He'll do his best by you; just make sure you bring someone to help, in case he's…" Hannity trailed off. "But that's not important now." Hannity shook his head.

"Hopefully I won't have much need of a doctor," Tara

smiled, "I've been learning herbalism."

Hannity leaned back in his seat and rubbed his chin briefly. "That's making medicine out of plants?" he asked, eyeing Pete.

"That's what I've been studying," Tara replied, unsure by the look on Pete's face if she'd said something wrong.

"You any good?" Hannity asked brushing some non-existent dust off the counter.

"I don't know. "I just study the notes I was left and the books I have. Though I do wish I could make some notes of my own."

"Why can't you make notes of your own?" Hannity asked, smooth as honey.

Tara looked momentarily embarrassed. "It's silly really. I don't have a pen."

Hannity let out a chuckle, "I haven't had many of those come through. People take them for granted. Let me think." Hannity scanned the shelves until he found a wooden box. It was carefully carved, but roughly finished. Hannity opened it to show her it contained a dip pen and a small jar of ink. "Apparently it was something a fella had for signing his wedding guest book that he never used. He traded it to me for a few eggs." He shut the lid.

"I'm afraid," Tara paused, "I don't have anything to offer you for that."

"This is on me. It should help you learn your trade and I appreciate the idea of a healer owing me a favor," Hannity assured her, holding out the box.

"I couldn't possibly," Tara shook her head.

"He's not kidding," Pete informed her, reaching out and taking the box for her. "He wants you to owe him a favor."

Hannity smiled his crooked smile again and Tara realized it was the one he used when something actually amused him.

"Now, is there anything you came in looking for?" Hannity asked Tara putting the salesman's smile back on.

"I didn't come with a list. Do you mind if we just look around?" Tara asked.

"Of course. But, keep in mind just because you don't see it doesn't mean I don't have it."

"I'll remember," she called to him as she headed towards the rack of clothing on the wall; surprisingly it was organized by size.

Pete trailed behind her and when she had found the section of her size he whispered into her ear, "That's one hell of a secret to be keeping."

Tara looked at him startled, "What are you talking about?" she asked quietly. To Hannity's credit when Tara looked at him, he flipped open some kind of ledger pretending to be busy.

"Are you really some kind of medicine woman?" Pete asked, shifting so he could talk with her face to face. Tara suspected it was also so they could stand in such a way that Hannity couldn't read their lips.

"I'm not sure I'd call myself that," Tara whispered to him, pulling a pair of jeans free from the rack and holding them up to herself. It was obvious that the cuffs were going to be too short, so she folded them back over the hanger.

"Forget what you call it, why didn't you tell me about it before we got here?" he hissed.

"I didn't think it was important. Rose gave me her notes in a ledger and some books on the subject before she left. There isn't much to do at night when you're alone other than study," she shrugged. "Didn't you wonder why I needed all of Rose's planters, or what was in that box of jars marked fragile?"

"I thought that was a bit eccentric of you to care about petunias at a time like that, but I thought it was because you were really attached to Rose."

"I am," Tara nodded, "but, Rose told me to take them all; that they were her medical garden."

"Do you have any idea what telling someone, especially Hannity about this means?" Pete asked.

"Not really?" Tara shrugged, smiling when she held a pair of pants up to herself that seemed long enough to cover her ankles. "Where does he put some kind of price on these?" Tara asked.

Pete rubbed his eyes, "The world doesn't work that way anymore. You're going to have to haggle. Stop changing the subject. What I was trying to tell you is that if you had some sort of dream of living a quiet life alone in the woods undisturbed, you'd better give it up now."

"Why is that?" Tara asked glancing around her.

"You just told the hub of information that you are the only person around that knows how to make medicine; a skill that even our good doctor doesn't possess. Do me a favor," Pete offered, "Let me do the talking when we leave. Hannity's going to want to keep you close. Unless you want that, I'll do what I can to keep where you're at a secret."

"How do you know so much about Hannity?" Tara asked.

"Because he pays me to be here a few days each week holding my gun."

Tara looked at him, startled. "You're a guard?"

"Normally a door guard, but sometimes I get a break and stand by the counter, or do patrols," he shrugged.

"Is that why you just left me out there?" Tara hissed.

Pete grinned. "Terry, that's the bald fellow, he's a pussycat. I knew he'd be a perfect gentleman. Didn't imagine you'd need me out there holding your hand."

"It didn't occur to you that I might have been scared?" Tara asked irritated.

"Of course it did, but you are the one who insisted I bring you, so I figured you were capable of talking to some door guards." Pete leaned in a little, "If you think Terry is the scariest thing you could come across in this town you are very mistaken. It's probably a lot safer here than anywhere else."

"How's that?" Tara asked.

"We'll have plenty of time to talk about it later," Pete assured her. "Let's get your shopping done so we can both get home before dark."

"I don't think it's right that you should have to pay for my things," she argued, looking at the jeans in her hand.

"I'm with Hannity on this one," Pete shrugged, "I like the idea of a healer owing me a favor."

"Is that all I am to you now?" Tara asked annoyed.

"No, but it's a bigger deal than you seem to think it is," Pete said, pulling a low-cut blouse off the rack and holding it up against her. Tara took it from him and hung it back up before pulling out a gray knit henley with long sleeves and three button in the front. It would be loose and comfortable to work in.

After some rummaging Tara asked Pete, "Where's the socks?"

"Socks? Nobody trades in socks, too hard to come by. It's amazing how much more walking everyone seems to be doing. Socks are kind of a commodity, like white sugar, or well, any food at this point."

"Doesn't matter. Kind of inconvenient though," Tara admitted. "Can you find me a sweater? Any color is fine, but I'll need to see the seams to see how it's put together. Wool or wool blend is best."

"What size?" Pete asked sliding down the rack.

"Doesn't matter. I'm just going to unravel it for yarn anyway."

Pete watched her for a moment, "You knit socks too I'm guessing?"

"Yeah, can't be that uncommon."

"I imagine not," Pete said watching her, "but, get two sweaters and if you make them both up into socks, you can pay your own way next time."

By the time Tara was finished with her shopping she had picked a pair of jeans, two men's sweaters in a neutral color palette, a gray shirt, a jar of molasses, and a few canned goods including two cans of fruit cocktail, one with extra cherries. Those were Pete's suggestion. Pete did the haggling, and even though Tara was fascinated by the process it made her feel tense just watching them. Oddly, the boys didn't seem the least bothered by it. Pete winked when Hannity called out to them before they made it out the door.

"Hey, I was thinking," Hannity said, as if whatever thought he was talking about had only just come to him, "I don't know where you're staying, but there are a few apartments that some of the fellas that work for me look after, just down the road from here. It would make it a lot easier on you… and your family, if you need a place."

"Don't worry," Pete assured him, "she has a place to stay."

"Well, I'd like to be able to send people who need her to find her, where is she?" Hannity asked absently brushing a couple of stray hairs off his forehead.

"I'd rather not send anyone to her," Pete told him. "If anyone needs her, you can send me to get her."

"That seems like a waste of time," Hannity sighed.

"Sir," Tara interrupted quietly, "I live alone. My husband deserted me." It gave Tara some small satisfaction to note that Hannity looked momentarily uncomfortable.

"My apologies miss," he said recovering quickly.

Pete glared at Tara briefly before continuing his debate, "It would be best if that didn't become common knowledge. Now can you see why I'm not comfortable sending any number of strangers to her home? There are courser elements who may take advantage of the lack of law and order around here. This is for the lady's protection."

"I can see your point, which is why she may be better off here where someone can keep an eye on her," Hannity argued, steepling his fingers in front of him as if praying for them to listen to reason.

"The lady's choices are her own," Pete insisted, "I think —."

"It was nice to meet you," Tara interrupted, turning and heading towards the door. She was tired of listening to the two of them arguing over her as if she was a child that needed to be minded. One more word and she was going to have a go at telling them both exactly what she thought about them.

"Yes, lovely to meet you. We'll see you again soon I'm sure," Hannity called back as she pushed the door open and stormed out.

Pete followed her out a moment later and took the shotgun that Terry handed back to him. Tara glared at him while she grabbed her skirt and began tying it roughly up into a knot.

"What an elegant debate," she scowled, "the subject of which happened to be how utterly helpless you both seem to think I am."

Pete's face broke into an infuriating half smile. "I'm assuming you want me to assure you that I have every confidence in your ability to defend yourself, but I don't." He didn't look away when her scowl deepened. "You might be happy to hear that it has nothing at all to do with you being of the fairer sex and entirely to do with the fact that unless you've had some serious training in the armed forces or law enforcement, I don't think you're ready for armed conflict. Even then, no one person is an army unto themselves. You can't always be watching your own back. Now," he added, throwing his leg over his motorcycle, "if you're going to continue trying to make me spontaneously combust with your eyeballs can you do it at the back of my head. I don't want to be on these roads alone at night either."

When Pete dropped her off at the cabin, true to his word he didn't stay; didn't even get off the bike, he just turned around and gave her a quick wave as he headed back down the driveway.

Alex had always said that Pete was honest, to the point of being blunt, an unapologetically straightforward man. Tara had thought it was silly. Pete was so quiet and always the first to lend a hand. Now she could see what Alex had been talking about. Pete seemed changed and Tara couldn't help wondering what had happened to him in the last few months. As she did the chores that evening, including washing her new pants, Tara wondered if she was the same woman she'd been six months ago.

CHAPTER 20

Tara could hear the motorcycle coming well before she saw it. Hurriedly she tied her hair back in a braid; that last time she'd gone for a ride it had taken her a long time to comb it out with her fingers. It was ridiculous, but she didn't even own a hairbrush. By the time the bike came to a stop in the yard she was sitting on the front step.

Pete pulled his helmet off and set it on the seat. "Are you armed?" he asked.

"Hello to you, too." Tara shook her head, "No, why?"

"You couldn't have been sure it was me and there you are just sitting on the front porch with no way to defend yourself," Pete admonished. "Are you wanting to get raped and killed?"

Tara cocked her head to the side. "Are you always such a mother hen?" she asked as she got up and walked toward him.

"This isn't a game," he hissed sternly, "I don't know why you seem to find this funny, but I'm being serious. You need to consider your safety more than you do."

Tara was smiling. "You finished?" she asked.

"No," he frowned.

"Doesn't matter. What you don't seem to understand is that this is my life. If I'm begging to be killed by some passing psycho by not being prepared it's my own business. If you've decided to be my father, I should warn you, nobody really liked him."

Pete's jaw clenched and the tendons in his neck stood out, "I'm sorry if I overstepped my bounds. I saw some things today I would sooner forget. It's not my intention to be so harsh." Pete's words were carefully measured.

"Are you out here because you missed me?" Tara teased.

"You are easily one of the most frustrating people I've ever met."

"Is that a no?"

"Hannity told me to come and get you," he said relaxing slightly.

"What's going on?" she asked, her demeanor immediately changed.

"One of his regulars came in looking for pain meds. She's not willing to see Doctor Farmer. Hannity thought you might go see if you can help her."

Tara felt momentarily panicky, but it passed quickly. What could it hurt? If she could help, great, if not, then maybe the woman would be willing to see the doctor.

"Oh, and I thought you might like these." Pete pulled two books out of his saddlebag.

Tara stepped forward feeling a bit guilty, "Survival medicine? What are these? Where did you get them?"

Pete ground the toe of his boot into the dirt while he glanced towards the woods. "I bought them when I got worried that something might be going wrong with the world, couple of years back. I thought you might get a lot from them since they are books about dealing with medical situations and emergencies in a SHTF situation."

"What is SHTF?" Tara asked

"Shit hit the fan."

"I guess it hit it good and proper already didn't it?" she said tracing the words on the cover of the book.

"It's absolutely everywhere," Pete grinned.

Packing the right supplies into Pete's saddlebags took her a lot longer than Tara had expected. She wasn't sure what she would even be doing. It was hard to pick what she should bring with her. When she finally felt she was ready Tara climbed onto the seat behind Pete. Thankfully, her denim insulated her slightly against their brief touches and she was much less self-conscious wrapping her arms lightly around Pete's middle. She smiled when she considered how deeply unfair it was that only one of them got to be made uncomfortable by this arrangement.

When they arrived at the address Hannity had given Pete it wasn't far from where Alex and Kate's house had been and, with a twinge, Tara realized how much she really missed them. The house itself was tiny with mint green siding and darkened windows, but thick smoke trickled out of a metal chimney pipe on the roof.

"You coming in?" Tara asked

"Nope, someone has to stay with our stuff." Pete dropped the kickstand and leaned against the bike like it was a chair.

"You just don't want to be in there," she grumbled.

"Nope, you won't see me making house calls anytime soon. You do what you do, if this is your thing, go, do it," he made a shooing motion.

Apprehensively Tara knocked on the cheap metal front door.

"Who are you and what are you after?" a woman's voice demanded from inside.

"My name's Tara," she hesitated, "Hannity sent for me to stop in and see you. He said you weren't feeling so well."

"You a friend of Doctor Farmer?" the voice inside asked.

Tara looked back over her shoulder at Pete who shrugged at her. "Actually I haven't had the chance to make his acquaintance yet."

"Good. You a doctor?"

"Nope just learning to be an herbalist," Tara admitted.

"That's plants and stuff right?" the door asked cautiously.

"Sure is. If you don't want me to be here, I can take off. I was just trying to be helpful," Tara called cheerfully.

A mumbling was quickly followed by the sound of the door being unlocked. The woman was young. Her slender frame was wrapped in a stained bathrobe and a very young boy with no pants on stood by her right knee. Her hair was disheveled and looked like it needed to be washed. The woman eyed her suspiciously before stepping back out of the doorway.

"Come on in," she said gesturing towards the couch.

Doing her best not to actually wrinkle her nose Tara followed the woman inside. The house smelled like smoke, with a light undercurrent of body odor, dirty socks, and stale urine. Tara's eyes followed the half-naked toddler and assumed that was the source of the latter.

"So," Tara said into the silence, "My name is Tara Hillcrest, it's nice to meet you...?"

"Susan," the woman muttered.

"It's nice to meet you Susan," Tara smiled, but the silence crept back into the room. After a terribly uncomfortable minute Tara decided that if she was going to do this she was going to have to practice her bedside manner.

"I hear that you haven't been feeling well," Tara prompted.

"Hurts to pee." Susan tied her robe tighter around her ribcage.

"Okay," Tara thought back to some of the things that she'd read. "Might be just a bladder infection, but have you had any unprotected intercourse lately?" Tara asked, trying to seem like it was the sort of thing she asked a complete stranger every day.

"You come to my house just to ask me if I'm one of them whores?" Susan asked irritably. "They're loathsome. It ain't no way to live. Only good Christian women until things get difficult. Well I can assure you that I ain't like that."

Tara was at a loss momentarily. "I never meant any offense," Tara paused, "I wasn't trying to imply anything. Just an important question to ask when dealing with the urinary system. I don't have the tools the doctor has. I just have to listen to what you tell me. It will help me narrow down what might be wrong."

"I ain't been with a man since Doc Farmer killed my husband," Susan glowered.

Tara looked at her abruptly, "He what?"

"You heard me, he murdered my husband," Susan spat the words out like they physically hurt.

At a loss Tara took a couple of deep breaths waiting for the woman to continue.

"You look like you don't know anything about what happened with the doctor," Susan smirked, "If you can call him that."

"I don't actually," Tara shook her head.

"Really?"

"Yeah, sorry."

Susan narrowed her eyes at Tara before she pressed forward. "About a month ago a fever and spots came to town. It was doing a lot of damage around here, but since the trucks weren't running they couldn't get any antibiotics in. So the Doc started rationing. He got to pick who got some and who didn't. Eventually he said he was only treating children, but I'm betting that he gave medicine to anyone who had enough for a bribe. He looked at my husband, weak as a baby, and said no, that he wouldn't treat him. Obviously, just because he didn't do the deed with his own hands, doesn't mean he didn't kill my husband."

Susan paused long enough to pick her son up and put him on her lap. "When supplies ran low he came and collected up donations of antiseptic for his instruments, 80 proof or higher. Now he sits around killing people and drinking up those donations. I hear he kills lots of people now. Guy died of gangrene couple weeks ago, after getting a cut stitched up. He ain't nothing but a butcher."

"I can see why you would be so upset," Tara soothed, but secretly Tara's heart ached for the doctor. If what this woman said was even partially true he'd had to watch a lot of people die because he wanted to give the children the best possible chance for survival. It would have been a hard call to make.

"This is going to sound like a strange question," Tara paused, "Do you have a clear glass container that you could give me a urine sample in?"

Susan's brow furrowed, "Like something sterile, you have a test kit?"

"Nothing so exact. In my teacher's notes she says that a bladder infection can often be diagnosed by viewing the urine with a strong light behind it."

"Whatever floats your boat. Let me go pee in a jelly jar for you," Susan sighed, walking out of the room.

Tara sat uncomfortably on the couch arranging and rearranging her hands while she listened to Susan wince and then let out a little moan from the other room. When she came in she carried a couple of inches of dark-colored urine in a jar. Tara held it up to the light and it was quite cloudy with an off-odor. It was so concentrated that she couldn't make out if there was any trace of blood.

"I feel fairly safe saying that you have a bladder infection." Tara handed her back the jar. "I also feel very safe saying that you need to drink a lot more liquid to flush this from your system than you are."

"If you knew how much it hurts to pee, you wouldn't ask me to do that. It's a little like pushing knives out. I'm not going to be doing that."

"I've had a bladder infection before," Tara confided softly, "You're right, it's a little slice of Hell on Earth. If you don't flush this from your system it can turn into a kidney infection, and then possibly kidney failure which, from what I hear, is an unpleasant way to die."

Susan looked at her. "That supposed to be funny?" she asked, "Cause, it's not."

"No. It's me trying to get you to understand how serious something like this can be. You need to drink. A lot. If your urine isn't clear when it comes out you're not drinking enough to deal with this."

"Can't you just give me something that will make this go away?" Susan complained.

"I'll give you something to help, but we don't live in the same miraculous world of medicine we did anymore. You can't sit down, take a pill, and expect to be all better. You have to be active in making yourself better; we probably should have been all along," Tara admitted the last part mostly to herself. "In the meantime I'd recommend that, if you can't wear loose cotton panties that are very clean, don't wear any at all. Drink so much that you decide you hate me and do what you can to acidify your urine. I doubt you have any cranberry juice, but it would be best. You can also use vitamin C tablets if you have any. If not, the notes say a couple of tablespoons of vinegar in water. Urinate frequently and try to keep the area very clean and dry. Do you have a small clean jar?" Tara asked.

"Sure," Susan said heading for the kitchen.

When Susan handed it to her Tara thanked her and told her she was going to go mix up a tincture.

"Did you get her all patched up?" Pete asked when Tara got back out to the bike.

"Move your butt; I need in the saddle bags. I'm going to mix her up some medicine," Tara said, shooing him away. She dug out Rose's ledger and flipped a few pages. Then she slid her fingers along the page while she read. "Yarrow and poke root for bacterial infections," she mumbled to herself.

"Not really any of my business I suppose, but isn't poke root poisonous?" Pete asked from where he hovered behind her.

"Actually, yes it is. That's why I'm measuring out only a tiny amount. It's dosed by the drop."

"Isn't giving people poison dangerous?" Pete asked peering over her shoulder while she measured out enough yarrow for seven days, while guessing Susan to be about one hundred and fifteen pounds.

"Sure is, that's why all pharmaceuticals were so closely monitored. The difference between helping and harming for a lot of things is very often an intricate game of amounts," Tara shrugged. "Most of the medicines that Rose used were completely safe and, in some cases, just food, but it says that this is the best thing for a bacterial infection. I'll trust her." Tara screwed the lid back onto the jar in her hand.

"Good luck."

Back inside, Susan took the jar while Tara wrote down the dosing directions on Susan's phone messages pad.

"Do you have enough clean water?" Tara asked, looking around. If she had to guess, water was harder to come by in town than it was at her house.

"Actually, if you could bring me some back from Hannity's I'd really appreciate it," Susan said handing her a bucket.

"Hannity makes you buy water?" Tara asked shocked.

Susan gave her a strange look, "Do you live in a cave? Where did you say you were from exactly?"

"Sorry, I don't live in town."

"Hannity had a well drilled near his store. It's free to anyone who needs it, but you have to plump it yourself. His guards watch the well; they make sure it stays free," Susan told her slowly, like she was talking to someone who doesn't speak the language.

"Well, then, we'll get you some and then be on our way." Tara headed towards the door.

"Wait! you didn't name your price," Susan said, chewing on the inside of her lower lip.

Tara thought about it for a few minutes, "You wouldn't happen to have a spare hairbrush would you?"

"Only about a dozen why?" Susan asked confused.

"I don't have one. I would take that as payment." Tara smiled.

"Seems pretty cheap for a doctor." Susan watched her with narrowed eyes.

"I'm not a doctor. I have no formal medical training," Tara smiled kindly. "I'm just making my best guess at how to help you. Besides, I need a hairbrush."

"Suit yourself," Susan said walking out of the room. Tara heard cabinet doors opening and things being moved around. When Susan came back in the room she was holding a wooden brush and comb. "It's the nicest one I have. It's boar's bristle," she explained, holding it out.

"Thanks, it's perfect," Tara smiled, carrying them and the bucket out to where Pete waited so they could bring Susan back some water.

While Pete pumped the water, Tara leaned against the building watching him. He made it seem easy but Tara's experiences pumping water were anything but that. She didn't mind not being the one to do it. While she picked at a fingernail she decided she had to ask, "Hey Pete?"

"Yeah?" he paused looking up at her.

"When I asked Susan about her sexual history she got really agitated and went off about whores who use to be good Christian women in town. What's she talking about?"

Pete looked down at the ground trying not to smile. "Are you sure you want to know?" he asked.

"Would I have asked if I didn't want to know?" Tara asked him irritably.

Pete picked up the bucket and carried it back to the bike, setting it on the rack behind the back seat and bungee strapping it down. "When the economy fell apart a lot of people were left starving. A few women in the area decided that they would rather give up their dignity than their lives, and often they have children to feed. So, some of them, ah," he paused looking for a way to put it delicately, "entertain men, in exchange for food."

"They sell themselves?" Tara asked shocked.

"Yup, sometimes for a little as a single can of food," Pete said sliding back onto the seat.

"Why would anyone do that?" Tara asked.

"If you're asking about the women, you've obviously never been worried about your kids starving. If you're asking about the men, you obviously don't have a lot of experience with men. Look," he said pointing to a house down the road, "That one does it."

"How can you tell? Or is it personal experience?" Tara

smirked.

"Yuck!" Pete frowned, "No. See the broom resting, bristles up, next to the door. It's like putting out a sign."

"I'll keep that in mind." Tara mounted the bike behind him. "Now, drive this thing easy. I don't want to end up soaked."

When they were back at Tara's home, she climbed off the bike and looked at Pete.

"Why didn't you tell me about the sickness?" Tara asked him, standing in front of the bike with her arms crossed.

"To be one hundred percent honest with you, I didn't really deal with it," Pete shrugged, pulling his helmet off.

"Did you isolate yourself?" Tara asked confused.

"In a manner of speaking… I wasn't really around much," Pete admitted.

"What does that mean?" Tara asked him growing irritated. "Sometimes you're the bluntest guy in the world, and others you're so obscure I can't make heads or tails of what you're hinting at."

"Well, Miss Grumpy, it's a long story and it's cold out here. We can go inside and have a cup of tea or we can talk about it later."

"I can offer you cold goat milk or water. Hot goat milk isn't very good in my opinion, but I suppose you can have that too," Tara sighed, heading up the steps and unlocking the front door before walking through.

"Cold goat milk is fine," he called from the doorway behind her.

Looking around, Tara felt deeply exposed. Her laundry hung to dry all across one end of the room. Her underwear prominently displayed along the line. On the table sat the leather journal her mother had bought for her. Open and still empty.

Pete didn't help. He paced around the room, not even attempting to hide the fact that he was looking at her things. When he was fanning through the pages of her empty journal she decided she'd had enough.

"Would you like to have a seat," Tara gestured towards the bed.

Pete raised an eyebrow and a small smile played at the edges of his mouth. "Are you trying to get me into bed?" he asked teasingly, "I should warn you I'm not that kind of man."

"Don't you worry your pretty little head, I wouldn't dream of trying to take advantage of you," Tara assured him. "Just think of it as the poor woman's couch. Unless it's escaped your notice," she gestured around the room. "I have no other seating."

"In that case," Pete said as he made himself comfortable half sitting, half sprawled across her bed. Obviously his reservations were all pretend.

Tara poured a cup of goat milk and handed it across the bed to him before she perched lightly on the edge of the mattress on the opposite end of the bed. "So tell me the long story,"

Pete looked at her and drank the cup of goat milk, handing her back the cup before he stripped his leather jacket off and tucked it and her pillow underneath him.

"It's a bit chilly in here," he said chafing his arms with his hands before pulling himself to his feet to open the door of the stove. Pete poked the fire and fed a couple of logs in adjusting the damper slightly.

"Are you finished?" Tara asked while he made himself comfortable on the bed again.

"Helping you?" he sniffed. "Yeah, with that attitude I think so."

"Stalling. Either tell me or don't, just quit with the suspense already."

CHAPTER 21

"This starts sometime around the beginning of the great recession," Pete said focusing on the ceiling instead of Tara.

"This really is going to be a long story isn't it?" Tara asked.

"Do I get to tell it or not?"

"Be my guest." She scooted back to lean against the wall.

"When the recession hit I started to worry about the fragility of our world. I lost most of my money market account and my 401K. If it could wipe me out I wondered what it was doing to everyone else. Anyway, it got me interested in the news, but the news sounded so insincere that I started looking at alternative media. Once I was there it became extremely apparent that something wasn't right in this world. Some of what I found was definitely sensationalist drivel, but when I started looking at the bigger picture, it was a bit frightening."

"Eventually I got talking about this with a guy who I met at the bulk store. He'd bought a little piece of land about an hour south of here. It turned out he was part of a survivalist community, so this fella' and I exchanged numbers and we kept in touch for a while."

"A couple of months later he invited me to come meet the group. They were an interesting bunch, and not the people you would expect. I assumed they would be a bunch of camo-wearing gun-nuts. In reality it was a lawyer, a couple of home-makers, some ex-military guys, a sales clerk, and a couple of guys who worked in the same insurance office. We had a potluck supper and discussed the sorts of items a person would want to have as trade in a post-apocalyptic world."

"That sounds interesting," Tara nodded.

"Funny thing is we got most of it wrong," Pete admitted, "Turns out toilet paper isn't the big deal we thought it was going to be. Neither is hand sanitizer. Most people are a lot more concerned about other things."

"I can imagine," she admitted, thinking of the journal hung from a hook in her outhouse.

"Really it's booze, lighters, any kind of food, and that sort of thing. A can of beans makes you a wealthy man." Pete sighed.

"Speaking of which, do you want some dinner?" Tara asked gesturing to the pot of beans she'd left simmering on the stove that morning. These were better than usual. The molasses they'd picked up at Hannity's made this practically baked beans.

"Absolutely."

After they had finished eating Pete continued, "After our introductions I started going to meetings when I could. We got together and went to the shooting range, or to take a self-defense class, we even went on a couple of survival camping trips. Those was pretty eye-opening for a couple of the people involved. It's amazing how many people in this world have never gutted a squirrel."

"You can count me among them," Tara admitted sheepishly.

Pete nodded. "I suspected as much," he continued, "We had agreed on pooling our skills and living on the same piece of land if things genuinely went bad to help each other build a community. Towards this goal, all of us were asked to convert a certain percentage of our money into silver so that we'd have a workable currency inside the group. We were also asked to have a certain amount of food on hand, and buy certain preps, we split the big things with a list. I began in earnest to convert what savings I did have into these things that I was going to need, then I worked extra hours whenever I could to buy more; above and beyond what I was required to have. As things got worse and especially when I saw you and your..." Pete stopped, and began again looking embarrassed, "When I saw my friends struggling I knew things were about to get bad."

"Okay," Tara nodded. At this point her financial troubles,

and even Jasper, seemed a long time ago in a different life, but she appreciated Pete's delicacy on the matter.

"When the world went dark the internet and phones went down and the gas pumps stopped running. I knew it was time to go so I boarded up my house and packed half of my preps."

"Why half?" Tara asked.

"Partially because I am not a trusting guy and partially because it was all that would fit on my truck. The things I left behind I hid. I gutted my washer and dryer and put food and supplies in the shells, did the same with the furnace. I even filled the ductwork anywhere I thought it was strong enough. When I got there I was nearly the last to arrive, and we were in the process of setting up shelter. We started out in a large military tent with a stove. It was awful, but we were spending the days building our community center out of logs like early American settlers. That's where all the food was going to be stored and where the fella who had gathered us was going to live, let's call him Mister Smith."

"You're not going to tell me his real name?" Tara asked surprised.

"Do you need to know it?" Pete countered.

"No."

"Then, no, I'm not. Stop interrupting," Pete retorted. "The moment the roof was on Mister Smith's community center he moved all our food inside where he kept it under lock and key. At first it seemed prudent to keep it safe. Then it became apparent that when we each finished our own places our food wasn't going to be returned to us. Mister Smith said that he thought it was best for the community if we were each given a daily ration from the collected supplies. That didn't sit very well with me since I brought more than my fair share, but I understood others who tried and failed to do as well as I did shouldn't suffer. Next, he collected up our silver and redistributed it evenly. Thankfully I left most of mine hidden. I still got back less than he took, and I feel comfortable saying he didn't give everyone an equal share, since all of us had less than we'd come with. When he told us we'd be pooling our guns and ammo, I packed what I had left and got the hell out of there."

"Really? Why?"

"Because that's what you would do before you kill people and keep everything for yourself," Pete answered gravely.

"You really think that was the plan?"

"I wasn't going to take any chances." Pete went quiet, as if her statements had completely derailed his story.

Tara waited listening to the silence before she cleared her throat and continued. "You know where their survival community is and they just let you leave?"

"They didn't let me anything. I nearly had to run Mister Smith down to get past him." Pete shuddered. "I was offered many assurances that if I ever returned I would not be welcome and very likely wouldn't survive the encounter."

"That's awful," Tara said tucking her feet under her.

"We all live with our own choices," Pete shrugged. "I thought I was doing the smart thing at the time. Just turned out not to be."

"Why didn't you ever tell anyone about the group?" Tara asked.

"Why didn't you tell anyone about your power being turned off, or Melody?" Pete inclined his head towards her.

His point was clear; so she nodded, but didn't say anything because she didn't want him to have an excuse to change the subject.

"Actually I did tell Alex at one time, but he didn't take me seriously. You have to admit that when that prepper show came out, preppers became kind of a joke." Pete looked as his hands. "I didn't really want my friends to see me that way."

"That's why I was so mad at Jasper when he told you about our money trouble." Tara stretched and paced over to look at the fire and adjust the stove's damper.

"I got that impression. There's no shame in it you know." Pete spoke softly now. "Being one of the early victims of a failing economy doesn't make you a failure. We're all in the same boat now."

"I know," Tara admitted. "It seems silly how much I wanted

to hide it now. I just wish I'd been better prepared." She fed a small log into the stove. "I have a question," she asked after a pause.

"What's that?"

Tara wandered over to the window after glancing at Pete, still sprawled on her bed. "Why did you help me before you left?" she asked as a crow landed in the treetop she was looking at. Silence sat heavy and pregnant in the room, but Pete didn't answer. "Did you hear me?"

"I heard you. I don't want to hurt your feelings."

Tara was surprised by this. Pete was blunt. It was in his nature. "Okay?"

"Honestly?" he asked.

"Yes," Tara answered before she had time to reconsider. Could it really be so bad?

"I felt sorry for you. Everyone abandoned you and you didn't have anything left. But mostly, oh, this is going to sound really bad. You know what, never mind, it's not important," he shook his head.

"Please?"

Pete took a deep breath. "When you told me you owned your own place I wanted you to owe me a favor just in case things fell through with my survival community. Just in case something happened to my house. I wanted somewhere to go and some food to already be there."

"How practical of you."

"Sorry."

"So it had nothing to do with friendship?"

"Not really," he admitted, "I hardly knew anything about you. You have to admit, we were never close. Truth be told, I thought you and Jasper were avoiding me."

Tara hadn't meant to giggle but she couldn't hold it in. To say that she and Jasper were avoiding Pete was an understatement.

"Did I say something funny?"

"No, it's just an inside joke."

"Inside of what?" Pete seemed confused.

Tara leaned on the wall behind her. "Nothing anymore." She

absently rubbed the spot where her wedding ring had once been. "Thanks for telling me. I was wondering why you were so willing to help me. I feel better knowing. You seem less suspicious." Tara smiled.

"Good, it's a relief not to have to hide all my mustache twirling and maniacal laugher anymore," Pete teased.

Tara glanced out the window. The sky was streaked with orange.

Pete followed her gaze and leapt from the bed. "Thanks for dinner," he offered quickly as he headed out the door.

Tara stared at him open-mouthed as he pulled his helmet on in the yard and started the bike. He was on his way down the driveway without hesitation.

"Goodbye, goodnight, and all that crap to you too," Tara mumbled to the window as he disappeared from sight.

CHAPTER 22

Pete visited routinely over the next few weeks to take Tara to town so she could help wherever she was needed, so she wasn't surprised to see his motorcycle pull up the driveway. The noon sun shone warmly on Tara's shoulders as she went to greet Pete, when he pulled off his helmet she could tell he was grinning broadly.

"What's going on?" Tara asked wiping her hands on her dress to dry them. She'd been out washing up after trying to turn over a section of her yard that she hoped would become a small herb garden.

"I have a surprise for you," Pete beamed, brushing some of the road dust off his pants. "Let's go."

"I hope it's a good surprise and not another case of projectile vomiting and diarrhea like the last time you took me to town. That house had a smell I won't soon forget," Tara answered squinting at him. "Aren't you supposed to be at the shop today?"

"Patrol actually," he clarified, gesturing towards the house. "Go change. You'll want pants," he smiled. "It's an amazing surprise, I promise," he assured her after he saw the look on her face.

"Pete," Tara squeaked. "We need to talk about your definition of amazing if we make it out of here alive!"

Pete had dragged her into a house in town with broken, boarded-up windows where he assured her nobody lived. She hadn't known what to expect, but this certainly wasn't it. The droning noise coming from across the attic space they were standing in was making her stomach quiver.

Pete was crouching next to her with a radiant smile on his face and a hand on her arm to keep her from turning to run away.

"They're beautiful aren't they?" he asked without looking at her and ignoring her previous statement.

"Pete," she whispered, "That's a lot of bees, a really lot of bees in a tiny little space, right here closed in with us."

"They're not closed in," he gestured to the window to their right, "They're coming and going. It's how I found them in the first place."

Admittedly Tara hadn't noticed the window. How could she? She hadn't looked at anything but the cluster since Pete pulled her to a crouch just inside the door of the attic to keep her from running back down the stairs.

"Okay, I'm surprised. It's a surprise. Can we go now?" Tara asked.

"Why would we go? It's an amazing opportunity."

"What's amazing is that you want to stand in a room full of bees," she hissed.

"I thought you'd be happy too," Pete frowned. "Honey is medicine, isn't it?"

"Well yeah," Tara hesitated. "Honey is antiseptic and the wax is used in making salves and things," Tara admitted.

"See," Pete nudged her.

"You're right. Now we know where some bees are," Tara nodded, "and we'll find someone to bring us honey and wax when they pull these babies out of here."

"Not even close. It's better than that. We get our own hive."

"How is that exactly?" Tara asked, dread flowing over her like a physical force while she waited for his response.

Pete reached over and slid a tightly-woven, lidded basket towards her. "Hannity already found me a Langstroth hive. I don't have any foundation for the frames, but they'll build their own eventually. They'll be our bees, because it's a hive that can be kept out at your place where they'll be safe."

"Please tell me that basket contains a tiny beekeeper who is about to tell us to wait outside while he takes care of this," Tara whimpered.

"Nope."

"Are you trying to get us killed? After all this grumbling at me about not protecting myself from lunatics? You, the lunatic, are going to get me killed by insects."

"You're not allergic are you?" Pete asked quickly.

Tara thought about lying just for a moment, but he read her face too quickly, she could tell by his smirk. "No," she grumbled.

"Well then, thanks for your vote of confidence, but I have skills you know nothing about."

I'm sure you do, Tara thought wryly. "Okay, but do these skills include attacking giant swarms of stinging insects?" she asked. "Because there are millions of those things over there."

"It's probably less than twenty thousand. Stop exaggerating," Pete soothed.

"Never mind… that makes all the difference in the world. Why didn't you say so in the first place? Let's go do this."

"You just have to be calm and know what you're doing," Pete instructed, pulling a small bundle of grass, cloth, and a strange-looking can out of the basket.

"Oh, good, then I'm not qualified."

"You won't be able to say that after today,"

"Pete, when it's just me against one of these with a rolled up newspaper, I'm still outmatched. Why would anyone want to take on an army?"

"Let's start by not swatting these," Pete warned her, lighting the wad of stuff he was holding and pushing it down into the can. There was some sort of bellows on the side and a hinged lid. "This isn't an army of bees," Pete clarified. "It's a colony. They are not interested in you unless you are threatening their hive, and they are amazingly tolerant of intrusion. Just don't start smashing bees, flailing around, or ripping things apart and they will barely notice you're here."

"I have a hard time believing that."

"Then let me show you." He'd been pumping the bellows on the side of the can until a bright flame jumped out the top. Then he closed the lid which had a spout and some thick white smoke immediately started rolling out.

"What's that?"

"A smoker for the bees. I was told that it keeps them calm because they produce a smell that tells the other bees that something is wrong. This smoke masks the smell, so they don't panic. I'm not sure if it's true," he admitted as he puffed smoke experimentally out of the spout with the bellows, "but it seems to work just the same."

Tara watched Pete approach the cluster slowly and begin wafting puffs of smoke on them. The first puff made them begin roaring even louder than they were before. Tara held her breath waiting for Pete to be engulfed by an angry cloud of bees. Instead he stood calmly with his face just a foot from the cluster looking at it. Turning to Tara he brushed his fingertips lightly down the side of a mass of bees. Still nothing happened to him. When he concentrated the smoke on the side, the bees pulled back to reveal some comb.

The comb didn't look anything like Tara thought it would either. It was white, not the deep yellow she'd expected. Instead of the rectangle that is always shown in pictures, it was a small disc the size of a saucer. With slow, steady movements Pete put his hand on the bottom of the comb and Tara cringed as bees began to crawl on his hand. Then he slid a knife out of his pocket and ran it across the top slowly, separating the comb from the rafter above. He brushed the bees into the basket with the side of a feather, and then set the comb aside before replacing the lid.

"That's all uncapped honey and pollen," he told her, licking his fingers. "It can't be stored, but that honey can be eaten right away or fed back to the bees."

"How do you know how to handle bees?"

Pete paused in the removal of another comb. "My grandad had some hives. I used to work them with him. None of the other grandkids would go near them so it was something just the two of us did together," Pete smiled at the memory. "He always told me that you couldn't work bees if you didn't respect women, and I thought it was the oddest thing to say," he paused to look at Tara before continuing, "Did you know that all the work done in the hive is done by women? The queen is the mother of the whole hive and without her they all die. The nurse bees, guards, scouts, honey, and pollen collectors… they're all female." While he spoke he turned his hand over to look at a bee moving busily along his palm.

"What about the boys?" Tara asked.

"The drones get all fat on honey and wait for a chance to mate a queen." Pete shrugged, and then smiled. "Actually they are such a burden that they're thrown out of a hive before winter so they don't have to be supported."

"Are you teasing me right now?" Tara asked.

"No, it's true. Do you want to see something beautiful?" He gestured her closer.

Seeing Pete stand in the group of bees without harm gave Tara a bit of courage. Her stomach had relaxed out of her throat without her even noticing, so she inched closer. "Pete?" she said, but froze when a bee buzzed near her face.

"You're fine," Pete reassured her.

"Pete," Tara began again, taking another slow step forward, "have you ever kept your own bees?"

"Yeah, briefly, but I lost them to colony collapse," Pete answered gesturing for her to squat down. When she did, Pete began wafting smoke on the bottom of the cluster. Tara knew that bees built combs in orderly lines, like in hives. But, this wasn't that at all. It looked like it had been planned and built by a bunch of drunk insects that liked surrealism. Combs bent and swirled organically around each other.

"How are you going to put that stuff in a hive?" Tara asked moving back to where she had started from.

"I'm not," Pete admitted. "I'm only going to keep the comb with a lot of babies for the hive. Those I'll wrap in to the frame with a light gauge wire. The rest I'm just pulling so that I can get the bees off them, and keep the honey and wax. Hopefully this way I'll get the queen in the basket. If I lose her, miss her, or squish her, we don't have a hive."

"Who'd have thought one bee in all of those is so important?"

Taking the cluster out of the attic took a lot longer than Tara had expected because every movement had to be slow and precise. There was nothing rushed or haphazard about what Pete did. By the time he'd gotten the last comb brushed off into the basket a cluster had formed on the bottom of the lid that he'd been replacing every time.

"That's probably the queen." He pointed at the cluster. When they left he tied the lid down tight and stuffed strips of fabric into the crack to keep all the bees securely inside. Back at Pete's house they loaded the truck with the basket of bees, a stack of white boxes with no bottoms, a lot of little wooden frames, and more pieces than Tara imagined would be in one of those simple-looking hives. There was a bottom screen and a board that slid out under it, an inner flat cover, an outer cover with metal on it for the roof, a feeder, and even a notched stick that Pete called an entrance reducer, though its necessity seemed unclear.

In just a short time they found themselves back at Tara's place and Pete had picked a sunny open spot on the edge of the clearing to set everything up. Pete had assured Tara that an angry swarm of bees wasn't going to fly out and kill them when the lid opened. But watching them calmly walk up the ramp he'd set up to go into the hive was something she had to see to believe. Pete crushed some of the comb and put the feeder full of the honey on the front of the hive. He told her that with frames of their brood wired in that it would smell like home so they shouldn't all fly away. Tara guessed they would have to wait and see.

For days after Pete left, Tara would find herself standing in front of the hive watching bees come and go through the entrance and the feeder full of honey get drained until it was clean. The hive made a peaceful hum and, on a warm day, it was a pleasure to lay in the grass and watch bees busily wandering in and out. The ones coming in had bulging yellow or orange sacks on their legs. Then others would come back out and drift into the sky, circling upwards until they were lost in the trees.

On such a day while Tara lay dozing in the grass near the hive Pete returned.

"Hey sleepy, where's your weapon?" he asked as she yawned and stretched on the ground.

"I was counting on my attack bees to protect me," she quipped with a pointed look while he scowled.

A low sound somewhere between a snort and a growl rumbled in him like a war was going on in his throat for control over what was going to come out of his mouth. Common sense appeared to have won out because instead of scolding her he took a deep breath and said, "Hannity sent for you. He's got someone for you to see."

"I don't normally do women." The young blonde who opened the door looked Tara up and down disdainfully. "But I guess I'm willing if you're willing to pay."

Tara's eyes traveled from the top of the bristles of the broom down to the handle on the ground. She should have expected something like this the moment she set foot on the porch and saw the thing, but until that moment she'd forgotten its meaning.

Tara glared back over her shoulder at Pete who shrugged. "My name's Tara," she said turning back and extending her hand, "Hannity sent me." The woman standing in front of her seemed familiar, but Tara was having a hard time placing her. She had thick garish make-up, unruly greasy hair, and was dressed in skin tight clothing that made her look like she was carrying a few extra pounds.

The woman looked at Tara's extended hand as if Tara had rubbed it in horse manure on the way to the door. "You're not what I was expecting, but you might as well come in anyway."

"Thanks." Tara stepped in and took a deep breath to steady her temper. She instantly regretted it. The inside of the house smelled terrible, like a backed-up sewer pipe.

"Sit," the woman gestured towards the couch which sat in the middle of a sea of trash in the living room.

"Thanks," Tara repeated with a little nod while she picked her way into the room.

"My name's Elizabeth," the woman said as she slid into a greasy-looking chair across from the couch and lit a cigarette. "Sorry, I'd offer you one," she said giving the cigarette a little wave, "but, after what I had to do to get it, I'm not willing to share. Sorry honey."

"No worries," Tara assured her as she fought to keep the disgust out of her voice. "I never was a smoker." Tara perched lightly on the edge of the couch, touching as little of it as she could manage without actually hovering above it.

"God, you're one of those health nuts aren't you?" Elizabeth asked rolling her eyes. The gesture was an exaggerated movement that made the woman's face look like a caricature under the cartoonish make-up. Tara stared, she hadn't meant to, but Elizabeth caught her and grinned in the uncomfortable silence, she was obviously missing her front teeth.

"I see the way you're looking at me," Elizabeth squinted at Tara. "You're thinking about my offer aren't you?"

"No."

"Don't kid yourself honey, everyone wants a ride," Elizabeth bit her lip and blew Tara a kiss.

"What did you need to see me about?" Tara wanted nothing more than to stand up and rush out of the house to someplace that the air was breathable and where this woman wasn't.

Elizabeth ignored Tara's question. "I can't have kids, that's a big seller now, and I don't turn nobody away." Elizabeth squeezed her breast while licking her lips. "I take 'em all. Skinny, fat, old, dirty, married, crippled... I don't care as long as I get paid. There's not much I won't do," she said the last bit with a proud smile. "Like I said, you don't want to know what I did for these cigarettes."

Tara was sure that she didn't want to imagine. "So, what's the problem that I might be able to help with?" Tara asked replacing the smile she'd allowed to slip from her face.

"This," the woman said kicking her knees apart and lifting her skirt.

Tara fought the urge to look away as Elizabeth pointed out the sores with her dirty fingertips. On the girl's left inner thigh was a tattoo of a purple feather. It's seemed ridiculous in the context and Tara's mind's eye imagined some disgusting purple bird inside the girl's most personal inner recesses. What the hell?

"If I had to guess," Tara paused, pushing her memory back through the pictures in the books Pete had given her and away from that disturbing bird, "I'd say it looks like herpes."

"Yeah, well, get rid of it," Elizabeth commanded, still holding her skirt aloft.

"It's not something you get rid of."

"Fine, can you at least get rid of the sores? They're bad for business," the woman demanded shoving her skirt down.

Tara fought the urge to yell at her. "You do know that you can spread that to other people?"

"The person who gave it to me didn't care and, I promise you honey, I don't either." Elizabeth put her cigarette out just before the filter and smiled with a raised eyebrow as if daring Tara to say something else.

"Do you have a jar?" Tara asked.

"Yeah, I just finished one of those little bottles of whiskey. One of my favorites gave it to me. God he's a big boy." Elizabeth smiled at Tara's discomfort while she dug into a small heap of refuse next to the chair she was sitting in. "Will this do?"

Several roaches had scattered and were still running in jagged lines across the living room. Tara nodded without looking at the container that Elizabeth held out to her. If it had held alcohol it was probably the cleanest thing in the room.

Tara dug in the pillowcase of supplies she'd brought with her for Rose's ledger and after skimming a few pages she pulled out a bottle of red oil. "I'm going to give you this because, if your sores are healed, you're less likely to spread the disease. But it doesn't guarantee anything." Slowly Tara poured some hypericum oil into the whiskey bottle. "Apply this topically, three times every day until the sores heal. Do it again any time they return," Tara sighed handing the bottle full of oil to Elizabeth, who snatched it with her grubby fingers.

"So, this'll have me back in business will it?" Elizabeth asked holding the bottle up to the light of the window.

Tara said nothing. She didn't care for Elizabeth's business. Instead she concentrated on packing her supplies and book neatly back into her pillowcase.

"I don't suppose you want me to do you a favor to pay for this do you?" Elizabeth held her fingers in a "v" in front of her mouth and wiggled her tongue obscenely between them.

Tara stood horrified with her mouth open for a few moments before she collected herself enough to respond.

"No," was all Tara could manage.

"Look at the superior little prude," Elizabeth hissed. "Think you're better than me do you?" she demanded, taking a step towards Tara, but a knock on the door stopped her.

Tara took the chance to grab her things and edge towards the door while Elizabeth answered it.

"Why, look who it is?" Elizabeth purred draping herself across the doorway. "I knew you couldn't stay away, Pete."

"Hello Elizabeth," Pete greeted her politely.

"I'm running some specials today," she smiled licking her lips before she continued. "A can of beans will get you a lot more than some veggies, for veggies you'll only get the hand. But if you have some fresh beef we can start with —."

"No, thank you," Pete cut her off. "I just needed to see Tara."

"Who?" Elizabeth asked.

"The young woman standing behind you," he pointed.

"Oh, her," Elizabeth looked back and forth between the two of them and frowned. "Whatever she's charging I'll do it for half-price."

"Excuse me? I'm not a whore," Tara glared at the woman.

"You think you're better than me?" Elizabeth bared her teeth in what Tara assumed was supposed to be a grin. "Your husband didn't think so."

"My husband wouldn't have touched you with gloves on,"

Tara sniffed.

Elizabeth grabbed a handful of Tara's hair and pulled hard. Instinctively Tara reached out and clawed at the woman's cheek. Elizabeth let go of Tara's hair and both hands flew to her face.

When she looked at her fingers she shrieked, "I'm bleeding!" Elizabeth's eyes filled with rage and she turned and lunged towards Tara, but she was stopped abruptly when Pete caught her arm. He twisted it behind her back and pushed her against the wall.

"What the hell Pete? You trying to break my arm? Don't you see that dumb bitch started it?" Elizabeth struggled briefly before she sat perfectly still, gasping.

"You all right?" Pete asked looking intently at Tara.

"I think so," she answered, rubbing her head. It had felt like Elizabeth had tried to pull out a chunk of her scalp.

"What about me? The bitch scratched my face," Elizabeth spat.

"You're going to learn to behave yourself or you're going to be out of this town. That's a promise," Pete informed her calmly as he let go of her arm. "Have you paid the lady?" Pete asked gesturing towards Tara.

"I'm a little short right now," Elizabeth grumbled, giving what may have been meant as a sultry pout, but it looked more like the woman's best impression of a mackerel. "She'll have to get hers later."

Pete frowned at Elizabeth, but she smiled back until he took Tara by the hand and led her out. The door slammed shut with vicious force just as Tara got clear. With annoyance Tara realized it was meant to hit her.

"What did you need to see me about?" Tara asked, trying not to physically shake with the force of her unresolved anger.

"Oh, I just needed to see that you were okay. I was keeping an eye on things through the window and it appeared to be getting a little heated."

"Thanks Pete," Tara smiled before she climbed on the back of the motorcycle. "It seemed like you two have some history, you're not one of her regulars are you?" she asked, knowing full well that he wasn't.

"That's nasty," Pete grimaced looking over his shoulder at her before they took off.

All the way home Tara waited to tease the rest of the story out of him. She was going to get to know Pete if it killed her. "So, if you're not a client, how do you know her?" Tara asked, standing in front of the bike before Pete could make one of his usual quick exits.

"We're still on about this?" Pete sighed.

"Yeah, were you friends?" Tara asked.

Pete frowned at Tara for some time before he answered, "She doesn't look familiar to you?"

Tara thought hard, but couldn't come up with anything. "I'm sorry, I can't bring her to mind," Tara admitted.

"She was a waitress at the restaurant I went to every day for lunch. You met her. She waited on us. You complained that she was making your uncomfortable."

Tara thought about it for some time before the face of the waitress arrived in her head. The waitress's hair had been clean and her makeup had been light and pretty, no wonder she didn't recognize her.

"You've both been through a hell of a lot in the last few months so I wasn't sure how things would go when you were in the same room." Pete shifted on the bike.

"What do you mean?"

"Last time I saw her was when I pulled the man off of her who had busted her teeth out because he'd decided not to pay."

"No, I mean why would it matter about us being in the same room? At the restaurant she seemed to hate me, and you act like you know why."

Pete looked at the ground and let out a deep breath. "I thought you knew."

"Knew what?" Tara demanded.

"About Jasper..." he trailed off.

Tara didn't want to hear this. "Was he sleeping with her?" Tara didn't realize she had shouted it until Pete flinched. She needed him to just be blunt like he normally was. "I'm sorry, but, how long did you know?"

Pete looked at the sky. "We ran into Elizabeth at the bar the first night we'd gone drinking together. She was trying to get my number. Jasper gave her his instead. Alex was in the bathroom at the time. He didn't know."

"Why didn't you tell me?" Tara's voice wavered, but she sure as hell wasn't going to cry over that bastard again, so she looked upward and cleared her throat.

"It wasn't my place to start rumors. For all I knew he just got a charge out of giving women his number. I mean we all have our secrets. I didn't know that anything had actually come of it until I saw them going into a hotel together."

"When?"

"I don't remember the date; after I dropped off the heater, but before Christmas." Pete shrugged. "I'm sorry I didn't tell you."

Tara waved his apology away. She felt sick when she thought about all the jobs and all the times Jasper had stormed off angry. How many times had he actually fled to the arms of Elizabeth, Melody, or any other woman that was there waiting? Another thought struck her. "No wonder," she shook her head staring at Pete.

"No wonder?"

"Every time he heard that you and I had talked he accused me of having an affair. He forbid me to speak to you." Tara looked down at the wheel of the bike that she was still standing in front of. "He didn't want you to get the chance to tell me."

"Sounds like something he'd do."

This was something that she should be mad about, but after he told her it was like her feelings flared quickly before turning to ash. She thought she should be mad at Elizabeth, and at Pete for not telling her, but mostly she wanted to be mad at Jasper for betraying her again, and again. Instead she felt nothing but hollow inside. Jasper was gone. He wasn't her problem anymore and there was no point in letting him destroy the life she was trying to rebuild.

"Are you going to be okay?" Pete asked.

Tara realized she'd been staring, unspeaking, for quite a span of time. "Yeah, I think I am."

"Good," Pete paused. "So, could you do me a favor and steer clear of Elizabeth. I don't want to have to break you guys up again."

Tara nodded.

"Can I go now?" he asked.

"Sure." Tara stepped out of the way and watched Pete slowly drive away.

CHAPTER 23

It was just a few days before Tara heard the motorcycle again. Hannity had sent for her to help a little girl in town with strep throat that was running a fever and refusing to eat. Tara gave a spray bottle of yarrow tincture to the family and went on her way with their gratitude and a leather bag. It was a large crossbody purse to carry her supplies in. Being able to keep a bag packed and on hand was a real help. The next time Pete picked her up was to see an older gentleman suffering from frequent heartburn. Her list of cures from Rose's ledger earned her a jar of wild blackberry jam.

"Tara," Pete called out to her as she was heading into the house after he dropped her off.

"What's up?" she asked, taking a couple of steps back towards the bike.

"I'm pretty much out of my gas reserves," he said matter-of-factly while he fiddled with the fingers of his glove. "I won't be riding out to get you anymore."

"What?" Tara asked startled. Some part of her must have known that this was coming eventually, but hadn't actually readied herself to deal with it when it did.

"If you want, I'll pick one day each week where I can walk out and escort you into town. People will still need you. Hannity can keep track of who."

Tara meant to say something right away, but it didn't happen. Not being able to ride into town with Pete on the back of the bike felt like a physical loss. "It's okay," she quickly pushed a smile across her face. "You don't have to walk all the way out here and get me."

"It's not a problem."

"It's fine, really. I'm a big girl and I can walk just as well by myself," she insisted.

"You need somebody with you," he replied just as firmly. What had been until that moment a friendly conversation had subtly changed. When she didn't say anything he continued, "I'll stop by sometime next week."

"That's fine," she answered, barely seeing him as he drove away. Tara was getting sick of being treated like a child.

It didn't take more than four days of solitude for Tara to start getting restless. She was turning over dirt for what she hoped one day would be the vegetable garden, if she could find any seeds for it. Tara had grown accustomed to being in town every couple of days tending to someone. She liked being useful, so she looped her bag with her herbal supplies over her shoulder and headed into town. She hoped the walk would be a nice change and soothe her restless spirit. She'd even put a couple of pairs of socks she'd knitted into the bag. Maybe she could trade them at Hannity's.

It was early afternoon before Hannity's came into view. Terry and Pete were standing at the door. She had to admit, Pete's demeanor as a guard surprised her. He looked serious and a bit scary. Tara paused at the end of the street before continuing forward. When Pete saw her, his face morphed from stern to angry. Tara took a deep breath and continued forward anyway.

"Morning Terry," Tara greeted him when she got near the door.

He smiled and hazarded a glance at Pete. "Do you have any weapons miss?" he asked cheerfully.

"She had better," Pete growled before she had a chance to

answer.

"Sure don't."

"And just why the hell not?" Pete demanded.

"The closest thing I have to a weapon is my kitchen knife." Tara smiled batting her eyes at him. "I'm not going to carry that around. What if I lost it? What if someone stole it? Then where would I be?"

"How is being dead a better option than losing your kitchen knife?" Pete demanded exasperated.

"I'm going to need to check your bag Miss Hillcrest," Terry ordered, holding his hand out. "Pete will give you the pat down," he said with the hint of a smile.

"Sure," she answered, handing her bag to Terry and holding her arms out for Pete to search her. Pete's hands on her waist, hips, and the small of her back were rough and angry. He didn't hurt her, but the sensation wasn't exactly pleasant. Tara slid her hand along the front of her shirt when Pete finished so that he could see there was nothing between her breasts. He nodded at her then moved back to his post at the door, refusing to make any further eye contact.

"Here you are, miss. You can go in to see Hannity," Terry said bemusedly, opening the door for her.

"Well, look who it is," Hannity called out. "What brings you here today?"

"I just thought I'd stop by and see if anyone needed me for anything. And I thought I'd trade these," Tara said slipping two pairs of knit socks out of her bag as she reached the counter.

"Nice." Hannity smiled turning one over in his hand. "Is there anything you're looking for in trade?"

"Garden seeds?" Tara asked hopefully.

Hannity leaned back and rubbed his neck. "I'm sorry, Miz Hillcrest. Seeds are more precious than gold. I only have a few and they are entirely for my own use."

"I was afraid of that," Tara sighed. "Can I just get a payment in food or silver?"

"Not a problem." He pulled a coin purse out of his pocket and counted out a small pile of old silver quarters onto the counter. "Is this fair?"

"It's fine," Tara answered distractedly without counting the money. She knew he was waiting for her to haggle, but her heart wasn't in it today. "Has anyone been in looking for me?" Tara was hopeful while she put the quarters in her pocket.

"Nope. Things have been pretty quiet around here," he assured her.

"I'll check back later this week then," she waved as she headed for the door.

Just outside the door, Pete's arm moved out to block her exit.

"What?" she asked mildly annoyed.

Pete's face had softened and he looked more like the Pete she knew than the one that had been at the door when she walked in.

"I'd like you to wait around until my shift ends so I can walk you home."

What Tara had been hoping for was an apology, not just him acting controlling more nicely. Who did he think he was? "I'll be fine," Tara snapped stepping away from him so quickly that she nearly bumped into a man who staggered a little to get out of her way.

"Dammit, Tara!" Pete yelled, catching her hand so she couldn't keep going. "Why are you being so stubborn?"

Tara fumed. "Get your damn hand off me. I'm sorry if I don't behave the way you want me to," she yelled as she pulled her hand free as he released it. "But, what gives you the right to be so controlling?"

"You haven't seen what I've seen. I'm trying to protect —," he began.

"I can take care of myself!" she cut in before he could finish his sentence. Turning, she strode away quickly so Pete wouldn't have a chance to argue further. He may have fed her and helped her for the last few months. He told her why he'd done that. She didn't owe him obedience.

As Tara reached the end of the block the man who she'd nearly bumped into earlier stopped staggering and stepped into her path.

"You're Tara?" The man's speech was labored, his breath stank of alcohol and he really needed a bath. His presence was nauseating. Tara breathed out quickly to get the smell of him out of her nose. He was tall and thin, with no muscle tone, and a paunchy little belly. His brown hair was standing up on the side of his head like he had something sticky in it. He looked to be in his mid-thirties. When Tara looked at the man's shirt, a little tremor of fear crept up her spine. The stains all over the front and cuffs were blood.

"Yeah, I'm Tara. Is there something I can do for you?" she asked in what she hoped was a calm and passive voice.

The man looked her up and down pointedly, "So you're the town witch?"

"Excuse me?" Tara asked taking a step back.

"Well," the man said taking a step forward, "What you do isn't medicine. I know medicine. I went through years of school and mountains of debt to learn it. Yet," he took another step forward and leaned in close enough that Tara could see he had some gray hairs in the stubble of his right cheek, "people around here seem to be tricked into thinking that you're helping them with magic, voodoo, superstitious mumbo jumbo, or whatever it is you're using." He swayed, nearly bumping his forehead against hers.

"You must be Doctor Farmer," she replied coldly. He wasn't at all what she had imagined. In her head she'd seen a kindly old man sitting up nights worried about his patients and fighting his powerlessness with every breath. Instead this pitiful creature stood reeking in front of her and she couldn't hold on to any of the pity she'd once imagined for him.

He leered at her. "And you must be," he paused to smile as if he'd already said something witty. "You must be awfully good in bed considering how many people you screwed out of real treatment." He chuckled while he pulled a bottle out of his pocket and opened it to take a drink.

Without thinking Tara snatched the bottle of whiskey from his hand. "At least I'm trying to help these people," she growled. "It's a hell of a lot more than you're doing you filthy butcher!"

"Hand that back to me witch," the doctor warned her as a dark cloud passed over his face.

"Not a chance butcher."

Farmer hesitated only a moment before he launched himself at her. Thankfully the alcohol made him slow and Tara sidestepped him easily. He fell on his face on the pavement with a howl and a string of expletives. The pounding footsteps approaching them were nearly drowned out, by the roaring of Tara's heartbeat in her ears. Before she could take a step forward Pete was hauling the doctor roughly to his feet.

"You sure do have a way with people," Pete said looking at Tara.

"Oh, that was nothing," she shrugged, "Doctor Farmer and I were just getting acquainted." She smiled at Pete as if nothing was out of the ordinary. "Would you look at that? He's fallen down and hurt himself."

Tara pulled a strip of clean cloth out of a plastic bag in her kit. "Let me put some pressure on that for you." She applied it to the cut just above the doctor's eyebrow that was already beginning to drip blood. Farmer struggled briefly against Pete's hands holding his arms behind his back until he looked defeated.

"How's that?" she asked the doctor condescendingly as she used his whiskey to clean the cut. She smiled when she saw him flinch.

After a moment he smiled back, then spat on her. Tara gagged as it ran warm down the neckline of her shirt.

Pete immediately grabbed the back of Jim's hair and pulled his head backwards until his ear was level with Pete's mouth. "It's time for you to go home." He released Jim's hair with a rough shove. "Go home, and don't bother the lady again. If you do, I'll find out about it," Pete warned, as he released the doctor.

Doctor Farmer stood on the sidewalk looking at Pete for only a moment before he seemed to regain his better judgement and hurried away.

"You okay?" Pete asked, turning his attention to Tara.

"Yeah, fine," she kept her voice even while she wiped the spit off her chest with a clean spot on the whiskey-soaked rag. What happened had rattled her, and not just the doctor; Pete's actions as well. "I just want to go home," she spoke tautly, shaking her head.

"You can wait inside until I get off work." Pete spoke softly.

"No, thanks. I want to go now."

"After that? Even after all that you don't see why I want you armed? You don't see why you should be escorted?"

"Would you like me to have shot the doctor?" Tara asked impatiently. "That seems like it would have been a bad idea to me."

"No, but what if the next guy isn't some weak drunk? What if the next guy is armed and scary?"

"Then I'm probably screwed anyway," Tara insisted trembling. The adrenaline was starting to wear off and she felt a bit weak. "I'm going home."

"You're impossible!" Pete insisted.

"I'll be fine." Tara headed off down the street briskly because she was done talking about it and she knew he wasn't. He wasn't the only one who could make abrupt exits.

CHAPTER 24

The morning was warm, warmer than most and Tara was uncomfortable even with the dying fire. Her blankets had tied her up while she had tried to kick them off during the night and it took her a couple of moments to get out of bed.

She grabbed a glass of goat milk for breakfast and headed out the door to cool off before she started on her chores for the morning. Outside, rain was sprinkling gently onto the yard as tiny birds picked enthusiastically at the softened ground. They sought out the fresh young grasses starting to grow under the dense dead clumps of brush, and the grubs waiting to turn into beetles in the summer. Everything seemed teeming with life except the bee hives, where she could see the little creatures just inside waiting for the sun to reappear so they could go back about their busy bee business.

After the chores, it seemed like a good morning for Tara to continue to educate herself about the local greens. In the planters that she had placed in a row between the house and the well pump, small green leaves were beginning to poke through the dirt. The comfrey roots she'd been given were planted on either side of the front steps and rosettes of leaf tips where shoving their way free. Everything around seemed to have so much potential. A couple of the trees that she could see in the clearing were starting to look hazy, their tiny new leaves softening the hard winter lines she'd become so accustomed to.

Not all of the young plants were easy to identify. Most of them were so small that she'd have to take a look at them later, but she'd found a patch of dandelion greens, which she noted were edible, but whose leaves were bitterer than the sweet chickweed. Her book said that as the flowers developed the leaves would toughen and need to be blanched before eating. A patch of plantain existed in a line between the driveway and the front door. It was also edible, but stringy. Tara spat the strings out after eating a leaf; they were too tough to chew without a great deal more effort than she wanted to put into it.

That's when she heard the engine. It didn't sound like Pete's motorcycle. Tara ran for the house and dug through the drawer until her hand closed around the kitchen knife. She stood frozen and panting for a moment before the idea of being trapped in the house scared her so much that she slipped out the back door into the line of trees. She heard the engine slow at the end of her driveway. It was the low throaty rumble of a truck.

Hands shaking, Tara put her back to the tree and took a couple of deep breaths to try to steady herself.

As the truck emerged into the clearing Tara smiled and walked forward out of the woods. It was distinctive, with its' round headlights, blue color, and voluptuous 1950's curves. Pete's truck.

By the time Tara reached the yard Pete was looking around panicked with his shotgun in his hands.

"There you are. You had me scared. The door was hanging wide open." Pete gestured before he tucked the shotgun back onto the seat of the truck. "Please tell me that you're actually armed this time."

Tara slowly raised the knife and held it out.

"See. How hard was that?" he asked.

"This is the second time I've nearly wet myself because you showed up here and you have the nerve to casually ask me that?" Tara grumbled.

"At least you're finally looking at the world the right way. It's that sort of thing that will keep you alive," Pete returned patiently.

Tara moved around the side of the truck. "What's all this?" she asked gesturing to the back. It was stacked tight with appliances, boxes, and sacks. Even in the cab, the passenger seat was so full she was amazed he could see out the window.

"That was me about to ask you for a favor," Pete sighed, "I'm looking for a place to stay."

"You couldn't come out here and ask me first?" Tara asked.

"Actually… this is me asking you first."

It wasn't until he was standing next to her that Tara got a good look at him. He was filthy, smeared with soot, and smelled of a sharp, acrid smoke. "What happened?"

Pete leaned against the bed of the truck. "My neighbors caught their house on fire sometime in the early hours of the morning. The town started a bucket brigade, but we just don't have the capability to do these things anymore. It didn't take me long to realize the writing was on the wall for my house too. I loaded as much as I could get in the back of the truck and pulled it out to the curb. Within the hour the tree between our two houses was on fire, then my roof. We stopped trying to put the houses out and just worked on trying to get a fire break in. People chopped down trees and tore out bushes. In the end we lost four houses. Everything is still smoldering, but I couldn't bear to leave my supplies sitting out any longer, people were starting to look at things."

"I'm so sorry," Tara came forward and put her hand on his arm. "It must have been awful."

"It wasn't fun. I'm not, of course, asking to stay in the house," Pete assured her, crossing his arms across his chest in such a way that she had to stop touching him. "I am more than happy to camp in the yard. I have a good-sized military tent, but I'd like to be able to lock my supplies in the shed or the house."

"After everything you've done for me, of course. Do you need help getting everything unloaded?"

"Sure, just be careful not to hurt yourself. A lot of these things are unusually heavy. They're just shells full of whatever I wanted to hide."

They decided it was smart to store most of the items as they were. A washing machine would garner a lot less attention than a large stack of grain sacks. Almost all of what they offloaded was stacked in the shed.

Out of the cab Pete pulled a pile of tools and the heavy fabric cover of a military tent. Then he paced out an area of ground about equal distance from the well as Tara's house stood. A two man saw helped them take down a few trees and Pete split logs while Tara ran the plane over them. By the time evening rolled around, they had a small platform, big enough for his tent with a slightly uneven rough floor. Tara was actually impressed. It looked a lot nicer than she figured it would. After that it didn't take too long to put up Pete's tent. She couldn't help noting that the space in her front yard looked very different with the olive drab tent shuddering in the breeze like her home's nervous friend.

Inside, Pete unfolded a cot and unrolled a sleeping bag on top of it. From a hook he hung his lantern and that was all the furnishings the small space held.

"You had to sacrifice your furniture for your supplies didn't you?" Tara asked.

"I wasn't too attached to much of it anyway," Pete assured her. "It's just stuff. I have tools, cooking supplies, and other things in your shed. But I'm looking forward to going to sleep if you don't mind." Pete laid the shotgun on the floor under his cot.

"I can bring you out a washtub and some buckets of hot water. I lit the stove a couple of hours ago and I've been re-heating some bean soup on it."

Pete shook his head. "A pan is enough for me to wash up. If you don't mind, a single kettle of warm water will take care of that."

In less than ten minutes Tara was back at the door of Pete's tent with a kettle of water and a bowl of bean soup. Pete had pulled an enamel dishpan that looked almost the same as hers out of the shed along with a bar of soap and a washcloth.

"Thanks." He pulled off his shirt and began pouring water into the dishpan. In the light of the lamp it was easy to see the goose bumps that rose all over his arms and chest, and her heart beat a little faster as she watched the taunt muscles slide under the surface of his skin.

Tara stood speechless for a moment as he began to wash his face, at which point she finally cleared her throat because she didn't trust herself to speak.

"What's the matter?" Pete asked.

"Nothing," Tara stammered, feeling guilty about watching him. "Just wanted to know where you wanted your bowl?"

"On the cot's fine." He ran the washcloth over the back of his neck before dunking it in the water again and ringing it out.

Quickly, Tara set down the bowl and slipped out of the tent.

In the morning, a knock on her door sent Tara nearly tumbling out of bed. She was on her feet halfway to the back door before she realized what she'd heard.

"Hey lazybones, wake up," Pete called through the closed door.

Outside, the world was still dark. "What's the matter?" Tara asked moving carefully to the front door where a dim light lit up the windows. Cautiously she unlocked the door and inched it open. Pete held up the lantern showing his face, he was clean and smelled like soap again.

"Nothing's wrong, I just stopped in to get breakfast started. "It's six in the morning," he told her pointing to his watch face. "Half the morning's gone already."

Tara watched him bleary-eyed for a moment then stepped back out of the way. "Pete?"

"What?"

"I think you need to start leaving one of your guns in here with me."

"I think that's a good idea. I'm glad you decided to be concerned about your own safety."

"Actually, it's so that the next time you decide to wake me at six in the morning I can shoot you," Tara yawned, rubbing the sleep from her eyes and attempting to smooth her hair back.

"You wouldn't shoot the man cooking breakfast," he mocked.

"Depends, is the sun up yet?" she asked pointedly.

"No." He started unwrapping a package of butter on the table that she hadn't noticed him carry in.

"Is that?" Tara leaned forward to smell the package. "I haven't seen butter in months, where did you get this?" Tara asked, her threats forgotten.

"Hannity owns a dairy outside of town," Pete informed her, producing a loaf of bread. "He started the trading post as a way to get rid of his own products and it just grew from there. He pays me in food most of the time. They're butchering a cow this week, everyone who works for him will get some beef."

"He pays people in beef, butter, and milk?" Tara asked incredulous. "No wonder all of you boys are willing to stand outside his shop and die for him."

Pete chuckled as he sliced the bread. "Yeah, he said he needs to keep his men strong." Pete flexed an impressive bicep.

"I see." Tara smiled as Pete began buttering slices of bread and laying them butter side down in the bottom of the frying pan.

"He's actually done a lot of work trying to keep the town together."

"I've seen what Hannity does," Tara nodded as she took an appreciative bite of the fried bread that Pete handed to her.

"He's involved in more than his little shop."

"Really?" Tara asked distractedly. She was more concerned with the butter than his answer.

"Yeah. He works with Pastor Richard more than people realize."

"Who's that again?"

"Pastor Richard runs that church in the middle of town. It's the soup kitchen and shelter. Hannity talks to folks who he knows have more than enough to get by to see if he can get people to contribute." Pete moved the frying pan off the top of the stove.

"What you really mean is that Hannity makes people contribute."

"Not at all," Pete answered, unamused. "All donations are voluntary. He himself is the biggest contributor. Perishables always go straight to the church if they don't get traded. He also gives regular donations of clothes, shoes, blankets, and that sort of thing. He would never ask anyone to do anything he's not willing to do."

Tara opened her mouth to start teasing Pete about how bromantic that sounded when she realized he might actually have a crush on the man. Pete had never said anything to her about his orientation before their world fell apart. It was probably even more important for him to keep his secret in these uncertain times. "It sounds like you really respect him." Tara sincerely hoped that he understood her meaning.

"I do think quite highly of him. He's shrewd," Pete smiled.

By the time they had finished breakfast the sun was creeping up the eastern sky. After the chores were finished Pete led Tara back out to the shed and pulled out the toaster. When he broke the bottom free, packages of heirloom seeds scattered onto the top of his dryer.

"Some of them are a couple of years old, but they should be viable," he assured her sorting through carrots, lettuce, watermelon, beans, and a pile of others. "I figured we could get some of the early season veggies in," he continued as Tara watched in delight. "Also in that small freezer over there," Pete gestured, "I have a pile of seed potatoes. I noticed you have a nice size garden, but I'm going to be cutting out some trees and making it bigger."

"What are you going to do with the trees?" Tara asked, touching the seed packets in wonder.

"I'm hopefully not going to live in a tent forever. As long as you don't mind I was going to get a cabin going, basically across from yours," Pete answered, sorting the seeds packets by planting dates like a deck of playing cards.

"Of course," Tara nodded, but for a nagging few minutes she hated the idea. The cabin, the clearing, the woods, this was her space. The idea of putting up another home bothered her, but it was Pete. How much safer would she feel knowing that he was just a quick yell away? Tara relaxed, if she could accept the end of her way of life, surely she could accept a neighbor.

Tara spent most of the day, with the sun warming her back, putting seeds into the dirt in orderly lines while they marked each row with sticks. The cold mud seeped into the knees of her jeans, but it felt good to be doing what she was doing. Her mouth watered when she thought of fresh lettuce, spinach, sugar snap peas, beets, turnips, and potatoes growing.

Tara realized as she watched Pete wiping some of the mud off his boots that she was happy to be working with someone. Most of the things that she'd done around here had to be accomplished by herself. This felt more like socializing than working. They made small talk about nothing important, mostly about plants and gardening. Pete made no attempt to hide that he really enjoyed gardening. The exciting moment when you finally start seeing your plants poking their way through the dirt in orderly lines, the funny shapes that root vegetables came out as... even the process of weeding. Tara was tickled. She'd always hated weeding. She hated it so much so that she hadn't had many gardens. If Pete found it as cathartic as he said then this was going to work out well. She already felt better about sharing her clearing.

CHAPTER 25

"I swear to God I meant what I said about shooting you Pete!" Tara shouted towards the front door when the gentle knock woke her up.

"You said you'd shoot me if I woke you at six, it's seven. Look it's a bright sunshiny day," Pete called back.

When Tara opened her eyes and peeked out the sunlight was just starting to creep into the dark of the room. "Oh hell," Tara swore sliding out of bed and unlocking the door. "If we're going to be neighbors you need to understand something really important about me."

"What's that?" Pete asked, carrying a pot of oatmeal in and setting it on her cold stove. It looked like peaches and brown sugar were swimming in it.

"Your breakfasts are the only thing saving your life," Tara warned him, flopping back onto the bed. "I'm not a morning person. I have never been a morning person. I will never be a morning person. If you decide to get me up before daylight there had better be bacon."

"I'll keep it in mind," Pete chuckled, spooning oatmeal into a pair of bowls.

Tara pulled her sweater on as Pete sat down on the bed and handed her one of the bowls. It smelled more like dessert than breakfast.

"Your food has been a lot easier to swallow than mine," Tara smiled, shoveling oatmeal into her mouth.

"Beggars can't be choosers," Pete shrugged.

"Not complaining, something is definitely better than nothing. It's just that suddenly I feel like I'm eating like royalty."

Pete laughed, "If there's any royalty left I doubt they're eating oatmeal."

"Why wouldn't there be any royalty?" Tara paused with her spoon halfway to her mouth.

"Our economy collapsed," Pete explained, scraping the bottom of the bowl and hopping up to scoop more oatmeal into it.

Watching him, Tara decided it was unnatural to be that energetic in the morning.

"I don't know if you noticed, but it wasn't called a world economy for nothing. It's very likely that if we went, we took half the world with us. I wouldn't be surprised if we are at war because of it. Problem is, until we see soldiers nobody will ever know." Pete sighed.

"Well, this is depressing." Tara took a deep breath staring into her bowl. "I'm going to take the initiative and change the subject now. What's the plan for today?"

"Actually, I was wanting to ask you about your neighbors," Pete replied as he finished his second bowl of oatmeal.

"What about them?" Tara asked confused.

"Who are they? Do you talk to them? Where are they located?" Pete asked in rapid succession.

"Actually I never thought to go out and meet my neighbors. I don't know any of them. I don't even know if anyone is still out here. I never hear anyone."

"You stayed out here alone for months and you never thought to go meet your neighbors?" Pete asked surprised

"My question," Tara gestured at him with her spoon, "Why would we want to, especially now."

"You want to; especially now," Pete emphasized, "Because we don't know anything about them. Maybe they can help us, maybe we can help them. For all we know we have thriving farms on all sides and you're out here living on rice and pancakes."

"Fine, I see your point," Tara admitted. "When do you want to leave?"

"After I get the chores done and get washed up."

"Good idea," Tara admitted. "If I'm going out to meet people I want to wash my hair."

When Pete came in to strain the milk, Tara carried out a kettle to the fire Pete had cooked the oatmeal on that morning. When she finished filling her washtub Tara handed the kettle to Pete on the porch.

"I don't have any curtains on my windows, so don't come to the door till I come out."

"Not a problem," Pete called over his shoulder on the way to the pump.

"I'm sure it's not," Tara mumbled to the empty space that he left behind.

Pete may have been okay with his washbasin baths, but Tara insisted on filling the washtub and being able to lower herself down in for a scrub. When she was as clean as she was going to get she brushed her teeth and hair and checked her reflection as she wove her hair into a loose braid. Pete had given her a small mirror and it was surprisingly nice to have it. Tara hadn't seen her face much over the last few months. The first time she'd peered in the mirror again she almost didn't recognize herself. Her cheeks were not as round as they had once been, and her eyes sparkled in a way she hadn't remembered seeing before.

Once she was ready she met Pete in the front yard where he was stirring the embers of a fire that he was trying to put out before pouring water on it again.

"How do I look?" Tara asked twirling before coming down off the porch. She had chosen to wear her dress and sweater. Her jeans were still crusted with mud from yesterday. The dress had a few stains around the hem and a tear that she'd patched. The long underwear beneath them was still in remarkably good shape. Her brown sweater was darned and not as well-shaped as it had once been, but she couldn't expect much more than that from something she wore nearly every day. A new pair of cream socks she'd knitted peaked out of the top of her boots.

Pete watched her twirl, "You look like you own a bar of soap; probably smell like it too, which is more than can be said for a great many people."

"You do flatter me so," Tara twittered melodramatically.

They decided that the best way to find some neighbors was to go out on the road and head either right or left until they found a driveway. A flipped coin led them left, away from town. Barely around the first bend in the road they found what they were looking for. The mailbox had two reflectors on it but no name, just a number. Each of them took a deep breath and headed up the driveway towards a house they couldn't see from the road.

The home came into view less than a minute into their journey. It was a two-story farmhouse with a tin roof and a wraparound porch. On the porch were a swing and two rocking chairs. In the driveway sat a small white economy car and a large black truck that looked to be from the late seventies. The lawn had at one time been well manicured, now it was already getting shaggy with spring growth. Elaborate flower beds were tucked against the house and a small rock garden near the driveway was full of little concrete angels.

Tara's hands were trembling. What if they got shot just for being here? She knew if she had a gun in the same situation she might shoot first and ask questions later, especially since Pete was wearing a rifle slung across his back.

When they reached the door Tara suppressed the urge to vomit from her nervousness and knocked lightly three times. After a space Pete stepped forward.

"Hello?" he called while knocked more firmly than Tara had, "We're your neighbors and we were just stopping in to check on you."

Tara leaned against the railing while they waited for some sort of response. Suddenly a large black and white short-haired tuxedo cat jumped into the window by the front door and let out a wail. Tara nearly fell backwards over the railing and Pete unslung his rifle and was holding it pointed at the creature while it pawed at the glass.

"Something's wrong," Tara told Pete pointedly.

"What do you mean?" he asked lowering the gun.

"There's no tracks in the mud except ours; nobody seems to be around, but there is a cat in the house that's still alive?"

"Maybe he has a whole bag of food," Pete replied hopefully.

"I'm sure that's it," Tara said sarcastically while a look of genuine horror began to spread over her face.

"Don't jump to the worst conclusion. Maybe they always come and go from the back. Maybe they have a field they're out working. They could be staying on one of the local farms for planting season. Maybe they're hiding, waiting for us to just go away."

"Maybe," Tara shrugged as they began their trip around the side of the house to find the back door. When they got there it was shut haphazardly and the frame was partially broken.

"I don't think I want to go in there," Tara moaned.

"Come on. We at least need to let the cat out." Pete tried the doorknob as he spoke. It turned easily in his hand and the door swung open. The cat was sitting in the kitchen looking at them. It yowled as they stepped inside, coming to rub himself back and forth across their legs. A heavy smell of rotting meat hung in the air.

"Where is everyone?" Pete asked the cat as they looked around the kitchen. The cabinet doors and drawers all stood open. One was pulled off and hanging by the hinge. As they looked around Tara noted that the cabinets had all been stripped of any food.

"That smell is awful," Tara gagged, stepping back towards the door.

"Maybe they had a big dog," Pete shrugged as he started forward through the kitchen.

"You don't believe that! Don't say it like you believe that!" Tara drug her feet reluctantly as she followed him.

The living room was cheerfully decorated in country plaids and angel figurines. In the corner was an entertainment center and newer game system that implied that someone in the house was probably in their thirties or younger. In the corner, a glass-fronted gun cabinet had the glass broken out of it and stood empty. Tara shuddered. A staircase along one wall led upstairs and through another doorway was the dining room. Inside was a very long table surrounded by ladder back chairs. A china cabinet in the same room was also filled with angels.

The smell was stronger the closer they got to the stairs and

Tara's legs shook as she climbed them after Pete. The hallway had a small landing with a couple of bookcases and a loveseat; off of it were two doors, both cracked open slightly. Pete pushed the door of the first room open and inside was nothing but a treadmill and some sort of fancy-looking exercise machine that Tara didn't know the name of.

The door of the next room had a crack in it like someone had gone through it with extreme force. Tara did her honest best to breathe through her nose as they approached it. Pete stood outside the door without touching it. Surely he knew what she knew.

Pete's hand shook nearly imperceptibly as he pushed the door open the rest of the way. He covered his mouth with his hand, his rifle hanging limply at his side. Tara took a step forward; she didn't know why, but she needed to see what he saw.

Just inside the door on the floor was a man, or at least what at one time would have been a man. Flesh was missing from the neck and shoulders and Tara shuddered with revulsion thinking of the cat. The man lay crumpled as if he had been clutching his middle in a wide pool of dried blood that was now brown and flaky on the carpet. The color of his skin made Tara feel queasy and she pulled her eyes away.

"Not again," Pete breathed.

Tara's focus had been too tight. The only dead body Tara had ever seen up close was in an open casket so she'd barely been able to look away. What she saw next made her gasp. The walls and ceilings of the room had sprays of blood on them and her mind tried to go blank when her eyes landed on the bed. The blankets were stripped and lay in a pile on the floor. In the middle of the bed lay a young woman, she was not beautiful in death, but from the picture on the wall of a smiling young couple, she had been in life. Tara's brain struggled to process the rest of what she saw. The woman was nude and each of her limbs was tied to one of the bedposts, blood nearly covered her skin and the flesh was pulling apart in dark areas that looked like gashes. One deep one on each thigh, both wrists and her neck. It took Tara longer than she would have liked, to comprehend that the sheets weren't supposed to be brown.

Tara didn't realize she'd been hyperventilating until Pete pulled her from the room and made her sit down in front of the window that he pulled open on the landing.

"Take some slow deep breaths," he instructed, pushing her towards the window by her shoulder.

"We're not even a mile from my house… When? Why? Did you see what was done to her?" Tara's words came out in a rush as she began to cry.

"It's not the first time I've seen something like that." He put his hand on her cheek and turned her head gently so that she was looking into his face. "Now you understand why I've been nagging you."

"It could have been me," Tara gasped.

"I know, but it wasn't," Pete spoke firmly. "It wasn't," he repeated until she focused on his eyes and nodded. He didn't remove his hand from her shoulder. "I'll get one of Hannity's crews to help me get these folks out of here and properly buried." Pete hurried over to pull the door closed. "I can't ask you to see that again."

When she turned to go down the stairs he caught her hand.

"Aren't we leaving?"

Pete hesitated and looked at the floor before he spoke. "I don't mean to sound ghoulish, but before we do that we'll have to salvage anything from here that would be useful to us. When the guys come out to help the house will basically be stripped."

Tara stared at him horrified, "What?"

"This is a different world and new rules. We're not going to be able to run to the store for every little thing. We can start with the bookcases; maybe there is something helpful or entertaining there. From there we can move through the house. Nothing that we leave here can save these people, but something we take may save us."

Tara shook herself and tried not to let the image follow her as she leaned over to the closest bookcase and began scanning the shelves. Mostly Amish romance novels, women's prayer guides, and cross stich pattern books covered the shelves. Tara didn't find anything, but the titles kept blending together because she couldn't focus. Instead she read the names over and over without remembering any of them. Pete pulled out a couple of auto repair manuals and a book on appliance repair.

"What good are those?" Tara asked.

"They're nostalgic and tradable. There are still people who tinker."

Tara had a hard time imagining people still clinging to that kind of hope in a world where this wasn't Pete's first time seeing something like what was in the bedroom and they were stealing a dead couple's books.

"We'll set what we're keeping on the porch in the fresh air," Pete said as he led her back out through the kitchen.

When Tara stepped out on the porch the cat looked up at her from where it was drinking from a puddle in the back yard. "I'm sorry," she said to it out loud. The cat was the only one left in the family that she could apologize to for stealing their things.

Tara set down the books and followed Pete back inside. "I'll go through the living room, dining room, and bath," he told her, leaving the door wide open and opening the kitchen windows. "Why don't you stay here and see if you can find anything useful in the kitchen."

Pete disappeared through the doorway and Tara stood numbly in the middle of the room for a few minutes before she began. All the cabinets yielded her were a large stoneware bowl, a metal spatula, a couple of big spoons, and two cast iron skillets. Above the refrigerator she found a few cookbooks and a hardbound journal of handwritten recipes. She took the journal reverently off the shelf and added it to the pile. An old tin she decided could be used for food storage was surprisingly heavy. Inside were several hundred new canning jar lids, without the screw bands. Maybe Pete was right, maybe some of these items could save them.

Tara turned her attention to what she'd assumed was a broom closet that had been standing partially open, but when she swung the door open the rest of the way, stone steps lead downward into darkness.

"Hey Pete, do you have a light on you?" she called leaning around the kitchen doorway. Pete stood up from where he'd been digging through the couch cushions and pulled a lighter out of his pocket then tossed it to her.

"What did you find?"

"A basement," she answered, heading back into the other room. With the lighter in hand she headed down the steps. A stone wall stood on each side. At the bottom a landing turned through a stone doorway and water lapped at the steps. The basement was flooded. At least she knew where the cat was drinking.

If the water was only one step deep she would be able to keep her feet dry for a while, her boots were waterproof. If it was deeper, she'd be wading through water with who-knows-what in it. At least it didn't smell particularly bad. Tara slid her foot down into the water and met solid floor before it came over the tops of her boots. Thank goodness for small favors.

Immediately in front of her were the useless sump pump, washer, dryer, and hot water heater. The surprise was what stood to her right. Along the wall that was shared with the staircase were shelves, and on them stood glass jars full of home preserved food. Whoever had killed the family apparently didn't want to get their feet wet or hadn't thought to look down here.

Tara ran back up the stairs to get Pete. "Food, there's food!" she shouted as she hurried through the kitchen nearly colliding with him in the doorway as he carried a couple of the ladder-back dining chairs out.

"Really?" Pete asked, obviously shocked. "How much?"

"I didn't count, but there's at least a few dozen jars, maybe more," Tara informed him, suddenly embarrassed by her delight. As the smile left her face she looked at Pete, "What's wrong with me?"

"Nothing," Pete assured her setting the chairs down. "The food is useless here, all it will do is rot. It will keep us from starving." Pete pulled a picture out of his pocket and held it out to Tara. "I didn't know if you'd want this because I don't know if it would make you feel better or worse. But in your case I can imagine it would help you to see the people who canned that food like this, not like…" he gestured upstairs and shuddered.

In the photograph that Pete had handed her were a smiling young man and woman sitting on the sofa with the cat. She was very pretty; with pale blue eyes, her hair was the yellow blonde of sunflowers. Her smile displayed strait white teeth, and made her eyes sparkle. Her husband was handsome, also blonde, but with hazel eyes. His features were the generic good looks of a mannequin, but he looked at his wife with such love. Tara smiled.

"A person who goes to the trouble of canning food obviously does it to keep it from going to waste. So, don't let it go to waste."

Tara nodded while Pete picked the chairs back up and walked past her onto the porch. While he was outside, suddenly an engine roared to life and Tara stumbled back up the stairs in a panic. When she reached the porch Pete waved to her from the black truck.

"It's got half a tank; we can use it to bring some of the supplies back."

Tara went back downstairs as her heart stopped hammering against the back of her ribs and pulled the boards off the windows to let some light in to the basement. She hadn't even noticed the boards on her first trip down there. In the light she could now clearly see the rows of jars. They were so pretty. Colorful rows of what looked like peaches, jelly, tomatoes, pickles, and a few things that Tara couldn't identify; but one looked like cubes of meat. Her mouth watered. On the next shelf over were lots of fairly clean canning jars turned upside down empty on the shelves. The pressure canner itself was sitting on the top shelf along with a large pot with a rack in it. She carried those up and out first.

When Tara started emptying the shelves she realized she hadn't guessed how deep they were. The jars themselves were stacked five deep and each one was carefully labeled on the top with the contents and date, all of which were from last summer and fall. By the time she'd carried them upstairs Tara could see they had over twenty jars just of deer meat.

Pete called out to her when she came out with the last load of deer, "Do me a favor and keep an eye on the legs, tell me if they're going to fall off the ramp while I winch this up."

Tara stared at him shocked, "How did you even get that out here?"

"There was a furniture dolly in the shed," he told her pointing to it on the ground.

Tara shook her head and watched as Pete winched a very nice woodstove up onto the back of the truck and tucked all of its connecting stovepipe around it. "This will work great in my cabin, when I get it built," Pete smiled.

By the time they had finished, Tara had packed all the jars, full and empty, into the back of the truck along with shelves from the basement, and then added all the things she'd already set on the porch. She was less concerned by what Pete had packed; most of what he'd picked out was for trading in town.

Tara helped Pete get everything unloaded and put away, but as she set up the shelves in her cabin and stacked the jars on them that Pete had insisted she keep for herself she felt very torn. On the one hand she stole food from her dead neighbor, but on the other hand, what else was she supposed to do with it?

Eventually she decided that when she went into town she would give a portion of it to the church running the soup kitchen. If taking it helped more than just her, maybe she could be okay with it.

Later, Pete walked in from the darkness carrying the small lantern. Even knowing he was coming, Tara was panicky when she heard him coming up the driveway. She couldn't relax until she saw him clearly in the circle of light that the fire made. He'd gone to town to get the crew to bury the neighbors. He'd left the black truck with Hannity after he'd helped take the bodies and belongings into town.

"It's done," Pete told her laying his rifle against the side of his truck. "The reverend let us all get washed up, but I didn't stay to bury them. They'll be taken care of," he assured her solemnly.

Tara nodded without looking up from the pot of deer stew she was stirring on the fire.

"What's wrong?" Pete asked, leaning forward slightly.

"Everything!" Tara started to cry. "Everything is wrong. Nothing is the way it's supposed to be anymore. People are being murdered. The world is all upside down, and I'm scared. Really, really, scared."

Pete moved towards her but stopped when they heard a small sound on the driveway. "Get inside!" Pete insisted while he grabbed his rifle and positioned himself behind the truck. Tara hesitated only a second before she ran through the front door and dropped low where she waited until she heard Pete let out a loud laugh.

Confused, Tara opened the door where Pete was standing next to the fire while a small shape crouched in front of him. It was the tuxedo cat. He'd wrapped himself into a small ball with his tail wrapped around his front feet and purred with his eyes closed.

"His name is Brom according to the appointment card we found on the fridge." Pete smiled, petting the cat.

"Did you show up for dinner?" Tara asked the cat.

That night they shared their dead neighbor's food with their dead neighbor's cat and tried to imagine that all was okay with the world.

CHAPTER 26

Tara wasn't sure how long she'd been screaming, but it was coming out in a strangled gasp. She clawed at the sheet that was on her, sure that it was the hands of the man that had been trying to tie her to the bed only moments before. The darkness didn't help.

Something slammed hard against her front door.

"If you're okay Tara open this door!" Pete yelled.

Panting she tumbled out of bed and scrambled across the floor. "I'm fine," she gasped in the darkness, but it came out strangled, she knew he didn't hear her. Tara tried to find the keyhole in the dark, sliding the key against the metal until it dropped into place. She turned the key and knob together.

Pete's hand found her arm and he helped her to her feet. "Are you okay? What happened? Are you hurt?" Pete asked in a string of words that all tumbled together.

Tara nodded several times while he repeated himself until she remembered it was too dark to see her reply.

"Yeah, I'm fine," she croaked feeling weak and foolish. "It was a nightmare. A man was tying me to the bedposts. It was so real," she admitted trying to catch her breath. "I'm sorry."

The hand on her arm slipped around her back and Pete pulled her against his chest. She was startled by the warmth. His skin was bare and she could feel the hammering of his heart, slightly off rhythm from the pounding of her own. She stood still in his embrace trying to calm down; relieved to be alive, not in any real danger. His heartbeat began to slow and he let go of her slowly in the darkness.

"I'm sorry," she told him again.

"It's fine. I'm just glad you're safe," he said in nearly a whisper. "I had nightmares the first time, too."

Tara lit the lamp that sat on her bedside table and turned to face Pete. He was holding a shotgun, and his hair was wild. When she continued her inspection she blushed hotly and hoped that in the dim light he couldn't see the color of her cheeks. All Pete was wearing was a pair of gray boxer briefs. He had really nice legs and… Tara turned away so as not to ogle him any further.

"If you're okay," Pete told her calmly, "I'm going to go back to bed."

Tara nodded.

"I'm right over there if you need me."

Tara didn't look at Pete but she assumed he was gesturing to his tent. "Thanks."

"Are you sure you're going to be okay?"

Tara nodded again.

"Goodnight."

There was no way Tara was going back to sleep.

Town was its usual collection of sounds and smells. In the distance a hammer rang against metal and horses huffed or whinnied, unaccustomed to standing still as beasts of burden. It was surprising the speed with which people seemed to adapt to this new way of life. Tara had to hand it to Hannity; he sure did know how to keep the wheels turning.

"Kylie!"

It was an unusual name and the voice shouting it had a familiar ring. Tara griped Pete's arm tightly, but he'd already heard it.

"Alex?" Pete yelled moving forward towards the church, the direction the sound had come from.

"Pete?"

"Where are ya' buddy?" Pete called, but Alex was already stepping out into the street. He looked more literally, and less figuratively, like a bear than he had before. Alex wore a shaggy jacket; his hair and beard both untrimmed, but he looked paler, and smaller than Tara remembered him.

The two men ran to each other for a crushing embrace. Pete lifted Alex off his feet and they seemed to do a little dance of joy while Kate and a couple of other people filtered out of the church.

Kate, whom Tara was used to thinking of as petite, seemed so fragile she wasn't sure she ought to hug her. But, Kylie had the blush and pink cheeks of a healthy little girl. Tara wondered how many meals Alex and Kate had missed to keep her looking like that.

"I can't tell you how happy I am to see you guys," Tara said wrapping her arms delicately around Kate. The top of Kate's head came only to her shoulder and her hair smelled like ashes.

"Finding you guys alive is more than we could ask. Where's Jasper?" Kate asked looking around.

"Chicago?" Tara shrugged.

"So he went?" Kate asked, drawing her mouth into a disapproving line.

"Yeah, he and Melody went together."

"He just left you here?"

"I refused to go with them. I thought I'd be in the way when they had their baby," Tara snorted.

Kate stared at her. "Hell with him! I never liked him anyway. I thought he was trouble."

Tara sighed. If everyone had known what Jasper was, why hadn't anyone bothered to warn her? "It's ancient history," Tara said distractedly. Her attention was drawn to the people standing several feet behind Kate.

Following Tara's gaze, Kate gestured them forward. "These are our friends, Jake and Tracy Fowler."

The couple was younger than Tara by several years. Jake looked tired and was streaked in grime, but when Tara stepped forward to take his hand he gave her a crushing handshake that made her flinch. He looked like he use to play sports in a not so distant past. Tracy had brown hair and eyes and was dressed in sensible clothing that looked like it might need a wash. In her arms was a baby, also pink and fat.

"Her name's Rebecca," Tracy informed Tara when she stepped forward to shake hands.

"She's adorable," Tara smiled. "I'm Tara. It's nice to meet you."

"I'll introduce you guys to Pete if he and Alex ever stop making out," Kate grinned.

"We're not making out, yet," Pete laughed.

"Can't a man miss another man without all your accusations, woman?" Alex asked, taking his hand off Pete's shoulder. "Wow, you guys look great! What's the secret to your success?"

Pete looked momentarily uncomfortable and he looked around at the people on the street who were now listening to the conversation. "Hannity is good to the men who work for him. Where are you guys staying?"

"Don't know yet. We went looking for you first. Turns out there is a wreck of burnt lumber just down the road that use to be yours. I can't tell you how happy I am that you weren't inside when that happened," Alex declared.

"Me too," Pete admitted.

"We were told Pastor Richard was the man to see about a place to stay and work." Alex was watching Pete intently. "I didn't know you guys had work available around here."

"We got lucky and we have a good infrastructure. There's farm hands and guard jobs along with some people with more specialized skills," Pete said eying Tara. "And, don't worry about a place to stay. Grab your stuff; you'll be coming out to stay with us." Pete stopped and turned to Tara. "As long as it's all right with you?"

"Of course," Tara nodded, though she wasn't actually sure about this. Where was everyone going to sleep? Not to mention the fact that she didn't even know Jake and Tracy. The idea of having complete strangers living in the middle of the woods with her made her uneasy.

"We don't have anything that we're not already carrying," Kate admitted, looking back and forth between her friends and husband while Kylie clung uncertainly to her leg.

"Tara was in town dropping off an ointment for a fellow, and

I was collecting my beef. If you want to wait just a few minutes we'll be ready to head back home. Are you up to walking about ten miles?" Pete asked.

"We can walk as far as we need to as long there's a place to sleep at the end of it," Alex assured him.

Later, as the group started out of town Pete turned to Alex, "How'd you get back here? What happened, if you don't mind me asking?"

"Do you want the long story or the short story?" Alex asked shifting Kylie to his other side to give his arm a rest.

"We have a long walk," Pete shrugged while the rest of the group walked in silence.

"When we moved in with Kate's mom it didn't take us long to figure out that was a temporary solution. I tried to join the local police force, but the job opening I'd heard about had already been filled. Fortunately I got on at a sign factory through the temp agency. I met Jake there. It was a real strange place by then. There weren't any women working there," Alex paused to shift Kylie again.

"You're getting sidetracked honey," Kate wheezed. Pete frowned while he watched her. Tara was worried that the poor woman must have been a good deal more hungry and tired than she had originally admitted.

"Actually that's how Jake and I got started talking. I thought it was really strange. I mean, if you look at most of the factories in the area they have always been half women, if not more. But apparently this old guy who owns the place was sure that the reason the economy was floundering in the first place is that women joined the work force. So, to do his part to fix things he just didn't hire women."

"How did he get around the laws?" Pete asked.

"He required proof of job ability and whenever a woman applied he claimed she failed the physical requirements, even if she was as strong as the next man," Jake informed them.

"Why didn't anyone say anything about it?" Tara asked slowly.

Alex looked pained momentarily. "Here's the thing about jobs; you know how hard they are to come by, and nobody there wanted to lose theirs. Not even me I'm ashamed to say."

Pete nodded. "Nobody here thinks less of you. You were telling us about the town," Pete prompted.

"Oh, yeah, right," Alex shook his head, "When the first wave of the inflation hit, Kate's mom told us very pointedly that it was time for us to leave. She said what we brought in wasn't enough to cover the extra food and she wasn't going to starve for us. Her own daughter and grandchild out in the cold because she was afraid of running out of rice and beans." Alex's face contorted in anger while the pause in his speech was filled with the sounds of shoes on pavement and labored breathing. Kate's feet were beginning to drag.

"Sorry," Alex said, "I don't know what happened to the old bat in the aftermath and I frankly don't care. When I was at work I told Jake what happened and he asked me that very night to come stay with them. They were no better off than us, but they were willing to share their last meal with us." Alex clapped Jake on the back with a large hand and Jake smiled. "That's why we brought them with us."

Tara nodded, but she was occupied watching Kate who was slowing down and lagging behind the group.

Alex beamed at Pete, "I can't wait for you guys to get to know each other."

Pete smiled at Jake. "I know I already like you if you took my buddy Alex in, he can be awfully hard to live with."

"Speak for yourself," Alex muttered and Pete grinned. "It was only a short time after the inflation started that the plant shut down," Alex continued smoothing his beard. "Most of the town shut down. Then in a couple of weeks the power went out. Apparently the coal plant couldn't keep getting shipments."

"Yeah, the power went out here just after that too, but at that point half the town didn't have power anyway. The price of it was running local businesses out," Pete explained. Tara grabbed

Pete's arm and pulled him back. Kate had stopped walking and was swaying slightly. Pete reached her side just after Tara.

"We need to stop," Tara called forward as Kate's knees buckled. "When was the last time she ate?"

"We all had a little something just before we got into town this morning, but I suspect that her portion went to Kylie," Alex said striding back to stand at his wife's side while Kylie wiggled to get down.

"Did you eat?" Alex asked his wife sternly.

"How can you ask me to do that when she was still hungry?" Kate answered quietly.

"Dammit woman, how can you take care of her if you can't stand up?" Alex demanded angrily.

"Here," Pete bent down. "I haven't missed any meals lately, if you can try to hold on a little that would be great. Otherwise, just try to lean forward onto my shoulders. I'm going to carry you piggyback."

"No, it's fine, I just need a minute to catch my breath," Kate told him as Alex lifted his wife from the ground.

"No arguments," Alex ordered her firmly while he helped to situate her on Pete's back.

"This way we can get the kids safely inside before nightfall," Pete explained to her over his shoulder.

"Okay," Kate mumbled against his back, obviously too exhausted to argue, which wasn't like Kate at all.

After Kate was settled quietly against Pete's back, Alex continued, "Once the power went out, it was chaos. The chain stores were all looted, and homes were being broken into. People were hungry, cold, and sick. But the thing that surprised me the most was how fast it happened," Alex sighed. "So many people died. There were bodies in the streets. Jake and I took turns keeping our house safe. We boarded up all the windows and all but one door. We spent days huddling in the dark with barely any heat or food."

Alex cleared his throat loudly a couple of times like he was trying not to get emotional. "That's when Marcus stepped forward. Marcus Harper was some sort of retired army general and he made no bones about the fact that he wanted to restore order to the town. He started by gathering folks to talk about what we should do as a community to come together and protect ourselves, and I'll tell you what he had to say sounded pretty good."

Jake scratched the back of his head, "Who'd have thought."

"Yeah," Alex nodded. "Within a few weeks he'd gathered a few of the ex-military men in town and they became a small police force. I'm not going to lie, I never let on that I use to be a cop. I didn't want to leave my wife and the kids unprotected while I did whatever was expected of me elsewhere."

"One of Marcus's first plans was to seize and redistribute all of the town's food. Now, I'm going to tell you that a lot of people were happy with this because they didn't have anything. But, a lot of others were really angry. They were having what they put aside for their families taken. He cleaned out the animals from some of the closest farms and slaughtered them a few at a time to help feed everyone. We all had a ration. We were each assigned a number and you had to show your ID and number to get your food every day. Not even by the week, by the day. When people started getting sick he imposed a quarantine and a curfew. Then he closed our boarders so that nobody else could come in. I heard some rumors that people who didn't obey his rules were getting killed, but it was just rumors. I figured he started them himself to keep people in line."

Alex paused again and took a deep breath before he continued, "Then they came for everyone's weapons to redistribute to his army. I assume this was because there had been a lot of grumbling about getting rid of the petty dictator. He told us that we didn't need them because we had him to protect us. Fortunately, "Alex paused, "for me anyway, he didn't start on my side of town. They were sweeping from one end to the other. The first of the resistance he encountered was within the first ten houses and he decided to make a very public example of the first dissenter. He executed the man in front of his wife and two boys in the middle of town. I wanted to fight, but my lovely and intelligent wife told me that everyone who could was either going to turn against him or run away. To keep him in power was crazy and to leave it to lawlessness again was suicide. Of course she was right. We took only what we could carry and slipped out of town through the woods before he could get his guards through the town. We took a chance there would be less chaos here."

Pete shook his head, "That's terrible. It's definitely easier here. It helps that one man doesn't hold all the power.

"What about Pastor Richard?"

"Pastor Richard does a lot, but nobody does more for the town than Hannity."

"Who's Hannity?" Jake asked, squeezing between Pete and Alex.

"He's just the guy that stepped forward to help and he does his honest best by the people here. He started his store to move his own products in town and donates his surplus to the soup kitchen and shelter that the church runs. He encourages all his guys to contribute a little if they can. I give some food every now and again, and Tara goes in to help the sick."

"He's a great man to work for. You should probably talk to him yourself. I'll take you to town in a couple of days after you rest if you want. He's always hiring guards even if they only work a day per week. We go through some training. A fair few of the guards are ex-military and they have worked out some training and workout routines that they run the rest of us through. We're not required to do it, but there's nobody that hasn't chosen to."

"So you guys are basically the town's police force?" Jake asked slowly.

"I'd say yes, and no. We're called guards, we protect things, but we're not out there enforcing a set of laws. The only thing we are asked to do is protect Hannity's and the church, certain citizens, and then protect others who we see in need of our help." Pete cleared his throat. "Hannity and the reverend are not picky about how people choose to live their lives as long as they aren't hurting each other. When we do step in to protect people and their property, the only thing we're asked to remember is that a man who steals to feed his starving family is not a bad man, he is a desperate one. A desperate man is dangerous, but he can be helped. To stop a man from stealing he can be fed and found work. A man that hurts or kills for his own pleasure is a dangerous man, he cannot be helped and he must be stopped."

Tara paused. The way Pete said it made her wonder if he'd been involved personally in stopping someone, and what that entailed exactly, but she wasn't going to ask him now in front of all these people.

Alex frowned, "I hope you don't mind my skepticism, but I do want to talk to him personally and have a look around town before I make up my mind to join his private army. I'm still a little weary of those kinds of offers."

"Of course," Pete smiled, "I was at first too and I told him so."

"Really?" Alex asked.

"Yeah, I couldn't figure out what sort of a benefit his apparent altruism seemed to have for him. He could have all the power and control the entire food supply if he wanted, but instead he seems genuinely concerned about making sure the hungry are fed, the cold are clothed, and the sick are tended. He only holds on to enough and he's not bothered with owning or having more than he and his family need."

"That's a man I would find suspect as hell right there," Alex said shaking his head.

"I asked him about it very bluntly and he was just as frank with me," Pete continued. "He told me that having more food than his family can eat and not sharing is just going to make people angry. All the money in the world won't buy him the most important thing in today's world."

"What's that?" Alex asked.

"Protection. Hannity told me that he's a family man and the best way for him to make sure that his parents, his wife, and his kids are safe is to make this town as safe as possible. Power does not create safety. If he chose to rule this place, he would not be safe. Feeding the hungry, clothing the cold, and healing the sick means that less people are hungry, cold, or sick. People who are less desperate are less dangerous. All of this comes with the added benefit that a great many people love him and feel they owe him."

"Makes sense," Alex shrugged. "But, power always corrupts. Even Hannity isn't incorruptible."

"If he ever becomes corrupt, I'll quit; remember I'm working as a job, not a conscript. He doesn't expect you to unquestioningly follow orders. If you disagree with him, he'll listen. He's never asked me to do anything I wasn't willing to do." Pete gave a tilt of his head meant to replace the shrug he couldn't manage with Kate on his back.

When the house came into view the others gave as close to a cheer as tired people could manage.

"Where'd you get this cute little place?" Kate asked when she'd been deposited on the front steps.

"My good friend Rose," Tara smiled pushing open the garden gate. They needed to have some lunch as soon as possible so that Kate and the others could sleep. Tara carefully gathered spinach and leaf lettuce along with some dandelion greens and chickweed. A nice green salad would probably be a welcome change from what everyone was used to. It wasn't long before Tara was setting a makeshift table that Pete and Alex had put together. They had a big bowl of greens, oil and vinegar dressing, a pitcher of goat milk, and some fresh bread with perfectly white goat butter. Goat butter would have been impossible had it not been for Pete's cream separator. Goat milk was naturally homogenized and so tended not to separate out until it had been sitting too long to taste good.

Everyone ate till they were full and to Tara's amusement spent a good deal of time talking about how nice it was to feel full.

She and Pete left the table long before anyone else to set up the sleeping arrangements. Tara's bed was big enough for one family. Pete carried his cot in for Tracy and they made a cradle out of a drawer from Tara's dresser for Rebecca, who couldn't have been more than six months old. They put the drawer on the floor between the cot and the blankets they spread on the floor for Jake.

After everyone was situated, Pete and Tara began cutting up the beef to preserve it. Half of it was going to be pressure canned, but Pete wanted to dry the rest out for a more portable snack. While they worked, Brom made himself a nuisance underfoot. The cat had decided to stay so Tara kept dropping gristly bits to the cat while Pete frowned.

"You're going to spoil that thing till it doesn't hunt."

"It'll hunt," Tara dismissed him.

More silence followed, but Tara had become wise to it. Pete talked or he didn't. If he didn't feel like talking, conversation was as difficult as trying to wrestle a bear. If she waited him out she'd know how much effort to put into it.

"Looks like we're going to need to make some more beds," Pete told her conversationally.

Good, she needed to talk to him anyway. "I wanted to talk to you about that," Tara said, lifting one of the jars and dumping the boiling water out of it so she could pack it with cubes of beef.

"About beds?" Pete asked, sharpening his knife again so that he could keep slicing off thin strips.

"About where I'm going to sleep. I couldn't ask anyone to leave my cabin, but there isn't room for another bed in there. And, you can't possibly expect me to sleep in a room with strangers," Tara pointed out as she poured boiling water out of the kettle over the beef and wiped the rim before she started on the next one.

"What are you after?"

"I think I should stay in the tent with you," Tara admitted blushing slightly.

"Oh?" he frowned.

"Is that a problem?" she asked, irritation replacing her

embarrassment.

"I'm not sure how I feel about sharing my space," Pete admitted honestly as he went back to slicing the beef.

"That's a joke right?" Tara asked. "You offered up my home to strangers and now you're not sure that you want to offer me a place out of the wind and rain?"

"I figured you would stay there with them," Pete continued frowning.

"What am I going to do? Should I cuddle in my bed between Kate and Alex, or lay on the floor with Jake?"

Pete shifted uncomfortably laying the knife down. "I'm being a hypocrite aren't I?"

"A huge hypocrite," Tara confirmed, keeping her voice as even as possible.

Pete spread his palms out on the table and looked at the backs of his knuckles instead of her. "I'll be honest with you… I'm not comfortable with the idea of sharing my space with you. But, you're right, it makes more sense to have the kids in the house and there isn't really room for you." Pete blinked a couple of times, "Okay, here's my rules. The first, don't touch me without my permission. The second, whenever you want to dress or undress, you'll need to hang a curtain in the corner. I will do the same. The third, if I wake you early in the morning, you aren't allowed to threaten my life. It's my home after all."

"I guess I can agree to that, though I agree to the last one under protest," Tara smiled.

"I also reserve the right to add rules as they become necessary, and protest or none, you agree to them or you sleep in the barn."

Tara stared at him in shocked silence. She couldn't tell if he was joking or not. He'd better be. This was her place, her home, and everyone here was her guest. Not the other way around. Tara took a deep breath, it wasn't worth a dispute. After all, she had a place to sleep tonight and so did their guests. That's what really mattered.

After a cold supper Pete and Tara spread two sleeping bags on the floor of the tent, which was the size of a small room. If it had been a little two-man tent Tara probably would have decided to sleep in the barn. Since she didn't know how long they'd be doing this, she decided that it would be best to bring her personal things over. At the cabin she packed her clothes, books, and Rose's picture into her box and carried it to Pete's place. It felt strange giving up her space, and even stranger to be sharing what little space she now had with another living human being.

That night Tara didn't sleep much. She listened to the unfamiliar rustling of the walls in the night breezes. On and off through the night Pete snored softly and Tara amused herself by wondering if he had some springtime allergies and what the best possible herbs for that would be.

CHAPTER 27

When the misty morning light crept through the tent's flap Tara was loathe to get up. This morning there would be people waiting for her. Up to this point this had been her own private world; except for Pete. She slept when she wanted, ate when she was hungry, and didn't have to think about privacy. Now her clearing in the woods felt small and confining. Tara hung the curtain that she and Pete had devised out of an old sheet. Pete was already out of the tent, probably cooking breakfast.

She slipped out of the flap, rubbing her eyes. Pete was standing over the fire stirring something in a deep pot. Everyone else was loitering near the porch. Rebecca was in Jake's lap and Kylie was looking for interesting things crawling through the grass that she could put in her mouth. Tara grimaced when the child spit out a pill bug.

"Good morning. How you feeling today?" Tara called out as she approached the group.

"A little bad about kicking you out of your own home, but other than that just a bit tired," Kate confessed.

"We noticed you moved your books and stuff out while we were sleeping," Alex pointed toward the cabin. "Why?"

Tara looked at Pete who didn't look up from stirring. "I thought it would be easier to keep the kids contained in the house." She shrugged, "There's not really room for a third bed. There will barely be room for a second."

Alex smiled back and forth between Tara and Pete, "So you found a better arrangement."

"It's a good temporary solution while I come up with something better," Tara explained; her confusion causing a little wrinkle to position itself between her eyebrows.

"Of course," Alex continued to grin broadly.

"Who's ready for some breakfast," Pete cut in staring at Alex. He was met with a round of hearty agreement.

"So what's the plan for today?" Tara asked Pete while they cleared the bowls off the outdoor table they had devised the day before. They'd already shooed everyone else inside to rest up. The group still seemed lethargic and sore, especially Kate.

"I want to go check out the other neighbors, see if there's anyone left in the area," Pete answered carrying the hot kettle over and pouring it into the dishpan that Tara set up.

"Why is that?" Tara asked him

"Because your hilly wooded plot here isn't going to sustain this many people. Maybe there's some nearby acreage up for grabs," Pete shrugged.

"Please don't tell me you're hoping all the neighbors are dead." Tara dropped the bowl she was washing into the water so she could turn on him abruptly.

"No," Pete was matter-of-fact while he swirled the rinse water around in the bowl he held. "There's a farm that borders this property and I was wondering who owned it and why the fields aren't planted."

"How do you know there's a farm?" Tara asked as she turned back to washing.

"I had to get the lay of the land. I wanted to know where the closest resources are. Did you know that you have a spring? It's just a trickle, but you might be able to use it to keep some of the dairy products cool this summer. We can work on cutting a path when we have some free time." Pete gave a dismissive wave. "This land is pretty much swallowed by the neighbor's currently fallow field and I was wondering if they're alive. If so, maybe they just need our help, or would be willing to let us use the land they aren't planting."

Tara shrugged as she handed Pete the last bowl.

"What?" he asked.

"Can't you take someone else with you? After last time I

don't really want to know if the neighbors are alive or dead. What if we find more of the same we found last time?" Tara shuddered even though the morning was warm enough that she wasn't wearing her sweater and Pete was in short sleeves.

"These are your neighbors, your community, and your best hope for survival. They need to know you, need to see you. I want someone to recognize you on the road and know not to shoot you," Pete advised her, dropping the flatware into a jar to dry.

"Okay, I see your point, but I'm going to be terrified," Tara assured him.

"Hopefully I can help you there." Pete smiled

Tara turned the gun over in her hand. "This isn't going to make me feel safer," Tara sighed. They were standing in the shed and Pete was kneeling on the floor.

"You do know how to shoot, don't you?" Pete asked as he dug in the duffel bag between his knees in front of him.

"Yes, I have a passing familiarity with plinking," Tara admitted as she turned the snub nose revolver over in her hand again before pressing the lever to drop the cylinder out; spinning it lazily a couple of times to view the empty chambers before she flipped it back into place. She'd done it to make a point.

"Good." Pete handed her a black object that was a complicated collection of straps. He zipped the duffel bag so this had apparently been the object he was searching for.

"What's this?" Tara asked.

"It's a concealed thigh holster. I don't want anyone to know you're armed. You go ahead and put it on while I get your ammo," Pete explained, opening one of the olive drab ammo containers that had been in the bottom of his gutted dryer.

Pete counted out bullets while Tara continued to stare at the holster. She didn't want to seem foolish, but she had no idea where all the straps went.

"Go ahead and put it on I won't watch."

"I'm not entirely sure how," Tara admitted.

Pete stood up and took the holster from her. "This," Pete instructed her, undoing a buckle at the top, "goes around your waist, these hold the weight in place, and these hold it to your thigh." He showed her the straps in quick succession. "Got it?"

"Sure," Tara told him reaching for it hesitantly. She wasn't sure. She just couldn't imagine how the straps were supposed to sit; she didn't even know where the black pocket was supposed to go exactly.

"Problem?" Pete asked closing the ammo can.

"I lied. I have no idea how to put this on," she admitted embarrassed.

"Here," he said taking it back again. "Go ahead and step in." Pete caught her left ankle and guided it into to the correct side of the pocket; it would be between her legs. His hands slid the strap upward higher than she expected until they were under her skirt and he was moving it out of the way so he could do up the buckle around her waist.

Tara's breath caught while she tried to remember which underwear she was wearing. It was a white pair of boy shorts trimmed in lace. Pete cleared his throat as his hands moved down to position the holster pocket. He moved it around from directly between her legs to just slightly in front of her thigh, but still close to the middle. She wondered briefly if it bothered him that she didn't have the kind of thigh gap that would allow her to wear it between her legs the way movie stars did.

"Let me know if these are too tight." The palm of his left hand was pressed against her inner thigh just under the holster, his fingers holding it in place. The straps around her leg were being tightened, but Tara was too distracted feeling her skin tingle and trying to control her breathing so he wouldn't know how overwhelmed she was by the sensation of his hands on her leg. How could she worry about how tight a strap was or wasn't?

Tara's cheeks burned while she tried not to watch his well-muscled body as he took the gun that she'd forgotten she was holding from her hand.

The sun peaked through the trees; birds sang, and the air smelled green, if green had a smell, spring would be it. Pete walked at her side, the gun on his back swinging against its strap.

The gun strapped to her leg felt strange and out of place on such a nice morning. It took more concentration than Tara had expected not to waddle. Frowning, she thought about how much she disliked the idea of fumbling under her dress for the thing. Pete had her practice drawing it a couple of times. It certainly hadn't gone the way she pictured it. Some sort of smooth movie spy gal she wasn't. Pete assured her it was better than nothing, but Tara imagined it as a good way to get killed. A one-handed draw was out of the question. The only draw that had gone relatively smoothly was when she used her other hand to pull her skirt out of the way first. To her embarrassment she'd also managed to flash Pete another good look at her panties when she did.

"You can stop right there. I promise you there won't be a warning shot!" a voice rumbled, pulling her from the embarrassing memory.

Tara stiffened as Pete stepped in front of her with his hands up.

"Hello, sir. My name's Pete and this is Tara," he gestured with a nod of his chin. "We're your neighbors and we just came to check up on you," Pete called out.

Over his shoulder he whispered to Tara, "Hold on to your gun when he takes mine. Try to look natural, don't fidget."

"Do you really think this old guy is going to rape and murder you?" Tara asked taking in the man's thin frame and silver hair which peaked raggedly out from under a wide-brimmed straw hat.

"Being old enough to be retired doesn't make a man less crazy, less dangerous, or less desperate, but he's often a lot more cunning," Pete mumbled moving his lips as little as possible.

"So, you brought that gun to be neighborly?" the man called out.

"Obviously it's a very dangerous world, but I don't mean you any harm," Pete called back cheerfully.

"I'm not sure I believe you. I know my neighbors and I'm gonna say you folks certainly ain't one of them."

Tara leaned out from behind Pete. "I'm living in the little cabin in the woods just down the road," she assured him, pointing back the way they'd come.

"You sure ain't," the old fellow called. "That place has been empty for years. If you are, you're squatting and we don't appreciate that sort of thing in these parts."

"I'm a friend of Rose Penderton, this was her husband's hunting cabin. She gave it to me before she left. I've got the deed at home if you need me to go back and get it," Tara assured him.

The man considered this for a moment before he lowered his gun. "Rose is good people," the man said slowly. "Any friend of hers is probably good people too." The man gestured briefly for them to approach. "Would you folks like to come inside for some tea?" he asked pausing to look at Pete. "Not that I'd like you to come in to meet my wife with your gun on your back, sir. She's liable to shoot you," he chuckled.

"Not a problem," Pete assured him, "I have every intention of being on my best behavior." As they approached the porch Pete slipped the gun off his shoulder and laid it gently against the railing.

An older woman in a blue dress met them at the door with a shotgun in her hands and a scowl on her face.

"Don't worry Mary, these folks are our neighbors, I invited them in for tea," the man explained calmly.

"That's what they say Fred, but you think it's true? I never saw them out this way before," Mary said narrowing her eyes at them through her gold-rimmed bifocals.

Fred gave her a sly smile, "They talked old Rose out of that falling down cabin."

"They knew Rose?" Mary asked.

"The young lady seems to, swears she has a deed and

everything."

Mary considered this, "Come on in. I've got some cooled tea, you folks want a glass?" she asked.

"We'd love some," Pete flashed her a charming grin.

When they were all seated comfortably on some blue rose-printed couches in a farmhouse living room with glasses of mint tea on coasters on the coffee table, Fred leaned back and spoke to Pete. "So you say you stopped in to check on your neighbors. Are we the first and what prompted this sentiment if you don't mind my asking?"

"Actually," Pete sat up a little straighter, "we headed the other way up the road and found a young couple."

"Mister and Missus Miles," Mary smiled, "lovely folks."

Pete looked at the floor. "Probably, ma'am," he spoke quietly, "but since they were killed, I never found out."

"Killed?" Fred asked shocked.

"Yes, sir." Pete nodded solemnly.

"So you were out this way looking for more bodies?" the man asked.

"Was hoping not to find any more," Pete admitted sincerely.

"Or make more bodies," Mary interrupted with a sour pucker on her face.

"Honest, ma'am, I was just hoping to help you. We couldn't help noticing that your field behind our place isn't plowed, but it looks like it was last year."

"Now son, let's be honest here," Fred frowned, "Why should I believe you want to help me?"

"We don't have any farmable acreage or seeds. We were hoping you do, and that we could help you plant it for a share of the crop," Pete answered.

"Why would you do that?" Fred asked, leaning back against the couch. "Why not just kill us and take it?"

"I like him," Pete smiled to Tara. When he turned back to Fred he spread his hands palms up as if to prove he had no weapons. "Because, sir, none of us are farmers. I don't know a thing about planting times, harvesting methods, or diseases. Your experience is worth more to me than the seed, or land, and

I can't kill you to take it."

Fred chuckled. "Son my fields are fallow only from lack of ability. I'm an old man with a questionable ticker and no blood pressure medication. Crazy part is, I use to make the circuit around the local heritage festivals with my plow team."

"You have a plow team?" Pete asked surprised.

"Don't do me a damn bit of good, but yes I do."

"Well," Pete paused to rub the back of his neck, "I don't know a thing about working a plow team, but I'd be willing to learn. Actually I have a few other folks who might be willing to help out."

"How many men you got living over there?" Fred asked.

"Just a couple," Pete admitted, "and their wives, but they'll need a couple of days to get their strength back. After that we can all be here."

"I don't really hold with the idea of women working the fields, but I guess sometimes you do what you have to do," Fred frowned.

"With any luck," Tara leaned forward in her seat addressing Fred, "I might even be able to help you with that blood pressure."

CHAPTER 28

The next couple of days saw Pete and Alex wandering the area searching for more neighbors or farmable land whenever they weren't working. Other than Fred and Mary, all that seemed to surround them was hilly woodland with nobody living on it.

Tara herself was surprised by how fast she seemed to be getting used to the constant company. She hadn't realized how nice it would be to have people around. Spending time with everyone really helped her feel normal.

On this particular afternoon Tara found herself in the garden weeding the grass out from between the leaf lettuce with Tracy and Kate while the fathers were watching the babies and making some lunch in the front yard. Tara was smiling to herself while the sun warmed her back. Weeding in good company wasn't so bad after all.

"How long have you and Pete been a couple?" Tracy asked, breaking the silence. "Was it before or after everything fell apart?"

"What?" Tara straitened up and dusted some of the dirt off her hands. "We're not a couple."

"Oh?" Tracy paused, "I thought —."

"He's gay," Kate told Tracy matter-of-factly.

"Are you sure?" Tracy asked as Tara bent back down to her row, wondering if she had been admiring him that openly. If so, she needed to pay attention to that. She didn't want to make Pete uncomfortable.

"Oh yeah," Kate winked.

"He just doesn't seem gay to me." Tracy shrugged.

"Obviously he's not a stereotype or anything, but yeah, we're pretty sure he's gay," Kate laughed.

"Pretty sure... or totally sure?" Tracy asked, taking her hat off and wiping her bangs back out of her face.

"Pretty sure," Kate admitted.

"Why?" Tara prodded.

"It's nothing I suppose, it's just the way he..." she paused, considering the right word shaping her hands in front of her like she was trying to build the word out of the air. A shrill whistle cut into their thoughts and Tara jumped.

"What's up Jake?" Tracy yelled.

"There's a kid out here on a horse, says Hannity sent him for Tara." Jake called peeking around the side of the house.

"Tell the kid I'll be there in a minute. I just need to get washed up and grab my bag," Tara called, hurrying out to the pump to wash her hands before running into the tent. Pete was sitting inside with a piece of paper and her pen drawing on the map he'd been making of what was around them.

"Where you off to in such a hurry?" he asked barely looking up.

"Someone sent for me," Tara answered as she pulled her hair loose to brush it and tie it into a tight braid.

Pete set the pen down, "You want me to meet you at Hannity's when you're done, walk you back home?"

"That won't be necessary," she mumbled around the ribbon she was holding between her teeth.

"Where are you going?" he asked.

"No idea." She picked up her sweater and tucked it into the top of her bag.

"I don't like this," he frowned.

"Don't like what?" she demanded.

"You just taking off to wherever. At least take the gun," he said as he walked over to dig it out of the bag of his clothes he kept by his sleeping bag.

"I'm not showing up at someone's sickbed with a gun tucked under my dress," she sighed.

"Then wear it on your hip," he insisted.

"I'll be fine, Mom," she rolled her eyes at him.

"Fine, do whatever you want, but don't come crying to me

when someone's eating your liver," Pete grumbled.

Tara rolled her eyes for him again making sure he saw it clearly before she left.

Tara's day was spent in a chair at the bedside of a little girl waiting for the child's fever to break. Most of the time she was staring out the window as the rain that had rolled in several hours before trickled down the glass.

When she tired of that she began re-reading some of Rose's notes. Every time she held the ledger in her hands she couldn't help picturing Rose as a young mother writing notes about formulas that her neighbors or mother may have given her. In her imagination Tara always saw Rose with her perfect hair from the black and white photo and bright red lipstick. Thinking about how much she missed Rose was sometimes like a physical pain, but at least she had this little piece.

"How's she doing?" the little girl's mother asked from the doorway, causing Tara to shut the book.

"She's resting," Tara whispered brushing a sweaty curl off the girl's cooling forehead. "Her fever broke a little bit ago."

The girl's mother swept in and laid her fingers lightly on her daughter's forehead. "God bless you," she praised Tara with a sincere smile.

Tara handed the woman a small cloth bag of herbal tea. "If her fever returns give her a couple of doses of this over about an hour. I wrote the directions on the paper." Tara handed her the note.

"What can we possibly do to repay you?" the woman asked.

"I noticed that you folks have goats —," Tara began

"I'm sorry," the woman interrupted, "we aren't giving you a goat. Do you have any idea what a goat is worth?" The woman sniffed.

"Actually," Tara sighed, trying not to be put off by the woman's abrupt shift in attitude. "I was going to ask if I could secure stud service for my doe. I noticed you have a male, and

I'm going to need mine freshened in the fall."

"Well," the woman considered, "I'm going to have to discuss the cost of something like that with my husband when he gets back. How can I reach you?" she asked.

"Leave a note with Hannity, he'll make sure I get it," Tara responded curtly.

"I hear something like this is your usual fee," the woman told her holding out a tin can with no label as Tara was putting on her sweater to leave.

"Only if you can spare it."

"We're probably not going to eat it," the woman admitted, "I don't even know what it is."

"I'm not too picky," Tara assured her with a smile.

"I wouldn't want anyone saying the Arthur family doesn't pay its debts." She nodded as if for emphasis.

"We wouldn't want that," Tara mumbled, stuffing the can into her bag as she walked off towards home. It never ceased to amaze her that some people didn't seem to get that this was a different world and that it wasn't likely that folks were whispering at PTA meetings and spreading rumors over the water cooler about one another. At least, she hoped they weren't. What was the point of the world falling to pieces if some of those things didn't go away at least for a while?

Water ran into her eyes and dripped off the end of Tara's nose. She was completely soaked through before the house she had left had disappeared from view. The drab darkness of a rainy day was giving way to the drab darkness of dusk, and it wasn't long before plumes of Tara's breath hung in the air and her teeth were chattering.

The road she was walking was unfamiliar to her; she'd only been on it when the boy brought her out here on horseback. Now that she was studying it, all it seemed to be was a dirt road and fence as far as she could see forward and back. When she finally passed a house she considered stopping, but fear moved her forward. All the horrible things she'd seen at her neighbor's place clung in her mind like mold.

As the last bit of daylight was fading from the sky she noticed smoke trickling lazily out of a culvert and light dancing in the ditch. Tara leaned down listening directly above for a short time, it didn't sound like the lair of cut-throats or thugs. Soaked and freezing she crept slowly down the embankment until she could see a couple of shadows inside the concrete tube.

"Hello?" Tara called moving cautiously in case anyone started shooting at her. Instead, two figures sat huddled over the fire neither of which seemed particularly bothered by her sudden appearance.

"Salutations and good evening miss," a young man who was so covered in mud that it was hard to tell that he was a person called out. He couldn't have been older than nineteen. He tipped a frayed top hat in her direction, but the smile he presented didn't reach the corners of his eyes.

"Everybody always gets the names wrong no matter what I says," mumbled the other shape that looked like a dirty pile of laundry, but sounded like a woman. She was hunched over something that was making a steady clicking sound.

"I'm not sure I understand —," Tara began before the young man cut her off with a quick wave and gestured for her to come into their shelter.

"Don't you worry about Violet," he smiled, showing crooked teeth. "Lettie's a bit confused sometimes. She's been a long time without her medicine," the boy explained sweetly.

"I got caught out in the rain. Do you mind if I sit by your fire?" Tara asked, wringing out the front of her sweater. She wasn't sure how she was supposed to respond to what the boy had just told her.

"We wouldn't want you to catch your death. Here have my seat," he offered, standing and dusting off the slice of log he'd been sitting on as if it were a velvet cushion.

As Tara arranged her skirt in the hope of getting it to dry faster, Lettie looked at her with a very serious expression.

"Daisies and roses have all the fun, but, if you're quiet we don't mind your air touching ours."

Tara nodded slowly and looked at the boy.

"She needs to concentrate," he smiled. "She's been working on her novel for ages. Click, click, clickity, click, she hates to be disturbed," he bobbed his head in the woman's direction.

After a moment of scrutiny Tara realized that the clicking sound came from a keyboard on the woman's lap that she hadn't noticed before. She would have called it a laptop, but most of the screen was missing and only a few wires hung out. Tara couldn't stop herself from wondering what kind of madness was being translated onto the invisible screen.

"She used to be the office aid for one of the local junk yards," the boy smiled distantly. "With her pills she was," he sighed, "a different person."

Tara's heart ached, "You knew each other before?"

"Yeah, she's my aunt," he informed her, only he pronounced it very carefully 'Ont.'

Looking up quickly Lettie yelled, "I bet you wanna' see my kitties!" She began frantically patting her pockets as if trying to find some on her person.

"No, ma'am," Tara answered carefully.

"I thought I told you it needs to be quiet here!" Lettie shouted. "Nobody asked you!"

Tara shut her mouth and wrapped her arms tightly around her body while her eyes found those of the boy.

"I told you she doesn't like to be disturbed," he whispered. "My name's Frank, by the way," he said offering his hand which he looked at then wiped on his shirt a couple of times; offering it again when he was finished.

"Tara," she whispered taking his slender hand in hers and trying not to notice that his shirt was probably already dirtier than his hand could possibly have been.

Pulling her bag open Tara reached in slowly and produced the can she'd taken in payment. "Here," she smiled brightly holding it towards the boy.

"What's that for?" the boy asked eyeing her cautiously.

"For your hospitality," she explained, holding the can up a

little higher hoping the he'd take it.

"I don't provide services," he grimaced putting a rather unpleasant emphasis on the word services.

"Good," she said, "I'm glad to hear that, but I'm not looking for any."

"Then what's this for?" he asked again, finally taking the can from her with his gentlemanly pretext forgotten.

"Eating I hope. To be honest I don't know what's in it, but it has a nice liquid slosh so it's probably not dog food."

"I'd take dog food," the boy shrugged.

"Then it can't really go wrong," Tara assured him cheerfully.

Frank slipped a knife out of his pocket and smiled at her oddly while he stabbed it down into the lid of the can making some rough cuts that made the lid come off shaped like a throwing star.

"Ta da!" he flourished the can before holding it out so that she could see it contained what looked like some kind of soup. The boy held it out to Lettie briefly before he set it on one of the cinder blocks around the fire to warm up.

The click of the keys on Lettie's lap drew Tara's attention while the boy threw the lid from the can into the fire. Lettie herself was staring at Tara as if she were a book and Lettie's eyes tracked back and forth across her face while she muttered like she was reading something to herself. It made Tara uncomfortable.

"The writing breathes you know," Lettie nodded, but after her last outburst Tara was unsure if she should answer or not. "You don't want to disappoint it," Lettie continued. "Worlds are written. Sometimes if you lift the rocks you can see the sentences. Yours is so sad, and it gets worse." Lettie shook her head. "Blood drips from the shelves doesn't it?"

Frank's hand slid down into the pocket the knife had disappeared into earlier as Tara froze. Leaning closer to his Aunt Violet he asked, "Are you saying our guest is dangerous? Is it time we bid her goodnight?"

"Course she's dangerous, all animals are, don't spook her." Lettie's brow furrowed as she stared at the boy. "I think she's a fixer, not a breaker. Hold on, I know I wrote it down here somewhere." While Lettie made some motions on the keyboard's mouse, Frank looked back and forth between the two women.

"I know she doesn't seem wise to you," Frank murmured to Tara, "but Lettie is an excellent judge of character."

"Nope, here it is, says it right here." Lettie nodded again. "She's not the sort for much killing. The blood on her isn't her fault."

"Just the same, show me what's in the bag," Frank told Tara, gesturing with a nod. When she began to pull it towards her, he got irritated. "No, throw it to me," he ordered, his face contorted.

"Please catch it, there are glass bottles in it that are very important to me," Tara pleaded.

When he nodded she tossed the bag with a slow underhand motion across the space between them. Frank snatched it out of the air; opening the flap roughly without letting her out of his sight. First he pulled out the roll of canvas she'd sewn to keep things organized, untying it to investigate the bottles with handwritten labels: Rose's tinctures. Some of her bags of loose herbs and jars of lozenges and pills followed. The ledger came out last since she often carried it in the bottom of the bag. After flipping through the pages for a minute Frank glanced at Lettie, "I think she's some kind of doctor."

"She has her own kitties?" Lettie asked patting her pockets again.

"Fix her," Frank whispered to Tara.

Tara stared at him, "I'm not a doctor. I just know some plants that help people."

"Fix her," Frank spoke louder this time.

"I don't know anything I can do for her, it's not in my notes. I help people with rashes, fevers, and heartburn," Tara implored. "I really don't know how to help her."

"Here," Frank barked as he scooped her things back into the bag. "Here," he tossed the bag back to her.

When Tara caught it she clutched it in front of her body like a shield.

"I gave it back. Now," Frank pointed, "fix her."

"You don't understand. I can't help everyone, I don't know everything. I'm still learning and I just don't know what I can do to help," Tara whimpered trembling, her pulse racing.

Frank stood with his arms at his sides, one hand in his pocket. He chewed on his lip while tears beaded up into his eyes. "But you can try," his voice wavered.

Taking a step back Tara shook her head no.

Frank ran his fingertips back and forth across his lips and paced, watching Tara. "I remember," he stopped and turned to her. "Co-pays, HMO's and all that." Frantically looking around, Frank considered her. "I don't have anything to give you." His eyes snapped back to hers. He took a step forward and pulled his shirt off over his head. It dropped with the top hat inside it at her feet. The knife from his pocket was clutched in his fist.

"The shirt off my back; dry clothes," he blurted.

Tara watched him speechlessly for a moment while his ribs heaved. "Please don't do that. It's really not about the payment. I just don't know what to do," Tara soothed.

Frank stopped with his hand on the button of his pants, looking down at the ground for what seemed an interminable amount of time. The silence was broken when Lettie began clicking quickly staring at some point past the scene in front of her.

Shivering, the boy looked at his hand as if he hadn't seen the knife he was holding before that moment. Slowly he folded the blade open and Tara's breath caught as the dancing light from the fire made it glitter. It was possible that it hadn't. It was just the only thing that Tara's panicked mind could focus on clearly so it seemed more important than it was.

"You have to try to fix her. I'm not asking," Frank commanded as his shaking hand turned the tip of the knife towards her.

Tara shook her head no again, too afraid to say the wrong word and set the boy off.

Frank stood staring at her, trembling. It could have been

years that passed, or just moments before the knife fell from his hand to the muck at his feet and he dropped to his knees with his face in his hands sobbing. He looked back up at her.

Tara turned quickly and fled out into the rain. It was too dark to run through the rocky stream bed, so she scrambled up the wet embankment towards the road. Every slipped step she expected the knife to plunge into her back, but when she reached the road nobody was following her. From where she stood, just audible over the pounding of the rain, she could hear Frank's jagged sobs.

Tara ran. She ran until her legs ached and she gasped for breath. Her toe caught something and it sent her sprawling facedown onto pavement. Skinned knees were common enough when she was a child that she knew she had a pair of them; probably both palms and her left forearm as well. In the dark, however, it was impossible to assess the damage. Sitting up, Tara hugged her knees to her chest for a moment before she began to cry. She couldn't remember the last time she'd felt so helpless. Cold rain and hot tears ran down her face as Tara pulled herself to her feet and continued towards home at a slow jog. At the end of her driveway Tara stopped and sat in the cold until she was no longer out of breath. On aching legs, she walked back to the tent and pushed aside the flap.

CHAPTER 29

The match flared to life against the side of the box casting dark wavering shadows around the inside of the tent. It was blessedly empty. "Thank goodness for small favors," she breathed as she lit Pete's lantern. The idea of Pete's 'I told you so,' wasn't very appealing and Tara wanted the opportunity to clean up in peace.

Just as Tara had imagined, she had scrapes and cuts on her knees and forearm, but her hands looked better than she'd expected. Brutally, she scrubbed the bits of grit out of the cuts.

When she finished she slid into her nightgown, picked up the lantern, and hurried to the cabin through the rain. There was no reason to leave people wondering where she was any longer than necessary.

The door opened to the light and noise of two families having dinner. "There you are!" Alex exclaimed stepping back out of the doorway to let her in.

"Look at you! Your hair's soaked! Come on in and have some stew," Kate called jumping up to take the lid off a pot on the stove and picking out a yellow stoneware bowl from the mismatched collection they'd gathered since they had arrived.

"Where's Pete?" Tara asked looking around at the faces in the room.

"Rescue mission," Jake answered.

"What's going on? Did Hannity send for him?" Tara asked worried.

"Actually, it's you he's off to rescue," Tracy explained, leaning her elbow on the table and her chin on her hand.

"We thought we'd convinced him not to go," Alex grumbled. "But, he appears to have slipped off just after dark."

"I'm guessing you two didn't cross on the road," Kate asked.

"No, he'll be heading for town and I didn't come from that way," Tara sighed. "That's going to be one angry mother hen when he gets back."

"A wet, angry mother hen," Alex nodded.

"Do you think he'll be okay?" Tara asked Alex as she stared out the window into the darkness, thinking about the night she'd already endured. There was no telling what could befall him between here and there.

"I don't worry about Pete," Alex assured her, "He can take care of himself."

Tara lay awake listening to the rain making ticking noises on the tarp that Pete had stretched out over the roof before he left. She wanted desperately to sleep but she was too worried, it had been hours since she'd dried off and crawled into her sleeping bag.

When the tent flap opened it was pushed by wind and rain. Pete stepped inside as the thunder muttered to itself. Tara could hear the water dripping from him onto the floor but she couldn't see him against the darkness.

"Nobody ate your liver I see," Pete said quietly as he lit the lantern.

Tara slipped out of her sleeping bag and readied herself to defend against whatever rude thing Pete was about to say, but when she realized how cold and bone-weary tired he looked she clamped her mouth shut and handed him a towel while he stripped off his jacket and shirt; leaving them in a wet mound on the floor.

"It's nice to know someone cared enough to make sure I still had my liver," Tara smiled weakly.

"It's not a problem," Pete shrugged as he moved stiffly, hanging the sheet and gathering some clothes from his bag.

When the curtain moved again Pete came out wearing pajama pants without any shirt and his hair tousled from rubbing some of the water out of it. As he reclined on his sleeping bag his eyes met hers in the lantern light.

"Everything went okay?" Pete asked

This wasn't what Tara had expected at all. He was supposed to berate her for not being home by dark; for taking risks; for making him tramp around after her in that terrible weather. Tara thought of Frank and Violet, but making Pete worry more wouldn't accomplish anything so she took a deep breath, shrugged, and said, "It went fine. Just took longer than I expected."

Pete nodded, but he didn't look away. "Good," he said finally.

She wanted to tell him how much it meant to her that he cared; that she couldn't remember anyone in her life caring enough to do what he'd just done. Tara's breath caught and she realized she might cry. Instead she took a couple of deep breaths to steady herself and said simply, "Goodnight."

"Night," he replied leaning over and putting out the light.

When Tara woke up, her hair was stuck to her face and her skin felt tacky. The night had warmed up considerably and, now with the humidity, she felt like she was breathing soup. Oh how nice it would be if she could roll out of bed and take a cold shower, but the best she could hope for was to roll off her sleeping bag and splash some cold water on her face. As usual, Pete's sleeping bag was already rolled up and he wasn't anywhere to be seen.

"Morning, sleepyhead!" Jake called as Tara slipped out of the tent. He was sitting in the front yard with his baby on his lap and Kylie at his feet pulling on Brom's ears.

"Where is everyone?" Tara asked, stretching as she headed towards the pump to splash some water on her face.

"Everyone went to town. Alex is joining the guards and my

wife wanted to see if she could get involved with some of the infrastructure projects they're working on."

"Really?" Tara asked surprised.

"She's an engineer by trade. She's a pretty good mechanic, too. I met her while she was up to her elbows in her car in our high school's parking lot. I decided I was going to be her hero and fix whatever she was struggling with."

"How'd that go?" Tara smiled

"I looked like an idiot," Jake laughed. "Learned a lot about fixing cars from her."

Tara took a deep breath. "I'm surprised they headed out without me."

Jake frowned. "It was Pete's call actually. He said you needed time to heal from whatever happened yesterday."

Tara looked at her palms, arm and knees. "He noticed that did he?"

"Yeah, what happened? Are you okay?" Jake asked, bouncing his daughter. "He seemed a little upset that you didn't tell him about it."

"I tripped on the road and fell on my face. I didn't think my gracelessness was worth mentioning." Tara blushed.

Jake shrugged, "Maybe you should tell him that nothing terrible happened. He was beside himself about your disappearance last night."

"I guess I should," Tara admitted. Beside himself seemed an unlikely state for Pete, so she chose to ignore Jake's exaggeration. Tara picked up her gathering basket and headed out to see if she could still find any dandelion roots and see what else might be in season.

"Want some company?" Jake called from the porch before she could step into the forest. He was standing up, cradling his baby in the crook of his arm.

Tara's immediate reaction was to tell him no thanks, she wasn't keen on company, but one look at his friendly expectant smile made a piece inside her shrug and ask if it would really be so bad. "On a nice day like today why not?" Tara gestured for him to follow her as she found a bucket for little Kylie to carry.

It was nearly dark before everyone returned from town. Tracy was so happy at dinner that she talked endlessly about the projects that needed doing that could really use an engineer. They were trying to figure out a way to pump uphill to a reservoir to provide a small living area in town with running water. It would be for the elderly and anyone who might not be in good enough health to be carrying buckets. But the project that she was the most excited about was a wind powered grinding mill that would be needed when the year's harvest started coming in, and the couple of old threshing machines they'd been able to dig out of people's barns that needed to be re-built. Simultaneously, Alex was talking about his new position with Hannity who'd been impressed with his background. Tara was only half listening to anyone. She was distracted by Pete. He looked like he was going to have a good long talk with her the moment they were alone. She was making her excuses in her head for later.

The most surprising thing about dinner, Tara realized when she put her fork down, was that it seemed so normal; a group of friends sitting around the table in the yard laughing, talking, and making plans. Fireflies played in the woods around them. Lamps lit everyone's faces with a muted glow, and the cat was asleep on the porch. A whip-poor-will called in the distance and frogs sang to them. Pockets of laughter burst now and again while people enjoyed each other's company. Tara closed her eyes and breathed deeply. She smelled dinner, a whiff of goat, damp earth, and the smoke of their campfire. For a moment it was the most beautiful perfume.

She grinned at Pete, who was watching her curiously; he shook his head and smiled back. And for the first time in longer than Tara could remember she knew that everything was going to be okay.

CHAPTER 30

Tara peeled the front of her shirt away from her skin to let some air in. Her clearing in the woods was perfectly still and the heat of the fire was oppressive on this mid-June day, but the strawberries and rose petals needed stirring. It was for a recipe they'd found in her neighbor's cookbook. With any luck, around the end of the year the group would be toasting with homemade wine.

Jake and Kate were at the table chatting while they sliced the rest of the strawberries to dry; the ones they weren't feeding to their girls anyway. Tracy and Alex had left early that morning for town. The two of them were gone nearly every day.

Pete had been next door all morning running the furrow between the rows of wheat and corn which were growing nicely. Now Fred was talking to him incessantly while he worked on the foundation for his cabin. The stonework was nearly finished. Pete wiped his forehead with his forearm and nodded absently. She couldn't hear what Fred was talking about, but Pete barely looked at Fred. If she didn't know Pete so well Tara would have thought Pete was ignoring him. He wasn't. Pete paid attention to everything, even when it seemed his mind was elsewhere.

Tara set the spoon down on their outdoor table and made herself comfortable on one of the tree stumps that served as chairs. In front of her was the basket of mint she'd collected while she was gathering rose petals. It would make a wonderful carminative tea, so she was tying it into neat little bundles to hang up and dry.

Brom sat up and looked at the road while he tucked his long tail around his feet. There was a rhythmic noise in the distance. He'd noticed it before her.

"Something's up!" Tara called to her companions. Jake

ushered Kate and Kylie into the house, pushing Rebecca into Kate's arms. A horse was coming down the road at a full gallop.

"Inside! Now!" Pete gestured to Tara to go in.

Fred moved forward, putting his shotgun to his shoulder. Pete pulled his gun from its holster.

Jake grabbed Tara's hand, "Please let's get you inside."

Tara nodded and let him lead her to the cabin, but the rider made it up the driveway before Kate could unlock the door to let her in.

It was Alex, both he and the animal were drenched in sweat. Tara hurried forward to pump a bucket of water for the poor horse.

"We have to go. Now!" Alex yelled, leaning down off the horse to toss a small gas can to Pete.

"What's going on?" Jake asked while Pete sprinted with the gas to the motorcycle he'd parked by the shed.

"Someone raided the White's Farm. One of the neighbors heard a volley of gunshots and ran into town for help." Alex panted. "We need to ride. Hannity's mobilizing all the part-timers, grab your gear and hop on."

"You want to start ahead and I'll grab a ride with Pete?" Jake asked as he headed towards the cabin to grab his gun.

"No, they want Tara on scene as soon as possible. Pete will get there faster than us." Alex fumbled with his reins while his horse danced under him in response to his agitation.

"Me?" Tara asked setting the bucket of water for the horse down suddenly.

"Grab your bag and as much bandaging material as you have on hand!" Alex pointed towards the tent, "We don't know what we're going to find out there."

Tara's heart pounded as she rushed around grabbing as many supplies as she could. She didn't know what she was expected to do to help. It wasn't like she had a lot of triage experience. She was the person who managed small injuries and day to day care. Hopefully she was just going to assist Doctor Farmer.

On the back of Pete's motorcycle, Tara clung so tightly to him it was causing them both to sweat. The wind ruffled her clothes and made her hair sting her face. She'd have preferred to braid it before they left, but there simply wasn't time. The state of her hair was going to be the least of her concerns when she got there.

Pete slowed the bike to a crawl and then turned off the engine just down the road from the White's farm.

"Why are we stopping?" Tara whispered to Pete over his shoulder.

"Please be quiet. I'm listening. I'm not just going to drive you into the middle of danger if I can help it. Hannity would never forgive me."

After a long pause Tara asked, "Why did Hannity want me here in the first place? I don't know what the hell to do for a gunshot wound."

"I'm not sure there's much anyone could do anymore, but you know a hell of a lot more about it than me," Pete told her solemnly. Pete hid his motorcycle in the bushes. "We'll walk in from here," he explained, creeping forward towards the driveway. "Stay behind me and stay low."

Pete moved agonizingly slowly up the driveway. By the time they got to the top, Tara didn't know what was worse; the fear or the suspense. Standing by the first storage building they saw a couple of horses with riders talking animatedly together. Pete joined them briefly before coming back to Tara's side.

"Those are Hannity's boys," Pete informed her as another rider dashed haphazardly up the driveway. It was then that Tara saw the first body. He was a boy; lanky, and probably not more than sixteen years old. She could tell from where she stood that there wasn't any life in him. On his chest was a pool of blood and there was a hole beside his left eye. Blood saturated the white gravel he lay in and white dust hung on it.

"I can't save dead boys," Tara choked to Pete. "Where's the Doctor? Aren't I here to assist him?"

"Doctor Farmer's not coming. It's just you."

Panic gripped Tara. What the hell was she supposed to do? She wasn't a doctor. While she thought of the implications she didn't even realize she'd started hyperventilating.

"Look at me." Pete grabbed Tara's shoulders gently and urged her to look into his eyes. "We're here looking for survivors, you and me. You'll do the best you can for them. I need to ascertain what happened. Can you keep moving?"

Tara stared at the boy for a short while longer, unable to pull her gaze away. When she finally looked at Pete she could see the urgency on his face and she nodded stiffly. She needed to take calm, slow breaths before she passed out right here.

"Keep low and follow me, I see someone else," Pete ordered her, moving forward towards the edge of the building. As several more of Hannity's men arrived and began splitting off into teams to patrol; Tara and Pete moved from body to body. All of them on the ground were already corpses. By the third, Tara had stopped gagging when she put her hand to each neck to find a pulse. As Pete and Tara rounded another shed she could see the house in the distance. The last time she'd been here in the dark. She hadn't realized how much open ground they had crossed; how many buildings they'd passed before they reached it in the truck. At Christmas it had been so quaint and homey. Today it wasn't festive. It felt like war. Like a minefield; every step possibly her last.

At her feet lay another body slumped with his head at an uncomfortable angle against the side of the chicken coop. He had a bucket of feed tipped on the ground near him. There was something familiar about this one, but he was so pale that she could not place him until she was bent down over the body. The man who lay on the ground in front of her was a slightly thinner version of the librarian who had helped her so many months ago. Tara wiped away a tear as she put her fingers on his neck. Startled she pulled her hand back, his skin was chill and clammy but there had been a fast, light fluttering; like the wings of a butterfly.

"He's alive!" Tara blurted out, startled.

Only one wound seemed obvious while she inspected him. Most of the other victims had two or more shots in them. The denim on the librarian's right thigh was saturated with blood. Pete flipped open a knife and cut the denim away from the man's leg. Blood oozed from the wound in the front of his leg, and the hole in the back.

"He's in shock; help me move him so that he can breathe better." Tara pulled open her bag and quickly folded a packing into the wound on the back of his leg. Pete placed a finger on it while she put a pad on the front. Tightly winding a bandage around the man's thigh, she tied it in place. Tara flipped the bucket over, scattering oats on the ground. She used this to prop his leg above the level of his heart.

"I know you. Aren't you the chicken girl?" the librarian whispered.

"Nobody's ever called me that before, but yeah, I guess I am," Tara whispered back.

"What are you doing to me?" he asked

"You got shot. I'm just trying to keep you from leaking blood all over. You need to keep that stuff," Tara smiled weakly, checking the bandage. It needed to be tight as he came out of shock; it was very possible he would start to bleed heavier.

"My leg hurts," he moaned.

"Do you remember what happened?" Pete asked, leaning in so the man could see him.

"Who're you?" the librarian mumbled.

"My name's Pete. I work for Hannity and I'm here to help you. If you could try to remember what happened around here I would appreciate it."

"My name's Steve," he nodded in greeting and Tara felt momentarily embarrassed that she didn't, until this point, know his name. "It was fast," the librarian told him, staring off somewhere into a past that Tara was glad she couldn't see. "I heard some popping noises and I'm not going to lie, I didn't realize it was gunfire. I just stood here listening, trying to figure it out. That's when Will dropped." Steve gestured to one of the corpses with a hole in its head.

Tara nodded. It must have been terrible watching his friends get killed.

"I heard a couple more pops and when I tried to run away my leg hurt like hell." He paused and looked away. "I'd like to pretend I was some kind of bad-ass, but when I saw the blood I started getting woozy and fell over. There were a lot more popping noises. I heard some of the windows breaking. I don't know if the Whites' were returning fire or not, all of this was pretty sudden. Around that time the world got all tippy and that's the last thing I remember. Now I'm wearing half my pants."

Tara smiled, but it died when Steve spoke again.

"How many of us are left?" Steve asked.

Watching his face Tara sat with her mouth open, unsure what to say.

"So far you're the only survivor," Pete informed him, sparing Tara the agony of saying the words.

"What?" The life was wrung out of the word as he said it. "How?" Steve swallowed twice hard. "What about the Whites'? Are they okay?"

"We don't know. We haven't made it to the house yet. Are you ready to try to get back to town? Doc Farmer is with Hannity right now and I can send you back to him." Pete told him matter-of-factly, reaching for the man's arms to get him up.

"Does he have pain medicine?" Steve asked tentatively.

"Who knows," Pete shrugged, "the chicken lady will join you when we're finished here. I'm sure she can give you something to take the edge off."

Tara glared at Pete. Steve's nickname seemed so derisive when Pete said it, but he wasn't even smirking.

Getting the librarian off the ground was difficult to say the least. He wasn't a small man, but eventually Pete carried him piggyback to the nearest rider. Between the three of them they managed to get Steve draped over the horse. Within a few moments Steve was a very uncomfortable passenger on a horse cantering to town.

"Ready to head for the house?" Pete asked, putting his hand

on Tara's shoulder.

Tara nearly jumped. She'd been preoccupied trying to imagine what she needed to do with Steve's wound when she got back to town herself. "Yeah," Tara nodded.

"There's a couple more guys between here and there, we'll have to check them." Pete paused watching her.

"With any luck we can find a couple more survivors," Tara smiled weakly.

As they started towards the house it became apparent they wouldn't. Tara bent down low examining a body whose arm was terribly mangled by a gunshot and a big chunk of his skull was missing. The grass was sticky with blood spray around the corpse. A couple of men on horseback headed towards the house ahead of them, the rider furthest back managed to fling mud on Tara as he passed.

Tara was wiping the mud off her hands with irritation when she was startled by a loud sound. It echoed, like a branch snapping off a tree, but louder. Pete knocked her sprawling into the blood-soaked grass and covered her with his body as another crack tore through the air.

"Hannity's order!" Pete yelled as a frightened horse jumped over them. The impact as the animal landed on the grass was jarring. Men with guns surged forward from behind them making a wall. The first shots roared out of their guns towards the house making Tara's ears ring as Pete pulled her to her feet. "Run!" he demanded causing her to stagger two steps as he pulled her. She quickly kept pace for fear she would be dragged if she didn't. "Fall back," he yelled.

When they slid behind the corner of a shed Tara heard a scream. Someone was hurt. She started out towards the sound, but Pete pulled her back; pushing her to the ground onto her knees with her head low. He was tight against her back, doing his best to wrap around her. There was a scrambling and a flurry of gunshots. Two men ducked behind the shed with them.

"Someone's hurt —," Tara started.

"He's dead," one of the men told her gruffly. "That guy's a hell of a shot. Got Jarod in the face, nothing anyone can do for him now."

"Military?" Pete asked.

"No idea, well trained though, we don't stand a chance against em' at all."

"How many?" Pete asked, his weight still pressing Tara down into the mud.

"Only saw one shooter; doesn't mean there's not more."

"I'd hate to think one man did all this," Pete stared at the bodies on the ground. "I don't think it's possible."

"Listen," the younger man who hadn't spoken yet said, "Whoever it is isn't laying down any sort of fire now. Maybe they don't have much ammo."

Pete sighed, "You know, Bob, whoever's in there has more ammo than he knows what to do with right now. Probably doesn't want to give away his position." Pete looked up and shouted, "Hold your positions!" Tara heard it echoed behind several other sheds.

"What's Hannity's order?" Tara asked over her shoulder to Pete, who had shifted away from her only enough to take his weight off of her, but not enough that she didn't feel like she was wearing him like a coat on a hot summer day.

"What?" Pete asked as if he'd forgotten that she could speak.

"You yelled it. What does Hannity's order mean?"

Pete shifted slightly, "Protect the medic."

Tara felt like a balloon rushing through the air let go by a careless child. "That was about me?" she gasped.

"Of course it was. You're the only person around here who knows herbal medicine. Hannity would have sent Farmer instead, except for the fact that he was falling down drunk," the younger fellow explained.

Tara gagged, "Jarod died because of me?"

"No," Pete corrected her, "he died because someone friggin' shot him. You didn't do it! You're just out here trying to help people."

"But —," Tara began again in protest.

"If you're going to blame anyone for him being out there in front of you, blame Hannity. He's offered extra pay to anyone who followed that order. If someone dies following that order he made a vow to help take care of their family," Pete huffed getting irritated with her.

"How did he make that deal with all these people in such a short time?" Tara asked confused.

"It's a standing order. You are one of several people in this community that Hannity's order applies to," the younger man offered.

"So all this protecting me that you've been doing is for profit?" Tara demanded looking at Pete.

"I'm not sure what you're getting at, but this is the sound of me not arguing with you about this in the middle of a gun fight."

Tara wanted to argue with him, but he was right. It was probably something they needed to talk about when they weren't in imminent danger. "So what do we do?" Tara whispered.

"We wait them out. We're not some band of crack-shooting heroes."

"What if they plan to do the same?" Tara asked trying to ignore the cramping in her legs.

"Then we're here until the night becomes our friend and we hope they don't have night vision scopes."

Tara frowned. "Do you think that's likely?"

"It's someone who is a hell of a shot. This isn't someone who took up marksmanship after things went to hell. He might even be military."

Tara nodded as the sound of an engine revving pierced the expectant silence. Tara was forced back down into the uncomfortable head-down position Pete had finally relaxed and let her out of.

"Where's it headed?" Pete asked his voice hoarse with a sense of urgency.

"It's going into the woods. There's a hole cut in the fence on our 11 o'clock," the older man replied, peering around the side of the building.

"Tell us when it's clear. Then I want our best shots ready to cover a team headed for the house," Pete called out.

Pete barked orders; Alex barked orders; a couple of other men that Tara didn't recognized barked orders. Men scrambled, but no gunfire came from any direction. They discussed their concerns about being flanked. Teams circled and searched, but Tara didn't get to see any of it. She was kept low and covered and everyone was too busy to tell her what was going on. It was like watching ants scatter after you pick up what they were eating, she wasn't sure at what purpose anyone was working.

"They need you!" a boy with a pimpled face told her, sliding to a stop next to Tara and Pete.

"Survivor?" Pete asked.

"For now," the boy answered looking a little ill.

"Let's go," Pete urged, pulling Tara to her feet.

Tara realized he could probably see the look of horror on her face while she considered the implications of "for now." Most of her didn't want to move, it was unlikely she'd actually be able to help a "for now."

Tara barely remembered the trip to the house. She was so wrapped up thinking about what she was going to see and worried about being shot that the boy was opening the side kitchen door before she knew it.

If fear had a smell it would be what she stepped into. Gunpowder, blood, and feces; those were the ones she could identify right away. Below that, raw meat, sweat, and other things she didn't want to consider. Tara squeezed her eyes shut and concentrated on not actually being sick. When she stepped down, something rolled under her foot. What she'd stepped on were two fingers with no hand nearby. Whoever had lost them hadn't stopped to do anything about it. Tara wretched, but managed not to be physically ill on the floor. She needed to look where she was putting her feet from here on in.

Pete offered her his hand, but she didn't take it. He didn't drop his hand back to his side until she was past him, but he didn't say anything about her rejection. There was blood all over the floor leaking from two young women that Tara didn't recognize.

To keep walking Tara had to remind herself this horror would end eventually. Like at the haunted house at the carnival when she was little. You just had to keep moving and finish walking through it and then it was over and it was amazing how you didn't think about it anymore.

"You can do this. I know this is hard, but you can do this." Pete whispered next to her.

Tara nodded. Breathing through her mouth, she hurried to catch up with the boy who was leading them around bodies. The rooms that had been so tidy and rustic were now covered in blood and disheveled. It was hard to believe it was the same house she'd come to with her husband for Christmas dinner.

The sound of someone moaning reached Tara before they got to the survivor. He was in the upstairs bedroom. When the boy pushed the door open Tara took a step back and bumped into Pete. Inside the walls were painted with fresh blood. On the floor, just inside the door was Bob; his shirt a bloody mess. It looked like he'd taken a shotgun blast to the chest. A pool of blood had leaked under the door and they were going to have to walk through it to get inside.

Deer carcass. Alex had shot one in the woods and everyone had cleaned it. That much blood could only be from butchering. It was on the bed, but Tara knew that couldn't be right. Nobody would do that on their bed. Looking closer at the carcass showed it wasn't an animal carcass, but a body that had Sharon's face. Her limbs were tied to the bedposts. She was naked; jagged cuts at the arteries. Shuddering Tara realized he hadn't cut her cleanly, he'd hacked at her. Two fingers on Sharon's left hand were missing.

"Over here," the boy called.

A young man sat crumpled over on the floor, moaning. Blood soaked him, most of it couldn't be his or he'd be dead by now.

"My name's Tara." She smiled, kneeling down next to him.

"I'm sorry about the smell. I think I shat myself," the young man gasped.

"You and everyone else," the pimple-faced boy stated dryly. "I wouldn't mind some clean underwear myself."

"Where are you hurt?" Tara asked, scanning him quickly, but he held his hands over his stomach.

"Got stabbed a few times. It hurts almost too much to breathe. I've been too scared to look at it. I know it's gotta' be pretty messed up." The man's breathing was labored.

"Okay, I'm going to need to see it," Tara informed him calmly, though inside she would rather have run away into the woods after the truck that had taken off than lift that shirt. "I'd like you to look away. I wouldn't want you going into shock now after all you've been through."

"You think it's going to look that bad?" he stammered.

"I can only guess at what it looks like. I see some blood; who knows if it's yours, a shirt, and some hands."

"Can you look at me?" Pete asked. "I've got some questions for you anyway."

"Okay," he winced as he slowly relaxed his hands from his stomach.

Something shifted under the shirt, and Tara's stomach rolled. She had to take a couple of deep breaths and allow Pete to talk.

"Let's start with you name?" Pete asked.

"Everyone calls me Bobby or Junior," he breathed.

"White?" Pete asked

"Yeah, this is my parent's farm."

"Do you know who did this to them?" Pete asked carefully as Tara began to very slowly peel the shirt away from the young man's injuries while he gasped.

The first thing she saw were jagged holes and several bits of severed intestine, along with a loop poking out of one of the holes in his skin that were still oozing blood, one hole was running in a trickle.

"Did what to whom?" Bobby asked confused.

"Your parents," the kid with the pockmarked face clarified.

"I'm sorry I don't have my glasses on, I'm nearly blind without them. What happened to my parents?"

"Did you hear anything?" Pete asked slowly.

"Not really I just woke up a little while ago. I passed out for a while. What happened to my parents?"

Tara slowly lowered his shirt. She couldn't think of a single thing that was going to help him at this point. Even if Doctor Farmer could perform such a complicated surgery, she knew Bobby would still die of infection.

"How bad is it, doc? You look like you've seen a ghost?" Bobby winced.

"I'm not a doctor," Tara chose her words carefully. "I'm just here filling in for someone else. There's not much I can do for you right now. We'll need to get you to the doctor before we know anything."

"My parents are dead aren't they? Did the man who stabbed me stab them too?"

"How much do you remember before you got stabbed?" Pete asked.

"Not much... It's all kind of a blur right now."

"That's to be expected," Pete comforted him before continuing, "Do you remember anyone with guns?"

"I'm sorry. I'm having a really hard time thinking strait. I'm really tired. Are my parents dead?" Bobby whispered.

"I'm sorry," Tara apologized, "they are."

Tears dribbled on the young man's cheeks. "They're really good people. Smart too," Bobby mumbled. Fresh blood was still spilling from his wound. Tara didn't apply pressure; it seemed cruel to prolong the inevitable.

"I know. I met them. We had dinner together. They gave me a goat named Greta," Tara spoke quietly.

"Goats are funny. That sounds like them," Bobby smiled slightly.

"Do you remember anything about what the man who stabbed you looked like?" Pete asked.

"I'm sorry; you're going to have to come back tomorrow. I'm too tired. I need to sleep. I have to trim hooves tomorrow."

"Goodnight, Bobby," Tara whispered leaning forward to give him a kiss on his cheek.

"Night, Mom," he sighed.

Tears rolled down Tara's cheeks, but when she wiped her cheek with the back of her hand a smear of blood came with it.

Staring at the blood from her face in revulsion, she listened to Bobby's last few breaths shuddering through him; like he was fighting to keep going. After several minutes of silence she leaned forward to check his pulse and shook her head. Then she collapsed in great wracking sobs. The man had died right in front of her and she'd let it happen, but she didn't know what else to do. They would never have been able to move him. She didn't have anything to give him for the pain. There was no way they could anesthetize him for surgery.

Pete rested a hand gently on Tara's shoulder. "There was nothing you could do."

She knew that, but that didn't make her feel like less of a failure. What was the point of her even being here?

"Speaking of goats," Pete turned to the boy, "Did you see any livestock?"

"Couple of dead cows, but that's it. Lots of tire tracks in the farm yard."

"Dead cows are a lot harder to move than live ones. The truck that was here was just what was left of the raiding party; the stragglers. It would have taken a lot of people and a lot of vehicles to clean this place out, there were a lot of cows. Have a couple of the guys load up the cows they left and take them in, then get the crews out here to bury the dead," Pete said as he steered her numb body out of the house.

While she walked Tara stared at the bloody tracks; all leading out of the room and thought about her bloody footprints in the room and down the hall. Her signature; her stain.

Out in the sunlight what she'd seen inside already felt less real. Men and horses went this way and that on errands that she didn't care to know about. Pete abruptly took off across the field but she barely noted his disappearance. Tara looked around into a sea of strange faces feeling lifeless and deflated.

"Tara!" Pete called, waving to her, "come here."

Tara hurried over to where he stood with several men and a couple of horses. "Terry's going to get you out of here. You'll ride to town and take care of Steve. I have a lot of things I need to help sort out around here."

Terry smiled down at Tara from the back of a brown horse who swished her tail and snorted as Tara took a step towards her. Reaching down, Terry caught her hand and quickly swung her up onto the horse behind him. "Hold on tight Miss Hillcrest," Terry called over his shoulder, "This mare's spirited."

Tara barely had her arms around Terry's broad body before the horse took off at a gallop towards town. The ride was rough enough that she was afraid if she opened her mouth her teeth would clack together. They couldn't talk and that was fine with Tara. She didn't want to talk. She didn't want to think. At least she was going away from the house, away from the horror. The sky above had soft puffy clouds, birds sang in the trees that crowded the fence lines on either side of the road, and green grass waved. A day like any other; oblivious to what had happened in the clearing. It seemed sacrilegious that such horrible things could happen on such a beautiful day.

CHAPTER 31

Tara realized when Terry let her down off the horse in front of the clinic that she'd never been in the building before. Boards covered the holes where two large windows had been, but skylights helped light the interior. The first thing Tara thought was that the waiting room looked wrong. The window that would separate the receptionist from the room stood wide open. Chairs were tipped on their side and the room smelled vaguely of vomit and needed desperately to be swept and mopped. That was the problem. A doctor's office was supposed to be clean and smell of disinfectant.

The door back to the examination rooms stood open and Tara followed the murmur of voices until she was standing in the doorway of a room where Steve lay on an exam table talking to a young man who was sitting with him.

"Holy shit, finally," Steve gasped. He went quiet and stared at Tara. "Wow, what happened to you? Are you still alive? Are you some sort of badass? Are you the kind of person they make movies about? Every time I see you, you have battle damage."

Tara glanced down at the blood all over her. "It's not mine," she assured him.

"Holy shit," breathed the young man sitting with Steve staring at her.

"I'd like you to meet my brother, Richard," Steve introduced, "Richard this is that badass chicken lady who appears to be some kind of doctor."

"I'm not a doctor," Tara admitted. "Speaking of doctors," Tara said glancing around the room. "Where's Doctor Farmer?"

"Hell if we know," Steve shrugged, "I've been sitting in here slowly bleeding to death and I haven't heard a thing from him. I thought he was still out at the White's."

"I'm going to need someplace to clean up and some help from him to look at that wound. I was told he was here," Tara frowned. "I'll be right back, sit tight boys."

Tara headed down the hall, peeking her head into room after room until she finally found what must have been his office; it stank of alcohol and body odor.

"Hey!" Tara kicked Doctor Farmer's foot. He was laying with his head down on his desk and an open bottle of vodka near him.

"Whad' da' 'ell ya' wan'?" Farmer slurred at her as he pulled his head off his desk, leaving a pool of drool behind. When he opened his eyes and actually looked at her he dropped his head back onto his desk. "I mean," he started again, "The hell with what you want witch. Get outta' my office."

"You have a patient to attend. A young male with a gunshot wound to the leg. He's complaining of pain and I'm sure it needs to be cleaned and examined."

"Then get out your little spell book and make him all better," Jim snorted, waving a hand for her to go away.

"Get your ass up right now!" Tara yelled. "They had to send me out as a medic in your place you useless piece of shit! I don't know triage! Think how many people could have died today because I've never had to make a tourniquet before? Because you couldn't do your job!"

"How many people?" he asked scratching his scalp under his dirty hair.

"How many people what?" she asked confused by his calm.

"How many people died because you couldn't make a tourniquet?" he asked, reaching for the vodka bottle.

"None," she snapped taking the bottle off the desk as his fingers touched it.

"Well then," he shrugged, "sounds like you had everything under control. By the way you have some brains in your hair." He gestured by her left ear.

"Under control?" she shrieked incredulously. "They were nearly all dead to begin with."

"Then what the hell do you want me to do about it. I can't raise the dead! You're the witch," the doctor snapped.

"I watched a man die and I couldn't help him. I wasn't equipped to do anything!" Tara snapped back.

"You've watched a man die. A man. Just one. Because you didn't have what you need. Why didn't you say so?" the doctor said sarcastically while he dug a quart jar with clear liquid in it out of his desk drawer and began unscrewing the lid. "You poor dear... I'm *so* sorry that you've had to watch one human being die because you didn't have what you needed to help him." The doctor took a gulp of the liquid in the jar. "But do me a favor," Jim sniffed then went silent staring at the jar in his hand. "When it's hundreds you find someplace to get your own booze, I'm not sharing."

Tara stared at him without any idea what she should say.

"What's the matter, witch? Your familiar got your tongue?" he sneered.

"I'm sorry," Tara spoke quietly.

"You don't have to apologize to me. I don't give a damn what you said and I'm going to forget it after you leave anyway," he told her, taking another drink of the liquid in the jar that made him cough violently.

"No, not for what I said. It's because I've never been in your situation before. Not until today. I'm called for rashes, and sore throats, and fevers. Nobody calls me when they've lost a lot of blood, or the injury is severe. I've never had to let someone die and I never had the power to save a person taken away from me by circumstance. I never wielded that kind of power."

Jim shifted uncomfortably in his chair holding the jar.

"I'm sorry, but you need to remember," she told him setting the lid back on the jar in his hands, "Empty cabinets doesn't make you less of a doctor."

Jim stood up from his chair and took an unsteady step forward until he was standing right in front of her. "If you're done talking I'm going to go take a piss, then I'd like you to stay the hell out of my office."

"Fine," Tara looked away. "But," she turned towards the door, "I'm going to go take care of your patient. Please check his wound if you sober up. I'll be back in the morning to check on him."

"Give him his wing of bat or whatever! Just try not to kill him in my office. I hate when that happens," the doctor called after her as she headed down the hall to clean Steve's wounds.

Tara still hadn't gotten to wash the blood off anything but her hands and arms. It made her skin feel stretched, puckered, and sticky. *These stains will never come out of my jeans,* she thought as she stared down at the blotches of blood covering her. She looked like she'd murdered a nice family and their dog. She shuddered when she realized that she hadn't, but someone else had.

When Tara pushed the tent flap open after she got home she was relieved that Pete wasn't anywhere to be found. He was probably still in town with Hannity's crew. Tara didn't want to see him. They had a fight that needed to be resolved and she didn't have the energy to have that fight tonight.

Brom slid in through the flap and made himself comfortable on Tara's sleeping bag. She smiled at him, glad not to be alone after the day she'd just had. At least Brom wasn't pretending to be her friend. "Nobody pays you to hang around me do they?" she asked, scratching behind his ears.

She wanted to sleep, but first she needed to get cleaned up. The fire still crackled outside; Kate had probably already made dinner on it. Tara fed it a couple of logs and swung the kettle out over the hottest part. In a few minutes she returned for it and poured it into Pete's basin. Tara stared at the sheet she was supposed to use to make a curtain for privacy, but she was too tired to care. Tara stripped bare and began scrubbing at blood that was so thick in places it came off in flakes.

The tent flap rustled and Tara tensed, but relaxed when she

recognized Pete.

Pete didn't relax, but instead stared at her open-mouthed. "What are you doing? Where's the sheet? I thought we talked about this? I thought we had an arrangement," he sputtered.

Sighing tiredly, Tara shrugged. "It seemed like too much work."

Pete turned his back to her. "If this roommate thing is going to work, we both need to follow our simple rules."

"I'm sorry. I'm dead tired; I barely have the energy to get this mess off of me. If I wasn't certain that there were brains in my hair I would go to bed right now. I don't see why it matters anyway."

"You don't see why it matters?" Pete growled at the canvas in front of him. "We had an agreement! That's why it matters."

"I'm sorry if you dislike naked women," Tara snapped, picking at something dried into her hair. "But I frankly don't care at the moment."

"What? Why would I dislike naked women?" Pete asked, shifting and crossing his arms, but not turning around.

"Since you're gay." Tara was tired of playing games.

"What?"

"I'm sorry, homosexual... whatever term you prefer. It never bothered me, you know." Tara slumped dropping her cloth back in the filthy water.

"I'm not homosexual," Pete sighed.

Tara froze, "You're not?"

"No. Why did you think I'm gay?"

"Things you've said about not being that kind of guy and having secrets. Nobody sees you with women and, well," Tara hesitated, "Kate told me that you are! That you haven't dated anyone since she knew you. That you disappeared every now and again to take on lovers in the city."

"Kate has a very active imagination," Pete told her pointedly. "Did it ever occur to you that if you wanted to know something about me you could just ask me instead of gossiping about me behind my back?"

"I didn't know you well enough for something like that to be any of my damn business back then," Tara admitted starting to get mad at his judgements.

"Then why were you talking to Kate about it?"

"I'm feeling a little judged here."

"You're feeling judged?" Pete huffed. "I have someone telling me my sexual orientation."

"Are you mad that I thought you were gay?"

"No, I'm mad that you didn't bother to ask me, then or now."

"It's not like you bothered to offer up the information either."

"I'm sorry. It's not a conversation I thought I needed to have. 'By the way I'm a man who is attracted to women'," he mocked.

"What am I supposed to think? You never gave me any indication that you are interested in women," Tara spoke through clenched teeth.

"That's because I don't involve myself with married women."

She hadn't meant to make it personal, but Pete did. It shouldn't have hurt, but Tara winced when he said it. She was still married, but only technically. Her husband had run off after less than half a year of marriage. Absently she rubbed her left-hand ring finger. She'd nearly forgotten. It seemed like a different life. If that's how he wanted this to go that was fine with her.

"Well I try not to involve myself with liars," she retorted, her voice full of snow.

"Are you calling me a liar?" Pete demanded with an edge to his voice. She'd hit the nerve she wanted to hit.

"What would you call someone who pretends to be someone's friend for money?"

"What the hell are you talking about?"

"Did Hannity tell you to keep an eye on me?" Tara demanded.

"Yes."

"That's my point," Tara shot back.

Pete took a deep breath, "Have you gotten dressed yet? I'd like to talk to you face to face."

"No."

"Why?"

"Because I'm still covered in dead men!"

Pete was silent for a few moments. "I can't do this with you like that. Would you please put some clothes on?"

"No."

Pete didn't say anything else. He simply shoved the tent flap open and was gone.

"Jerk," she muttered.

Tara stared at the place Pete had been standing. Hot tears were streaming down her cheeks even before she realized she'd begun to cry. It was too much. This was all too much. She sunk slowly to the floor and began to sob. All of this time Tara thought she and Pete were friends. Pete's friendship reminded her that the world wasn't all terrible, but now she knew Pete was only there because he was paid to be. How could she have been so stupid?

CHAPTER 32

The next morning, as she promised, Tara was at the clinic bright and early. She'd walked into town with Alex and Tracy, leaving Pete behind to work on his cabin. She didn't want to talk to Pete, let alone spend the whole day with him. Not like he'd offered to walk her in or anything. He never even came back into the tent that night. She guessed he'd slept in his truck. Tara felt out of sorts because now everything felt like a lie.

Well, not everything. What she was doing now was still very real. She could still help people, and she didn't have to be paid to be there, unlike some people.

"How are you doing this morning, Steve?" Tara asked walking briskly into his room at the clinic without knocking.

"I'm sore."

Tara was happy to see that a new bandage had been wrapped on the wound. "Did you do that yourself?" she asked gesturing to it.

"Nope, the doc came in to look at it really early this morning. He said I got lucky. The bullet missed the bone and any major blood vessels. Said it's just soft tissue damage, so if we can keep it clean I'll get to keep the leg," he smiled. "He even said you did a really nice job on it, but that I wasn't supposed to tell you that."

"Well then I'm glad you didn't tell me," Tara winked. "But, I want to warn you, he's not kidding about keeping it scrupulously clean to keep the leg," Tara warned.

"Really, I thought he was just messing with me," Steve whimpered, looking solemn.

"Nope, we don't have any antibiotics." Tara said laying out some of her supplies. "But I have some yarrow, some echinacea, and a little garlic I'd like you to take. I also have some honey here."

"Hot damn," Steve said reaching for the jar.

"For your wound," Tara clarified, snatching the jar out of his reach. "If you eat it we can't use it on you. Hopefully with regular cleaning and sterile dressing changes we won't have any problems," Tara patted him on the shoulder. "But if you start feeling feverish let the doctor know right away."

"Not a problem I got faith in you guys," Steve smiled. "But when can I go home. This place stinks."

Tara chuckled, "Do you live alone?"

"Nope, I moved back in with my mom and brother."

"Then probably as early as tomorrow, but the doc is really in charge of that, so it's his call," Tara shrugged.

"Hey, did you ever actually get those chickens you were after?" Steve asked while Tara measured out his medicine.

"No. It's funny, but everything happened and I never actually got the chance." Tara gave him a glass of liquid.

He threw it back like he was taking a shot and gagged. "That's awful."

"I know this stuff tastes pretty bad."

"No, I mean not getting the birds must have really ruffled your feathers," he grinned.

"I'm not doing this again," Tara smiled. "I'll be by later tonight to check on you and make sure you get your medicine." She gave his hand a squeeze.

"Speaking of which," he stopped her as she turned to go. "You guys said something about pain killers."

Tara stopped, "Sorry, I almost forgot."

"I didn't," he grumbled.

"We'll start with some willow bark tea and I have a couple of other tricks up my sleeve if it doesn't help," Tara assured him as she pulled Rose's ledger out of her bag to look up the dosing information.

After her check-in with Hannity to see if anyone needed her,

Tara found herself with time to kill. With yesterday's events still fresh in her mind she wasn't going to be wondering around by herself outside of town. Alex and Tracy wouldn't be heading home until the evening, which during these longest days of the year wouldn't be till quite late so she decided to go for a walk.

Tara's unstructured wondering through the town reminded her how much it had changed. There was a stable not far from Hannity's store. Hitching posts were starting to pop up. Bicycles were everywhere. Someone had opened a blacksmith shop down the road and the steady sound of metal hitting metal rang clear. In the distance there were the sounds of industry. Tracy's mill was going together with remarkable speed. She and several others in the community had designed it from some old pictures they'd found in the library.

The library was still there, minus a few romance novels that had become bum fodder or fire starters. Nobody sat at the desk anymore, but people wandered in and found a book every now and again.

By the time she realized where she was going her walk had taken her full circle to the church. She stood at the bottom of the steps looking up into the open double door. Tara knew why she was here even if she didn't want to admit it to herself. It had been where her mind was all day.

Inside the main room the pews had been re-arranged into an order that made no sense to Tara, but probably did to the people sleeping in them. There was a hall leading out of the room and at the end of the hall on the right was a door. When she knocked a pleasant voice called out, "Come in."

"What can I do for you?" Pastor Richard asked without turning away from the tea he was pouring into a cup from the tray on his desk. It was a heavy wooden desk, the kind that was meant more as sculpture than furniture. The room was also finished in a dark paneling that made the room look severe and gloomy, like it was already judging you for your sins. It had obviously been designed with electric lights or a siege in mind as there was only one small window.

Richard himself was the opposite of this room. He was a real salt-of-the-earth man who kept his doors open to sinners and good Christians alike with no judgement. He was slightly pudgy, but had become less so in recent months. His jeans were loose, the extra size being taken in by a belt. Over that he wore a simple blue t-shirt and a warm smile on his lined face. His hair had at one time been dirty blonde, but now it was mostly white.

"Oh, Tara," he said when he turned around, "Can I get you some tea?"

"No thanks," she gave a dismissive little wave.

"Make yourself comfortable." He gestured to the dark leather couch in corner of the room. "If you can on a day like today," he joked as he pulled his shirt away from his neck and mopped his brow with a handkerchief.

"Thanks," Tara replied, tucking her dress's faded fabric carefully under her as she sat. She had no desire to stick to the leather.

"So what brings you in to see me today?" he asked.

"Well," she stared at the wall, fidgeted, and then paused to think about how she wanted to say what was on her mind.

"No need to be embarrassed if you've come here for a little counseling. I've spent months listening to things even I wouldn't have imagined," Richard prodded, putting on a friendly smile.

"What would I need to do to get divorced?" Tara asked all in a rush.

"Divorced?" he confirmed leaning back in his seat. "We haven't had a lot of call for that. As a man of God I'd like to say first that the vows you've made before God are very important. Secondly it needs to be remembered how important a partner is to help with the work every day."

"I know," she paused, "but my husband left me back in January for another woman."

Richard looked momentarily confused. "I'm sorry I thought you were married to Peter Hatcher."

"Pete?" Tara stared at him, "No. What gave you that idea?"

"I thought you were living together and I'm making no judgments here," he assured her.

"We do. Pete, Alex, Kate, Kylie, Jake, Tracy, and Rebecca have been staying with me," Tara informed him.

"Of course, that's very kind of you to take in those who are in need."

"Thank you," she said, "But I'd really like to know what I can do about a divorce? I know you are in charge of record-keeping for the town, so I figured you were the man to talk to."

"Yes, I suppose I am," he sighed. "If you can get him to come here and express his desire to end the marriage I can get things recorded as such."

"That's going to be a problem," Tara frowned. "They went to Chicago… or that's where they were headed anyway."

Scratching his chin, Richard leaned back to think. "Without him here I don't think I can reasonably grant you a divorce."

"How can that be right?" she interrupted, but he held up a hand so she fell silent.

"I think," he said, "that, given the state of the world right now, if your husband doesn't return within one year of when he left, it would not be unreasonable to assume that he is dead."

He nodded his head, "Yes that should be adequate time for him to return. A man who hasn't returned for his wife inside of a year is probably dead. Return in February and I will record him as dead and thus nullify whatever marriage vows had existed. We will not have to draw up a one-sided divorce which I simply can't condone."

"Thank you," Tara replied solemnly, but inside it was like a weight had been lifted, even if it was only a small one. Not that it made a difference to anyone but her. "Do you mind," Tara asked, "If we keep this conversation between us?"

"Not at all," Richard smiled at her, "If there is one thing I can do it's keep a secret."

The rest of the day passed quickly and without bloodshed in

Tara's little corner of the world. Before she knew it she was trailing after Tracy and Alex, who were chattering happily like birds while they walked along the dirt road on the way home.

"Something wrong?" Alex called back.

"What?" Tara asked, shaking herself out of her head. She'd been lost between emergency treatments for infection and Pete's words about not getting involved with a married woman. Why had he made it personal?

"I asked if something was wrong." Alex repeated. "Are you having a hard time getting yesterday out of your head?"

Happy for an easy explanation Tara nodded.

Alex walked back to put an arm around her shoulders, "As a cop I've seen terrible things. Some of the worst were the car wrecks. I don't want to describe what several tons of metal smashing does to a human body." Alex winced, "But I had to learn to compartmentalize. When I was at work, my mind was at work. At home I tried to keep myself from thinking about anything but my beautiful wife and then my beautiful daughter. I'm not going to say I was always completely successful." Alex shrugged, "but living in the moment is a place to start."

Tara felt guilty that the moment she'd been living in wasn't so much about the horrors she'd seen... and they had been horrors. Those already seemed surreal, like she'd watched them in a particularly bad movie. Now that the movie was over her brain tried to glaze over it. What she'd been thinking about was the stranger that lived in the tent with her at night. If he was dishonest about his motives for being around her how could she trust him?

Alex was looking at her expectantly so Tara nodded. "I'll try."

"If you ever need to talk about it, I'm here for you," he soothed, giving her shoulder one last quick squeeze before he let her go.

"Thanks," she smiled, though she had no intention of talking to him about what was really on her mind.

When Tara walked into the tent that night the flaps were open to invite the breeze in. Pete sat on a stool reading shirtless in the last light of dusk. Tara understood his reluctance to light a lamp; even a little more heat would have been unbearable. Pete never looked up, didn't even acknowledge her.

That was a game that two could play. Tara hung the curtain and changed into her nightgown then went about brushing and braiding her hair without looking in his direction. The silence was like smoke seeping into all the cracks and surrounding everything.

Pete closed his book with a snap that made Tara jump and he dropped it forcefully on top of the pile. He looked fixedly away from her while he walked past her and lay down on his sleeping bag with his back to her.

"Night!" Tara snapped as she lay down on her sleeping bag. His reply was even more silence.

CHAPTER 33

The problem with summer, Tara decided, was that it had a way of stealing away whole days to hot sweaty work. On this particular day Tara's entire body ached from the unfamiliar motion of using a scythe. She'd spent all morning working side-by-side with her friends cutting hay for Greta. It now lay spread in Fred's field smelling sweetly of cut grass while it baked in the summer sun. They really should have started this more than a month ago, but it had taken quite a while to locate a couple of scythes.

Across the clearing, Pete was diligently working on his cabin. He'd been spending all of his free time since they had fought working on it. Tara didn't know if his intention was to avoid her, but it had been working. Pete had barely said more than a sentence at a time to Tara in weeks.

Shade pooled under the big oak tree at the edge of the clearing where Tara sat watching him work. The walls of Pete's log cabin were up and chinked with thick clay mud. A frame supported a tarp that served as the roof. Shutters covered the holes in the walls that would one day house windows if Pete could find some.

Today's project was to finally hang the heavy door. It had been saved for so long because Pete had to commission some hinges robust enough to hold it from the town blacksmith.

Tara set Rose's ledger open on her lap so that she at least looked like she was doing something. She would let the others help Pete without her. It would be hard for the two of them to politely ignore each other if she was helping him too.

There were a few false starts and a busted knuckle for Jake, but by the time the first fireflies darted through the woods Pete's door swung freely in its frame.

Dusk already darkened the interior of the tent Tara and Pete still shared to an eerie gloom when Pete wandered in silently as he had every night for the past few weeks. Normally he would lay down facing the wall and ignore Tara for the rest of the night. Not that she had offered him any friendly greetings either. Even when they had to work together or travel it was done in silence. Tara scarcely looked at him.

Today he stood watching her. "Tara?"

The sound of her name snapped her attention to Pete. "Yes?"

"Good news." His voice held a tone that implied that whatever he had to say was anything but.

"What?"

"I'm finally going to be out of your space," Pete informed her, picking up the trunk he'd built that held most of his personal possessions.

"Oh?"

"I have a door so I think it's time for me to move to the cabin." Pete nodded several times as if he expected her to say something.

At first Tara wasn't sure what she should say. "You're moving tonight?" was all she managed. It's not like Tara didn't know he was going to move, but some tiny part of her still expected they would be moving to the cabin together. They may not be getting along, but she was still his job wasn't she?

"Yeah, I thought I should move as soon as possible." Pete announced calmly.

"You don't even have a roof."

"I know, but I can make one. I have the tarp until it's finished."

"I see," Tara nodded slowly. She'd been acutely aware the moment he took the tarp off the tent, because now when it rained the roof pooled and dripped.

Pete ducked out of the flap of the tent with his trunk. He'd be back in a moment for the rest of his things, but she allowed herself to let out a groan in his absence. Tara hadn't planned for this eventuality. She wouldn't have a house come winter. It was already late summer, what did he expect her to do?

Pete made several more trips picking up his things. All that Tara had were her books, her sleeping bag, her herbal kit, and her box that held her clothes and personal effects. When Pete at last picked up his lantern he hesitated before setting it back down.

"You can use this. I'll stick to candles for now."

Tara nodded. How did she keep ending up here?

"I bet it feels good to have your own space again," Pete offered with a brief smile that didn't reach his eyes.

"Sure," Tara mumbled. Was he messing with her? Did he say that to start a fight?

"Something wrong?" Pete asked quietly as he stood by the flap of the tent watching her.

"No," Tara shook her head quickly.

Pete stood in silence for a few moments before he turned and disappeared. He still wasn't any better at goodbye.

"My space my dying ass," Tara grumbled looking at the olive drab walls of the tent. They were perfectly motionless in the night's oppressive heat. How could anyone call this tent her space? Everyone here was her guest, not the other way around. Yet, here she was living like a squatter on her own land. Would Pete let her stay here and freeze this winter? He had more compassion for her when she was nearly a stranger than he did now. Not only that, he was rejecting her again.

Several days passed and life went on. Tara made a trip to town with Alex, Kate, and Tracy while Jake played his frequent role as babysitter. Kate had been planning a soiree to celebrate the completion of the mill. Tracy's crew had somehow managed to get it done before the harvest. Tara had stopped checking in on Steve, but he cornered her outside of Hannity's and presented her with his payment. It was a hen and rooster in a cage. The hen was a puffy-faced tan thing and the rooster was striped like a barred rock. Tara had insisted it was much too much, but he wouldn't let her give the birds back to him. She didn't know how he'd refrained from making chicken jokes at the time.

The morning of the party Tara leaned back from the tomatoes she'd been slicing and wiped her forehead. Cicadas sang even at this early hour of the morning. All around the clearing a gentle breeze bent the goldenrod tops still dressed in green on this early August day. Bees buzzed around the liquid the tomatoes leaked and the chickens bathed in the ashes from last night's fire.

Everyone but Pete was already in town. The others had headed that way the night before, but not until they peeled the tarp off Pete's roof and took it with them. Tara had to admit she was delighted. It served him right. She and Pete had been left behind to mind the animals, as neither of them had a hand in the town gathering, and a goat doesn't milk itself.

The steady sound of Pete splitting shingles from one of the cedar trees he'd cut down paused at the other end of the clearing.

"Is the food ready to go yet? Pete called, unbuttoning his shirt as he headed in her direction.

"Yeah," she frowned, sliding the last of the tomatoes off the cutting board into the bowl they were taking with them. It was the day of the festival and she'd made a veggie salad as their potluck contribution.

"I'm going to get washed up, are you going to change before we go?" he asked draping his shirt over his shoulder before wiping his forehead with it.

"Yeah, I'm going to get cleaned up at my place." Her words tasted like irritation while she gestured towards the tent. Pete nodded and headed into the cabin while Tara made a face at him behind his back and wished he would keep his damn shirt on. It was hard to seem cold and distant while she was molesting him with her eyes.

After a refreshing cold scrub, Tara fished her new blouse out of her box. She'd been looking forward to today since she'd learned about it and had taken the blouse in payment for treating an infected ingrown hair. The blouse was gray silk in a simple pullover style that fluttered against her skin as she moved.

Without a mirror to see herself in she could only imagine what it looked like on her, but she didn't really care, she still enjoyed how it felt. Tara brushed her hair until it was soft, but it was still damp when she twisted it up into a loose roll that she pinned in place.

Pete was waiting for her on the porch of her old home where the others lived now. He was already holding the bowl. His eyes roamed from her face, down her blouse, to her jeans, and finally landed on her boots before he looked back up to her face. Pete himself hadn't dressed up. He was still wearing his usual work boots, jeans, and a t-shirt. This one was brown.

"Ready?" he asked without comment on her new blouse or anything else.

Tara nodded and sighed. It was going to be a long walk, but it was a nice day. The air smelled sweet and dusty, birds sang, and cicadas droned. But, for the first time in a long while she knew nothing unpleasant waited for her when she reached town.

When Pete and Tara got to town they wandered to the outskirts where the mill had been built. Here a stage had been constructed in the middle of the road and tables full of food lined one side. Mismatched chairs and tables had been assembled on the street where children chased each other squealing between them. Alex and Kate hurried to greet them. Kate looked radiantly happy.

"How did you manage all this?" Tara asked Kate, who took the bowl that Pete offered and arranged it with the others on the table.

"People love a good party," Kate beamed.

Kate was right about that. A large crowd was already milling

about, eating, talking and laughing. On the other side of the
street were several booths selling homemade goods. One of the
closest, which appeared to be doing some good business, was
run by a young couple and was just a few stacked barrels behind
a table with a sign that read, "Ale."

Pete was watching the same booth. "Nothing like keeping
track of a bunch of drunks," he sighed.

"You're not working tonight are you?" Kate groaned. "I
thought you were going to join us and have some fun. You've
been wound so tight lately."

"You have seemed pretty stressed," Alex told Pete. "Maybe
you should see if you can get the night off."

"Sorry," Pete shrugged. "I volunteered to keep an eye on
things and I can't back out now."

"Well I'm here to party," Alex announced to his wife, who
was now frowning. "Besides," Alex leaned in as if telling Pete a
secret, "I can't leave my wife out here tonight. She got a band
together and I wouldn't want a riot to start over who gets to
dance with the prettiest gal in town."

Pete smiled at Kate, "Just give a shout if you need me to
shoot anyone for you."

"I'm sure that won't be necessary," Kate assured him. "Now
get out of here, we don't need you anyway," she huffed before
smiling and winking at him.

"I'm going to go check in with Hannity," Pete nodded,
turning away. "I'm sure he has a plan to keep you party animals
in line," he called back over his shoulder.

As the day got started it reminded Tara of a county fair.
People traded and chatted, there was a horse race, and livestock
competition. People competed at arm wrestling, sawing logs,
and even knife throwing.

In the late afternoon Tracy got to pull the levers that put the
mill's sails in motion to a great cheering from the crowd. Tara
was relieved to see that there was enough wind to get the main

event going. It was so hot and sticky she could swear there hadn't been a breeze all day.

As twilight set in the musicians took to the bandstand while lamps, lanterns, and torches were lit all around. Tara watched Jake and Tracy twirl to the music until she caught sight of Kate and Alex, both couples looked so happy.

"Can I have this dance?" asked a familiar voice. The young man pulled his top hat from his head and tried to let it roll down his arm in a complicated motion. Instead it ended up on the sidewalk. He shrugged and picked it back up.

"Frank?" Tara asked, though she couldn't have forgotten him if she'd wanted to.

"At your service," he declared, bowing.

"You don't have a knife on you?" she frowned scanning the crowd to see if anyone might be paying attention to them.

"Certainly miss," he continued unabashed, "but it will stay out of sight in my pocket where it belongs." He hesitated briefly and cleared his throat. "On that particular matter I would like to offer you my deepest and most heartfelt apologies." He offered Tara his hand as the fiddler began a lively tune that Tara couldn't place.

"How's Violet?" Tara asked, hoping to change the subject.

Frank bit his lower lip and looked up. "She wouldn't come, but she told me to tell you the stars are screaming."

"What does that mean?" Tara asked sliding one of her hair pins back in place.

"I haven't the slightest clue," he smiled reaching for her hand since she hadn't taken his.

"I think I'm going to sit this one out." Tara refused politely but firmly.

"Oh come on and have some fun," he encouraged, giving her wrist a tug. "Who knows what screaming stars will bring. We could all die tonight," he smiled.

The hair on the back of Tara's neck prickled as she pulled her hand free.

"Is this man bothering you?" Pete asked stepping close to Tara out of the crowd.

"I'm not here to bother her at all," Frank said indignantly. "I already explained to her that I'm just here with a message, and that I won't take my knife out this time," Frank smiled, patting his pocket.

Frank's hand was still on the front pocket of his pants when Pete grabbed him roughly by the front of the shirt. "I think you should explain what that means," Pete said in voice that sounded a lot calmer than he looked.

Frank huffed and rolled his eyes. "I did. I'm only giving her a message. I don't want to scare her again."

"Again?" Pete glanced at Tara, but turned his attention back to Frank quickly.

"I told her I was sorry," Frank looked down sheepishly. "I thought the knife would help her think better. I just wanted her to help me. I didn't really want to hurt her." Frank looked towards Tara and frowned. "Beautiful things aren't meant to be broken."

Pete gave Frank a shake. "How about you focus on me right now." Pete inclined his face towards Tara without taking his eyes or hands off of Frank. "Did he threaten you?"

Tara crossed her arms and glared at Pete, "He only asked me to dance."

Pete slowly released the front of Frank's shirt which he smoothed down, patting the boy in the center of the chest rather hard when he'd finished. "I want you to leave," he ordered, brushing some imaginary lint off the boy's shoulder. "But," he continued holding his index finger up in front of the boy's face, "if I have any reason to think you want to hurt this lady I will find you, and I don't care what was meant to be broken."

"Then I shall take my leave of you, sir. I have no desire to be around a ruffian of your sort," the boy said adjusting his top hat before turning to Tara. "Good evening to you, madam." Frank bowed low to her before striding off.

"I take it you two know each other?" Pete said crossing his arms.

As they stood watching Frank disappear, Tara took a slow deep breath to calm down. Pete was pissing her off.

"We've met," Tara nodded, not wanting to get into the story. Not while Pete was still full of adrenaline. She was worried he'd go after the kid.

"At knifepoint?"

Tara shrugged.

"How the hell am I supposed to keep you safe if I don't even hear about you being held hostage by a knife-wielding lunatic?"

"Don't you think that's a little dramatic? I wasn't a hostage. The boy is definitely not all there. But I would hardly call him a lunatic."

"So he was just showing you his knife's craftsmanship?" Pete huffed.

"He put the knife down on his own the last time I saw him. It wasn't the first time I've had a knife in my face and I tell you what; they just don't make these knife-wielding lunatics the way they used to," she smiled.

"That's not funny." Pete frowned at her.

"Why are you lurking around spying on me anyway?"

"I wasn't spying on you. You just happened to get into trouble." Pete's frown deepened.

"Oh, it's not spying when it's your job?"

"What's wrong with you tonight?" Pete demanded. "I just stepped in here to help you."

"Has it ever occurred to you that maybe I don't want your help?" Tara raised her voice enough so that the people closest to them stopped to watch what was going on.

"So I'm supposed to stand by and watch you get hurt?" Pete demanded.

"Well, you wouldn't have to watch if you would just leave me alone," Tara snapped. "I don't need you."

"You can handle creeps like that kid without me?" Pete asked calmly.

"As a matter of fact I was fine."

"It didn't seem that way from where I was standing. You looked terrified.

"Then go stand somewhere else!" Tara panted, unable to control her anger. "Whatever Hannity is paying you to watch me

I'll pay you twice as much if you'll just leave me the hell alone."

Pete's brow furrowed, "What?"

"Just go away," Tara demanded, not caring who heard her.

"Fine," Pete spat, turning abruptly and pushing his way through the crowd. He disappeared into the mass of bodies.

Tara slumped while people around her stared at her open-mouthed. Why couldn't he understand she didn't want him pretending to care about her? It was too confusing.

When Tara looked up she caught sight of Steve making his way towards her.

"Hey," Steve greeted her smiling.

"Hi, Steve. How's the leg?" She asked, noting the tin cup in his hand.

"Sore sometimes, but I could probably manage a slow dance or two."

"I'm glad to hear you're getting around well," Tara answered distractedly.

Steve held up the tin cup, "Want a drink?"

"What is it?"

"Liquid courage. It's to help me ask a pretty girl to dance."

"How's that working?" Tara asked him, amused.

"Well," Steve sighed, "I've gotten as far as getting the courage to talk to her but then I chickened out because I'm scared her goon will mug me too."

"Why does she have a goon?"

"I don't know. I thought it was her boyfriend, but now I have no idea who the guy is to her," Steve shrugged.

"Maybe it would be a lot less complicated if you just go ask her," Tara smiled weakly. Her mind was still on the fight she'd just had with Pete.

"Okay," Steve paused, "Who's the goon you yelled at?"

"What?" Tara asked in surprise.

"Is he your boyfriend or what?"

"No, he's not," Tara snapped.

"Okay," Steve held up his hand. "No need to get mad at me. I was just following your advice."

Tara sighed. "I'm sorry."

Steve nodded then stared at her expectantly.

"What?"

"Well?" Steve held up his palms and nodded.

"You wanted to dance," Tara smiled.

"I guess if you insist I could be persuaded to dance with you." Steve slid his hands lightly around her waist while she put her arms on his shoulders. Their awkward shuffle was a parody of every school dance Tara had ever attended.

Steve stared at a point off in the distance over her shoulder for nearly half a song before he spoke. "The doctor came by to check on me yesterday. He seemed sober."

"Sober?" Tara asked surprised. "Are you sure?"

"Yeah," he nodded. "I'm sure. He asked me what you'd used on me. I hope it wasn't some kind of trade secret because I told him. I even told him how disappointed I was that you smearing my thigh with honey wasn't some sort of kinky thing," he grinned.

Tara slapped him lightly on the arm. "No, I don't mind you telling him what I did for you. I really wish it was something he and I could do more of," Tara admitted. "He knows so many things that I've never had a chance to learn. If he had medicine at his disposal again he might be able to really help people."

"Does someone have a little crush on the doctor?" Steve teased.

"Hardly," Tara rolled her eyes at him. "He and I exist in a state of loathing."

"I think he's around here somewhere. I don't mind if he cuts in. I could just —."

Steve's teasing was cut short by the sound of several people shouting, and then a high-pitched shriek. On the other end of the dance floor some tables were knocked over and what looked like a brawl began to spread.

"Let's get out of here. I'm a lover; I don't do that other stuff," Steve beckoned pulling her away towards the food, but someone grabbed Tara's other hand.

"A man's been stabbed with a fork, I think. You need to be heading for the clinic to assist Doctor Farmer." Pete paused long enough to give a disapproving frown to Steve. The sound of someone screaming and some breaking glass interrupted him. "From the sound of things I'll be sending more your way soon."

Tara nodded and turned to leave, but Pete's hadn't let go of her hand yet. "If I don't come and find you at the clinic before you leave there, come and wait for me at the church," he instructed before he dropped her hand abruptly and hurried towards the scuffle. Tara nodded again even though he wasn't looking at her anymore. Tara didn't go directly as she was told; she had to stop and make sure that Pete was okay and the fight was dying down before she slipped off to the clinic.

"You're here under your own power... you can't be hurt too badly," Doctor Farmer barked when she came in the door. His hair was combed and he even appeared to be wearing a clean shirt.

"I was sent here to help you," Tara informed him.

"I was afraid of that," he grumbled, striding towards her quickly. He grabbed her hand and slapped a wad of clean cloth into it before he pushed it hard against the wound on the arm of the man he'd been tending when she walked in. The man howled in pain. "Now hold pressure on that until the bleeding slows so I can check out some of these other miscreants."

Tara stood obediently holding pressure on the arm of the groaning man while she watched the doctor work. He moved methodically around the room starting with the bloodiest patients while injuries slowly filtered in. Alternately he called people fools and idiots.

"It's broken," the doctor informed a young man sitting on a chair in front of him. Without further talk he pulled the man's arm up and, after making some minor adjustments, he gave a tug. The young man shrieked while the doctor ignored him. He felt the injury again. "Don't move until I put a splint on it," he instructed the man, who was now crying like a small child. After he'd wrapped the injury he proceeded to tell a few patients that their injuries weren't severe and he couldn't fix stupid so they needed to go.

Tara's eyes followed the doctor as he continued. She was determined to learn whatever she could glean from where she stood. Farmer was holding a slender man's hand, examining the palm when a chill ran down Tara's spine. Behind the skinny patient was a man who was both broad and tall staring at Tara.

She nodded at him hoping that he would look away, but it didn't seem to have an effect. The doctor poured some alcohol in the skinny man's cut and told him he could go. While they left Tara only glanced at the pair, but the bigger man hadn't stopped staring at her.

She didn't relax until the door closed behind them. It didn't take much longer for Doctor Farmer to finish assessing the injuries. He sent most of them away after a quick pouring of alcohol on open wounds and whatever hateful thing seemed to parade through his head came out his mouth. Afterwards he re-joined Tara.

"Has the bleeding stopped?" he asked.

"I think so," she answered, pulling the wad of cloth slowly away from the man's arm so that Doctor Farmer could see. With a pair of tweezers the doctor removed what looked like a few bits of the man's shirt from the gash.

"It's pretty deep. He could probably use one of your potions to stop the infection," he stated as he poured alcohol into the wound, causing the man to grind his teeth and groan.

"I didn't bring my bag," Tara admitted, feeling foolish. She hadn't expected to be working tonight.

"Without your little charm bag, you're useless to me," the doctor admonished.

Tara watched him probe the injury mercilessly. "I can bring my supplies first thing in the morning —."

"That's fine," he cut her, off turning his back to her. "I'll see you then."

"Don't you want my help?"

The doctor scanned the room quickly. "No new patients have come in. I can clean some cuts without anyone holding my hand.

Since you are neither a doctor nor a nurse; you are nothing more than a gawker who's in the way. I don't need you underfoot. Go home," he ordered with a dismissive little wave.

"Who'd have thought you're a bigger asshole when you're sober," Tara taunted.

"Thank you for your inexpert opinion, but I suppose it's the only kind you can offer." He smirked wrapping the stab wound in a clean bandage and not bothering to look at Tara.

Tara stood staring at him trying to think of a witty retort, but none came to mind. After a moment her opportunity had passed so she just continued to watch him in angry silence.

"Either you're deaf or stupid," the doctor said glancing at her after tying off the bandage. "You seem to hear just fine so I'm going to assume it's the latter. I recall telling you to be a useless lump elsewhere."

Tara was tired. All the day's excitement; the people and now this. She felt so bone-weary tired it was like all the fight had fallen away. She didn't need to best him; she just needed to get back to the church so she could go home.

"I wouldn't want to get in your way," Tara spat heading towards the door.

Farmer looked at her suddenly. "I'm glad you understand," he replied, looking momentarily confused.

"Goodnight." Tara only said this because 'go to hell' wasn't appropriate in front of the patients.

The doctor gave a vague nod in her direction as she headed out into the chilly evening air and turned towards the church.

"Oh my God, help! Please help me!" the yell of a woman echoed as feet pounded on the sidewalk in the near total darkness. Tara squinted around. She'd only walked a few blocks from the clinic, but her mind had been so occupied she barely knew she was walking in the right direction.

"Help me!" The woman shrieked again as she hurried towards Tara. She emerged from an alley not far behind her and

Tara was surprised to see it was Elizabeth. Her first thought was that something had probably gone wrong with a client. Maybe someone didn't pay her.

"What's wrong?" Tara asked as Elizabeth reached her side and breathlessly clung to her arm.

Elizabeth's eyes were wild in the pale light from the sliver of moon. "It's Pete," Elizabeth gasped, "There's so much blood, I..." The woman panted several times before she continued, "I... it's spraying. I don't know what to do."

Tara's mind went blank, as if she could think hard enough to un-hear everything.

"Hurry," Elizabeth pleaded.

"The doctor," Tara whispered turning back towards the clinic.

"I'll get him. Hurry, you have to save him. He's down there," she gestured back into the alley.

Terrified of what she would find; that she wouldn't know what to do, that he would already be dead, Tara sprinted forward. Adrenaline pushed her down the alley, running blindly in the darkness.

"Pete can you hear me?" she called. He must have been on his way to get her. This was all her fault. Her heart clenched when only silence answered. Tara turned a corner and nearly ran into a wall. She scrambled against a couple of locked doors before she realized the ally was a dead end. Blindly she groped around.

"Pete, oh please Pete where are you!" she shouted in her frustration. Had she passed him? She gagged at the thought.

"Tara?" Elizabeth called.

"Where is he?"

"I told you I'd pay you back," Elizabeth chuckled.

"What?"

Tara didn't get an answer, didn't have time to think. The movement was so sudden she never got a chance to fight the momentum before the meaty hand bashed her head into the wall. She didn't even have time to register the pain before everything went black.

CHAPTER 34

"You know what I love on a woman?" a deep voice breathed into Tara's ear. The breath quickened while he appeared to be waiting for some sort of reply. "Blood," he rumbled just before a slimy tongue slid up her cheek, over her closed eyes, and onto her temple where the pain exploded like fireworks in the dark. Tara cried out.

She was lying on the ground; her ankles and wrists ached and throbbed. When she strained to pull her face away the movement caused a pain in her head so intense she had to fight the urge to vomit.

As she forced her eyes open she became aware that a very large man was sitting on her pinning her body down. His face was so close that all she could see were his perfectly strait, yellow teeth streaked in her blood as he grinned.

When Tara struggled weakly to get up she became aware that she was bound at the wrists and ankles. The man stopped her movement by pushing her hard against the tiles beneath her. They were no longer outside. They were inside a building that was dirty and abandoned. A water stain marked the acoustic tile next to the cheap light fixture above them. On the floor next to her face was a broken frame that held a torn cartoon frog, but no glass. That was all Tara could see of the room. It was lit by a single candle nearby. The man on top of her was taking up an unrealistic amount of space and casting the rest of the room into the darkness of his shadow.

Tara opened her mouth to scream, but a massive hand was pressed over it. She could taste his skin; dirt, salt and the intense copper tang of blood on his palm. She gagged and let out a low whimper when something cold pressed against her neck.

The man sat upright, still pinning all but her legs down hard;

like he was trying to grind her bones through the floor. His shirt was saturated with blood, and his hair stood out wildly matted with it. His arms and face were smeared as if they'd been hastily wiped clean, but it still looked thick and sticky on his neck. Where had it all come from? His eyes were wild above his excited grin.

Tara kept staring at his smile, with those perfect teeth. It bothered her that they must have received a lot of dental work. She couldn't make that make sense in her head. Monsters couldn't have dentists.

"That my dear," the man spoke slowly as he pressed the cold metal against her throat, "is a very sharp knife." Tara winced. She felt the drip of blood before she was even aware that he'd made a cut that now burned as a short line on her throat. "That's just a taste of her, my darling." He leaned in so that his lips touched her ear as he whispered, "I promise if you struggle I'll fuck you with it."

When he leaned back to look at her again he was smiling. "I did it once," he chuckled softly. "It made a mess and she was dead before I finished." The man smiled wider when Tara gagged. "It's okay sweetie," he soothed trailing his fingers down the side of her face, "I'd like us to be together while you're still alive. Dead girls rot too fast. You just can't have a lasting and meaningful relationship with one. So, these are special circumstances."

Tara stared at him, trying to get control of her breathing. She was beginning to get light-headed from hyperventilation. Her hands felt numb. "Still alive," echoed around in her head. He was going to kill her.

"You're not even going to ask why this is special?" he asked, "I'm hurt."

Tara was looking around frantically. She had no interest in talking to him. She needed to get out of here. She had no idea what to do.

"Hey!" he shouted, snapping Tara's attention back to him. She panted at him, wide-eyed. "That's better," he praised, brushing some of her hair back off her face. "I just wanted you to know that I appreciate how much you wanted to be here, and that your friend helped to set us up. Most of the time I have to be the one to pursue my relationships. You're the only one who has ever pursued me. I've never known a woman who wanted me to bestow my honors upon her so badly."

Tara struggled to understand what he was trying to say. Between her fear and his rambling he wasn't making any sense.

"You look confused. Oh well, I guess I didn't ask your friend about your intelligence." He looked away for a moment. "You do need to understand that now that we're married I do own you completely."

"Married?" Tara's lip quivered.

"Till death do us part," he pinched her shoulder with his fingernail drawing blood.

Tara gasped.

He continued, "My brother said the words over us and your friend was the bridesmaid."

"Elizabeth?" Tara whispered as realization dawned.

"Normally she just gives my brother things and he gives her food."

"Things?" Tara repeated slowly.

"Mostly names and places that we might like to visit. She has sex with men and they say stupid things to her that she shares with my brother. She disgusted me."

"Disgusted?" Tara asked. She was afraid not to respond to him. Maybe if she kept him talking he'd change his mind about what he was planning to do.

"Yeah, disgusted," he frowned. "She took something beautiful and made it ugly by making people pay to take it. It's gross because nobody owned her like they should."

The man laid his head briefly on Tara's chest where he could surely hear her heart pounding. "You don't have to pay for what you already own."

Tara closed her eyes. She didn't want to see what he was doing. Didn't want to know what was going to happen. She had no idea how to stop him.

"Open your eyes sweetheart," he coaxed, sliding the knife's

flat edge gently back and forth across her neck. "I didn't want to get too excited and finish this too soon." He paused looking momentarily embarrassed. "I took care of a little something with Elizabeth while you were sleeping. She was disgusting so I did it fast. I didn't even bestow my honor on her. I promise I saved that just for you. I hope you don't think this makes me appreciate you any less. She didn't mean anything to me."

Tara whimpered while she forced her eyes open to look at him again. Part of her wished that whatever he was about to do he would just get it over with.

"You're not mad about what I did with your friend are you?"

Tara shook her head no. She didn't want to upset him.

"Tell me you still love me," he nuzzled his nose against her collarbone.

What the hell was wrong with him? Still love him? She didn't love him, but those teeth so close to her throat made her gasp.

He leaned back away from her, "What's the matter? Aren't you going to stroke my hair and tell me how much you love me?"

Tara looked at the binding on her wrists. "How?" she asked him meekly as she held her hands out to him.

"Silly me," he paused with the knife on the rope. "You'll be an obedient wife if I do this won't you?"

Tara nodded and he slid the knife through the rope with a little ringing sound as it broke. The man laid his head on her chest with the knife against her side, the tip poking into her skin. Tara's hands shook while she looked at his hair. Slowly she lowered her left hand onto the sticky mess on his head. She patted him gently.

"Don't worry dear, I'm not just some brute. I'll give you some foreplay like you deserve," he whispered quietly sitting up to look at her as he slid the wide blade away from her side and teased it into the front of her shirt. "Remember not to move," he ordered as he cut the fabric away slowly over her breast. Tara didn't dare move a muscle while the cold metal of the blade was on her skin. She trembled while he cut the rest of her beautiful silk shirt away in slow agonizing strips. He brushed the blade over her bare skin, making tiny cuts around her belly button. The man smiled when he cut her bra away in the same slow way he'd done her shirt. When he laid the edge of the blade next to Tara's nipple, she bucked and pulled her shoulder back.

The man growled; a terrifying sound, while he clasped his hand over her mouth and sliced the side of her breast before laying the blade on the outer side of the same breast. Tara's sobs escaped unevenly and muffled from his hand.

"Listen," he growled, "I mean for you to lay still and stay quiet. If you didn't have such nice tits I'd cut the damn things off," he spat. "I want us to enjoy ourselves. If you struggle how am I supposed to know you're having a good time?"

Tara squeezed back tears. If staying still kept her alive she could stay still. She could endure anything in this moment if she got to the light of morning intact. Maybe he'd wait to do what he was going to do if she passed out? Maybe it would buy her time to imagine a way out of this? Tara fluttered her eyes closed and willed her body to go as limp as possible. He enjoyed her fear, maybe if she didn't offer it he'd leave her alone, or at least get things over with.

The man bit her lightly on the cheek. Then he bit her hard on the collarbone. When she didn't respond she felt his hot breath on her ear. "You look at me right now or I'm going to slide this knife inside you," he whispered. Tara didn't respond, and to her relief, he didn't put the knife anywhere. "It's okay dear, you can sleep. I don't mind. I'm sorry I can't wait to be with you. But we'll do it again when you wake up. I want to hear you scream."

He didn't stop cutting her clothes away as she had hoped he would, but he did it faster and cut her less than he did when she'd been watching him. It didn't take long for her jeans and underwear to be removed. He cut the binding on her ankles then continued making small cuts in her skin. The knife was on her even when he removed his weight. It stayed too close to her arteries to imagine that she might get away clean if she tried to run.

Tara kept her eyes closed and her face slack as the man slid his hand slowly down to her ankle and lifted her leg so it fell

open. Even though Tara knew what he was about to do, she
didn't move. After he moved her other leg she heard the rustle
of clothing and then some pressure on her chest where the blood
was pooling from her damaged breast. She fought with all her
will to keep her face slack when she realized he was lubricating
himself with her blood. A moment of tense silence later
something slid into her and it hurt so terribly that it could very
well have been the knife's blade. It took her longer than it should
have to realize that it was only his flesh, as it both ached and
burned like fire. It took every bit of Tara's concentration not to
let her face show the pain she was in.

This went on for a short time while Tara listened to her
pounding heart and imagined it was drums, somewhere in the
wild darkness, far out in the woods, away from here. Then it
happened, her heart leapt as she felt the hilt of the knife rest
against the back of the knuckles on her left hand. He'd let the
thing go to steady himself as his grunting was getting louder.
Tara moved her leg slowly and carefully, going with his motion
so that it would be in his way. At the same time she wrapped her
fingers around the hilt of the knife. When he stopped and leaned
out to move her leg out of way, it had to be now.

She brought the knife up and forced it into his side as fast as
she could. It cut in easier than she had expected. There was a cry
of rage and agony and Tara realized that they were both making
it. He scrambled weakly at her hands while she pushed, slicing
through his belly. Hot wet blood ran across her knuckles and she
could smell shit. As he doubled over clutching at his wound
Tara scrambled back holding the knife.

"But you're mine. You gave yourself to me," he sputtered
curling up tight on himself; his pants still obscenely around his
knees. "You think you can kill me?" he gasped between jagged
breaths.

Tara stayed firmly pressed against the dirty wall behind her.
"I just did," she spat.

"You can't. I saw you all covered in blood where we went to
get the cows. You were beautiful. You wanted me. Why else
would you have painted yourself that way?" he gagged and then

began to cry.

"I don't know what you're talking about," Tara spat.

"Yes you do," he sobbed. "You love me. You're my wife."

"No," Tara seethed at him, easing slowly away from the wall. "I'm not your anything."

"But, you can't kill me," he spat. "God will never allow it."

"That's a mortal wound. You'll be dead soon enough no matter if you believe it or not." While she spoke Tara groped along the wall; she was sure she'd seen a door. As her hand closed onto the door knob she paused. He was sputtering and making mewling noises now, and they enraged her. Someone who claimed to have so casually taken the lives of women was now crying for his own. For a moment she had the urge to go back; to stab him until the blubbering ceased. In her rage she felt that nobody should cry for his death, especially not him.

The realization of her fury scared her. She flung open the door and stumbled out into the darkness. The night breeze made her cuts burn and a howl began from behind the door that had just closed next to her.

Tara slipped between the buildings while her mind reeled around what she needed to do now. She'd never make it home the way she was, naked and barefoot, but her most primal instincts told her to get as far away as she could as soon as possible. So, like a ghost, she headed towards the center of town until she found herself standing in front of Hannity's, which was barred and dark.

She turned away and found herself facing the church. The colored glass windows sparkled with a warm glow. It had never looked as inviting as it did now. Tara had slipped up the front steps and had her hand on the door before she ever stopped to consider the commotion a naked, bleeding woman in a group of strangers might cause.

Hugging the wall of the building, she headed around to the back; less public access. Maybe she could figure out where the donated clothes were kept before anyone even noticed what had happened.

Easing the door open into the back hallway Tara was

surprised by the lack of security. But, just as the thought formed, footsteps echoed just around the corner and Tara hurried backwards through the first door on the left. The moment the door closed she knew she'd gone the wrong way. Several sharp intakes of breath were punctuated by the sound of a slide being pulled to chamber a bullet. She was panting, too panicked to think.

"Don't shoot," a gruff voice ordered and Tara knew without turning around that it belonged to Hannity. She stood frozen with her hand still on the door knob. She couldn't be shot after what she had just survived. Another voice ordered her to drop the knife.

Tara looked down at the knife for the first time since she'd stabbed the man with it. She didn't even realize that she'd still been carrying the thing. The blade was nearly a foot long and covered in gore. Tara willed her fingers to let go of it, but instead she just stared at it dumbly.

"Young lady, may I have the knife?" a soft voice asked from several feet behind her. Tara couldn't do more than nod. She didn't know where the gun was. Her body coursed with adrenaline, but she allowed Pastor Richard to ease the knife out of her fingers.

Tara turned around slowly, and realized nobody there knew who she was. Her hair was filthy and stringy with blood, and she couldn't imagine what the rest of her looked any better.

"Tara?" Hannity breathed, shocked. He turned abruptly. "Don't just stand there," Hannity barked at the young man who was now holding the gun pointing towards the floor while staring open-mouthed, "Get my wife!" As he spoke, Hannity hurried forward unbuttoning his shirt and sliding it around Tara's shoulders when he reached her. He turned and nodded to the pastor, who slipped quietly out of the room with the gore-covered knife in his hand.

Hannity's sharp brown eyes met Tara's. "Who did this?" he asked gravely.

Pounding feet sounded in the hallway and the door was flung open hard enough that it bounced off the wall. Pete stopped in the doorway. His breath caught as his eyes moved from Tara's bloody hair matted to her forehead, down the cuts showing on her body, and back to the smears of blood on her thighs. Tara swayed with the force of her relief, Pete was alive.

"I volunteer for this assignment," Pete intoned with a voice like ice.

"It's yours of course," Hannity nodded. "Now," he turned his attention back to Tara, "Do you know his name?"

Tara shook her head, "No, but he's a dead man."

"Yes he is," Pete assured her.

"No, I mean I gutted him," Tara clarified, holding out her bloody hands. "If he's not already dead, he will be soon."

"Where?" Pete asked her with an unnerving calm.

"Your favorite diner," Tara told him as she realized why the building had seemed so familiar. As fast as the words left her mouth Pete was out the door, nearly knocking over a slightly pudgy woman with very kind blue eyes who had been on her way into the room.

The woman wore a bright smile that faltered only slightly when she looked at Tara. "My name's Laurie Hannity," she told Tara, squeezing Hannity's hand briefly before reaching for Tara's. "We'll get you all cleaned up and bandaged."

Tara let the woman's soft hand urge her forward. She was alive. Pete was alive. Was anything else really important?

Steam rose off the tub and sweat beaded on Tara's skin while she sat curled around herself in the hot water. The older woman bathed her, carefully cleaning her wounds. When the door creaked open Tara's head snapped up, but it was just a young woman carrying a towel and a stack of clothing.

"I'm sorry, Mom. I couldn't find any panties or socks for her, but I thought this dress was awfully pretty and I think these shoes might fit."

"Set them there," Laurie instructed her daughter, pointing to a table in the room. "Oh and," she said, stopping her daughter before she could slip out of the room. "She needs more care than I can give her."

"Yes, Mom," the teenager nodded pulling the door shut.

Tara had never been in Hannity's home before. She'd never met his family either. They were underground, under the bank, in a series of vaults. *It made sense why he would make this his home,* Tara thought, looking at the concrete walls.

On her way in she'd seen three kids; the eldest daughter, who had just been in the room, a younger daughter, and a little boy who couldn't have been more than five years old. He'd watched her open-mouthed as her mother led Tara through the main room wrapped in a ruined blanket.

"Let's get you dry darling," Laurie said, helping Tara up out of the tub full of pink water. As she was wrapping up the door opened a crack again.

"She's in here," the girl said stepping back out of the way to let Doctor Farmer in the room.

"Oh hell no," Tara growled pulling her towel tight around her body.

"I have other things to take care of too," the doctor sneered briefly before his voice softened to a whisper as he studied her skin, "...Witch. Geeze, you look like hell. What happened to you?" the doctor asked as Missus Hannity shooed her daughter out the door and slid out herself.

"I killed the bastard," Tara answered bluntly, her voice flat.

"I'm sure you did," the doctor grunted, setting down his bag. "It was bound to happen eventually with your lack of medical training. How about you tell me what he did to you before you killed him." Farmer asked digging out a bottle of alcohol and some clean strips of cloth. "Cause it looks like you got in a fight with an angry pack of cats."

Tara stared at him, unwilling to say anything.

"I was told you'd probably need stitches." Farmer sighed, "Let's see it."

"No way, butcher!" she huffed, pulling her towel tight enough that she winced.

"Don't flatter yourself woman, I just want to see the damage.

Don't get your panties in a bunch."

After a brief glaring contest Tara let the towel fall away from her wound. The doctor moved forward and inspected the side of Tara's breast. "It's a nice clean cut," he nodded, "When I'm done you won't have much of a scar."

"Either that or my boob will fall off," Tara sniffed.

"Just put one of your little potions on it," he mused, laying out some tools.

Tara gasped as he began sewing her cut. She hadn't expected it to be so painful. "Sorry that I can't offer you anything for the pain. As I've mentioned before I'm out of medicine," the doctor said cutting the last thread.

Tara adjusted the towel and began to pull it back up over herself while the doctor watched her closely.

"The only skin I've seen so far that's unmarked is your face." The doctor paused. "You were raped?"

"Why does that matter?" Tara huffed.

Farmer stuffed his hands into his pockets and looked at the floor. "I'd like to assess the damage."

"Don't you think that's a little personal?" Tara asked.

"I'm not getting fresh!" Farmer scoffed, looking insulted. "I'm trying to do my job."

Tara whipped her towel off onto the floor, "I guess you don't want to have any secrets between us?"

The doctor raised his eyebrows. "That was not my intention," he clarified, picking up the towel. "Will you consent to further examination?" he asked.

"Why not, I've already had one madman look at it today, how about two." She eased herself down into a chair.

To doctor Farmer's credit he didn't look embarrassed by her behavior, even though she'd been trying to make him feel that way. Nor did he say anything while he examined her except that he was sorry when it hurt. "It's nothing that won't heal," he assured her when she picked up her dress and held it up. "But I wouldn't engage in any intimate activities with your partner for at least three to four weeks."

"Not a problem," Tara smirked. "My husband left me more

than half a year ago for a younger woman," she told him while she slipped on the light green dress and began to button up the front. She had to thank Hannity's daughter for picking something so light and easy to get into. It still hurt as she slid it over her damaged skin.

The doctor had turned away. "I'm so sorry."

"I'm a big girl you didn't hurt my feelings. It was a long time ago," she assured him.

The doctor was leaning forward on the table with one hand held to his face. Tara stared at him for a moment in silence before she realized he was crying.

"Have I missed something?" Tara asked stepping forward.

"I feel like this is my fault," Farmer blubbered between sniffles. "I didn't think about your safety. I didn't let you stay long enough for your friend to come back for you. I sent you out alone at night. I'm jealous of you... of what you can do. You sometimes make me feel so useless and I put you in danger over my stupid pride," he sobbed, the words all coming out in a rush. "I'm so sorry," he gasped with his head down. Tara could see tears dropping to the floor.

His tears made Tara feel weak and helpless. Panic gripped her as she watched him. She had to get out of this situation as much as she'd needed to escape the last one.

"I don't need you to feel sorry for me," she snapped, snatching up her shoes and storming out the door as she began to cry. She couldn't be any more vulnerable in front of him than she already had been. She had to go. She felt like she couldn't breathe.

"Dear!" Missus Hannity called as she rushed past. Tara didn't even slow down. She couldn't. She needed to go. Missus Hannity took a step towards her while she fumbled with the door, but Tara flung it wide and ran through slamming into Pete who stood waiting just outside.

He held his hands out unthreateningly, but with the intention of impeding her without actually touching her. "Wait, what's wrong?" What happened? Are you okay?" he asked all in a rush while she stared at him blankly.

It had taken Tara a moment to recognize Pete. He had blood on his shirt, none of which appeared to be his.

"I have to go," she breathed wild-eyed.

"Okay, just give me a second to let —."

"No. Now!" she gasped. "I need to go."

"Follow me," Pete offered her his hand.

Tara stared at it without understanding before she decided finally to take it.

Everything after Tara took Pete's hand was blank. Like that moment of contact had flipped a switch in her head and her brain turned off; maintaining basic life support only. Tara knew they must have walked, but not very far.

"Hey Avery," Pete called in greeting to a man Tara had not seen until that moment sitting in a chair under an awning.

"I didn't expect to see you here," the young man called back, "and with such a beautiful lady." He gestured to Tara. "Are you trying to torment me?" Avery grinned, showing a set of brilliantly white strait teeth, a striking contrast against his dark skin. Tara stared at those teeth and shuddered. Would she ever be able to look at a smile without the hair standing up on the back of her neck?

Pete gave her hand that he was still holding a gentle squeeze and stepped between her and Avery in a very subtle way. She was breathing too fast and shallow.

"Avery, you know our love can never be," Pete joked cheerfully while he unlocked the door in front of them.

Tara looked around. They were at a motel, standing outside of room number five.

"Of course I know that now. I can't compete with Tara." Avery pouted comically before smiling again.

"I'm sorry."

"Oh well," Avery shrugged.

"Goodnight," Pete called.

"Wait, I just needed to ask," Avery's smile faltered only

momentarily. "Are you okay?"

Pete looked down at himself. "Yeah, it's not mine."

"Is it something I need to know about?" Avery asked.

"Just a clean-up," Pete shrugged. "We can discuss it later."

"Gotcha'." Avery nodded before Pete ushered Tara inside and closed the door behind them.

CHAPTER 35

Inside the motel room the air was still and stiflingly hot. It was also the kind of dark that didn't show outlines, so Tara stood quietly while Pete moved away from her to do something she couldn't see.

A scraping sound was followed by a flare when Pete lit a match. Tara's eyes were drawn to the edge of the room where he stood next to a small table and two blue plastic chairs. On the table was a small oil lamp with a metal base; functional instead of pretty. There was only one bed, a cheap pressboard nightstand, and in the back of the room a door that Tara assumed led to the bathroom. Near the table was a set of flimsy metal shelves that had been added to the original décor.

On the shelves were a selection of canned goods, a can opener, two sets of eating utensils, a camp stove, a bottle of propane, a couple of buckets, a bottle of lamp oil, and what appeared to be several changes of clothes.

"Where are we? What is this place? Who's Avery? Why is he out there? Why does he know who I am? I thought you weren't gay," Tara said in one breath.

Pete chuckled while he pulled the curtain aside and opened the room's two large windows. Tara was relieved to note that he had put bars over the windows that appeared to be made out of metal porch railing. Instantly the breeze flapping the curtains made the room more habitable.

"What order do you want me to answer those in?" Pete asked leaning against the wall by the window and gesturing for Tara to sit on the bed.

"Start with Avery."

"Avery works for Hannity. He's a guard. That's what he's doing right now. He sleeps in room four during the day and guards this place at night. Avery knows you because he was there at the White's farm. He told you about Hannity's order. I'm a little surprised that you don't recognize him." Pete paused to let her think.

Avery's face didn't seem familiar to her at all so she shook her head.

Pete smiled warmly. "It's okay. The last time you met him was a pretty traumatic day, too. It might come back to you when you've had some time and a good night's sleep." Pete shifted, looking down at the mess on his clothes before continuing. "About that last one. I may not be homosexual but Avery is." Pete shrugged.

"Are you sure he's not just kidding around?" Tara asked. "Getting the wrong impression sometimes happens." She looked sheepishly at the floor.

"Firstly, he asked me to attend the dance with him. Secondly," Pete hesitated and took a deep breath. "Secondly, he was crying the night of the attack at the White's. He told me that he and Bobby White were supposed to go on their first date that weekend away from the farm since Bob senior did not approve."

Tara stared at him. "Avery must hate me. I let Bobby die."

"Actually," Pete said, moving towards the edge of the bed but not sitting down, "Avery knows that you offered Bobby comfort and that was the best anyone could do for him in that moment."

Tara nodded, but it was a hard thing for her to believe.

"As for where we are," Pete paused. "Do you mind if I get cleaned up while we talk?" Pete held out the front of his shirt with a disgusted look on his face.

"Don't let me stop you."

Pete nodded and took a bucket off the shelf before opening the bathroom door. Tara wandered over to the doorway since Pete left the door wide open. It didn't really look like a bathroom at all. All the fixtures had been removed. At the end of the room a section of tile was missing where a tub had probably been. Now the space was occupied by two plastic fifty-five gallon barrels. Just inside the door was an outline where the paint was now the wrong color where the sink was missing. Below that were two pipes cut off and welded shut. The drain hole was capped. On the floor, only a couple of feet over from that were a discolored shape on the tile that had probably been the base of the toilet. The pipe in the center of that shape was also capped.

Pete had set his bucket on the top of one of the fifty-five gallon barrels. When he noticed her standing in the doorway he said, "Let me give you the tour real quick." Pete pointed to a bucket with a toilet seat on it. "This is the facilities, just put a scoop of sawdust from the box in when you use it," he instructed, pointing to a plastic container next to the bucket.

"An indoor outhouse," Tara nodded.

"Yeah basically," he admitted. "Over here is the water, he told her as he took a small cap off the top of one of the barrels. From next to the barrel he produced a siphon pump with a plastic squeeze bulb that he had attached a longer hose to.

Pete used the siphon to fill the bucket half-full of water. Then he turned and walked out of the bathroom while Tara went to sit back on the bed.

Pete carried some clothes back into the bathroom and pulled the door half-way closed.

"You were going to tell me what this place is?" Tara called.

"Well actually," Pete paused while Tara heard some clothes rustling. "This is my place."

"What?"

"I'm sorry I never told you," Pete admitted, "Hannity gave me this place when my house burned down. His wife owned the motel. Actually they gave a room to everyone who lost a house that day."

"So you're telling me you had an actual room with an actual bed and you were sleeping in a tent in the woods? I thought you came to stay with me because you didn't have any place to go,"

"I never said I didn't have any place to go," Pete called over the sound of sloshing water. "I just asked to stay with you."

"Why?"

"Practical reasons. Your isolated location and land gave the advantage of hunting, trapping, and garden space. I know this next part makes you mad, but it was also a chance for me to come out and help watch your back."

"I understand," Tara said flatly. "You moved out to my place and looked after me to get paid more for protecting the medic."

Pete looked at Tara around the door. "Is that honestly what you think?" he asked gently.

Tara looked away from him while her thoughts raced. "I don't know what I think anymore," she stammered. "I thought we were friends, but I found out you were being paid to be around me and I felt so stupid."

Pete disappeared behind the door again and, after a quick rustling, he came out to stand in front of her wearing just a pair of jeans. "Why do you keep on talking about me being paid to be around you?" Pete asked, sitting on the edge of the bed. Rivulets of water trickled down his chest.

"Because of Hannity's order!" Tara shot back crossing her arms then gasping in pain.

Pete scooted closer, but not close enough that they were touching. "I am your friend," he assured her offering her his hand, which Tara ignored. "Hannity doesn't pay me to be around you."

"Really?" Tara asked, narrowing her eyes.

"You can ask him if you don't believe me," Pete soothed.

"If you're not getting paid, why have you been helping me?"

"I guess to start it was because your pain was like a mirror of my own suffering. I hated that happening to you. You seemed so nice. After I got to know you better…" Pete smiled and looked away, "It's because I couldn't bear a Tara-shaped hole in my life." Pete took a deep breath and looked at his bare toes that he flexed on the carpet. "I would die to protect you." He paused and looked at her before putting his head down in his hands. "For whatever good that does you now."

Tara's eyes traced the pattern of cuts on her arms. "I'm okay."

"You don't look okay."

Rubbing her eyes Tara looked back at Pete. "I can't tell you I'll be all right tomorrow, or the day after that, or the one after that." Tara rested her fingertips against Pete's arm. "But I can deal, right now, in this moment. I'm not ready to think about all the moments to come."

Pete nodded, but said nothing.

Tara stared at the wall for a long moment before she continued. One detail had been eating her up. "Pete, I let him do it. I just laid there. I was so scared of him, and his knife, that I didn't stop him." She hadn't meant to tell Pete. She hadn't planned to tell anyone. But thinking about the moment that she lay still and let that man enter her made her feel nauseous.

"Hey," Pete said sharply. "Don't do that to yourself. You did what anyone would have done. You didn't *let* him anything."

"But I —," she started.

"No," Pete knelt on the floor in front of her so that she had to look at his face. "You did nothing wrong. You are alive. Whatever you did to stay that way was, in that moment, the right choice. That man was a monster and you did what you had to do."

Tara sniffed, "Then why do I feel this way?"

"Because some beast violated you," Pete soothed.

"Pete?"

"Yes."

"Can you not tell anyone that?" Tara sniffled again. "I don't think other people will understand."

Pete nodded slowly. "You haven't done anything you should be ashamed of, but I respect you and your wishes. It's your choice what you tell people and what you don't." Pete stood up. "We all have our secrets."

Tara watched him walk back into the bathroom where he closed the door halfway again.

"What's your secret Pete?"

Water sloshed in response and Tara wondered if he'd heard her.

The bathroom went still and they sat there until the silence itself seemed to be making a noise to fill the space.

"I've thought I should tell you about that many times," Pete admitted. "But each time I was afraid of what you'd think of me if you knew." There was a sigh from behind the door. "Now I don't want to frighten you."

"Why would it frighten me?" Tara asked stiffening.

"Because I spent nearly a year of my life in prison."

"Why?" Tara asked slowly.

There was another rustling and a sigh. "For two counts of assault."

"Did you do it?" Tara asked.

"Yes. One of them."

Tara sat silently, listening to her breathing before a rustling started behind the door again. Pete walked out dressed in a fresh pair of jeans and a white t-shirt. Tara stared at him, unsure what to say.

Pete pulled out one of the chairs at the table and turned it to face the bed before slumping down into it. He looked exhausted. "I guess," Pete said to the silent space between them, "I should tell you I used to be married."

"Really?" Tara asked startled.

"Is it really so hard to be believe?" Pete asked, his face softening.

Tara fiddled with one of her buttons. "I guess I never considered it before now."

Pete chuckled. "Well I was. She was my high school sweetheart. Cliché I know, but we were in love. She was one of the prettiest girls I'd ever seen. When I finally got the courage to ask her out she told me no."

"That's not where I saw that story going," Tara smiled leaning back.

"I know," Pete nodded, "Turns out she was dating some gorilla. So I did what any pathetic teenage boy would do."

"What's that?"

"I became her friend," Pete smiled shaking his head.

"Does that work?" Tara asked

"Just the once so far." Pete stared at her for a moment longer than was comfortable before he appeared to shake himself and continued, "I was there for her when things ended with the gorilla, then the lump, and finally the bear. In the end she asked me to prom. The rest is history. We got married a few months after graduation."

Pete stretched before he continued, "Neither of us went to college, we just moved in together and played house. The first couple of years were wonderful, but, after that, I guess she started to get bored with me. She started complaining that I wasn't trying hard enough. I wasn't making enough money. I didn't go to the right parties or spend time with the right people."

Pete leaned forward and put his face in his hands before he rubbed his eyes and sat back up. "It started to fall apart in the usual ways. All the signs were there, but I didn't see them." He stared at his hands. "My world revolved around her."

Pete stood up and wiped his palms on his jeans. "Are you hungry?"

"No." Tara shook her head. "If you don't want to tell me I won't be mad at you," she offered.

"No. I want to tell you," Pete frowned.

Tara patted the bed.

Pete sat down and continued, "By the time we'd been married about three years she started to gain a lot of weight, didn't hold a job, and she seemed angry all the time. I probably didn't help. I began avoiding her. Any time we were in the same room for more than twenty minutes a fight would start."

"Did you get divorced then?" Tara asked.

"Not yet?"

"Why?"

"Because I still loved her more than anything. I knew we could work things out eventually. Things went like this for another couple of years, until she got a new job and actually held on to it. She started taking care of herself again, she lost weight, started doing her hair, wore make-up. I was happy she seemed to be pulling herself out of her depression."

Tara waited, but Pete didn't say anything so she took the opportunity to lay down. When she did Pete got up and blew out the lamp.

"Pete?"

"Yeah?"

"Will you lay here next to me?"

"If you want me to."

Tara could feel Pete's weight shift the bed. Silence filled the room for so long that listening to it started to make Tara's ears ring.

"What happened?" she asked carefully.

Pete's voice was more hushed and he continued haltingly, "I came home from work on lunch to throw a roast in the crock pot for dinner. I wanted to surprise her for her birthday." Pete paused again. "Her car was in the driveway. I could hear them as soon as I walked in. They were in our bed, in our room."

Clearing his throat, Pete continued, "The man was older than me by at least ten years, skinny, with thinning hair. I found out later that he was her boss. I remember staring at the top of his head because I couldn't stand to look anywhere else. They didn't even notice me until I said her name."

Pete went quiet, but Tara didn't want to interrupt his silence, or intrude on his thoughts. A few minutes passed before he continued.

"In retrospect I wish I'd just walked back out without saying anything. The man demanded to know who I was, in my room, in my bed, with my wife. When I didn't answer he wrapped himself in a sheet and poked me in the middle of the chest calling me a son-of-a-bitch. I lost it."

Tara could hear Pete shift in the darkness. She wished she could see his face.

"I don't remember hitting him the first time," Pete admitted. "My wife was screaming and there was blood on his face. Then I hit him again, this time in the chest, then his side. When I put my fist in his stomach he was sick on my carpet and it made me angrier."

Pete sighed, "About this time my wife threw herself on me naked, crying, and shrieking. She was clawing at my back and arms with her fingernails. I caught one of her wrists and told her to stop. I didn't even recognize her in that moment. I'd never seen her look at me with such hatred. She went for my face with her other hand and I pushed her down onto the bed. She glared at me and I remember she started to say something to me, but I didn't care what it was. I was more interested in the man on the floor. I picked him up again, but he looked so pathetic. He was naked and crying. I couldn't hit him again, so I shoved him back against the wall and walked out."

Tara listened to Pete breathe. It was faster than it should have been. She wanted to comfort him, but she didn't know what she could do, so she sat still and listened until his breathing calmed.

"I sat in my truck until the police arrived. They took me away in handcuffs. When I was in holding I found out that my wife was charging me with assault. She claimed I threw her around, threatened her, slapped her, and a couple of other things. They had photographed some marks on her, but I didn't put them there."

"Is that when you met Alex?" Tara asked quietly.

"Yeah, he was the only cop who seemed to believe me. He told me she seemed too smug when she was telling her version. I hadn't even tried to deny beating her lover so he deemed me more honest. In the end it didn't matter. I refused to make a deal, but I was found guilty of both assaults. I was served my divorce papers while in lock-up. I gave her everything she asked for except alimony. I never wanted to set foot in that house again anyway. Once I got out I would chat with Alex every time I was in to see my probation officer. He did a lot to help me get my life back together."

"Is what happened with your wife the reason you don't date?" Tara asked slowly.

"I guess so," Pete admitted. "I never realized that my dating or not dating was so interesting to other people. I guess I look at a woman and when I see what is good and beautiful in her I think of my ex-wife. Then my brain slides forward to when this woman is going to use me and betray me. I basically never get to the conversation stage."

"That's oddly romantic," Tara smiled in the darkness.

Pete moved again, shifting the bed. "Romantic is not the word I would use. I was thinking pathetic."

"You let your love for her break you apart. You said it's the good and beautiful that makes you turn away. I've never imagined a man capable of that depth of devotion." Tara rubbed her left-hand ring finger in the dark. Jasper probably never even missed her. If Jasper was even still alive at all.

"I really loved her," Pete confessed, his voice tight.

"Thank you," Tara said quietly.

"I don't understand." Pete cleared his throat.

"For telling me your secrets. For being here. For being who you are. It really helps."

"I'm sorry I couldn't be there when you really needed me," Pete whispered.

"You're here now,"

Neither of them interrupted the silence that followed for quite a long time.

"Pete?"

"What?" he answered groggily. He'd been falling asleep.

"Is he dead?"

"Yes."

"Who killed him?" Tara's voice quavered betraying her.

"Are you sure you want to know?"

Tara was relieved that he'd asked. It was one more thing she didn't want to think about. Had she killed a man? Had Pete? "No. I don't think I want to know," she admitted.

"Okay."

Tara wouldn't have thought she could sleep, but with Pete close enough to reach out and touch she slipped into a dreamless darkness.

CHAPTER 36

A knock on the door startled Tara awake while Pete jumped to his feet. The entirety of her skin felt like it was badly stitched together. Tara gasped but Pete held a finger to his lips while he peeked out the window with a pistol in his hand.

"It's Avery," Pete announced while she got painfully to her feet and smoothed her hair and clothes.

"Pete, you awake?" Avery called through the door.

"Yeah. What's up Avery?" Pete asked.

"Can I come in?"

Pete looked out the window, scanning the courtyard before he unlocked the door. Avery slipped quickly into the room before closing the door behind himself.

"Pete we have a problem," he paused looking at Tara.

"What's going on?" Pete prompted.

Avery looked pointedly at Tara, but Pete nodded so he continued. "The Breakfast Man is at it again."

"Shit," Pete breathed, "Where?"

"In town," Avery winced.

"What?" Pete glanced out the window as if he expected to see something horrific. "Where?"

"Excuse me?" Tara stepped forward to join the men. "What the hell is the Breakfast Man?"

Avery stared at Pete, who looked momentarily embarrassed. "It's what the guards have been calling the man who murdered your neighbors, the Whites, and three others."

"I don't understand," Tara looked back and forth between the two.

"Serial killer," Pete mumbled apologetically.

"Like cereal for breakfast," Avery added.

"It's okay I got it when he said it," Tara paused. "What the hell guys?"

"All the other things people were calling him were just too awful," Pete shrugged.

"What I've seen of him is pretty awful," Tara grumbled.

Avery looked back at Pete. "They are calling in everyone in town. Sweeps are being conducted, guards are posted, and Hannity has requested you on scene."

"Why you?" Tara asked.

"Because I'm the only one who has seen all five crime scenes," Pete answered her softly.

"Really?"

"Yeah," Avery nodded

"Who found the victims?" Pete asked as he strode to the other end of the room and started pulling ammo out of boxes under the bed.

"Only one victim this time; Jessica found her while on patrol."

"She okay?" Pete asked. "Did she have any contact with Breakfast Man?"

"She's shaken, but no. She only found the body."

"Thank goodness," Pete sighed. "I hope none of us come up against this maniac alone. You ready to go?" Pete asked, turning to Tara.

"I heard about what happened to…" Avery trailed off while watching Tara's face. "Do you think it's a good idea to go to the crime scene today?"

Pete glared at Avery. "I'm not leaving her here with the Breakfast Man around."

Avery led the way while Tara tried not to think about the fact that every step burned. Her cuts pulled and there was still some swelling she was trying to ignore that was making walking a challenge.

"I got you, you're it!" shouted a little girl who ran into an even younger boy in the yard next to them pushing him to the ground.

"That's not fair! I'm telling Mom!" the smaller child yelled back.

Tara smiled, they were surely siblings. Kids were so resilient. Here they found themselves in a world unlike the one they were born into, but they played like nothing had happened. Tara briefly envied those children. She shuddered when she thought where she was headed. Avery was leading and Pete was behind her; like a strange line of ducks. Or like she was a prisoner. Tara looked around.

"Are we going to the clinic?" Tara asked Avery as it came into view around the corner.

"No, but not far from it," he said gently.

Guards were milling around the alley. The same alley Tara had been lured into. She froze suddenly, causing Pete to bump into her. One of the guards was being sick into the gutter while his friend patted his back and murmured something.

Tara didn't know what was said because her heart was pounding in her ears; drowning out the noise of the scene in front of her.

Pete and Avery were talking to each other, but Tara had no idea what about until Pete stepped in front of her.

"Stay here," Pete whispered.

"Are you out of your mind?" Tara breathed. "I'm not going to just stay here. Do you know where here is?"

"Where is here?" Pete asked gravely.

"This is where I was taken!" Tara gasped.

"I don't think you should go in there. I don't know what we're going to find," Pete told her firmly.

"I don't care. I'm not staying here!" Tara hissed.

"Then I wouldn't presume to tell you what you need to do." Pete looked at her sympathetically, holding out his hand.

Tara took it, and she didn't let go as they started down the alley. It looked completely different in the daylight and Tara could already see Hannity, Farmer, and Pastor Richard standing in a group discussing something animatedly between them.

"But the question we need to be asking," Hannity insisted, "is why he would change his strategy now."

"Maybe he was interrupted," Richard offered.

"If that's the case we could have a witness," Doctor Farmer nodded gravely.

"I think we should start knocking on doors; every door in town if we have to. We need to know if anyone saw anything; if anyone can identify him." Hannity nodded.

"Everyone was in town last night. Even the rural families." The pastor added.

"We'll just have to do what we can." Hannity shrugged. "He must be stopped. He's gotten bolder."

Tara's breath caught. On the ground behind them was a mess. Presumably a body. Rope stretched from an air conditioner on one side of the alley back to the body and another disappeared behind an old trash can on the other side. As Tara continued to walk, pulled forward by a force she could not describe, she saw there was more rope. Another stretched to a door knob, and another a small awning. The alley smelled like blood and viscera. A smell Tara had come to equate with the cleaning of animals and, as the morning was heating up, an underlying bad smell like the beginning of decay.

"Pete!" Hannity scolded, "What in the hell do you think you're doing?"

"She wouldn't stay behind," Pete announced defiantly, gripping her fingers.

Doctor Farmer's face was twisted in anguish when he saw her. She wasn't sure she was going to be able to talk to him anymore if he always looked at her like that.

Pastor Richard and Hannity started up the alley towards them.

"After your ordeal I'm sure this is hard to see," Hannity soothed.

Tara didn't respond. She was still looking at the scene on the ground in front of her. The body was slashed at the throat, and each of the major arteries in the limbs. Just like her neighbor, just like Missus White, but this one was still dressed and the face had been stabbed so many times there was basically nothing left of it.

The trunk as well, but on the left inner thigh was the purple feather. She could barely make it out under all the blood.

"It's Elizabeth," Tara whispered.

"Yes, we know," Hannity assured her putting a hand on her shoulder.

"No, you don't know. It doesn't matter. The search doesn't matter. She's dead. He's dead. That could've been me!" Tara panted shaking her head and stepping away from Hannity.

"It's not you," Pete told her firmly.

"But he killed her," Tara whispered. "He told me. He was covered in her blood."

"What are you trying to say?" Pastor Richard asked gently.

"The man who raped me. He told me he killed Elizabeth."

"Why didn't you tell us that last night?" Hannity asked.

"I didn't realize he meant he killed her. He said something about having taken care of something with Elizabeth. He said he did it fast. I thought they'd had a transaction," Tara admitted.

"What does Elizabeth have to do with all of this?" Pete asked

"It was a trap. I was on my way back to the church when she stopped me," Tara paused, her voice tightening as she balled her hands into fists. "She told me to go down the alley and I did. That monster was waiting there to take me."

"You went down a dark alley at night with nobody around because Elizabeth told you to? Were you drunk?" Pete asked solemnly. His voice had sounded calm, but just a hint of flint crept in.

"She told me you were dying." Tara paused because she couldn't underline the word in the air so that he could understand why she was so upset. Tara put her hand on his arm and repeated, "Dying. She told me your blood was spraying. I wasn't going to stop and ask questions. I told her to get the doctor and I ran because I thought it was true." She could feel his muscles tense and he took a couple of deep breaths before he spoke.

"I see," Pete whispered.

"Good," Tara said calmly.

"I'd have done the same in your situation," Pete nodded

slowly.

Tara let what he said flutter between them like a moth around a candle.

"There's something else you should know," Tara said, turning back to Hannity.

"Yes?"

"He works with his brother."

"Who is his brother?"

"I don't know, but I saw them in the clinic together," Tara nodded at Doctor Farmer.

"Which one? There were a lot of people at the clinic last night." Farmer frowned.

"Remember the big guy standing behind the skinny guy who had a cut on his palm?"

"Jesus. The brother's name is Wayne," Doctor Farmer blurted. "He runs a church north of town. They took in a group of displaced folks."

Hannity stepped forward and took Tara's free hand in his. "We have some business to take care of. Would you do me the honor of meeting us at the shop in about an hour?" Then he turned away from her. "Men," he said to Pete and Avery, "Would you see that she gets there safely."

It had taken Hannity considerably more than an hour to arrive at his shop that afternoon.

"I'm sorry," he apologized to Tara, who had been sitting in front of the store relaxing with Pete, Avery, and Terry; the men guarding the door. Terry had been telling them a big fish story. If the fish was as big as Terry said then it would have been a threat to life and limb.

Hannity looked more than a little tired. "Come on in." He gestured them inside while he unlocked the door. Pete and Tara followed him quietly while Terry and Avery stayed out front.

"We have a plan of action," he nodded gravely.

"Can I ask why we weren't involved?" Pete asked.

"I thought that Miss Tara has been through enough, lost enough," Hannity sighed rubbing his eyes. "But, I'll admit I'm not very good at this sometimes."

"No, I'm glad you left us out of planning what's going to be done. Whatever happens, more people are going to die."

"Yes," Hannity nodded gravely.

"Do you mind if I ask what's going to be done?" Pete asked.

Hannity dragged his hand through his hair. "We're going to have to be careful. We're no army, and Wayne's group has proven itself to be pretty lethal. So we're going to do some reconnaissance. If we can take them by surprise we'll do it as carefully as possible."

"By take them you mean..." Tara trailed off.

"Probably kill them, yes," Hannity nodded.

"Why," Tara asked.

"If they pose an observable threat, which I can imagine they will," Hannity rubbed his temples, "this is the only justice we have available to us."

Tara's face flickered thought a series of reactions, but she chose not to say anything.

"So why are we here?" Pete asked

"I thought you would want to know what was decided. Also I have something that belongs to Tara." Hannity reached behind the desk and pulled out a long leather sheath and belt. Inside the sheath was a knife.

"That's not mine," Tara corrected him, confused.

"Yes it is." Hannity slid the knife out of the sheath.

It was the knife she'd stabbed her attacker with; the knife whose blade had decorated her body with cuts. Some of them she would probably carry as scars. "I don't understand."

"Many warriors take a trophy from their fallen enemies." Hannity held it out to her. "It's your choice if you want it."

"Thank you," Tara responded solemnly as she took it. Gently, she fastened the leather belt around her waist.

"It suits you," Pete smiled.

"Also, your friend out front," Hannity nodded at the door, "Terry. He was a Navy Seal. He said he'd give you some lessons on how to use it effectively.

"That would be a good thing," Tara nodded.

"And Pete," Hannity smiled. "Take some time off."

"What?" Pete demanded. "There is important work to be done."

"Yes, and I believe you have an obligation as a bodyguard," he said looking back and forth between Tara and Pete, "and a harvest to bring in."

Pete nodded obviously conflicted.

"Pete, Tara," Hannity paused holding his palms out. "Go home."

CHAPTER 37

It was the first chill raindrop that hit Tara's cheek that made her eyes flutter open in the morning. It made her wish they had remembered in the madness of the last couple of days to get Pete's roof tarp from town. In front of her, still lying on his sleeping bag on the floor, was Pete. He was on his back with his hands tucked behind his head. He took a deep breath and smiled as the rain sprinkled down harder.

"It's raining," Tara said without moving off her sleeping bag. It seemed obvious, but he acted oblivious.

"I know. Isn't it wonderful? Don't you love the smell of the rain?"

"I guess I never really thought about it," Tara admitted, squinting up into the sky. Pete made no move to go anywhere.

"I know. I never really thought about it a year ago either. I was too busy working, eating, and sleeping. The only time I ever thought about the rain is when it meant we couldn't get a job done, or I left my truck window open." Pete rolled onto his side to look at her. "Now I think about the rain; the smell, the sound of it on the leaves. I listen to the wind. I watch the clouds. I smell the grass when we cut hay. It's wonderful. It makes me feel alive."

"You're not going to feel so alive if that hay doesn't last the winter, or the crops fail, or if someone shows up here wanting what we have… like the Whites," Tara admonished picking up her sleeping bag. She was going to need to hang it on the back porch of her old place to dry.

"I think that's part of what makes me feel so alive. It's all so temporary, but then it always has been."

"Life hasn't always been this hard," Tara sighed.

"Hasn't it?" Pete asked innocently. "So there wasn't any

crime, or hunger, or sickness. You didn't fear for your safety, or find yourself scraping, working two jobs, and still barely getting by?"

"I see your point," Tara smiled while Pete stood up and spread his arms as if to embrace the sky itself."

"So, the world isn't really worse, it's just more direct, more honest if you think about it." Pete smiled at Tara.

"Are you drunk?" Tara giggled.

"No, but I could be if I wanted to. I don't have to be anywhere but here." Pete shrugged dropping his arms to his sides as the rain began to pour down harder.

"We're getting soaked," Tara said pulling at her clothes that were starting to stick to her skin.

"Good, let's do that then," he told her as a bird began to sing nearby. "I used to worry about following all the rules. I used to think I would work every day, each day exactly like the one before. I would do that until one day when I would retire a worn out old man, never having done more than just get by. Every bit of my struggle and sweat would benefit the board of directors and the bankers. I would never build anything. I wasn't important. Now you know what?" Pete had to nearly shout over the sound of the rain.

"What?"

"Now I work for me, and for you, and for them," Pete said pointing back to the old shack where Alex, Kate, and the others lived. "We all work together to make this shit work. We all need each other in ways we never did before."

Tara wiped some of the water off her face and couldn't help sharing Pete's infectious smile.

"You know what else?" he asked, offering her his hand.

"What?" she asked as she took it.

Pete surprised her by pulling her towards him. "It makes me feel good."

"Me too."

"Shhhhh listen," he murmured as he embraced her and began to sway.

It did feel good to matter. To have a place she belonged; for what Tara realized was probably the first time in her life. Her world felt right as she danced with him in the rain.

 Denise Terriah draws inspiration for her writing from her interest in old-fashioned skills and her hobby farm. She lives in the Midwest with her husband, twin daughters, and an ever-shifting menagerie of pets and livestock; all of whom have been subjected to a wide array of weird-tasting herbs since she took up the hobby of herbalism. Thankfully they don't seem to mind. *As It Ends* is her first published novel.